"A wildly imaginative science fiction odyssey, always compelling, it works on a lot of levels, and they all come together like clockwork in the end. Highly recommended."

—Scott Hawkins, author of *The Library at Mount Char*

"Enchanting, captivating, intriguing . . . none of these do *The Raft* justice. Strydom's fresh voice and confident prose will completely engross you. A stellar debut!"

—*New York Times* bestseller Jason M. Hough, author of *Zero World*

"Strydom's debut subverts postapocalyptic fiction with a scathing parable of pain and paranoia . . . reinvigorates the genre with a suspenseful concept and intimately realized characters. [A] sucker punch of a novel."

—*Publishers Weekly*, starred review

"If you think you've seen it all, read it all when it comes to dystopian fiction, you really haven't; not until you've experienced *The Raft*. I was enchanted, awestruck, and ultimately moved by Fred Strydom's rip-cracking debut."

—Nick Cutter, bestselling author of *The Troop* and *The Deep*

"This eerie debut about one man's search for truth, even though what he finds may hurt more than it heals, features a protagonist with raw emotions and a strong voice, carrying what could be a convoluted plot to an unforgettable ending."

—*Library Journal*, starred review

"This novel really is a masterpiece. It's different and haunting. It's devastatingly good. And it's beautifully put together. If you don't read another SF novel this year, shame on you. If you do, make it *The Raft*."

—John Love, author of *Faith* and *Evensong*

"One of the sharpest premises in 2016 . . . *The Raft* is a must-read."

—*B&N Sci-Fi & Fantasy Blog*

"F***ing fantastic. The writing, from start to finish, is wonderful. *The Raft* is easily the best book I've read this year, and one that I'm not sure will be topped."

—*We the Nerdy*

"*The Raft* was a refreshing, unique read. [I] can see it sticking with me for a long time. I look forward to seeing what Fred Strydom writes next."

—*Christy's Love of Books*

"A strong debut in the genre and sure to interest SF readers in general, and dystopia fans in particular."

—*Booklist*

"Riveting and moving science fiction . . . I read *The Raft* in one sitting."

—*Rant and Rave Reviews*

"A must-read, even for hardened 'realist' readers."

—*Aerodrome*

"A writer to watch . . . a philosophical adventure story that takes the reader into a terrifying world where no one can remember who or what they are. . . . A brilliant book, and one not to be missed . . . a rollicking good dystopian novel."

—*Cape Times*

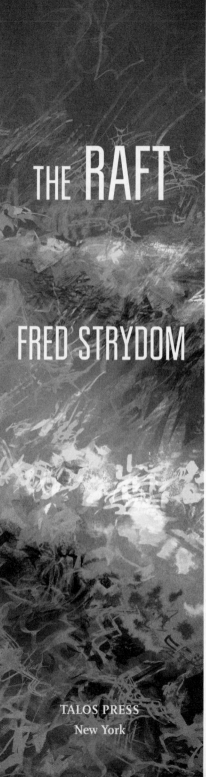

THE RAFT

FRED STRYDOM

TALOS PRESS

New York

Talos Press books may be purchased in bulk at special discounts for sales promotion, corporate gifts, fund-raising, or educational purposes. Special editions can also be created to specifications. For details, contact the Special Sales Department, Talos Press, 307 West 36th Street, 11th Floor, New York, NY 10018 or info@skyhorsepublishing.com.

Talos Press® is a registered trademark of Skyhorse Publishing, Inc.®, a Delaware corporation.

Visit our website at www.talospress.com.

10 9 8 7 6 5 4 3 2 1

Library of Congress Cataloging-in-Publication Data

Names: Strydom, Fred, author.
Title: The raft : a novel / Fred Strydom.
Description: First Talos Press edition. | New York : Talos Press, 2016.
Identifiers: LCCN 2015050141 | ISBN 9781940456607 (hardback)
Subjects: LCSH: Regression (Civilization)--Fiction. | Memory--Fiction. |
   Science fiction. | BISAC: FICTION / Science Fiction / Adventure. | FICTION
   / Science Fiction / General.
Classification: LCC PR9369.4.S85 R34 2016 | DDC 823/.92--dc23
LC record available at http://lccn.loc.gov/2015050141

Paperback ISBN: 978-1-940456-88-1
Hardcover ISBN: 978-1-940456-60-7
Ebook ISBN: 978-1-940456-61-4

Interior illustration by Sylvain Sarrailh
Cover illustration by Mujtaba Sayed
Cover design by Claudia Noble

Printed in the United States of America

For Bronnie . . .
My compass, my journey and my destination.

A tree in the clouds

Remember Jack Turning—

I fell out of my dream.

It took me a while to figure out where I was, where I had fallen asleep. It was the familiar scratch of sand beneath my clothing that first became apparent.

The beach.

I sat up and looked towards the sun. It was sinking into the ocean, layering the sky in uneven smears of purple, yellow and red. The day was ending and I'd already spent most of it asleep, which meant I'd spend most of the night awake. Again.

"Do you know about the alp?"

The deep voice belonged to the large and swarthy man sitting beside me. Ropes of sun-bleached dreadlocks lay slung over his shoulders and down to the small of his back. His name was Gideon and he was as much of a friend as I could claim to have had in that peculiar place. Still, I knew so little about him—where he'd been born, where he had originally lived, or what it was that he loved in this world. I didn't even know his last name. All I knew was that he had been taken to the beach as I had, all those years ago, and that, like all of us there, he was a far and unconquerable distance from where he truly wished to be.

Through his hair, one eye glistened back at me, the mossy green of pond water. He slid his feet into the sand in front of him and wrapped his arms around his knees.

"No," I replied. I dusted the sand off my shoulder, trying to seem unaffected. I wondered how long he'd been sitting there, watching me sleep. I wondered if I'd said something I perhaps shouldn't have.

"It's a creature," he said, "that sits on the chest of someone who dreams. It squeezes all the breath out of the body. There was such a thing on your chest while you slept."

"I wouldn't know," I said.

"Well, maybe you know this story," he went on. "There was once a cabinetmaker who lived in a place called Bühl. Have you ever heard of this place?"

I shook my head.

"At night he'd sleep in a bed in his workshop. Around midnight, something would crawl onto his chest and sit on him until he could hardly breathe. After several nights of this, he discussed the matter with a friend. The friend advised him to stay awake in order to catch this märt. So he did. The following night he lay awake in bed, waiting, and as the clock struck twelve, saw a cat slip into his room through a hole in the wall. The cabinetmaker quickly blocked the hole. He caught the cat and nailed one of its paws to the floor. Then he went back to sleep. In the morning he found a beautiful woman sitting where the cat had been. She was naked and one of her hands was nailed to the floorboards. He was so taken by this woman that he decided to marry her. Many years later, after they'd already had three children, he returned with her to his workshop. He pointed to the blocked hole in the wall and said, 'My darling, my love, mother of my children, it was from here that you came into my life.' He bent down and opened the hole to show her. And as soon as that hole was opened, the woman changed back into a cat, ran out through the hole, and was never seen again."

"I didn't have a dream."

"Maybe you did and maybe you didn't, but there was a märt, my friend. Anyway, it is okay to talk about our dreams. I think it's a good thing."

He spoke with such authority that, for a moment, I believed him. I believed it was fine, regardless of what we had so frequently been told.

"No one can stop you from dreaming, Mr. Kayle. But go on. Let us dream and hide our dreams from each other as we've been told. It is ironic, yes?"

"What is?"

Squatting on his haunches, he dusted his large dry hands together. His hair rolled over his shoulders as he swivelled in his spot towards me. The dreadlocks on the right of his head blazed; to the left his face was caged in twisted bars of shadow.

"They wish us to keep our dreams a secret from each other, to keep them trapped inside us, when it really only makes us dream more. They are making sly, beautiful women of our cats, no?"

Gideon stood and turned his gaze to the shifting ocean. I stared up at his broad and towering form. There were very few people on the beach as large as Gideon, even fewer with the capacity to command the respect that he could, in his own quiet way.

"Strange days," he murmured under his breath, possibly only to himself. He used his foot to smooth out the print his body had left in the sand, as if in denial of ever having sat beside me, and began to walk away. "Mr. Kayle," he added, looking back over his shoulder, "the märt on your chest. I've seen it before. Stealing your breath in your sleep. For now, know that it is getting bigger, my friend."

At that, he set off along the white sand towards the group of communers at the end of the beach.

They were going about their usual business, dancing around their colossal fires, yelling their prayers, invoking their stars. Whether they were finding the answers to the questions in each of their steps and mantras, I didn't know, but I wasn't even sure that was the point. Perhaps I had missed something. Perhaps it didn't matter whether they ever truly understood this broken world, only that they considered themselves privileged enough to be seekers within it. For some that may have been enough.

A warm wind whispered in my ear then slipped away, gesturing me to follow it to some secret place. I got to my feet and trudged up the dune towards the road. Ahead, a rusted signboard read WELCOME WELKOM BETTYSBAAI. Over time, the wind and the rain had faded its colours and eaten into its metal surface. It creaked and teetered from a pole, each geometric letter glaring like the vacant eye of a dead god, a fallen Argus without sway over a nameless world.

The sun had already been swallowed whole and night was draped over the land. The large bonfires along the shore licked the darkness between the silhouettes of anonymous men, women and children—strangers to each other, strangers to themselves–dancing and chanting the last rites for their left-behind lives.

Andy, is that you?
  Dad!
There was a soft rap on the tarp of my tent.

My eyes adjusted to the dimness. Each of the objects in my small space solidified into hard tokens of reality. The crooked silhouette of a person quivered on the side of the tent. I climbed out of bed, opened the entrance, and was hit by the cool night air. Standing before me was a young girl, clenching a shabby teddy bear in her right hand, chewing on the nails of her left.

At first I thought the girl was my daughter, but realised such a visit would be impossible. My daughter was not here. Not on the beach. Not even in the world. My daughter was long dead and this was someone else's child.

"Did they send you?" I asked as I stepped out. It was still dark but I had no idea for how much longer it would last. I could see the last ribbons of smoke rising from the dying fires in the distance and hear the crackle of enormous embers beneath the babble and murmur of the ocean. The singing and dancing had ended. Most of the communers were asleep.

"Do you have a name?" I asked. She shook her head. "Does your bear? He's scruffy."

I wondered how long she had been on the beach, how long it had been since she had seen her family. Did she even remember them, and did they still remember her? Not that it mattered. The longer she stayed, the sooner their faces would become little more than worthless apophenia: Jesus in a slice of burned toast, Mother Mary in a frosted window. She was on the beach and on the beach she would remain. She'd grow up. She'd assimilate. She'd receive her reports and be conditioned to commune. You could bet your life on it, if it were still your life to bet: we were all there to stay.

The girl turned and ran, vanishing into the blackness. I threw on a sweater, grabbed my shoes and made my way up the rickety wooden steps, half-sunken in the dunes and their dull tufts of fynbos shrubberies. I stepped off the sand of the beach, slipped on my shoes, and hiked the winding clay path ahead of me, guided only by the light from the lone white house on the hill.

"What fraction of God's powers would satisfy you?"

The light of an overhead lamp beamed down on me as I sat in a lone chair in the centre of a stark, featureless room. The rough stone walls were white and bare and a wooden fan *thopped* uselessly above the interrogators' table, accomplishing nothing more than the shifting of stale air.

The skin beneath the plugs attached to the sides of my head was beginning to itch. A myriad of white wires extended outwards from each plug. Each wire ran into the port of box-shaped machines tucked away in the shadows; each machine did its part to facilitate my examination. An enormous grey box to my left generated printed reports based on my physiological responses to their questions.

"Could you repeat the question?" I asked, my voice flat.

The questions were always strange and elusive—difficult to answer directly. The most recent one had come from a man with an old, croaky voice. Six others, faceless, indistinguishable, sat behind their table, taking notes in small dockets. The faint glow of the moonlight through the window outlined the silhouettes of their heads and the curves of their shoulders. One of them was wearing baffling headgear, a rigid, geometric, cage-like device.

"God," he said again. "What fraction of God's powers would satisfy you?"

"No fraction," I replied automatically. I'd studied *The Age of Self Primary* so thoroughly I could extract the correct answer with little conscious effort. "None of it. That, and the power of God, cannot be measured in acts."

I watched as the grey box spat reams of paper into a tray.

"Explain," said a woman sitting at the opposite end of the table.

"The concept of a theistic God is based on omniscience, omnipotence and omnipresence. God is infinite. Infinity cannot be portioned. There is no percentage that can be subtracted from infinity and redistributed."

"What about numbers?" another woman asked. "Numbers are infinite and yet they can be . . . portioned, as you put it."

"Yes. The permutations of numbers are infinite but the numbers *themselves* are finite. There are only nine of them, excluding, of course, the representation of zero. Asking me what I could do with a fraction of God's power would be like asking what I could do with the numbers one, two and three—without having access to the other six. Such thinking is paradoxical. Nihilistic. It would lead to chaos. And historically, it has."

A few heads nodded and a figure in the middle of the row jotted something down.

"And what is your understanding of the power paradox?" one of them asked.

Words left my mouth although I could barely remember what they meant. Those lines from the scripts flew out like a language merely recited phonetically—shards of jagged and transparent glass. Philosophies memorised, dead on arrival. I paused, my tongue swollen, my mouth dry. I longed for a glass of water, but there wouldn't be a drop until I was done. They knew all too well: it was more difficult to deceive them under physical strain. Eventually I managed to speak again:

"Man has always been unable to differentiate between true power and the trivial struggle to reposition himself within a predetermined framework. We have never known true power. We have never come close. True power cannot be based on hierarchy because the simple act of positioning oneself above another will always rely on the positioning of those below. True power doesn't rely on such a symbiosis. It doesn't need it. True power is absolute."

I paused and licked my lips. "But Man was obsessed with finding the answers to his questions without considering the possibility that it was the questions he posed, in fact, that were incorrect. This presented a problem."

"How?"

"Plotinus was correct when he stated God could not be reached intellectually."

"And in that regard, what is it we're attempting to accomplish today, with The Renascence?" the old man asked.

"To deconstruct the questions, find the flaws in them and then disown them—to exist within the answer itself, free from the inanity of our primitive curiosities and hierarchies."

A third woman: "And what of natural selection? Isn't life itself based on the survival of the fittest? On hierarchy?"

"Yes, but natural selection is only the first stage. Evolution demands more. In the end, we will not need to be the fittest, for competition itself will cease to exist for us. Subsequently, we will neither disown nor denounce the remaining organisms with which we share the planet. We will simply exist in a state of being of which they will have no concept and to which they will have no access, on an alternate stream of time, within the one true reality."

There was a moment's silence before they all nodded in agreement.

"Straight out of the scripts. Almost word for word. You're very impressive," the man with the headgear said. He scrawled on his paper. "You are academically gifted but you are still . . . questioning. That is your weakness. Added to which, we're not entirely convinced that you have surrendered yourself to the truth. We're not sure you believe in it." A pause. "Even if you can recite it."

The machine whirred again and printed out the latest results on me.

"Tell us something." Another man spoke for the first time. His voice was the most calculating of them all, and the driest, as if he'd never once in his life expressed any sentiment of joy. "Have you been dreaming?"

"Yes."

"Of what?"

I paused to consider my response, even though the machine was already churning out my true response in numbers and graphs.

"My son," I replied. "Andy . . ."

"Tell us about your dream."

This was always the most difficult part of the test. No scripts to call upon. No quick answers. My dreams were all I had, all that was left of me, and soon they'd be handed over to The Body, just like everything else.

One of them tapped a pen on the table, impatient for my response.

"I'm walking in a beautiful forest," I said, squinting from one shadowy face to the next, doing my best to sound neutral. "That's how it starts. How it always starts. There are many tall trees, but I see one in particular in the centre of the forest, enormous in width and height. It's taller than the rest. This tree extends far beyond the canopy of the forest. Its trunk disappears into the thick white clouds above. At my feet, a red shoe is lying in the dirt. It's a child's shoe. I recognise it as my son's, then look up and realise he may have dropped it while climbing that tree."

"How do you feel at this point in your dream?"

"My emotions?"

"Yes."

"Excited. Hopeful."

"Go on."

The grey box rumbled and spat. The moon had moved beyond the glass doors behind the seated examiners, leaving the room in a disquieting dimness.

"I decide to climb the tree, thinking he is at the very top of it, perhaps sitting on a branch up in the clouds. To my surprise the tree is easy to climb even though there are no branches at the base of it and the trunk is perfectly cylindrical, too wide for me to wrap my arms around. My hands and feet clasp firmly on to the bark as I ascend. I continue climbing. As I enter the foliage of the surrounding trees, I notice children sitting in the higher branches—children of differing ages. I do not recognise any of them. They ask me if I am their father and I tell them I'm sorry, no, I'm not. And then I continue. Eventually, I exit through the top of the trees and am able to see the landscape in all directions. The trees go on forever, a boundless plateau. There is no curve on the horizon. It is flat and it is infinite, and I continue climbing."

"How do you feel at this point?"

"Nervous. The height begins to worry me. My hands and feet aren't gripping as firmly as they once did. My confidence begins to . . . lessen."

"Do you give up?"

"No, I continue."

"Go on."

"I look down. I feel dizzy. I tilt my head and can see I'm about to enter the clouds. The branches and foliage above me are barely visible now, but at least I know how far I have to go. I press on. Soon, I'm in it, surrounded by cloud. I call my son's name but there's no response. I climb some more. Call some more. Nothing."

"How do you feel at this point?" a voice shot out.

"Disappointed. Desperate."

"Go on."

"For a while I sit on a branch. I sit there . . . by myself, at the highest point of the world. Above, the sun is beaming through the clouds, but as time passes, whatever it is that beams through feels less like the beam of a sun and more like the glare of a giant eye. The shape of it becomes clearer. It's an orb. A planetary orb hanging in the sky. It speaks to me. It has a voice, and the voice it uses is my own and at the same time not my own. The voice is calming. It tells me I will not find my son there. And then it mentions a name."

"Whose name?"

"Jack Turning. The voice repeats the name over and over again. It tells me to remember Jack Turning, but I don't. I can't."

"Do you know this name?"

"No. I don't. At least, I don't *think* I do. The orb continues to tell me things. A feeling of hopelessness comes over me. I'll never see my son again, I think. Perhaps it wasn't his red shoe. I'm spent. I have nothing left. I give up. I lean backwards and fall through the clouds."

"Your feelings?"

"I have no fear. I know it will all be over soon. I'll hit the ground and it'll be over. But then, suddenly, I see him. Andy. He's there. He was on the tree trunk the entire time, climbing up after me. I'm slowing as I fall. I have time to turn to him and call his name . . . and he turns . . . and he looks me in the eye. But it's too late. I pass him and my speed builds . . . the ground rushes towards me before . . . I wake up."

For a moment, I was no longer in the room. I could hear the voice of the orb. I could feel the fall and hear the wind. I could see Andy's face, his bright green eyes in his young, unblemished face. I was filled with guilt and the anguish of falling from him as my hands clawed madly at rushing air, watching the distance grow as the tree shot up into the sky above.

"And what do you feel when you wake up?"

"Guilt," I replied in my forced monotone, aware of how I'd failed to seem impartial. "Despair."

"Well," the woman said. "For the moment, do not concern yourself. We'll give you something to help you."

The man with the metal contraption rose from his seat and walked to me. He held out his hand and it fell into the single beam of yellow light. He was holding a small plastic bag filled with dark, dried and crushed red leaves.

"It's a temporary solution, until you've adjusted to your new state. Have a few leaves before bed. Wash it all down with water," he said.

I reached up slowly and took the bag from him.

"They'll prevent you having dreams."

I stared at the bag of leaves I'd been told would wipe away the orb, Jack Turning, the clouds, and my son's face in a few daily gulps. Then I nodded up at him.

I had to remind myself, The Renascence would see the transcendence of Man. The age of truth after the age of lies, and we'd been assured we'd never go back. Not to the way things were. Not to the way we had been for all those years, roaming like stray animals on some long dark night of fear and avarice. No, The Renascence would inaugurate the future of our existence, and the future was glowing bright.

"Thank you," I said, and wrapped the bag in my fist.

Walking back from the white house, I felt the biting cold that signified the final few minutes before sunrise. I hurried down the path towards my tent. The large blue moon rippled on the surface of the flat ocean. The stars peered down from their posts, waiting to see what I'd do next.

I grabbed the bag of red leaves from my pocket and looked at it. Then I opened the bag and tipped them all out. Each leaf was whisked upwards and carried away by a breeze, flecks in the blue light of the moon, like the ashes of all the dreams they had been prepared to extinguish. I watched until every ort disappeared into the night. Then I unzipped my tent and went inside to sleep.

Moneta asks two favours

The heat of the day had already begun to fill the tent. I sat on the edge of my bed, curling my feet and cracking my toes. My body felt tighter and heavier than it had the night before, probably from the lack of sleep.

I finally forced myself to stand and the bed creaked, the mattress popping back into shape. I looked around my confined space. Each small object and ornament sat in its rightful place: a shelf of tattered books and a stack of unfinished drawings beside a broken mug of pencils. There was a small chest of drawers containing a few items of clothing. A red umbrella with missing spokes leaned like an ageing charmer. Beside it, a shoebox of clippings from *National Geographic* magazines recovered from the cabin of a boat wreck. There was also a glass jar filled with coins, a set of broken headphones, and a rusty old army knife that wouldn't close anymore . . .

(*The Renascence is not a law, Kayle. It's a choice. A collective choice, isn't it? A choice we make together. Material hoarding was resigned to the Age of Self, whether or not the people of different periods were able to see it for themselves. The secular people of the technological period prided themselves in having little in common with the henotheistic people of Ancient Egypt—with their ideas of an afterlife and their pantheon of gods—and yet both seemed intent to die in mounds of their possessions. Don't you see the hypocrisy in that kind of behaviour? Rest assured though, Kayle: in The Renascence, when we die, we'll leave nothing behind)*

I ducked my head and stepped outside. My eyes took a moment to adjust to the bright light as I sauntered through the narrow spaces between the tents, passing familiar faces as they went about their morning chores. A large woman dunked her clothing in an old bucket. She churned the dirt out of a soapy shirt, her bronze arms pumping like the rhythmic shafts of an engine. There was the smell of jasmine, sawdust and spices in the air, and steam rose from tinny pots warbling over gas burners.

As I left the commune of tents and stepped out onto the beach, the sea breeze nibbled at my legs and arms like inquisitive, invisible creatures. I shaded my eyes with my hand; the sun was high enough for it to be midday. The sand beneath me was already hot between my toes and, at the far end, the faint shimmer of a heat mirage weaved like a chorus of ghosts.

I walked along the water's edge with my pants rolled to my knees. I crouched and cupped the water in my hands to dab the back of my neck. Seagulls hovered and cried above me, chasing each other between the rays of the sun. At the end of the beach a group of people stood huddled like the Moai statues left by the inhabitants of an expired empire, gazing forever out over the ocean. It would have been an odd sight had I not already known the object of their fascination: they were watching the rafts.

I could just about make out the floating rafts bobbing over the small waves.

I counted three of them.

Each raft had been attached to the pier by a length of rope. The offenders had been tied down at the wrists and ankles, forced to stare only at the sky while they thought about their offences. Pumped full of hallucinogens and bared to the heavens, forced to wait until the universe dripped itself in, filling each with a sense of purpose, realigning them with The Renascence.

Although I knew nothing of the men on the rafts that day, a rumour had spread of their having vandalised the white house two mornings earlier. They'd scrawled defamatory comments on the walls in mud, but I hadn't seen the words for myself. By the time I'd awoken, the evidence had been removed. Their sentence was delivered with no deliberation. No prolonged trial. No testimonies. A direct and unchallenged judgement by the one dictatorial panel of voices that oversaw us: *Guilty— Separation by the Raft.*

Offenders could drift for as long as three days before being pulled back to shore. No food. No water. Pounded by the wind and the waves. Frozen in the cold or burned in the sun. Sometimes the icy rain fell so hard it must have felt like hot iron shot on their exposed faces. And while the rest of us could scarcely imagine such a battering, we sensed it was the stillness of a quiet night that affected them most. We'd heard about it. Watched them raptly. Wondered.

"Kayle."

Surprised, I turned.

It was Moneta, standing a few feet behind me. She was an elderly woman with ash-grey hair tucked behind a green plastic peak. Her overalls were grass-stained, the tips of her fingers browned by soil.

"I wonder if you wouldn't give me a hand," she said.

Moneta needed me to move bags of fertiliser and fill pots, and I followed her to the botanical garden, a glass dome set back from the beach. The dome housed countless varieties of flowers, herbs, vegetables and small trees. I'd often seen children assist with the pruning, picking, planting and cleaning, but only Moneta knew how to make her autotrophic friends truly bloom into silent wonders.

As I entered the dome, I was hit by a flurry of scents: the perfumes of the brightly coloured flowers, the wetness of loamy soil. The air was thick with humidity, which probably kept Moneta's skin as supple as a much younger woman's. That, and her lifestyle: one of calm and commitment.

She explained where the bags of compost and the enormous clay pots needed to be moved to, and I hauled and dragged her heavy pots and filled a large empty wooden crate with soil and fertiliser. Once I was finished, I stepped outside to wash my hands in a bucket of water. I lifted my face to the sun. It slipped behind a single cloud—throwing grey on everything—and I continued to stare until it returned to blind me. I dried my hands on my pants and walked back inside.

"Oolong tea?" Moneta asked as I entered. She was sitting at a small wrought-iron table. She had prepared a pot of tea and two china cups, each overturned on a daintily patterned saucer.

"Yes, please," I said.

"Well, have a seat then."

She poured each of us a cup of tea. I lifted the cup to take my first sip, my thick finger squeezing through the narrow handle. We sat quietly for a while, and the silence didn't seem to bother her. There was little deemed appropriate to talk about anyway.

"They gave me a hard time in the beginning," she said. "You know, with my garden."

I nodded. I was sure they had.

"It took me a while to explain that my garden would not be a possession of any sort. I have no interest in owning these plants as *things*, you see."

"I see."

She looked to the side as she spoke, and I felt as if I could have been anyone, really—any willing ear. Finally, she turned to me.

"Thank you for helping," she said.

"It's my pleasure," I replied.

She smiled and sipped her tea. She surveyed her garden—the ferns, flowers, vines and vegetables—like a parent keeping an eye on her children in the park.

"Let me tell you a story," she said. "Would you indulge an old woman and her story?"

I shifted uncomfortably. Moneta and I had hardly said a word to each other before that moment. We'd greeted each other on occasion and I had assisted her once or twice before, but we were far from what one might consider close. "What kind of story?"

"A story I need to tell. To someone else and to myself, one last time."

I looked through the glass wall and saw the others on the beach. They seemed far enough away and I was almost certain the two of us were alone.

"Okay," I said.

"I hope you will entertain my story. It may be a bit long. I imagine it will be. But I must tell it the way I want or I will not want to tell it at all."

"All right."

She lifted her cup and watched me carefully as she sipped. Then she smiled.

"Thank you," she said. "I'm not sure you know how much this will mean to me, but it does, it will, and I thank you. I'll make us another pot."

The man in the woods

I was born in the middle of the last century, and I suppose that makes me—oh, I don't know—a hundred-and-some-odd years old. I'm not really sure anymore. I never thought I'd get to this age, or that I'd get here feeling the way I do. But life, I've learned, is like a cat that comes and goes as it pleases, making you think you own it when it is only in *its* best interest that you believe so.

When I was twenty years old, I thought I was an adult. At thirty, I thought I was somewhere in the middle of my life. Forty, I knew it all. At fifty, I cared less, but only because I assumed the majority of my life was behind me.

Ha! Well, you can understand where this is going.

At fifty, I wasn't even halfway through it, and yet I'd anchored myself with my preconceptions. Given each little moment and event its weight, only to find that most of my experiences were not anchors. They were balloons, floating up to the sky as the years breezed by, out of my reach.

I rarely understood where I was in my life. When I married at the age of twenty-two, I believed married life was my destiny, for then I believed there was such a thing. When I had my first child, I thought he would be my entire reason for being.

And for a time, both he and my husband were, and would have continued to be, had death not robbed me of them both. My husband was killed in a road accident seventy or so years ago and my child was taken by cancer twenty years later. I never had grandchildren. I never remarried. I have no family. My younger sister passed away about forty years ago in her sleep, of old age, I've been told.

And yet, I am here. Alive.

What has it all been about, the whole silly business of my life? I can honestly not tell you.

Funny, isn't it?

But none of this concerns me. And neither, I suspect, does it concern a young man like you.

No, what I want is to tell you one story.

Only one.

Of all my balloons, this is the only one I hold on to. The rest are floating, up in the sky. It is the only story I can recall with absolute clarity. I cannot tell you what it means, but that doesn't concern me. All that matters is that it's the clearest memory in my head, and for that reason alone, I wish to tell it.

I was raised in a small town; at the time it was called Tsitsikamma. In the language of the Khoi-San people this meant "place of water." It sat near the coast, an incredibly woodsy place. That's what I remember most: rolling hills blanketed in dense forest. The ground was covered in moss and chips of bark. The air smelled of damp and tree sap. One large highway weaved through it, but you'd never know until you were standing right on it; the woods swallowed that highway right up. Even the sound of passing trucks and cars couldn't make it too far beyond the edge of the woods, certainly not as far as our cabin.

Before Tsitsikamma, we lived in a town called Kroonstad. My father was the manager of a factory that made cardboard boxes and my mother stayed at home to take care of me. I don't recall much of Kroonstad, but I do remember the many boxes my father brought home. There wasn't much money to spare, so boxes were often the best my father could provide as gifts, and I rarely complained. I kept myself occupied building fortresses, robots and motor vehicles. Other times I played marbles with myself at the bottom of an enormous and empty bowl-shaped swimming pool in the middle of the housing commune.

I kept out of trouble with my parents most of the time, except for when I brought some injured animal into the house without permission. Once I even managed to hide a few bats in a box, until my mother tipped it over while cleaning. Needless to say, bats were not her favourite of my friends, and she ended up running around the house with a broomstick, trying to shoo a pair of disorientated fruit bats from the corner of our ceiling, cursing and scolding me as she did.

I look upon my time in Kroonstad with reasonable fondness. But when the box factory went under, my father lost his job and we were forced to move. As a child, I questioned little: I simply packed my things, hopped in the back of our old car, and was driven out of Kroonstad to my new home in the thick, dark and marvellous woods of Tsitsikamma.

Our new house turned out to be nothing like our old one. Instead of the flat, concrete commune in Kroonstad, where most of our neighbours were large women with rollers in their hair who leaned over the fences chain-smoking, our house in Tsitsikamma was a log cabin in a deep forest clearing, where the neighbours were large birds and bugs who chirped and clicked from the trees and the bushes.

The house itself was not really a *house* but a lodge for tourists and travellers. My father hadn't bought the business; it belonged to his older brother. He'd offered my father a position as manager of the lodge, as well as a couple of rooms for us to use while my father worked there. I was a small child at the time, so it is difficult to say in all honesty that it was an *enormous* house, but at the time it certainly seemed so. There were six rooms, each with four or five bunk beds. Three small rooms with double beds. There was a communal room with a bar and a pool table below a big poster of a man sitting in a red Cadillac. The communal kitchen was full of tinny old pots on the walls and a ceramic rooster that perched on top of the fridge. Behind the lodge there was a large outside area where guests could sit on hollowed-out logs and braai meat on open fires, talking and singing into the early hours of the morning. The place was rarely ever full, but the backpackers and vacationers trickled in and out steadily over the course of the first spring we were there.

Most of them were young men and women who needed an easy and affordable place to rest en route to somewhere else. Sometimes they'd arrive wishing to spend a night and would only leave after three days. Sometimes they'd book a room for three nights but leave on their first morning. All sorts arrived but we had no real trouble. My mother and father argued a few times in the first couple of weeks, mostly about money, I suppose, but that didn't last long.

After a time everything settled down as each of us explored some fresh and exciting aspect of this new life. My father had found a guitar stashed in a storage shed and was suddenly strumming old tunes around the fire at night, entertaining guests when the vibe was right. My mother took up painting, but spent most of her time taking care of my new sister, Carly. And I soon learned there was far more to do than play with cardboard boxes, marbles, and even bats. The woods, stretching on in all directions, were a treasure trove of curiosities. And I, a reckless and uninhibited explorer, planned on discovering each and every last one of them.

Over time, I grew used to the endless trees, the untidy forest floor, and the inquisitive looks and nods from the local wildlife. It had been my father's idea for me to keep a notebook to write down whatever I saw and heard in the woods, and I adopted his advice with great zeal. Armed with my pencil and my notebook, I would wake up early and take a stroll, exploring and documenting all the woods had to offer. Every morning I went deeper in, sought out some new route, and found a perfect spot to lie in the shade and chew on the end of a pine needle.

Beyond the woods were more woods. I never came across anyone else on my rambles. I was told that the woods ended in a cliff-face drop into the raging ocean, but I had never seen it for myself. After the first few weeks of going out as far as I could, I assumed the edge of the cliff was a great deal further than I could ever walk and so there was no need to worry about it.

When I left the lodge I would always start at the same point—a path that led from our tiny car lot—but as soon as I was beyond the range of my mother's kitchen window, I would divert left or right. Most of the time, it felt as if the woods led me, they set my path, and in that way I came to trust them, since the woods rarely led me to trouble.

Rarely, but . . . No, I cannot say *never*.

On one especially hot summer morning, I left the lodging with nothing but my notebook, a pencil and a banana, and began one of my regular walks. I turned off the path and headed down a leaf-laden slope. I grabbed a rough tree trunk and slung myself to the next trunk, and then the next one, and the next. I continued, light on the balls of my feet, all the way down. I looked up. Birds. Their silhouettes could have been mistaken for leaves were it not for their nimble darting from branch to branch.

In the woods there were all sorts of birds.

A book from the library had a picture of each of them, and I always made sure to keep an eye out. I had seen Knysna loeries, emerald cuckoos, olive woodpeckers and even a couple of barn owls. Funny how I still remember those names. Whenever I saw one, I wrote it down in my notebook and drew a picture of it. One day I even came back to the lodge with a baby robin that had fallen out of the tree and broken its wing. My father helped, but warned: *Be careful out there, Moneta. The forest is not a playground. It's a place full of living things, all fighting to survive in this world. Do not expect the loyalty of anything fighting only to survive.* He warned that even plants, harmless as they appeared to be, would attack an intruder if necessary.

Plants have had to survive this world just like everything else. Don't make the mistake of thinking they are weak or useless things.

He told me about prickly thistles and poison ivy and plants that would make me very sick if I ever ate them. I listened to my father and pondered his warnings, but still felt safer in the woods than anywhere else. As far as I was concerned, if everything in the world was fighting to survive, the forest couldn't be any more or less dangerous. To me, the forest was a place of safety. A sanctuary.

So there I was on that hot morning in my sanctuary. I jumped over puddles, picked flowers, dodged the gossamer webs of small spiders, and finally decided to eat the banana. I munched and ducked under low branches, munched and climbed over fallen boughs.

Once I had finished my banana, I worried about throwing the peel on the ground, but remembered the peel was just a plant too. It's only inside buildings and on concrete pavements that banana peels are considered litter; not out there. Certainly. My forest would take that peel back into itself. The bugs would come out and break it down into bits, and once they were done, the trees would finish the rest. That's how it worked. And it was at that moment something else dawned upon me, something I've carried with me to this day: a peel on the floor of a building isn't litter at all. The *buildings* are the litter. Nature can't use bricks and mortar. In the end, it's the buildings that will never be taken back because the world will never have any use for them.

I threw my peel over my shoulder and soldiered on.

The light above me cut through the leaves like spun gold. I could tell the sun had climbed a great deal since I'd taken off. As I walked I thought about chores I still had to do back at the lodge: sweep out the foyer, restack the pamphlet rack, unpack the boxes of vegetables and put them in the pantry. Just the thought of it bored me and I decided I'd continue for another few minutes before turning back. I still hadn't come across anything new, although I had seen a few sparrowhawks, which was always a treat.

It wasn't long, however, before I came across a new surprise: a small, shallow brook, gurgling its way to the distant ocean. It was only a few metres wide and not very deep, but brooks were always great places to spot things you otherwise wouldn't see: kingfishers perched on rocks, pools of tadpoles, little black sucker-like things that slid on their bellies and seemed to live off lichen.

I got down on my knees at the river's edge and drank some of the running water. It was cool and refreshing. I stopped to breathe, wiped my mouth on my sleeve, and as I lifted my head, was startled by a long, dark reflection rippling on the water. I looked up.

A man was standing on the other side of the river.

I lifted my head slowly and got to my feet, keeping my eyes on him. He was high up on the opposite bank, staring down at me. There are some things I don't remember as clearly as others—that is only natural, I suppose—but I will never forget my first impression of that man on the other side of the stream. The image of his body is burned into my mind just as a black mark is left in a plank of wood by a soldering iron. I remember how tall he was, and gangly—a lamppost dressed as a person. If you'd asked me then I would have told you he was seven feet tall, maybe taller. Perhaps it was the way his legs seemed to blend into the ground rather than rest on it. I could barely tell where he ended and his sinewy black shadow began.

He was wearing a long dark trench coat and he had his hands in his pockets. From where I was standing I could not make out the details of his face. He said and did nothing. For a moment I thought my eyes were playing tricks on me, that he was a being conjured out of nothing but light and shade, but I quickly dismissed that possibility.

The funny thing is, I felt no fear. You may find that odd, but don't forget, I was a young and innocent child. Quiet men standing on riverbanks didn't scare me. Loud, barking, snapping things like dogs were more likely to send me off in a sprint.

From across the water, I asked his name, but he said nothing. He didn't move. I asked if he came there often and finally he nodded. That gave me the go-ahead to continue asking questions. I asked where he was from and he shifted his head to his left, telling me. I asked if he had a home and he shook his head slowly—*no*.

Eventually, after running out of questions to ask, I told him it had been a pleasure meeting him, I was going home, and turned away. As I walked from the river, I looked back over my shoulder. He was still in his spot, watching me go. I waved and continued on, through the woods, back to the lodge to deal with my chores.

That night I could not get the man out of my head. I remember sitting at the dinner table, rolling peas on my plate with my fork as my father talked about something or other and my mother fed my sister in her high chair. I hadn't told them about the man in the woods. There didn't seem to be any need to do so. He was just another one of the many woodland curiosities I kept to myself. I guarded my time in the woods the way one guards a diary full of secrets that may never mean as much to anyone else as to oneself. I confided in the woods the way the woods confided in me, revealing each of its marvels so faithfully.

After dinner I went to my room, climbed onto my bed, and stared through the window at the moon. I thought about where he could have come from and what he wanted. I was struck by sympathy for him. He had seemed so alone. Not just alone in the woods, but always. Anywhere. I struggled to imagine him knowing *anyone,* which was not an assumption I'd made about anyone up until that point in my life. What was most clear was that I needed to know more. I decided then I would return to the brook the following day.

But in the morning, I was less enthusiastic. The previous day seemed like many weeks before. I couldn't trust my earlier opinion, that he was nothing more than some harmless woodland curiosity, but the weather was beautiful and sunny, promising a day of good things, so I grabbed my notebook and pencil, ignored my concerns, and set off to find him—not that there was any reason for him to be in the same spot.

At first, I struggled to retrace my steps. It wasn't often that I felt the need to take a route I'd previously taken. I liked to set out and see where my feet would lead me. That day, I tried to remember where and when I had turned. I found it surprisingly difficult. It didn't really concern me though; whether or not I found the brook, I was in good company. The birds chirped and the leaves rustled. Small creatures scurried beneath the dried leaves on the forest floor. Above, trunks creaked and teetered in the wind like old men with bad joints. I found a large stick and used it to plough my way through bushes, through small swarms of miniature flies that did little but tickle my face. It was not long before I felt warm and needed a drink of water.

I heard the chatter of water on stones and stepped through the bushes. I hadn't spent any time exploring the edge of the stream the previous day. I was longing to see a frog or toad out in the woods and hadn't yet been lucky. Perhaps today would be the day . . .

He was there. The man. It had momentarily slipped my mind that I had set out to find him, and yet there he was. Standing just as before, in his long coat, his hands in his pockets, still on the other side, but a few metres closer. He was no longer high up on the bank but right at the water's edge. I could now see his face. He had a long head, like a horse's, but his features were sharp and lizard-like. His pale skin was stretched too tightly over his skull, his ears too big and his neck a little too long. Now that he was closer I could see that he was, in fact, very tall—taller than anyone I'd ever met. He was hunched over slightly, his long wizened neck undulating. He cocked his head to the left like a nosy bird. His face was expressionless, his lips taut and thin, indistinguishable in colour from the rest of his skin.

I said hello. He said nothing in return. He cocked his head to the right. I sighed and looked away.

His lack of reaction disappointed me. I asked why he wouldn't speak. He didn't reply. I asked if he could, in fact, speak at all. He shook his head, no. Without thinking, I stood a step forward, but he became agitated and stepped back, shaking his head violently. I said there was no need to be scared of me, that I wouldn't hurt him, but he did not seem convinced. For a few minutes we simply stood there, our eyes fixed on each other.

I pointed at a green bird in a tree. I told him it was a Knysna loerie. It didn't seem to interest him. I looked down at the water and saw a small shoal of silvery fish whip between the rocks. I asked him if he liked fish. Nothing.

Frustrated, I said if he wouldn't speak, I'd leave. Still, he offered only silence. I waited for him to signal that he wished for me to remain. Nothing. Fed up, I turned and headed back into the woods. As I did, though, for reasons I could not—and still cannot—fully explain, I looked over my shoulder and promised I'd visit the following day. Then I left.

As promised, I returned the next day and met him at the brook. He was closer still than the day before. In fact, he was in the middle of the stream now, unperturbed by the water sloshing about his knees. He simply stared as I talked on and on, about my father, my mother and sister, our house in Kroonstad, and what had brought us out to Tsitsikamma in the first place. I told him about the birds, the bugs, the trees and the plants. I assumed he was listening the entire time, though he continued to extend nothing other than the occasional nod and shake of the head. Soon, I simply forgot he was there at all. I got lost in my stories, punctuating my babbling with expressions like *you know what I mean?* and *isn't that wild?*

Finally, he reached into his inner breast pocket and when he pulled his hand back out it was tightened into a fist. His action startled me. I'd been sitting on the riverbank, not expecting a response, and was now propped up against it. Carefully, he opened his enormous white hand and rolled out his long, bony fingers.

In the middle of his palm was a small frog.

I sprang to my feet. I so wanted him to show me up close. He didn't. Instead, he extended his open palm as if it was the frog's fleshy white throne, and tipped it over. I gasped as the stiff body rolled over, out of his hand like a ball, and *plopped* into the water.

It was dead. He'd pulled a dead frog from his pocket. The frog floated down the river on its back, arms and legs splayed, white belly up, and disappeared behind some rocks.

My hands flew to my mouth and I let out a wheeze, yet even then I didn't fear him. I was like a mother whose child has made a horrible undercooked breakfast for her. Or rather, the owner of a cat both appreciating and detesting the dead pigeon left on the stoep as a gift. After the frog was gone, I let out an uneasy giggle and thanked him, my voice dubious.

He smiled. It was an awkward smile that stretched from ear to ear. His cheeks pulled back like two thick curtains. It felt physically forced, but earnest. It seemed to pain him, smiling in such a way, but I was pleased he had offered it.

I announced that he needed a name. Everyone needs a name, I told him.

I decided his name would be Burt.

Burt, the man in the woods.

A few minutes later, I left Burt and returned to the lodge.

At the dinner table that evening, I still said nothing, but was in better spirits. My father had invited a nice young Dutch couple to have dinner with us. Afterwards, he pulled out the guitar and played his songs. I could tell where the night was going; a couple of bottles of wine had been called to duty. The more the chatting and laughter grew, the more tired I became. They hardly noticed me leaving. I switched on my bedside lamp, climbed under the covers, grabbed my grubby notebook, and turned to a new page. I drew a picture of Burt smiling his big banana smile and wearing his long black coat. I drew myself, standing beside him. I filled the rest of the page with tall green trees and big, bushy plants. The land and sky teemed with birds and bugs. They were all huddled around us, faced inwards, keeping a watchful eye.

The following day I returned with food.

Burt was standing even closer, still in the water, but on my side of the brook. I had brought a tuna-mayonnaise sandwich my mother had made.

Now, the only thing I hate more than tuna is mayonnaise. My mother told me to not be fussy with food, because one day I might not have the choice. I replied that when the day came, I'd eat the tuna-mayo sandwich. Until then, I'd take advantage of my options. At which point my mother shoved the wrapped sandwich in my hand and said, *The day's come, smarty face.*

I'd taken the sandwich reluctantly, but now I had an idea: I'd offer it to Burt.

I placed it on a dry rock between us and waited. He lowered his head and looked at it.

I said, *Go on. It's for you.*

He looked up at me and down at the sandwich. He whimpered softly to himself, almost pitifully, and I encouraged him again to take it.

Then, unexpectedly, he lunged. His long arms flailed like two long windsocks as he leaned to grab it from the rock. I stumbled back and tripped over a branch, falling onto the mushy bank. I watched with wide eyes as he ripped the cling film with his teeth and stuffed the sandwich messily into his wide, cavernous mouth. He ate voraciously—his big jaw opening and closing violently—as if he feared the bread would try to escape his clutches. His throat made gurgling sounds as he pushed the food in. Once it was finished, he licked the mayonnaise off his hands, working his long pale tongue into every crease and wrinkle of his palms and fingers.

Then he was done, and he snapped upright like a switchblade. He narrowed his eyes at me and licked his lips.

He groaned. He wanted more.

I shook my head to say, *Sorry, I don't have any more.*

He groaned again, his head jerking like a chicken.

For the first time, I felt scared, acutely aware that I knew nothing about the man. There was no way to anticipate what he would do next. He shifted under his coat, the bones in his shoulders *clacking* like pebbles dropped on pebbles as he twisted his head up and to the left, then up and to the right. He chattered his teeth, *clack-clack-clack-clack,* like the novelty toy dentures you wind up and set on the floor. *Clack-clack-*

clack-clack. Birds fluttered away from the branch above him. His tongue rolled out of his mouth; his eyes widened to the size and shape of large coins.

I struggled to breathe. My heart beat faster. My body knew what my mind couldn't fully register: I was more than nervous. I was scared.

His left foot moved forward. Then the right. Then the left. *Clack-clack-clack-clack*. My hands scrabbled for purchase on the bank behind me, I pushed myself up with my feet, crawling backwards as fast as I could. He was gathering speed, lurching towards me, hands out, grabbing at air.

I'm sorry, I told him. *I don't have any more.*

He wailed from his throat, disappointed and aggrieved. I continued to crawl backwards, realising he was not going to stop. He was begging now, yowling for food and no matter what I said he would not accept that I had nothing left to offer. He would not stop. I flipped over and dug my feet into the mud. I would have to run.

Moneta, it is time to run for your life, I told myself. *This is what you must do. No time to think it through, Moneta. Run.*

And so I did. I ran.

If there's one bit of advice I can give you, it's this: take care of your body. People forget it's the only one they've got, flippantly putting all kinds of poisonous things into it, never doing enough to keep it fit and strong. People don't realise that when it finally gives in, there is no replacement. That's it. *You've ruined it, rotted it away, and now you're stuck in it, my friend.* People also don't realise that, yes, they will get older. Their bodies will weaken and there will be some things they won't be able to do, like climb a tree or jump over a fence. Or run. Oh, I would give anything to be able to run again. Anything to have my young legs, my young lungs and my young heart! And let me tell you, as a young girl, I could *run* all right. On that hot summer morning, in the thick, evergreen woods of Tsitsikamma, with gangling, lizard-faced Burt ploughing through the woods after me, I ran.

I ran like I'd never run before. I hurtled through that forest. Each tree was a rushing blur. The air pumped in and out of my lungs. My heart thumped against my rib cage as I clambered up slippery muddy banks and splashed through puddles.

I ran as fast as I could, but running in fear is not like running to win a race or get in shape. Running in fear, your legs are never fast enough for your racing mind. I had no idea how far he was behind me, if I was losing him, if he was gaining on me, or if, at any second, his bony hand would snatch me by the shoulder and jerk me to the dirt. I simply ran and hoped. I hoped I'd make it out of the woods in time. I hoped I'd be able to burst into the kitchen and throw myself into my mother's arms. She'd be standing in her apron over a boiling pot of something good. She'd throw her arms around me and I'd cry. She'd rub my back and tell me, *It's okay, sweet pea, everything's going to be all right.*

But I was not in the kitchen. I was not even in the lodge. I was in the middle of the woods. The man in the woods was an unknown distance behind me, with legs so long it probably took him only one or two steps to cover my five or six. I didn't stand a chance.

I glanced over my shoulder.

There he was, ten to fifteen metres back, his arms and legs flapping like cooked spaghetti as he tore through the woods towards me. He let off a sound, a cross between a growl and a groan. Fury and despondency filled his wordless utterings.

Strange, yes? And possibly hard for you to believe. But it is what happened next that you may struggle with most. I wouldn't blame you. As I grew older I somehow convinced myself that it hadn't happened—that it was the wily invention of a child's fancy—but these days, in these late years, I have come around. I now know that what I came to witness that day occurred just as I remembered it. This is another of a long life's little lessons: there is no greater ignorance than the belittling of a memory for the sake of what you believe to be the truth at *that* point of your life. Once you decide the events of your past did or did not occur in the way that you once believed, you harm yourself in ways you cannot fathom.

Oh, young man. Take this with you: tread lightly. Your memories are what are left of your experiences, and a memory that has been tampered with is not easily fixed. It took me the better part of a hundred years to remind myself of exactly what happened that day in the woods. A hundred years to identify and then dispel all of the supposed *insights* I'd accumulated since then and restore my memory like a conservator restores a weathered old painting, stroke by careful stroke.

Remember that.

As I ran through that forest, something mystical took me over.

I always knew I could run, but I was no longer simply running. I was moving through the forest as if I had designed it myself. I knew every part of it. I anticipated every upcoming hole in the ground—every slippery slope, every fallen branch. I leaped from rock to rock. I swerved effortlessly through the gauntlet of trees and bushes. It felt as if I was running on air, as if the forest had uploaded the obstacle course in my head beforehand, or I had done the exact route a thousand times before. The woods opened up. I flew through a thick bush, barely touching it. I cannot explain how I managed this, but I did. The bush was riddled with thick thorns, but it left me unscathed as I slipped through it.

I looked back and saw the man crash into the same bush. The thorns ripped through him, shredding his coat and his skin. He howled as he smashed through the dried hedges and burst out with two thrashing fists. Once he was out, he continued running after me, cut up and bleeding, yet seemingly oblivious to the pain. I ran ahead of him.

I flitted through a clearing of tall grass and small shrubs. My bare legs were exposed to a poisonous ivy, but suffered not even the slightest reddening of the skin. Those rough leaves brushed past me like soft strips of cotton cloth.

The man rushed into the same grasses and crashed into the thick underbrush, landing on all fours. I spun to see him. The ivy was not nearly as forgiving to him. He wailed like a baboon in a trap. The ivy ran across his face, grazing and infecting him, intensifying the pain from his cuts. His screams echoed through the trees.

Now, I've felt ivy; it stings, but his was most certainly *not* a normal reaction. In just a few short seconds his face had reddened and swelled like a boiled tomato. On the mound of each of his lumps, white blisters began to form. His left eyelid bulged and drooped. His thin, indistinguishable lips were at once very distinguishable—fat and red.

I swear it.

Some people may tell you it is impossible, that ivy would never affect one so severely, but let me tell you, I saw it. It was as if scalding hot water had been poured over him. He yelped like a small dog, struggling to breathe as he slowly got to his feet. Even his hands were no longer long and white, but inflamed and disfigured. With a madman's gusto, he staggered on towards me, his hands swimming through the damp air, his eyes glassy and unfocused.

I gulped and took a few quick steps back as he edged closer, reeling and panting. He threw himself against the trunk of a tree and wrapped his arms around it. His throat was so bloated it must have been virtually impossible to breathe. He wheezed and whistled, his face pressed against the bark. His lips and eyes drooped from his face like slivers of raw fish and yet I could still see an intensity in his face. There was still a busy and incensed mind inside that failing, bloated vessel, that was for sure.

My father's words came back to me: *Plants have had to survive this world just like everything else.*

He saw me—or perhaps he simply sensed me—and pushed himself off the tree with whatever strength of will he had left. I moved backwards. He swayed as he took a few steps, confused, battered, blistering, but still intent on stalking forward.

Don't make the mistake of thinking they are weak or useless things.

A flying insect buzzed around his face, and he swatted blindly at it. The insect circled his head, infuriating him. I saw then that it was no harmless fly that had made its acquaintance. It was a hornet.

The hornet landed on his face and stung him. He shuddered, froze in his spot, and shrieked. I looked up. A second hornet was spiralling down from above. Then, a third. Soon there were hundreds, literally *hundreds* of them, descending from the trees and engulfing him. He flung his arms madly and let off a high and unearthly screech. They stung him in the neck and face. They slipped beneath his clothing and plunged their stingers into his body. He beat himself with his fists, throwing himself forwards and backwards, spinning on his spot like a top, yapping and wailing as they flew into his mouth, as they stung him in the eyes, as they injected their poison into his blood.

He tried to walk but at that point he could barely stand. His legs began to wobble, and then he dropped to his knees.

I grabbed my chance to leave.

With the sound of his screams following me, I ran back to the lodge as quickly as I could. The light of the sun lit my path. The bushes and trees parted. The wind escorted me. I ran flat-out for almost fifteen minutes.

My mother was drinking tea at the kitchen table, reading the paper. I burst in, sweating and panting. I left muddy tracks all over the floor. She pushed herself back from the table and stood. I ran into her, just as I'd imagined, and then I cried. She asked me what had happened. She asked me where I'd been, but I said nothing. She kissed me on the top of my head, rubbed my back in circles, and said to me the words I'd ached to hear, but at that moment they were the most impotent little words I'd ever heard: *It's okay, sweet pea, everything's going to be all right.*

A mother gives up

"It took me only three or four days to go back into the woods," Moneta said, sitting at the iron table with her hands folded neatly on her lap. "But the woods were a different place. And I was a different person."

Our tea was finished. It had been a while since I'd had tea, and I'd enjoyed it thoroughly. Moneta had undoubtedly used her own leaves. It had been strong and invigorating.

"Did you see him again?" I asked. As difficult as it was to believe the man had truly been attacked by plants, I had absorbed every word of her story. In fact, she'd not so much *told* her story as had it seep from her, filling the air until we were both steeped in it, like the steam from our cups.

"When I went back into the woods I decided to return to where I'd left him. It took me more than an hour to get there, far longer than it had taken when I ran out of the woods. I retraced each of my steps with dread. I didn't know what to expect. Somehow I imagined he'd still be kneeling in the centre of the clearing, swatting at the hornets, but there were no piercing screams, no more buzzing. Even the brook in the distance seemed to have stopped gurgling. The woods were uncannily still, as if the trees had withdrawn into themselves, in mourning perhaps, or shame.

"And then, there he was. His dead body lying in the grass, still in his tattered coat. But what was most interesting was the underbrush. The grasses. You see, in the few days since I had left him, the plants had covered him. From what I could see of him: his arms, his legs, his hands, his feet—all that wasn't obscured by his coat—they'd somehow grown over him, tied him down, either in an attempt to hide him or prevent him from standing. He had been wrapped, swaddled like a mummy in green bandages. If not for his black trench coat, I may have had trouble finding him at all.

"I stood over him for a few minutes, studying him. He was lying front down, his legs and arms bent and twisted. The plants hadn't yet swallowed his head—it was turned to the side and his eyes were open and glassy, like a doll's, looking at nothing. Surprisingly, I felt both sadness and guilt: sadness that he'd been punished for possibly not knowing any better, guilt that I'd run from him in the first place. He hadn't hurt me. He'd only frightened me, and I wasn't certain my fright alone had warranted his long and agonising death. But I knew too that I had had no choice. And the woods, it had seemed, had had none either. I sat on my haunches, tilted my head, and looked down into his eyes. He looked right through me. I expected him to blink, but he didn't. He just lay there, a sad scarecrow who had fallen over. A beached sea creature. It was the first dead body I had ever seen."

I listened as she spoke, but couldn't help studying the small details of her face: the thin lines running down the sides of her nose, her grey eyes calm and wise, old inside a face that looked considerably younger.

A young boy ran to Moneta's side. Short and wiry, he had a dark complexion and thin, tousled hair. She turned and beamed at him, and patted his cheek.

"Hello Junyap," she said. The boy smiled back and then looked at me. I had not seen him before. "Say hello to the nice man," she told him.

He greeted me in English, politely on cue, although I could tell he was not an English speaker. He said something to

Moneta in his own language and she replied. They kissed each other on the cheek and then he left her side.

"He's been in my care for a few months now. He's a special little boy. Very sharp. He lives here with me and helps me with the plants. He loves them, just as I do. He once told me that his favourite memory is of his grandmother, sitting barefoot on the lawn of their old house, singing and pulling out weeds. It sounds like she was a warm and beautiful woman. We've been teaching each other our languages, Junyap and I, but he's catching on quicker than I am. Children: they're sponges."

She watched him as he picked up a watering can and moistened the soil of the large wooden crate I had dragged in earlier.

"He was separated from his family—his mother, father, sister and two older brothers—and yet he has never cried a tear. He loves them dearly, but he is a realist. Pragmatic. Some may mistake it for aloofness, but I have come to understand him; he is a survivor. Astute. And yet, somehow, a gentle soul. So much so that there is no one else I trust more to take care of this garden after I am gone."

She smiled and then turned to me. "Do you have any children?"

It was the first time she had enquired about me. As simple as the answer was, I felt lost for words. Eventually, I nodded and said, "Yes. A son."

"Do you know where he is?"

"No."

"Do you dream about him?"

I paused and said, "Yes."

"And somewhere out there he is dreaming about *you*. It's nice to have a place to meet, hmm? Come, let's take a walk."

We left the table and walked through the garden. Moneta glided slowly between her green companions, loving each with a gentle touch, leaning over now and then to smell a leaf or a flower.

She went on to speak about the plants, telling me again that they, like people, have their friends and their enemies. It is important to have both, she said, because that's how life pushes itself forward. Chamomile encourages other plants to increase their essential oils. Rosemary protects cabbage and beans but dislikes potatoes. Basil brings the best out of tomatoes but can't stand being near rue. There are allegiances and rivalries in the plant kingdom, just as everywhere else.

Eventually, she came out with: "Some say that in tropical areas a corpse left above ground can be stripped to clean bone in under two weeks. Invertebrates do most of the damage."

She stuck her finger in the soil of a small fern and smelled it. She rubbed two fingers together to remove the soil and then continued along the path.

"Well, I returned to that place in the woods only four *days* later, out of curiosity, and he was gone."

"Gone?"

"No body . . . and not one bone. Nothing, except for that horrible black coat. Entirely gone."

I frowned. "What do you mean?"

"He was taken in, of course," she said.

"You mean . . . ?"

"Obliterated. I know. It's difficult to believe. But those woods had broken him down and pulled him in, like my banana peel . . . all signs of him ever having existed were erased."

"That's not possible," I said.

"No, I suppose it isn't. And yet . . ."

She called to Junyap and instructed him to do something. He nodded and ran outside.

"Such a good boy," she said. "Yes, well. The man was gone. The woods had taken him, and I think I know why."

"Why?"

"Because he was a mistake."

The sun was high overhead, piercing the glass dome, the air hung warm and unmoving. I had no idea how Moneta could spend so much time in there. I wiped my forehead with the sleeve of my shirt and puffed a warm, wet breath into the warm, wet air.

"There *are* mistakes. Even in nature. Things that do not belong. The man in the woods—if he was a man at all— was a mistake. He was never meant to be. I know that now.

I don't know where he came from, or where he belonged, but I've come to accept that some things don't come from anywhere, don't *belong* anywhere. Some things are simply not meant to exist at all. And nature does not take kindly to such abominations. So he was taken. Wiped off the earth. Like mopping up spilled milk. Two weeks. That's how long it took for the man in the woods to be removed. The trees, it seems, will take the body of a dead thing as quickly as they want it, or want to get rid of it."

Moneta lifted a hand to my face and stroked the side of my cheek. The skin on the tips of her thin fingers was feathery and dry.

"You're young," she went on. "You will see a lot in your time. I can tell. Most of it will slip away from you as the years go on. Don't concern yourself with what slips away. One day even the sun will burn out and everything will go dark. This earth will be a rock. We will be ash. There'll be no meaning left behind us, no clue that we existed. There will be no answers, but more importantly, there will be no more questions. Until you realise that, you'll never puzzle out what it means to be alive. I don't know it all, but I know that much. So do yourself a favour: leave it all behind. The whole silly, sorry mess of it, and be alive while you can, hm?" She tapped my face and turned back to her plants. "Oh good. Finally. The dahlias are coming out. I've been so worried about them."

She said nothing else. Her final announcements baffled me. They seemed to be in contradiction with what she had said earlier, that memories were not to be tampered with, that the truth of the moment was all that mattered. Now, according to Moneta, nothing mattered. One day, we'd all be ash, and our memories would go along with us, to a meaningless end.

So why bother with the story at all?

I looked around me, lost in a daze. There was nowhere else I had to be—I had no chores for the day—but I sensed Moneta was once again in her own world, strolling like a sheltered queen through the courts of her green kingdom. Her story had been told, I'd moved her bags of fertiliser, dragged her wooden crate, and it was probably time for me to leave. I said goodbye and she smiled absently.

As I stepped out of the glass dome, a cool sea breeze ran over me. Seagulls flapped against the sun, twirling and squawking. The white foam of the blue ocean soothed the hot sands of the beach. In the distance, the three rafts bobbed on the shimmering water—three brown spots, like flotsam.

The scene was tranquil, the offenders seemingly inert, but I knew better. There was nothing passive about being out there. Nobody returned from the raft the same person they'd been before. Something deep within their minds was lost or altered. I'd seen some of the liveliest members of the commune reduced to vacant-eyed loiterers, passive and submissive. Others would do nothing but stare at the ocean for hours on end, as if they'd seen something out there the rest of us could never comprehend. Some retreated into themselves completely, petrified to even greet anyone, let alone dishonour The Renascence and risk being sent back to the rafts. Others would reveal the truth in nightmarish screams as they slept. I'd lie in my tent and hear them moan and shriek, knowing everyone else was hearing it too. It was clear that the physical torture of being on the raft was relieved only by a sort of madness most of us hoped we'd never experience.

Still, something was lost in the spectatorship, like looking into a glass of water and forgetting water is the birthplace of life. Or listening to an old woman's story and remaining oblivious to what the Greeks had called her pneuma, the Hindus her atman, the Christians her soul.

Junyap ran to me. He held out a peach-coloured envelope and I took it from him.

"What's this?"

"Sunsengnim. Yi-mo says you must open it, but you mustn't open it now. Yi-mo says you'll know when. She trusts you. Yi-mo trusts you because she's told you she trusts you. Do you understand?"

I nodded.

He grinned with relief. "Nice to meet you," he said.

"It was nice to meet you too."

At that, he darted away from me to resume his chores. I looked at the envelope and slapped it against the palm of my left hand. It was light. I wondered if it was connected to her story about the man in the woods.

You must open it, but you mustn't open it now.

I walked away from the botanical garden and back down towards the beach. Moneta's strange story swirled in my head, displacing the emptiness with which I had awoken earlier that day.

The next day, it poured. The rain fell in hard sheets, hammering the land and sea. Thunder rumbled from some far-off place, not so much a boom as a deep groan within a groan, lost within its own rolling echo. Lightning struck the water in the distance like a blue crack in the invisible wall that separated us from the rest of the world.

I sat under an awning beside Gideon, watching the rain. We said nothing. We simply watched and listened. The rain chattered endlessly on the sand and drummed on the tarps of the tents, showing no sign of letting up. Beyond the rain, a thick greyness had fallen, leaving only dark muddled shapes without texture, as if everything had become a weathered old photograph of a place we used to know.

I turned to look at Gideon. He was staring out intently, unflinching as the thunder rumbled again. I drew in my legs and hugged my knees tighter.

Each of the small tents on the beach glowed a faint orange, the lamps within providing the only few dabs of colour in our gloomy, achromatic world. There were no chores to be done. The offenders on the rafts had been pulled back in. The rations of food for the day had been handed out. Now all we could do was wait the weather out.

My mind replayed the details of Moneta's story. I couldn't work out why she had chosen me to tell it to.

I thought about telling Gideon, but a deeper part of me said it would be a mistake. I had been entrusted with her story, and though she had not told me to keep it to myself, I sensed the many specific details of her memory were her prize. A memory like an old heirloom that needed to be polished every day and kept in a safe place. The story had been shared in incredibly vivid detail. No one on the beach had told me anything like it before. Whatever I could possibly repeat would undoubtedly be a mere shell of her living, breathing memory—and that, above all, would be the real wrongdoing.

A part of me also knew Gideon appreciated my company precisely because of our silences. I rarely understood what was going through his mind, but for some reason, we'd been drawn to each other's quiet company. One of the instructions to the commune was to minimise conversation, but sometimes I thought only Gideon and I sat willingly without needing to talk. In another time and another place—a place where sharing a dream or spreading an idea was not only accepted but encouraged—my guess was that Gideon and I might still have been friends, and we'd still probably not need to natter about every passing thought.

"Look," Gideon said, looking out into the rain.

"I know."

"No, *look.*"

I squinted and saw a man running through the pelting rain, coming out of the grey like an apparition.

It was Daniel.

Daniel walked briskly ahead of us. He was a young man with a lanky frame and the gaunt face of someone at least ten years older. I knew him to be keen to impress at times, but honest and competent. I had liked him since the first time we'd met.

He was yelling, but his words were barely audible beneath the clatter of the rain: "Nooit! It has to be moved! If it dies, it won't be long before it becomes a health risk to us all! But it's not going to be easy!"

The pellets of water beat against my face. My eyes fought to stay open. I ran my hand through my hair, slicking it back, and glanced at Gideon beside me. The water didn't seem to hassle him at all. I looked back along the beach. The commune of tents was far behind us, a cluster of orange dots in the dimness. I wondered how much further we had to go.

Daniel continued: "I don't know how we're going to do this! Maybe with rope! Maybe rope and a lot of men!"

As he marched ahead, his feet threw up brown crowns of water. He pointed towards a mound of boulders up ahead. We still weren't sure why we had been called.

We climbed carefully over the rocks. Foamy water rushed into the gaps below, churning and slapping against the dark stone. My hands struggled to get a grip on the slimy surfaces. As I reached the top the object of our undertaking came into full view: on the shore ahead of us an enormous swollen body lay beached on the sandy shore.

A whale.

Daniel had mentioned nothing on the way over, but not even his obvious eagerness could have prepared me.

It was a black mountain, stretched out, slumped-down flesh crushed by gravity. The rain cascaded over its sides as it moaned and emptied its blowholes in fine, hissing sprays. A thick fin hung limp at its side like the unusable remainder of a gigantic, clipped wing. Near the edge of the sand the black serpentine tail rose, flapped once, and crashed back down. The longer I stared, the less it looked like an animal at all. It was unearthly, almost god-like—something that could just as conceivably have fallen from the sky as washed up from the ocean.

"Have you ever seen such a thing?" Gideon asked.

"No," I said, shaking my head. "Never."

I hopped to the sand and Gideon followed. Daniel ran ahead and climbed up the side of the whale. He stood atop, hands akimbo, looking as if he'd like to stick in a flag and proclaim it the New World.

"Come on!" he shouted.

It rose ever upwards and outward. I could see nothing of the beach or ocean beyond, only a black wall stretching into the sky and across the world. The thought of it passing weightlessly over the watery surface of the earth filled me with fear and respect for the ocean's secret, unexplored depths. But the same ocean had spat it into this heavy, alien netherworld, perhaps in banishment for some broken rule understood only by the creatures of the deep.

I laid my hand gently on its rough exterior. I had never felt anything like it. Coarse in some places, smooth in others. Still, it was all wrong. This was not where it was supposed to be, and it was clearly in pain.

"He's right, Mr. Kayle," Gideon said, standing a few feet behind me. "It has to be moved back. It can't stay here. If it dies here it'll cause problems."

I ran my fingers along the grainy, curved wall of its long body. It was peppered with clusters of white callosities. Finally, I reached its eye. Its large eyeball rolled in its socket and I leaned to peer into it, as if through a window.

"So, how we gonna do this?" Daniel yelled from above.

"I don't know," I said, but I wasn't sure he'd heard me. "We'll need more of us. And rope. She's not going to last long. She'll probably die of dehydration."

"How did you know?"

"Know what?"

"That it's a *she*?"

"I don't know. Is it? A guess."

"A good guess!" Daniel yelled. "Come to the back and see for yourself!"

He walked the length of the whale and jumped to the sand. I looked at Gideon, a man of few words, but could tell he was just as overwhelmed.

"Go on! Take a look!" Daniel shouted. "Underneath!"

Together Gideon and I followed Daniel to the rear end. I leaned over and Gideon dropped to his haunches.

The tail and y-shaped fin of a calf hung from the mother, lying still in the water. Barely half of it had been pushed out, the head was still inside. It was dead—that much was certain to us—before even having taken its first breath.

"You know why she did this, right? Got herself all beached up?" Daniel said. "Magnetic fields! Disrupted echolocation systems! Electromagnetic activity. I'm telling you! There's tech being used somewhere. The grids are back up. They're not telling us, but there's *tech* being used by *someone* out there."

The ocean raced up on either side of the whale mother, lifting the baby's lifeless tail for a moment (offering the illusion that it was still alive) and then retreating. "So, should we take it out? I mean, out of its mother?"

Gideon and I held back an immediate reply. The rain continued to hurtle so ferociously hard that at one point I thought it had turned to hail. The ocean foamed, folding over itself and charging the shore, passing our knees as it came up and sucking hard on us as it went back out.

"Not right now," Gideon said. "That's my feeling on this. For now, we need to think about getting the mother back into the water, if it's even possible. The baby is gone. We can't waste time. Also, she could bleed to death if we try. I don't know these things. Maybe it's already too late."

I agreed with Gideon. We needed a real plan.

Ultimately, we came up with less of a plan than a next step: Gideon and I would remain at the whale's side while Daniel ran back to the commune to call for more help.

Daniel nodded at that and swiftly left.

Later, when the rain had finally stopped, he returned with around sixty large men, the log-herders who kept the beach fires stoked. They carried all the rope they'd been able to gather. Gideon and I stepped aside and allowed them to co-ordinate the task.

They discussed how they'd go about it, and then hurled thick ropes over the whale's body. For the next hour or so, the men moved over and around her like a group of ants commandeering the corpse of a big, black beetle. In the end, satisfied the net of ropes was sufficiently fixed to her, they called on everyone to assist in the pulling. Gideon and I stepped forward and lined up to grab our section of the rope.

One of the men shouted a count, and we pulled. We dug our feet into the sand and urged each other on with grunts through clenched teeth. As time moved on, however, it felt as if we'd convinced ourselves we could reposition a mountain with little more than the determination of madmen. Others joined—bigger men than myself—and I gave up my position. I joined Daniel on the hillside, where he had been observing us the entire time. Sweating and drained, I collapsed next to him.

"How do you get a fifty-ton beached whale to move?" he asked offhandedly, leaning on an elbow and chewing a piece of grass. I didn't say anything. He stared out and said, "You ask it *really* nicely."

I turned to watch. Down on the beach the seventy-odd men appeared Lilliputian beside the colossal whale, and despite their efforts, hadn't moved her at all. She moaned and the sounds of her distress reached us in a high-pitched wail. Even the small movements in her tail had ceased.

"She won't go," Gideon said, walking up to us. His shirt was spattered with dark patches of perspiration. "We can forget about this. She won't go anywhere."

I was afraid to agree with him. I watched as the biggest and strongest log-herders in the commune heaved and pulled to no avail. Too much time had passed—she was slowly being crushed under her own weight, waiting for it all to be over.

By the time the clouds parted to reveal the clear patches of a starry night, the group of large men, exhausted and without any new ideas, finally gave up. One stood and said that it was no use. That they had tried their best. They'd hoped the rising tide would assist in floating the whale back out, but it had sunk too deeply into the sand. There was nothing more to be done. In the morning the whale would be put out of its misery, doused in oil, and burned. If they couldn't move it, they'd raze it to the ground, he said, since there was no other way to guarantee it didn't become a decaying health hazard. Everyone agreed and then swiftly decided: they'd end her and set her alight at dawn.

With no need to consider it further, they rolled up their ropes, left the mother with the carcass of her unborn calf, and marched up the beach to their tents for the night.

The rest of the night was peaceful and soundless.

I was lying in my tent and staring at the blank ceiling. I pulled my blanket up to my neck and clutched it firmly with my hands. The image of the calf hanging from its mother wouldn't leave my mind. This image was spliced with another: a terrible memory of my own, few of them that I had left. As I lay there, caught between sleep and wakefulness, memories and images slipped into and around each other:

My wife is running from the side of the road with our daughter in her arms. It's dark and I can hardly see them. But my daughter's body is limp in her arms, and my wife's high-heeled shoe comes off her foot as she hurtles towards me through the small bushes. She's screaming. No, not screaming. It's a suffocated yelping I've never heard her make. Between the yelps, she's saying, *Oh my god, oh my god, oh god, oh my god* . . . and then I see that calf in the whale. I see my daughter. And my wife's standing in front of me. She shows me my daughter . . . and it's the whale calf, and my daughter.

And they're dead.

I opened my eyes in the dark and breathed softly.

Amid the silence of a sleeping commune, I heard someone cough. The coughing stopped. All that could be heard was the purring of a quiet ocean. I turned to my side and stared at the silhouettes of my few belongings. I felt incredibly alone. I was not meant to be there.

I whipped the sheet away from me and sat up in my bed. I rubbed my face with my hands and sighed, sprang to my feet and threw on my pants. I grabbed my shirt off the corner post of my bed and put it on. Moving carefully in my dark tent, I found my way to the paraffin lamp on the floor. I lit the wick with a match and the flickering light of the flame revealed the details of my makeshift dwelling.

I took my paraffin lamp by the wire handle, unzipped the tent, and stepped outside, into the brisk night air. I walked quietly through the sleeping commune.

The clouds had broken away from each other and were now hovering on the horizon. Millions of stars flickered against the black night, the moon was full and large, beaming bright and blue and dripping over the wrinkled surface of the ocean.

My lamp swung in my hand as I made my way along the cold, wet sand. I crossed the beach, climbed over the boulders, and approached the black giant.

The whale heaved as she breathed, droning softly now. I stopped beside her and placed the lamp on the sand. The orange light flared against the side of her body, revealing each of her barnacles. I laid my palms flat on her. I pressed my face against her side and felt the weak vibration of her enormous heart. Closing my eyes, I absorbed her movements. My breathing slowed until I could barely feel it enter and exit my body, and a calm enveloped me.

I pictured her back in the ocean, where she had belonged: a weightless beast moving effortlessly with her pod, bursting from the waters, touching the sun, twisting, and crashing back in. Once, she had been free to roam every shore on the planet, every dark and unchanging abyss, to bask in the warmth of the ocean's surface, but now . . .

I put my back to the whale and slid down to the sand. I tipped my head back, turning my eyes to the sky. A comet appeared, trailed across the deep dark blue, and vanished into nothing.

Day Zero

On a warm Thursday morning in early November, Kayle Jenner got out of bed and kissed his wife goodbye. Sarah always left earlier for work than he did. He'd sleep in while she did her hair and put on her carefully selected outfit. He'd bury himself deep under the white duvet, all the while enduring the banshee shriek of the hairdryer and the irregular trot of her heels across their wooden floors. Just before she walked out the door for work, he'd muster his first bit of strength for the day to rise from his bed, compliment her on her looks, and see her off with a kiss and a wave.

On that particular morning, he stood at the door with his hands tucked into the pockets of his grey bathrobe and watched her walk to her autovehicle. The metal chimes hanging from the ceiling of the porch played a jangling tune in the morning breeze. The sun fell through the wooden slats above him and cast glowing stripes across the deck.

Kayle leaned against the doorframe and took in a deep breath. His wife really did look fantastic in her black shirt and ruffled orange skirt. Her hair was done up just the way he liked it, in a ponytail, with two curls falling softly on either side of her face.

The door of the AV opened. Sarah turned back and smiled at him, offering an awkward half-wave as she held the top of the car door. She had taken to wearing her large sunglasses, and he wished he could see her eyes. Was she wearing them deliberately, to protect him in some way—to save him from some emptiness she couldn't bear to show? Kayle sighed, and forced a smile.

Ever since the accident, Sarah hadn't quite come around to reality. He knew she blamed herself. She should have been keeping an eye on their Maggie. She should have realised their daughter had climbed out of the backseat and made her way to the road. Sarah was the one who'd been sitting in the front, reading some magazine when it happened. That was what she kept going back to, even though Kayle reminded her over and over that he'd left the back door open. *If only. I should have.* The same endless litany.

In the days and weeks that followed, both he and his wife were connected by the stark reality of their pain, if nothing else. They tried to talk each other through it. They saw somebody, some counsellor. It was considered healthy for them to pour out their grief in tears and nightly wails and fits of remorse—but then Sarah stopped, as if she'd cried herself dry and turned to dust. She shut down. She wandered the house in a trance. Her ability to care about the rest of her life slipped away with everything else. Now, five months later, there was little improvement. Heaven knows, Kayle was hurting as well. He missed his baby girl and went to cry in the bathroom, but for God's sakes, he was *trying*. For Andy's sake, if for anything and anyone. Was she even trying anymore? Could she be so selfish? Was *he* being selfish? He didn't know what to think—who was right, who was wrong—but anger welled up in him like warm, thin bile as he watched her. He turned and went back inside, flushing it away.

He walked into the kitchen, instructed the room to play Abbey Lincoln and put on the kettle for a cup of coffee. The twiddling jazz piano filled the house. While the water boiled, he went down the hall into his son's room and woke him for school. Andy sat up and rubbed his eyes, against the whole idea. His father patted him on the shoulder and told him to get up and be in the bathroom in three and a half minutes, *big guy*, before returning to the kitchen to prepare breakfast.

Kayle's first lecture was only in a couple of hours—enough time for the two of them to have breakfast together and for Kayle to drop Andy at school before going to the university.

Andy sat at the kitchen table. He watched as his father plated up his eggs and the slice of toast that had had some advertisement for women's shoes etched into it by their smart appliance. He smeared his butter over *Up to 60% off all high-heels at Guillian's!* and bit into it. They sat and ate their breakfast together, saying little. Kayle asked about school and Andy's answer was predictable; for him school was always the same old drag. They finished their breakfast, cleared their plates, and Andy went to pack his bag while Kayle shaved and changed. He grabbed a red shirt and chose a blue tie, a combination Sarah had always disliked, but she'd already left. She'd probably remark on it when he came home from work. By then he'd have been gone all day, offending everyone's good taste. By then it would be too late.

The music haunting the rooms was now Beethoven's "Adagio un poco mosso." It escaped the windows through the soft white curtains that waved gently in the cool wind. Outside, Brandy and Whiskey, the two horses in their paddock, stood apart from each other and nibbled on the grass. Beyond the paddock, the green land rolled forever beneath the brilliant yellow sun.

Andy climbed into the backseat of the AV and dumped his bag at his feet. Kayle placed his hand on the ignition screen and the car hummed to life—the red bars on the solar-electrometer climbing as the car charged itself for the day's driving. Kayle sighed and leaned his elbow on the lowered window, rubbing his face and pinching the bridge of his nose. He studied the blank expression on his son's face in the rear-view mirror. The boy was staring back at the house. It rested on its overgrown plot like a primitive Woodhenge from a time nobody remembered.

Andy hadn't been doing well. His grades had slipped. His friends had stopped calling. He was obviously wrestling with his own emotions. Not only had a daughter been lost, but a sister too. Kayle had to remember that, and keep remembering that. He had to be prepared to be patient.

The car beeped—it was ready to serve them. Kayle lowered the brakes and headed for the gate at the end of the gravel driveway. As he hit the narrow track leading to the public road, a cloud of orange dust hid the beams of the horse paddock, shrouding the shrinking house.

Kayle switched on the radio. A female news broadcaster was halfway through a story he had caught drift of a week earlier: Chang'e 11, the Chinese space-mining vessel that had left earth almost forty years earlier—the one that had famously lost communication and vanished without a trace—had somehow returned. According to the news, what was most peculiar was that the crew of nine astrominers had virtually no recollection of where they had been for forty years. Even stranger, they had not aged a day. It was a fascinating story and one that had captured the imaginations of people around the world. According to the news, however, the Chinese government was keeping it under wraps. There was growing international pressure on China to release more details (arguing that the return of Chang'e 11 constituted a case of global security), especially since the vessel had been back for a while and the world had only recently been allowed to know these few details.

Kayle struggled to care about any of it. He was tired of his students asking what he thought, of the teaching staff sharing their speculations. As for the push from Western governments, well, to Kayle it sounded like little more than old men using some dull, political pretence to validate a childlike curiosity for the other kid's new toy.

He drove through the familiar countryside of Tulbagh, passing twisted woods and open pastures. The sun sparkled on the hood of the silver autovehicle and the pitch of the engine's smooth hum grew in proportion to its acceleration. Kayle turned into the town and drove through the narrow streets.

He passed the local cafeteria and the shoe shop, the bank and the small police station, and the memorial square where people sat on the concrete steps behind the fountain and ate their packed breakfasts in the bright morning light. As the AV turned in and out of streets, Kayle saw familiar faces preparing to open their businesses for the day. Some of the shop owners waved as he passed, and he nodded or waved back.

Kayle rubbed his chin, glanced again at his son in the mirror, and pulled up outside the schoolyard. As usual, the road was packed with double-parked autovehicles, the pavements crowded with mothers urging children into the school yard. Children hurtled to meet their friends, their dark rucksacks hanging from their backs.

Andy opened the back door.

Hey, big guy, came Kayle's reminder, and the boy leaned over the front seat and kissed his father on the cheek. Kayle held him close for a brief moment before letting go. Then Andy sprang from the car and slammed the back door behind him, disappearing into a mob of chatting mothers and hyper-excited children.

Kayle drove back the way he came, but stopped at the local store to grab a small carton of milk. He made small talk with the old man behind the counter, wished him a good day, and left. As he drove he continued listening to the news about Chang'e 11 and the astrominers; the media were repeating what little they knew, adding tidbits of new information as if each was a revelation.

Kayle drove under an arch of trees, overhanging full and green, casting a blanket of shadow speckled with leaves of light. The tint of the windscreen automatically softened in the shade. Kayle passed through the suburbs, watching as residents took out their trash or hurried their tardy children into the backs of large AVs. A man raked leaves. Two women, one bobbing a shirtless young boy in her arms, chatted over the fence between their houses.

The newscaster droned on: the latest speculation on the Chang'e 11 story was that a large and unknown source of energy seemed to be pulsating from a location in China. There were concerns over radiation. The Chinese government had neither confirmed nor denied that the strange radiating energy had any direct relation to Chang'e 11 . . .

Kayle entered the small business district of the town and the tint on the windscreen adjusted to the direct glare of the sun. He pulled up to a traffic light and stopped. A few other AVs pulled up beside him. They waited together for the lights to change.

Kayle did a quick mental review of his upcoming lecture, "Secular Voices in Ancient Israel."

His thoughts were interrupted by an odd sensation building inside his head. He blinked his eyes hard and forced a yawn. It was nothing. Perhaps he hadn't had enough water to drink. Perhaps he'd eaten something that hadn't agreed with him . . .

The sides of the streets were busier now, families, young stragglers, old couples walking their designer dogs: the blood of human life was pumping through the concrete veins of the town. On the radio, the newswoman was still talking, her voice distorted.

Kayle switched it off.

He touched the side of his head. He was feeling dizzy and the first pangs of a headache were creeping in, not so much a pain as an aching heaviness. He must be coming down with something. Or perhaps it was stress—"The Silent Killer" that the posters in the doctor's office warned against. After all, there was tension at home, he'd been having peculiar dreams. Perhaps he was having some kind of psychosomatic—

s c r e e e e e e e e c h

It rang through his ears, the sound of two metal plates being scraped against each other. Kayle shook his head and shut his eyes, trying to force the sound back to the cruel place it had come from.

This isn't normal. This isn't right.

His hands clutched the wheel. He opened his eyes. The large woman in the vehicle to his right was grabbing her face, shaking her head. The same symptoms as his. *No. That doesn't make sense.* It was just a coincidence.

He looked to his left. The driver in the next lane was forcing two fists into the temples of his head like the clamps of a wood-shop vice.

The traffic lights were green, but nobody moved. People on the sides of the road had stopped. Families, stragglers, old couples—everyone suspended in a state of agony. Some were leaning against store walls, clutching their skulls. Some were bent over, throwing up on the pavement.

Kayle didn't understand. The noise, the dizziness, was originating from inside *his* brain. So how could they all be hearing and feeling the same thing? He tried to hold the thought but the screech in his head was intensifying and his eyes were becoming frighteningly sensitive to the harsh morning sun. Sunlight struck him like an angry god, cutting through his retinas, reaching in to ruin him with a single touch.

Kayle sat immobile now, completely paralysed by the sound and the light and the aching heaviness. His last rational thought before blacking out was of his son and his wife. Were they in a similar state, wherever they were? Would he ever see them again?

A man nobody on earth knew opened his eyes. He was sitting behind the wheel of a car. At first he did not know enough to register he'd awoken at all, only that there was light pouring into his head. A wall of light and a wave of sounds that eventually organised itself into shapes and allowed him his first bit of sense.

He was looking through a windscreen. The windscreen of a car. Beyond, smoke rose and spread, stretching up from the crumpled bonnets of two wrecked vehicles.

The man closed his eyes, calming himself in the darkness. He knew he could not keep them closed. He would have to open them again.

When he did, the world was clearer, but not his understanding. Gradually, a thought entered, and then another that tried to say the same thing, until he became aware of one thing only: *Wrong.*

Everything was wrong.

He held out his trembling hands but did not know who they belonged to, where the scar on the back of his knuckle came from, how many years had weathered his skin. He fixed his eyes on the two cars that had smashed into each other. They were smoking and steaming as if they had engaged in some violent kiss that had bound then broken them forever. But the man did not know they were cars at all. He could not recall their shapes nor did he know the purpose they served. They were strange physical abstractions, signifying nothing. He knew nothing, understood nothing. Nothing of himself or the world.

He turned, saw a large woman sitting in the car beside him, in the front seat, staring into space. She turned, looked at him, no expression on her face.

Their gaze shared nothing but mutual bewilderment.

The man had to get out. He had to breathe.

He looked at the side of his car. No handle, no button. He pushed hard—it wouldn't open. He looked around. A rectangular glass screen, the blue outline of a hand. He lifted his hand, looked at it. The hand on the screen . . . The same shape as *his* hand. He pressed his palm down, onto the glowing contour. The side of the car opened, startling him. He stepped out. He stood and the blood rushed to his head. He swooned. Steadied himself. Breathed deeply, then looked around.

A line of cars stretched out behind him. Each dazed occupant looked back at him. The man scanned the street. People, ambling slowly, dragging their feet. Drifting in a quiet stupor.

The man walked forward, stumbling into the sides of cars. He looked up to the sky. Wispy clouds drifted overhead. The sun shone strong, exposing an absurd, meaningless world.

The man wandered to the side of the road. A few people huddled silently in the shade. The small group proved a strange mix of people—an old woman, a young dark-skinned boy, a man in a grey suit and yellow tie, a portly woman with large breasts sagging under her baggy t-shirt.

The man squinted at her chest. There were colourful words on her shirt, but he could not read them. Squiggles and shapes. Meaningless . . . like everything else surrounding him.

Still, the clouds drifted and the sun shone as usual. The buildings were still standing, food was still cooking in the pans on stovetops in restaurants, the televisions in the shop windows were still flickering. Not a leaf of a tree had moved out of place.

He walked along the street. The details of the new world around him filled his blank mind: flowerpots on the windowsills of white shops, chalk scrawled on a black signboard, a steel gate swinging on its hinges outside the boutique. He recognised none of these objects.

He caught his reflection in the window of an electronics store. A man with a hard jaw, a wide sharp nose, sad and sloped eyes—the face of a stranger. He pushed a finger into the fleshy centre of his cheek. His mirrored likeness did so too. He was, indeed, looking at himself. His eyes refocused and a television image swam forward on the visual-glass—the studio background for a weather channel. No weather-person was standing before the image to offer predictions for the week's forecast. All he could see was an indecipherable map and a smattering of mystic numbers.

He approached the open doorway of a grocery store, stopping to peer inside. There were people in the store. A few people sat on the floors of the aisles, opening packets from the shelves, eating the contents. Tins rolled across the tiled floors. A lone baby cried in a shopping trolley.

The man sauntered further down the street. A fire hydrant spurted water into a gutter. *Thirsty.* The man realised he was thirsty. He got down on his knees and drank from the gutter, cupping the water in his hands. The blue tie around his neck dropped forward. He grabbed it and studied it quizzically. He pulled at it, but the peculiar accessory only tightened on his neck. He slipped his fingers into the loop around his neck and tugged outwards until it loosened. Finally, he whipped it up and over his head and threw it on the ground.

He walked on.

He passed three more car wrecks: a small silver one mounted across a lamppost, a white one with its side stripped by a brick wall, a long black one that had shattered the front window of a food mart. Two of the drivers were standing in front of their wreckages, staring indifferently at the crumpled steel boxes. The third driver, still in the car suspended diagonally against the pole, was still in his front seat, unconscious or dead. The man spared a glance for them all but did not stop walking.

He climbed over a low wall and into a public park. His sweaty skin cooled in the shade of dense green canopies. Dead leaves wheeled across the ground in a warm wind. The sun cut through the leaves above, spindles of light spearing in and out of the gaps.

In the centre of the park, between the trees, an old woman was bent over a refuse drum, rummaging through trash. She pulled out a black wrapper dripping with yellow liquid, and put it in her mouth. She sucked on the plastic and turned to look as the man in the red shirt went by.

The man walked through the park and out onto the narrow winding roads of a small residential area. Large houses, tucked behind bushy front yards, beige outside walls crawling with pink and purple bougainvillea, gimmicky postboxes, an unmanned length of hosepipe lying like a snake on an outside lawn, water looping into the grass. The man swung his head from side to side as he walked, but still he saw nothing familiar.

The man walked. Suburb after suburb, a stretch of road lined with restaurants and cafeterias, a pool hall, an art supplies shop. He crossed the perfectly green grass of a school rugby field, walked beside a concrete canal. The more he saw of the world, the less he grasped. His head was filled with more and more unrelated details and none of them added up to a helpful sum of this strange world's parts. The complexity of it all exhausted him. When his feet began to hurt, he stopped to sit. When he grew bored, he walked on. He did this for most of the day.

Once the sun had moved almost all the way across the sky, burning at its worst, he came across a bridge. A group of people were lying in the shade beneath: men and women in suits, children, teenagers, office workers, schoolteachers, policemen—a random assortment of people. He ducked under the bridge to join them and sat, finally out of the scalding sun. The people under the bridge looked at him silently. He remained there until the sun went down and the world was swathed in darkness. The group curled up close to each other, holding on like hopeless refugees from a faraway place they could no longer recognise as their home, and went to sleep.

In the morning the sun returned and one by one they awoke and left the underside of the bridge. The man woke and watched with tired eyes as each person ambled away. He lifted his head from the concrete and wiped away the bits of sand and stone embedded in the skin of his cheek. He cricked his neck and his back, and then made his way out into the vivid world. He was no closer to remembering where he was or how he had come to be there, but now he felt something other than confusion: a mist of despair swirling up and around him.

As he walked, he encountered a few more of the world's mundanities: an unattended fruit stall, a black dog chained to a post, barking frantically from behind a wire fence, an abandoned merry-go-round creaking softly in the wind.

A few hours later the man in the dank red shirt came across something that finally brought him to a stop: the sight of a woman walking towards him. He paused and stared at her. She stared back at him. She was wearing a black shirt and a ruffled orange skirt. She had long bleach-blonde hair. The roots were beginning to show and two curls framed her face.

She was beautiful, he could register that much, but he was interested in more than her beauty. Something deeper had caught his attention, something he could not understand, like the details of a dream that had been forgotten but that left the waking soul with a lingering sense of incomprehension. He couldn't shake it: this woman seemed different from everything and everyone else in the world. This was someone with whom he was somehow connected.

He was now directly in front of her. They looked each other over like two curious animals. The sense of connection was stronger now, but still, he could not frame it into a single idea. Instead of a searing, single beam focused through the curve of a magnifying glass, his recognition of her was like a wide and warm blanket of sunlight bathing him in warm hope and possible meaning. Comforting, but nothing would ignite.

They held hands, turned and walked along the street. The man felt a greater sense of calm now. The woman seemed calmer too, but they made no comment on it.

Eventually, having walked alongside a stretch of twisted woods and open pastures, they saw a brown house sitting at the top of a hill. There it was again—a sense of connection, this time to the lone structure. They made their way up the gravel driveway past a paddock and two galloping horses and came to a stop in front of the large wooden building.

The woman looked back at the man, her face anxious. Letting go of her hand, he stepped onto the front porch. The light through the slats above cast glowing stripes on the wooden floorboards. A wind-chime beside the door jingled softly. The man cupped his hand on the window. There was nobody inside. There were things—furniture, vases of flowers, a fireplace—but no person. He moved to the front door. Next to the door was the same panel he had seen in the car, the one with the glowing blue contour of a human hand. He placed his palm on the screen. With a beep, the door opened.

The man took a deep breath, and entered warily. The smells that filled his nose were instantly familiar, though nameless. Wood. Lemon-lime furniture polish. Flowers.

The woman came in after him. For a while, they stood there. Various objects radiated weak pulses of familiarity. The woman picked up a pink scarf from the sofa and held it to her nose. In the kitchen: two plates, dried crusts of old toast. Broken eggshells in a plastic bowl, water dripping into the sink. The man reached out and tightened the tap without thinking. Only afterwards did he register that he'd remembered what to do. A small memory, returned without warning.

The woman joined him in the kitchen. She was holding something in her hand—a photograph in a wooden frame. In the picture the man saw himself and the woman bright against the backdrop of a snowy range of mountains. They were wearing goggles and yellow woollen hats. They were smiling and holding each other and it was clear that those two people in the photograph knew each other better than the two people now standing in the vaguely familiar house.

She handed him another framed photograph. Once again he saw the two of them, this time lying on a red and white blanket under a tree. She was buttering a roll. He was wearing sunglasses and sporting a beard, lying on his back, his arms crossed behind his head. There were two other people in this picture: a young boy and girl. The boy lay sprawled with his head on the woman's legs, sipping on a juice-box and looking at the camera. The young dark-haired girl was behind the woman, her hands draped over the woman's shoulders, her cheek against the woman's neck.

The man instantly felt the same connection he'd felt with the woman in the street.

No, not the same. Stronger.

He knew these children.

The man shoved the framed photographs back into her hands and dashed through the house. The woman followed him. He charged into one of the rooms. A large empty bed, a wardrobe, clothing, books, sporting equipment—nothing felt significant. He left the room and swung open the door of another. The walls of the second room were green, filled with more colourful objects than the rest of the house. Posters crowded the walls. A trophy stood on a shelf. Clothing was scattered on the floor. In the centre of the room was a narrow bed, and on it, he finally found what he sensed he had been looking for—the first thing he had felt the need to locate in two days.

A young boy was curled up on top of the duvet, fast asleep. The man did not see the girl. She was probably somewhere else. He'd find her later; he was almost sure of it. But here was the boy, for now. The boy from the picture.

The man reached his hand down and touched the soft brown hair on the boy's head, and a word entered his head. A word like the first drop of rain in a desert. Out of nowhere and without warning. A word that he thought, and then recognised, and then said out loud.

"Andy."

Invisible idiot

I wasn't certain how long I had been sitting on the sand with my back against the beached whale. It felt like I had been there for hours. I expected the first warm slivers of sunlight to arrive at any moment, but the long night was still full of stars.

Various thoughts had drifted in and out of my mind as I'd been sitting there—aimless things, disconnected, each as unclear as the reflection of a face within the oily swirl of a floating bubble.

Something caught my eye and I looked down.

A small white crab scuttled sideways over the sand beside my leg. It passed under the warm light of my lamp and held up its pincers as if ready for a fight. Two black eyes bobbed back at me from their miniature stalks. They twitched as they scoped out the surroundings, and I was made suddenly aware of the small creature's simple perfection—its candid existence. Nothing could seem more natural, more a part of the world. I reached out my finger and touched its broad chitinous back. It hurried off, back into the dark.

"Hey!" I called after it.

I stared up at the stars, deceptively close to each other, actually light years apart, at vast and varying depths.

"I once saw a whale," I found myself saying. It came out without my thinking. I expected the whale to respond in some way. Of course it didn't. Undeterred, I went on: "I was with my son, a long time ago. We were on the beach and the whale was far out at sea, but he was thrilled anyway. Just to know it was there, even if he couldn't see much of it.

"He loved the beach. I'd take him there whenever I could. I'd sit up top and watch him run from the water, make shapes and sculptures in the sand. He'd chase the seagulls and poke the crabs. He was never scared. He'd dig holes and fill them up. He'd laugh and wave his small hands, as if he was standing on the deck of some large ship leaving a harbour. Then, after a long day, he'd return to me, throw himself into me, and I'd dust him off and we'd go home."

I stopped. The words died in the dark. I looked to my side, but the whale did nothing, showing no sign that she either understood or cared. I hadn't expected anything else.

"We'd go . . . *home.*" I added the last word carefully, forcing myself to remember the concept. I lifted my head again and sucked in the air.

My son.

Where was he? Was he okay? Did he even remember me, or was I disintegrating in his mind the way he was starting to disintegrate in mine, like the ink on paper left in water? Already my daughter's small face had begun to fade, but that was different. The last time I'd seen her, it had been in the open casket at her funeral, and ever since that day I'd wished I hadn't: the pale face in that tiny coffin had somehow annexed my memories of the one I'd known before . . . before the car had come screeching around the corner . . .

The whale moaned weakly, a low sound that came from deep within her. I put out the lamp, closed my eyes, and listened. The sound moved through her and then through me. The cry of longing. A mother's mourning. I curled up in a foetal position beside her. My eyelids grew heavy and, back to back

with a dying mammal marooned on the lip of the world, I quit
on my mind and coasted off to sleep.

*I was in a room of some kind, or perhaps it was a cave. It was large
and dark and I couldn't see any walls. The only reason I knew it was
a closed space was because my breathing bounced against something
and echoed back at me. Constant drips of water from some place
above me formed puddles on the floor, exuding the fumes of damp
rot. I swung my head from side to side, craning back, trying to see an
exit, but there was none. I attempted to extend my hands to touch
the sides, but my arms wouldn't move. I shifted my shoulders, but
felt nothing at the ends of them. The realisation hit me: I had no
arms, not even stumps. A surge of panic rose inside me like a septic
froth, and I told myself it didn't make sense, that I really should
have arms, but there was no consolation in my reasoning. I was
in a lightless space, with no windows and no doors and no arms to
feel my way through. If you trip and fall, it's going to hurt and*
be difficult to get up, so whatever you do, stay on your feet . . .

Hey you. *A voice crept out of the dark. Startled, I whirled around.
The voice was soft but coarse and phlegmy.* You have something to
eat for me? A sandwich, maybe?

Who's there? *I spun to my left and then twisted to my right,
peering into the heavy darkness.*

Calm down, will you, *the voice replied. It coughed, clearing its
throat.* It's not like I'm not stuck in here as well. Do yourself a
favour. Take a seat.

*I moved one foot forward and struck something hard. It was the
leg of a chair—the one from the white house on the hill, instantly
recognisable. I slowly lowered myself onto the padding.*

How about that sandwich then?

I'm sorry, *I said.* I don't have anything.

There was a gurgling sigh. Fine, *croaked the voice.* So here we
are, just the two of us.

*Water dripped from above onto my forehead, slipped warm and
thick, like saliva. Hardly a few seconds later, it dripped again in the
same spot.*

Do I know you? *I asked.*

The voice cackled, then let out a long sigh. I once met a girl, *it said,* in the woods. She was sitting at the river, drinking water. I watched her for a bit, doing nothing, and then she saw me. Yeah, she was scared at first, but she came around eventually. Ha, children, they do know how to trust, don't they?

What's your name? *I asked.*

Jack, *the voice said.* My name's Jack Turning.

I'm Kayle.

Well, it's a pleasure meeting you, Kayle. *He coughed again, sputtering.* Too bad about the sandwich. I do love a good sandwich. *A glob of warm water ran over the curve of my face like a fat tear.* Where are you from, Kayle? *he asked finally.*

I don't really know.

Yeah, me neither, *he replied.* I was just kind of here one day. Weird, huh? So, where you heading?

I shook my head, then, realising he couldn't see me, added, I don't really know.

Eh heh, *Jack's voice chortled.* Looks like you've got yourself a case of the dunnos. Okay, okay—you dunno where you've come from, dunno where you're going . . . do you at least know where you are?

I said nothing.

Kayle, let me ask you something, *he said, and I wasn't sure what he had gauged from my silence.* You seem like someone who can give me a straight answer.

All right.

Tell me. I was once told I was a mistake. That I did not belong in this world. That's why I sit in the dark like this, where no one can see me. But here's the thing: if I was such a mistake, if I didn't belong, as I was so rudely shown, what makes you—any of you—think you're any different? What makes you so sure that one day, fed up with your shit, nature's not going to swoop down on you all and take you all out? Hm?

I had nothing to say. I didn't want to tell him that the thought had occasionally crossed my mind.

And if you are—if you come to the realisation you are a mistake in this world—will you have the courage to go willingly, to remove yourself of your own accord, or will you stubbornly remain, in stupid denial and against the will of nature?

I paused and thought about it. I don't know.

Of course you don't. I mean, you wouldn't know until the bushes ripped off your face and you were covered in hundreds of angry hornets. You wouldn't know until then, would you? Oh yeah, then you'd know, but by then it would be too late.

A deep grumbling rose in the room. The foundation was shifting. Jack's voice grew to make up for the steady, rising boom.

Unless you finally decided to listen to that nagging voice in the deepest part of you, fighting to be acknowledged: that voice that says, hey you, Kayle, be honest; what good have you ever been to anyone?

I craned my head and watched as the wall on one side of the room opened, a widening split in the darkness. It was suddenly clear to me: I wasn't in a room at all. I was in the whale. For a moment, I was able to see the moon through the open mouth, hanging impotently in the sky. And then I caught sight of the edge of the horizon.

No, it wasn't the moon.

It was something that looked like the moon. An impostor. An alien orb, cream yellow like the infected conjunctiva of a giant eye. It was watching me. It was also my last image of the outside world before the water rushed inside. My guts shifted to my chest and snatched my breath: the whale was diving under, descending, taking me down into the cold murkiness of the ocean.

Icy water crashed over my body and lifted me from the chair. Floating around, trapped in the belly and breathing my last breaths, I was filled with nothing but a terrifying certainty the end would be coming soon. But it never did. Death wouldn't take me. Instead, I was shaken about without even the arms to struggle, submerged in the water-filled belly, drowning but still living. Fully aware in the watery blackness, and alone.

By the time the men returned in the morning, the beached mother was dead. I had no idea when she'd slipped away.

When I struggled awake, just after sunrise, she was no longer breathing. The men arrived with two drums of oil. They dug a trench around the body with shovels. As the morning went on, a small crowd began to form around the carcass, no one speaking but everyone scrutinising the scene. I wondered if, like me, they were waiting for nothing else but to *feel* something. To feel anything.

I stood back from the crowd, up on the embankment, watching from afar. The large black lump didn't look like the same whale from the night before. The awe was gone, and with it the notions of fallen gods, of mystic giants, and other such romances of the heart and mind. Now, surrounded by people and exposed by the sobering light of day, it looked like nothing more than a big, dead animal. A rotting husk.

I felt nothing.

I looked over my shoulder. Gideon was near the tents, sitting on a wooden bench and cleaning his tools. To my left, Daniel had perched himself on the branch of a tree, giving himself the best view; the crowd around the whale had already deepened so that some in the back were struggling to see anything.

Four men climbed atop the whale and had the drums passed up to them. One of the men said something to the crowd, perhaps warning that the fire would be large, but from where I was standing I couldn't hear anything. Two men to a drum, they proceeded to lift them and tip them over. The slick black oil ran like treacle. They walked the length of the whale, making sure that all of it was covered in the dense fluid. Some of the oil dripped and ran out like thin black tentacles into the ocean. The men climbed off the whale and held up their hands, ordering everyone to stand back.

A tug on the sleeve of my shirt.

Beside me was the same girl I had seen at my tent in the early hours of the morning, two days earlier. She was still clutching her furry companion.

"Hello," I said to her. "Hello bear," I added, tugging twice on its brown ear. A moaning sound came from her throat and she pointed up to the white house on the hill. She was probably mute; I hadn't yet heard a sound come from her and her lack of speech seemed to extend beyond mere shyness. Nevertheless, it was clear I'd been summoned.

I glanced at the crowd on the beach below, nodded to Daniel to let him know I was leaving, and trekked over the embankment up to the house on the hill.

"We've been concerned," said one of the heads from behind their long steel table. "There have been inconsistencies."

I shifted in the uncomfortable chair. Once again, the plugs and wires siphoned my thoughts and squirted them into the big grey box beside me. It rumbled like some anxious creature, foaming out its reports.

My first thought was that the summonsing was connected to my night alongside the whale. The Body had its eyes: we were always being observed, no matter where we were and what we were doing. I'd often spot someone staring a little too long, making a note, loitering where they clearly had nothing better to do than spy.

"I couldn't sleep," I said. "I'm sorry."

"No," the woman said. "This isn't about last night. That does not concern us now, though we will continue to monitor your inconsistent behaviour. What concerns us is more serious, I'm afraid."

My mind was blank and I frowned, trying to recall. Then it dawned upon me: Moneta. Her story.

"You were seen with Moneta in the garden."

"Moneta asked me for a favour. To move a few pots," I said.

"But what did you speak about? You were seen conversing for quite some time."

I wasn't certain how to respond. I couldn't betray Moneta by telling them everything, and yet I couldn't keep it from them either. The machine would read my anxiety.

"She spoke about her plants," I said as calmly as I could. "She was worried about them."

"What was she worried about?"

"They aren't growing properly. She's been having some problems with the dahlias. She spoke about how some plants need to be near other plants, particular ones, that attention needs to be paid to the partnerships."

"Partnerships?"

"Between the plants."

They said nothing for a while, scratching notes in their dockets.

"Was that all?" one of them asked.

"Moneta's getting old. It's difficult to understand some of the things she says." Again, they scrawled in their dockets. "I'll be more careful next time, though, not to indulge an old woman's careless conversation."

"Well, unfortunately, the problem is even greater than that. Moneta has gone missing . . ."

They paused, waiting for a physical response. They didn't get what they expected; my sudden surprise registered on the machine, and thus, so did my alibi.

"She hasn't been seen since yesterday and it seems you were the second-last person to speak with her. We've questioned the assistant, but he says he doesn't know. We've sent scouts. We've looked everywhere. We are not pleased by how things have transpired. The conversations and such. You can understand our concern, yes?"

"Yes."

I thought about Moneta. She had offered no thoughts about leaving. And then I remembered what she had said, the curious finality of her words. *A story I need to tell. To both someone else and myself, one last time.*

"We need you to be very careful over the next few days," said the man with the metal gadget on his head. "We'll be keeping a closer eye on some of your actions. Until this is all cleared up, of course."

"Of course."

I wondered whether The Body had made it all up, said that she'd disappeared in order to test me in some way, but I too was capable of providing my analyses of others; they were puzzled and troubled, all right. They weren't faking it. They said nothing and had me sit for a couple of minutes while they looked for any fluctuations in my report. They waited for some secret to slip through the cracks of my subconscious and into their mechanical mind reader.

"That's all for now," said the old man at the end of the table. "We may need to call you back, soon. Do not go far."

I walked back from the house and picked through my memory of Moneta's story, but could recall no hints of a plan to escape. It was difficult enough to believe a woman of her age could get very far. Behind the beach was nothing but steep mountains and barren, endless roads. We were fenced in, they'd told us. The Body had its eyes (enough eyes to know I had spoken to her in the first place) and even the most careful of us would be captured before covering any meaningful distance.

I looked back to make sure I wasn't being followed. All I could see was the roof of the white farmhouse as it sank into the shrubby knoll. I slid on the muddy footpath and stepped onto the skewed stairs leading to the encampment of tents on the beach.

I still had the letter.

Checking over both shoulders, I slipped inside my tent. I zipped up behind me, lifted a pile of books from my shelf and grabbed the letter. I sat on my bed and tore open the short side of the envelope. Carefully, I reached inside and slid out folded sheets of white paper. I unfolded the pages and read Moneta's words.

To whomever you are

Firstly, thank you. I am writing this before having even spoken to you and yet am deeply grateful to you for having offered your time, patience, respect and discretion. You would not be in possession of this letter if I had suspected otherwise of you. I would not even have bothered telling you my story, let alone given you this letter. So again, my deepest thanks.

Secondly, if you are reading this, I am no longer on the beach. Unfortunately, my whereabouts will not be disclosed to you in this letter. I apologise for any disappointment. I am not keeping it a secret out of disrespect for you, but out of respect for myself. In this strange world, we are born alone and we die alone. And while we use this as an excuse to force ourselves upon each other, I believe there is some natural, overlooked importance in embracing some elements of our seclusion instead of trying to disown them. There are some things we need to keep to ourselves, things no one else can or should know, so that we are able to maintain a more meaningful sense of self. We need our secrets. Our individuality. I'm too old and have been around for too long to worry about the oneness of everything, despite what they've been telling me—how we are all heaps of the same stardust, having followed the same tired line of evolution. One divided example of the same configuration of amino acids and protein molecules—forget it! Couldn't be bothered. What a terrible waste of sentience, honestly, to get caught up in all that!

I have already told you my one clear memory. You have heard about the parents, the move from the house in Kroonstad to Tsitsikamma, the lodging for the backpackers, the man in the woods, and how he was so violently removed from the earth. I remember this memory almost perfectly. I remember the smell of the cabin and the woods. The light, the sounds. And the feelings: joy and curiosity and fear. Of all the times, of everything that has occurred in my long years here, it is this time I recall the most. The problem, however, lies in precisely this fact. You see, even though I remember this memory, there is something I must confess: it is not *my* memory.

Now, this may confuse you, and I cannot assure you that I will be able to offer any clarity on the subject, but I will tell you what I know for now. Perhaps, in your time, you will find the answers to some of the questions this raises, but know that I have been unable to find the answers for myself, and frankly, have no interest in doing so.

Everything about that memory occurred just as I said, but the truth is, it did not happen to me. I have never lived in Kroonstad. I never moved to Tsitsikamma. And I did not meet the man in the woods. I cannot tell you to whom these things actually happened, but it wasn't me.

Simply put, someone else's memory somehow found its way into my head.

As time passed, this alien memory grew in my mind, became stronger and clearer, and somehow sucked the nutrients out of my other memories (my own memories) like some thick weed. There are still other memories in my head, memories of events I know actually happened to me, but they are weak and frail things, barely attached.

Now, you may think this the senile confabulation of an old woman. If you can look no further than this assumption, I am afraid there's little I can do about that, but know this: there is something happening on this beach. Believe me. Something is happening to us—to all of us—and I think the fact I have someone else's memory, so sharp and ingrained that it may as well be my own, is somehow linked to this *something*.

This memory is also the reason I have decided to leave the beach. You can't imagine what it feels like to realise that the one thing you remember about your life did not actually happen. It could be assumed that sharing someone's memory could be understood as an enriching, communal experience, but nothing could be further from the truth. It is with loneliness that I am leaving this beach. Loneliness and regret. If the one thing I remember about my life is not actually mine to remember, I see no reason to prolong my stay.

I didn't tell you about this earlier, in your company, because I needed to say it out loud one more time as if it *was* my memory, to hear it from my lips, to know how I felt. If you are reading this, it means I have made up my mind. It means I have quit this lie. As I have already warned you, however, what I am telling you is somehow connected to what is happening on the beach, as well as in the rest of this unusual world. Beware of what they say. Examine it carefully to see, if you can, what it is they mean. Keep your eyes and ears open. Absorb each moment. One day, the world will no longer be recognisable to you. Without a memory or two you can trust, you will be forced to leave it a stranger.

Finally
Moneta

Flipping the final page, I saw nothing else. I read her letter again and then fanned out the pages on the bed. I leaned back on my pillow and looked up at the ceiling. A moth was tacked in the corner—it had been there for two days. I stared at it until its furry body and flat grey wings became sharper—almost hyper-real—the perfect emblem of a tattered and unmoved world.

It seemed ludicrous to accept that Moneta had somehow received someone else's memory, like a radio transmitter picking up some unknown signal.

It couldn't be possible, I told myself.

It didn't make sense.

I sat up on my bed and rubbed my face, wondering what to do next. My eyes swept the tent, seeking familiar things, things I recognised and could rely on to simply be what they were. My broken umbrella. My box of pictures. My blunt knife. But whereas once they might have served to balance me, they now sat like cold dead stones at the bottom of the ocean. Magic charms that had lost their magic. They held no power, didn't mean anything, and I no longer knew why I'd once thought to keep them.

Stepping outside, I looked about; the area was quiet and empty. I thought about telling someone about the letter, but who, and why? Besides, that seemed the wrong thing to do. And who would believe it? I wasn't even sure I did, though the letter had suffered no lack of coherency.

As I walked, the commune remained eerily still. Everyone was at the whale and many strange contraptions, rigs and workstations stood unattended. There was always an array of tasks to be managed in the commune. Anyone with a proclivity for handiwork had been assigned to the building of the tent frames and furniture. Evening meals were prepared by four men who recalled they had once been Swedish and had worked as chefs. A team washed our dirty clothes in vats of filtered seawater provided by the overseers of a rickety, clanging desalination system. A group of fishermen made and hauled the lave nets and three women sat on stools outside the infirmary, waiting to tend to the occasional broken bone or fever. Nothing was ever adorned or embellished. A stick of primed wood never saw a lick of paint and nor was a meal ever garnished. The commune was a place of bareness. A practical bone yard. And now, without a soul in sight, the place was even gloomier than usual. It seemed for a moment that all activity had not been postponed but permanently abandoned, as if everyone, all at once, had come to the realisation they'd been living on a stage of cardboard props, none of which really worked at all.

I continued walking towards the botanical garden.

I didn't think I'd see Moneta, but there was no other place to look. I thought again about her story—each inspired detail. I thought about her running between those trees, and long-legged Burt chasing her the way some horrible thing chases you in a nightmare. Tearing through those bushes until the bushes began to tear through him. Now, perhaps old Moneta had chosen to run again, run from this commune the way her memory told her she had, that day in the woods.

But was there anywhere left to run?

A warm wind passed through the trees, ruffling the leaves and startling brightly coloured birds. They took to the sky like shreds of a rainbow. Below, an arcade of palm trees shuffled in the stiff breeze. My path ran alongside the beach and then snaked between the trees. Soon, the glistening glass dome came into view. I passed through the wild grasses and could see Moneta's plants through the shimmering glass walls.

Junyap was hobbling awkwardly out of the front door, carrying a blue bucket, tipping his body to the side to counter the weight of it. He wiped the sweat from his forehead and flapped the top of his shirt to pull cooler air in. He caught sight of me. I waited for a reaction, but he did little but stare. I redirected my gaze to the dome.

Everything seemed to be as it had been when I'd left it: the perfect green ferns, the vegetables, the bushels of herbs, the radiant petals of the flowers. And there were the bags of fertiliser, the pots I'd moved and the large wooden crate I had dragged.

The crate. The six-foot-long crate was now packed with soil and blanketed in tufts of large-leafed plants.

(*The trees, it seems, will take the body of a dead thing as quickly as they want it, or want to get rid of it*)

I swung to Junyap to confirm my conclusion. He placed the bucket on the ground beside him. Holding my gaze, he raised his right hand and put a finger to his pursed lips . . .

Sssshhh.

A chill ran through me, but I nodded. I understood, immediately and completely. There was nothing left to be said: I already knew more than had been intended. Any questions would only betray Moneta's final wish.

Unhurriedly, and without looking over my shoulder, I strolled away—away from Junyap, away from the greenhouse—and back through the long green undergrowth towards the path.

The weather was changing again. As I made my way back to the commune, the wind whistled listlessly overhead. But it was also carrying something. Something that made me sick to the bottom of my stomach. The wind, an unscrupulous messenger spirit flitting over the ocean and beach, carried the stench of oil smoke and burning flesh.

Extracts

(Excerpt from the *The Age of Self Primary*)

The day every person on earth lost his and her memory was not a day at all. It couldn't be slotted in a schedule or added to a calendar. In people's minds, there was no actual event—no earthquake, tsunami, or act of terror—and thus whatever had happened could be followed by no period of shock or mourning. There could be no catharsis. Everyone was simply reset to zero.

This moment of collective amnesia could not be understood within any context because it was the context itself that had been taken away. There was nothing anyone could do to repair themselves because they didn't know what was broken. Before the resetting, they had created for themselves lives of routine and were motivated to participate in the world because they knew where they had come from. They knew what they were capable of doing and clung on to the mistakes they'd made like the maps of dangerous roads they knew not to take. They were driven by their aspirations as well as the fears they'd built up over the course of their lives like solitary fortresses on the peaks of mountains. But with no recollection of their aspirations, no remembrance of their fears, they were not propelled at all.

And so everything stopped. Industry. Commerce. Politics. Religion. Technology. They could no longer remember what their gods had needed of them. They no longer knew how to use the machines they'd once made, let alone how to improve upon them. Money was of no use because the values of various notes, coins and currencies could not be designated. So they became loiterers. Ghostly wanderers, doomed to haunt a world that no longer belonged to them.

When a few memories did begin to filter back to them, gradually and in no particular order, there was, at first, a mood of hope. Some families drifted back together. Homes and towns were faintly remembered. People hoped that over time enough memories would return to remind them of what their purpose had been before the resetting. Their memories would show them the significance of the lives they were supposed to now resume. But even as memory upon memory slunk back in their minds—a familiar face, a friend, a place from their childhood, a talent and a job they had once done— the purpose of their existence did not follow.

Instead, as they hunched down, picking up each new memory like the charred and scattered remains of a burned-down house, they were filled with a new sense of despair. The despair of realising the things in their world did not add up to any whole, and that there was no meaning in any of it. All the things they'd been desperate to recall were little more than the trivial knick-knacks of a species that had not lost—in that one global moment—any meaning, but that had never had any real meaning to begin with . . .

II

A functional version of earth

Finally, I am on the raft.

I've seen so many others out here before and been curious about the experience. Now I am here: tied down at the neck, wrists and ankles. Spread open like the Vitruvian Man. Eyes fixed on the sky. Mouth dry. Skin beginning to burn. Stomach digesting what's left of my final breakfast, as well as the hallucinogenic flower I was forced to ingest a short time earlier.

Soon, that flower will begin to take effect.

When it does, my thoughts will start to slip. My reason will lose its shape and my ideas will fold like a sheet of paper, forming finally into an elaborate origami figure I will not understand. I probably won't even realise it's happening (that's the point, I suppose)—I'll just slide into it.

I feel the cold seawater rise through the gaps in the logs. It wets my back, and retreats. The water dries in the sun, caking my skin in salt and aggravating my sunburn. Beneath my leather constraints, my neck, wrists and ankles are beginning to chafe. The moisture between the pelt and my broken skin forms warm and sticky incubators for infection. With my head fastened, I can't see how bad the blistering has become. I can only feel it.

There is only one thing I'm capable of seeing.

The sky.

I've been staring at it for hours now. I have no choice. The blue is a blank wall. It fills my vision, a maddening thing that goes on forever with no depth. No corners. No shape or texture. It could be a centimetre in front of my face or a million kilometres away. It is so absolute and empty that after a while it doesn't look blue at all—just another strange form of nothing. Am I really seeing it at all, or am I losing my sight . . .

No. Focus. Hold on.

I can't let such notions take control of me. I need to ground myself with facts, with what I know.

I've seen plenty of others cast out on the rafts, attached to the pier by about a hundred metres of rope, so that's one thing I know: I'm not far out at sea. I may as well be, though. I can hear nothing from the shore, see no land, no matter how far I roll my eyes. I know the three others are floating beside me, each on their own rafts for committing the same offence, but I can't see or hear them either.

Calling out won't matter. We are too far away to distinguish anything more than muffled shouts—but really, what is there to say? Shouting will only dry our throats.

That's the last thing we want.

We have no idea when we'll be pulled back in, our recalibration complete, but sooner or later the thirst will come, regardless of the anti-diuretic compound we've been given to conserve our fluids. We'll feel the dryness in our mouths and throats long before our bodies reach the critical stages of dehydration.

Hold on, Kayle.

The sea moves, a restless, gelatinous creature. I am disturbing it in its ancient sleep. I am glad I'm not suffering motion sickness. That would be devastating, and is a horrible thought: if it becomes unbearable—all the rocking back and forth—there's always the possibility of retching, up, and onto my own face . . .

I don't want to think about that either.

Three birds fly overhead and across the blue wall. They are so high I can hardly see the movement of their wings. I zone in on their small dark bodies, relishing each tiny flutter. They fly in a staggered formation, three rafts on their own blue sea, the projection of a more functional version of Earth held up against mine.

Then they are gone, out of range, and I am once again alone. Strapped to the raft, drifting in blue limbo, with nothing more than my thoughts . . .

So what *do* you remember?

This is what you remember . . .

You were on the beach.
It was late in the afternoon.

The sun was low in the sky, blistering the horizon with redness. The clear blue water hushed gently, and you were crouched beside it, watching a young girl use a wooden branch to draw a picture in the sand. Is that right? Yes, that's right. It was Angerona, the mute girl. Her new name, the one you'd given her, since she had no name of her own. Angerona: the goddess of inner voice, a permanent finger to her lips to conceal the secret name of Rome that could not be spoken aloud.

And what was she drawing?

In the sand, she was drawing a house.

A house on a hill.

There was a long winding path from the bottom of the hill to the crooked front door. Beside the house she drew four crosses in a row, tombstones, or possibly crucifixes, but that place—that house, path, hill and those four crosses—had been her home. That much was clear to you.

She held out the stick and you took it from her. She rubbed out her drawing with her foot and flattened the sand.

Draw yours, her face seemed to suggest. Your house, Kayle. Your home.

You shook your head. You couldn't, you said, you didn't remember, but that wasn't true. Finally, you took the stick from her hand, put the end to the soft sand, and reluctantly drew a line . . .

The line became a house. *Your* house.

You drew a long fence, and the fence became an enclosure and you scratched two horses in the sand. You wondered if she could tell they were supposed to be horses. You were never much of an artist. You gave up on the horses and drew a tree beside the house, and then a number of small, round apples.

At that point you stopped. You were done.

No more, you said. *I'm sorry. I'm too tired right now. Maybe later, okay?*

Angerona smiled, understanding and accepting, and you put your hand on her shoulder. She nodded, waved, and dashed across the sand. You examined your drawing: a house, a tree, two horses. Then you scuffed out the lines with your foot until there was no hint of what had once been there.

You decided to go for a walk—by yourself.

You needed to clear that picture out of your head, so you left the beach and went towards the woods. You were used to taking walks by yourself, but this time you found yourself going in a direction you had never taken, the route laid out perfectly in your mind. The idea of going that way wasn't so much a thought as a voice, the words clear enough to almost be heard. *Go,* it said. *Go into the woods, Kayle. Follow your feet and go into the woods. It's time to pay back what you owe. So go, Kayle, between those crooked trees. See what you can see . . .*

You walked under the swaying palms and along the winding path. You reached a river and crossed without rolling up your pants. When you looked over your shoulder, you could no longer see the beach or the ocean and the trees had changed from a few hanging palms into a thick forest, blanketing the mountain.

As you walked you thought about many things, mostly about life in the commune. You were walking away from the beach and it was as if you were putting it all behind you. Not that you imagined you were escaping right then (you were sure you'd know if you were doing that), but something told you that when you came back to the commune it would seem like a different place and you would be a different person.

As you walked, you thought about Moneta.

It had been three months since Moneta left and despite endless searching, her body had never been recovered. All causing more fuss than The Body were prepared to allow. Thus, The Body sent out a message telling the commune that she'd drowned at sea while attempting an escape. That wasn't true, of course, but it did the trick. Everyone settled down, as if their imaginations had been shot with tranquilliser darts. Routines promptly resumed. Rusted trawlers arrived every few weeks with new communers. Large bonfires burned on the beach into the early hours of the morning, each a small sun at the centre of lonesome bodies dancing in orbit. The tide came in and went out. The white house watched. Dreams owned the night, dullness, the day—and still, everyone waited.

As usual.

The slope grew steeper and you reached for tree trunks to haul yourself up. The orange light of the low setting sun cut through the trees, tracing jagged silhouettes on the bark. Apart from the crackle of twigs and leaves there was no sound, no wind.

But there was another sound, wasn't there?

It brought you to a stop. You first thought it was an animal of some kind, but then you heard it again. A human voice. A woman.

You edged around a tree and saw a man on his knees. There was a woman lying on her back, her bare legs arched upwards. A man knelt between her legs. You moved closer. He was helping her deliver a baby.

A twig cracked and his head snapped towards you. His eyes were wide with sudden panic. You told him not to worry; you wouldn't tell anyone. He said nothing and continued attending to her. You asked if you could help. He ordered you to grab the canteen beside the tree and give her water. You did as he asked. There was a thin strip of white cloth hanging over the canteen and you used it to wipe the sweat from her forehead. There was a blanket on the woman's chest and he told you to spread it underneath her. You followed this instruction without question.

The man was a few years younger than you. His long hair was swept back and there were deep lines in his forehead. He seemed to know what he was doing.

And the woman?

The soon-to-be mother was a young woman named Jai-Li. You had seen her before. She'd stood out on the beach, not only because of her pregnancy, but also because of her striking physical features: leaf-green eyes, pale white skin and long sleek hair so impossibly dark it occasionally glimmered blue in the moonlight. You hadn't met the father of her child (you were quite sure she'd arrived pregnant), but could have been mistaken. For all you knew, the man at her side was the father.

Okay, okay, he encouraged her, *almost there.*

She strained to push, lifting her head, clamping her jaw and gritting her teeth fiercely.

Breathe and count back. Breathe and count, Jai-Li.

A slick bulge began to appear, and the mother screamed as the sides of her cervix stretched around the infant's body. The man guided the child out, cradling its head with one hand, working the delicate body out with the other. Minutes later he held the child in his arms. The mother's pain subsided and she threw her head back and exhaled deeply, exhausted.

A boy. Perfect. Ready to simply be.

Startlingly, upon first sight of the child, its entire future flashed before you: every yet unknown pain and joy. Every scraped knee and stolen kiss, each moment of heartache and laughter, triumph and disappointment. And the questions too—all of the many, many questions to come. Your projections made you feel as if you were staring down on him from somewhere high above, an ancient eye in the sky. He would never know you, but you could somehow see him—and all of his years—in a way he could not yet see for himself.

The man removed a thin membranous film from the newborn's face, allowing the passages to be opened. He asked you to take two short pieces of string from a small wooden bowl beside him and tighten one of the threads around the umbilical cord. Next you tightened the second piece, a notch up from the first, creating an air-locked segment. Finally you took a pair of scissors from the bowl and cut through the sealed section of the cord.

The newborn breathed in and then, as if exposed to the alien atmosphere of an alien planet, he gasped and cried out in alarm.

What happened after that?

You stayed in the woods. You helped the man pitch a tent and guide Jai-Li into it.

You sat against a tree.

The man sat opposite you, his knees drawn up. He said his name was Theunis, and he thanked you. His face was soft and warm, his eyes creased by crow's feet and underscored by deep blue shadows.

On the slope of the mountain beside you, Jai-Li and her child slept in the tent.

Theunis was willing to speak to you, but his choice of words and careful tone made it clear that he wasn't going to give away too much, say the wrong thing. He told you he'd met Jai-Li less than a month ago. Before that he had known nothing about her but she'd asked for his help. *When a pregnant woman asks for help there's not much more you need to know,* he said.

What kind of help? you asked.

An escape, he said. *She's leaving the beach, the commune, and I'm going to help her.*

She had no intention of returning. If she didn't leave immediately after her child was born, the baby would be delivered to some unknown guardian in some unknown location . . .

You couldn't help feeling doubtful, could you? After all, people *had* tried to escape in the past.

You asked what made her think she'd get away with it. Theunis didn't reply. He stood and said again that when a pregnant woman asks for help, there's not much more you need to know. He walked over to her tent and pulled back the flap to check on Jai-Li and her child.

How did they plan to escape, you wanted to know.

A rowboat, he said. *She needs a second oar and I haven't even begun working on it. When it's ready, I'll take them down to the cove and then . . . well, then they're on their own. Jai-Li hasn't mentioned where she plans to go . . .*

He seemed anxious to end the conversation, so you didn't ask him anything more. He said he was glad you had come, but stressed the importance of keeping everything a secret.

I'm going back, he said, *for food and water. You stay here and keep an eye.*

You thought it was a good idea. Jai-Li would probably sleep all night and you would make a small fire for warmth, and to keep the baboons away.

Quite suddenly, he clasped you by the shoulders. *The only thing left to be in this world is a martyr,* he said in a rush, as if he couldn't hold the thought in any longer. *One day we'll look back and be forced to ask ourselves what good we've ever been to anyone.* He nodded quickly but said nothing more. Then he took his hands off your shoulders and made his way down the slope, towards the beach.

You gathered twigs and dried branches and prepared a small fire beside the tent. Then you sat against the tree and watched the small flames flicker.

(*The only thing left to be in this world is a martyr. One day we'll look back and be forced to ask ourselves what good we've ever been to anyone*)

Theunis's words lingered. It was difficult to fathom why you'd been so ready to help. You felt as if you'd been swept away by the hope of accomplishing something, anything at all. On that beach, in that commune, purpose itself was the desired end. You'd arrived at the beach hoping to come to an understanding of your new place in a meaningless world, but contrary to every new idea and belief The Body had encouraged you to espouse, it was only then—safeguarding that mother and her child— that you felt any semblance of the long-promised "meaning." But there was more to it, you knew. More than the hope of your own worth in a world that no longer saw the merits of worthiness itself.

You had held a baby in your arms, once upon a time. You had held your son. Your daughter.

You'd lifted them in the air and made them each a promise you were naive enough to believe you could keep. A promise of protection. A promise of love. Of never leaving. Never forgetting.

Night leaked across the sky.

The fire settled into itself, nibbling steadily on the wood. The glowing embers sputtered and sparked in the endless dark and your eyes grew heavier with each passing moment.

But just as your eyes were about to close completely, you saw something that shook you to wakefulness.

A tall dark figure emerged from the trees—a man standing behind the fire.

His long, black, buttoned-up trench coat hung to the forest floor and he looked as if he was drenched in oil and it was slopping over his feet. The sharp features of his pale face shimmered in the low light of the fire. He was not a *normal* man. You were not convinced he was human at all. He towered like the long crooked shadow of a bony giant, fixing his big white eyes on you. Long arms rose slowly at his sides. White hands appeared at the ends of drooping sleeves, then moved slowly to the centre of his coat. Skeletal fingers grasped the edges and parted the sides ceremoniously, like thick, dusty curtains drawing open on the stage of a grisly old theatre house.

An empty stage . . . As his coat opened you could see no body in that coat. Until, deep from the shadows of the hollow space, a young boy materialised. You stared as he took form in the brushstrokes of the fire's light. He saw you sitting against that tree and stared dreamily back at you.

Andy.

The boy was about seven years old, maybe eight. He was wearing a striped t-shirt and khaki shorts. His thin hair, milky brown and soft, hung just below his eyes and curled around the ears. Andy, familiarly unkempt, the way he looked after spending a long summer day outdoors. The way he looks *whenever* you think of him.

He mouthed something.

I'm sorry, big guy, you said. *I'm sorry, but I can't understand.*

He moved his lips again and the meaning of his muted words became clear:

Find me.

It wasn't until a low whine from the tent shook you to consciousness that you realised you'd been dreaming. You looked over to the trees. The man in the black coat had vanished. Only sparks and faint wisps of smoke remained, drifting above glowing logs of wood.

Another faint cry, reminding you why you had woken. You made your way towards the tent and pulled back the flap. Jai-Li was sleeping on her back, her child in her arms. She was stuck in some nightmare and you could see the sheen of perspiration on her tightened face in the dim yellow light.

You touched her gently. She opened her eyes and looked around.

It's okay, you said. *You had a bad dream.*

A moment later, reality settled in. She sighed and looked down at her child.

Finally, she said something. Your name.

Yes, I'm Kayle, you said.

You explained that you'd helped Theunis, that he'd gone back to the beach.

You wondered then whether everything had gone according to plan. Theunis had been gone for a while. Perhaps he was lost, had been injured, or . . . perhaps something worse. Perhaps he'd been caught.

She asked if anyone had seen them, if there was any reason to think The Body knew about her being up in the woods, and you said you didn't think so. No, they were fine. Everything was fine.

Are you okay? you asked.

She said she was glad you were at her side, not one of the other communers. This took you by surprise. You knew each other, but not well. Nothing more than each other's names. How could she be glad to have you, a near stranger, be the one person beside her?

She'd seen you on the beach, she said. *You can tell a lot about someone without exchanging a word. In fact, she said, conversations are full of lies anyway. People pretending to know things, not know things, to care or not care about one thing or another.*

No, she'd seen you around. She had observed you, once asked someone your name. You were unusually quiet, she said. Private. Calm. Thoughtful. Not so much in a state of sadness as a kind of hopeless *emptying*, like water evaporating from a reservoir in a place with no sign of rain.

You were taken aback. Mostly you were surprised you had been singled out.

She rubbed her eyes.

You asked about her nightmare, if she remembered what she had been dreaming, but she said it was difficult to explain.

That's when you told her: *I had two children . . . once. A girl and a boy. My girl died. She was hit by a car when she was five years old. We were on our way to a lodge. My son needed us to pull over, he had to pee. She climbed out of the back, wandered up to the road, and then I saw headlights. Like two glowing eyes. I saw the lights before I even heard the car. It came speeding around the corner, slid out, and hit her. Killed her on impact. And the driver . . . The driver just continued on. Didn't even slow down. My boy . . . my boy's somewhere else in the world right now. In some other commune, I suppose. I don't know.*

Here was a mother hiding in the woods with her child, and you barely had the courage to speak of your son. Your daughter was dead, but your son—he was alive. You no longer had the power to protect him, so you'd swaddled him in denial like a newborn sent down a river in a basket. You weren't keeping him in your heart. You were letting him go, and the truth of your actions was poisoning you little by little, every day.

What were their names? she asked.

My daughter's name was Maggie. My son's name is Andy.

When last did you see him?

I don't know. I don't remember. It's been a while.

She smiled—the tender smile of the mother she had already become—and then she reached up to touch the side of your face.

Find him. Never give up. Find your boy and bring him back to you.

She said she now knew she needed to tell you her story. She couldn't explain why, except that something told her it would guide you. The sense of her own story's mysterious import on your life seemed to overcome her for a moment, like sunlight abruptly touching the cold bottom of a dried well.

Rest now, you said. *Tell me later.*

She shook her head. *No*, she said, *I need to tell you now.* You helped her sit up against the wall of the tent, slipped a pillow behind her back. She settled her child in her arms. He shifted and murmured and she stroked the ridge of his nose, just between his eyes. He quietened and she leaned back and exhaled.

That's when Jai-Li, speaking in a low voice and holding her sleeping infant, told you her story.

A life in the sky

M y father was a talented businessman.
That was no secret.

No one could take that away from him.

But that was as much as one could say about my father with complete certainty. Anything else—well, that depended on whomever was speaking. His partners or proteges may have added he was a leader. Perhaps even a hero. The media may have contended he was one of the top however-many influential people in the world. My mother may have said provider or, sometimes, victim. But if you had asked me, rest assured I'd have said my father was the coldest and most soulless person I had ever known.

That might surprise you. Even shock you. After all, what kind of reasonable daughter would speak about her father in such a way? Well, unfortunately, that's the way I felt; no sentiment rolled off my lips more easily.

You see, my father was the CEO of a corporation called Huang Enterprises. You may remember the company. It was always in the news for some new breakthrough or another. At one point there wasn't a pie Huang didn't have its finger deep inside—space travel, genetic engineering, nanotech, asteroid mining, terraforming; they had the monopoly on it all, as if existence itself was up for sale. There wasn't the leaf of a tree or scale of a fish that didn't have Huang's barcode imprinted into it, that wasn't owned or patented. And my father, as head of this monster, was the Ozymandias of his empire. King of kings, a wrecked colossus. A fair enough comparison, I think, considering the anticlimactic outcome of it all.

But no man achieves in a single lifetime what Huang Enterprises achieved. The corporation had been in my family for three generations before my father assumed position as its puppeteer and, in some ways, its sad puppet. Three Huang men at the helm of this corporate monstrosity, each of them with their own brand of cold-hearted genius. Behind *them,* it must be added, three generations of unfortunate women to mop up their muddy footprints.

Like me.

I was born on the 152nd floor of the largest city-scraper in the world. You may have seen it. Or perhaps one like it. In the end there were a few of them around and for a while they were quite the fad. Those monolithic towers must seem comical to behold these days—dark, empty and unused—but back then they were glittering megaliths of human ingenuity.

Our one was known as Huang-345.

Not very creative, I know, but then my father was committed to creating a legacy of its own mythological proportions. There was never any need for clever references to Babel and Yggdrasil, associations made with similar towers around the world. Not using my family name directly would have been seen as an offence to the end goal of our efforts: to be the inarguable rulers of the universe, the name and force against which all other names and forces would be measured. A family suffering the ultimate delusion of grandeur, some criticised—but then, given all of the Huang family's accomplishments, who could honestly reduce their achievements to some cliched flight of imagination?

The city-scraper itself was unmatchable: three hundred and forty-five floors of glass and steel that raced two and a half kilometres into the sky, piercing heaven's side like the Spear of Destiny. It was as wide as two of those old football stadiums and as self-sufficient as a small city.

The first hundred and fifty floors housed over a thousand apartments and houses, the most luxurious equipped with swimming pools and gardens. The next thirty floors had two schools, a university, a hospital, a bank, a shopping mall, a theatre and a playing field. Above them: an ice rink, a cinema complex, dozens of restaurants, and a park complete with trees and a pond for swans to float on. These were followed by seventy floors of "work rooms," conservatories, laboratories and agri-pods, where the majority of the residents (largely scientists and engineers) earned their keep by designing products, growing food, harvesting organs, and experimenting with new technologies—all for the benefit of and under the "good" name of Huang Enterprises.

Each floor was lit by a holographic, sun-like orb that passed across the ceiling at an illusory depth, giving the sense of great space above us—one impossible sky stacked on top of the other, accessed by twelve white vertical tubes. The tubes commuted between floors, each carrying up to forty people at a time. They could get from the top of the tower to the bottom in less than two minutes if necessary.

In essence, it was a city in the sky.

It was also the only home I ever had or ever knew.

From the day I was born until I was a young teenage girl, I remained in that city-scraper, not once stepping outside into actual, unpatented air and sunlight. That didn't bother me—not initially. I mean, we accept the world with which we are presented, don't we? For most of my childhood I never concerned myself with life outside because the idea never lingered long enough to excite me. *Outside.* Just as we have it on good faith the rest of the known universe is inhospitable for humans, I grew up believing that the rest of the world was an inhospitable place for me.

Besides, the tower was safe. It contained everything I could possibly need. For a while, I even felt comfortable. I found my way around with ease and grew accustomed to almost every steel inch of it. There always seemed to be more to explore, though, but then, if one is blessed with an ever-curious nature, anything can be explored in endlessly greater detail. That was something I learned from my mother. The plant and animal life in the park didn't just come into the world and simply *be*, she once told me. Nor did they reveal each of their secrets in one go. No, they grew and changed and fought to survive, constantly facing the gauntlet of existence, and I observed as much of this as I could with mounting passion.

Although everyone my age was at school during the day, which was when I was *allowed* to actually leave our house, there were always familiar people to speak to in the more residential parts of the tower. Ticket conductors, restaurant owners and grounds-keepers, they all knew the young barefoot girl in the pink and yellow dresses flitting about the tower, and they treated me with distant graciousness. It was only much later that I questioned the motives of those overly polite residents. Perhaps most of them deferred to me because I was the daughter of the CEO—but at least this allowed me to gain access to most of the floors and facilities quite easily. Most of the doors of the tower were open to me, and I stepped through them willingly, with a trusting insouciance.

In fact, in the entire tower, there was only one area I had no desire to explore and roam: my father's office.

"Office" really isn't the word. The room was the Hall of Valhalla itself: incomprehensibly spacious with almost nothing inside. Extraordinarily high ceilings supported by six colossal, shimmering marble pillars. Marble floors. No art. No decor. In some comically hyperbolic way, the obscenely large space was completely bare apart from my father's small desk.

The tiny desk sat at the furthest end of the space and it took a person about ten minutes to cross from the large double doors to where he was sitting. It felt much longer than that, though. The walk was a silent one, and when I made it I felt as if I was walking to the gallows. But my father? Part of me believed he covered it each morning to remind himself of how far he'd come in life and how much further he still wanted to go. A form of mental self-flagellation, I suppose. A purging of apathies.

If the distance ever became a problem, or an annoyance, he'd know to keep his level of commitment in check.

On the left side of the room, instead of a wall, there was a gargantuan pane of tinted glass that ran the entire length and height of the office. All that could be seen through it was the surface of an endless carpet of thick white clouds, the vast and unblemished universe above, and the bellied curve of the earth in the distance.

Predictably, it was magnificent.

Magnificent, and yet I hadn't ever seen my father spare as much as a glance at any of it.

Bent over his desk, he burrowed into his work, in a perpetual state of not-wanting-to-be-disturbed, his hard acne-scarred face barely moving. Two black beady eyes flickered intensely as he dragged and tapped digital documents on the large clear screen that hovered in the air above his work space. His maroon tie rested in a perfect knot around his neck like a patient noose. He was a man of terrifying precision, not so much a person as a bloodless vessel for some mathematical, chaos-phobic force in the universe.

That is the most persistent image I have of my father.

On the other hand, the memories of my mother are more complicated, and it is about these memories that I truly wish to speak. In my mind there are two versions of her and each wrestles for dominance.

The first is the mother of my earliest years—when she was a beautiful woman full of life and energy.

Hand-in-hand we'd walk through the park on the 188th floor and she'd often stop to show me a flower or a butterfly, something or another. She taught me what she knew. She would crouch beside me and her hair smelled of honey, her skin of rose oils. Her hands were powdery and soft, with long piano-playing fingers capable of the lightest and most assured touch. When she smiled, her lips parted effortlessly, revealing perfect white teeth. Her eyes were a red-brown colour I haven't seen before or since.

Sometimes I would lie on my stomach on her bed and watch as she sat at her gold dresser to dab on her blush and pencil in her eyeliner. She'd catch my eyes in the mirror and blow me a kiss. Staring at her with my chin in my hands and my bare feet kicking back and forth, I'd imagine she was a dancer preparing to debut in some spectacular show.

But there was no show.

No one to impress with her efforts.

She did it only for herself, if for no other reason than to remind herself that she was still a woman, regardless of my father's lack of attention.

I was young, but it was obvious enough.

The only time I really saw my mother and my father together was at dinner. Around him she would become different—unusually quiet or agreeable. From across the table she'd sometimes slip me a wink and a smile, before returning to her stoic and refined poise. I loved it when she did that. It made me think of the awkward silence over dinner as a game we were playing, to see who could act the stuffiest and most dutiful the longest. But my father, guzzling his meal at the end of the table as if it was nothing more than fuel poured into some giant engine, never had a clue.

After dinner, however—once my father had returned to his office—the two of us would laugh and chase each other around the house, letting out all of our pent-up mischief and giddiness. We'd collapse into each other's arms on the bed and I'd twirl her long dark hair around my finger until I drifted into sleep.

I'm sure you'll believe me when I say those first few were the best years of my life. There's honestly nothing I would have changed. But things did change, as things always do.

One morning she woke to the sensation of a tingling in her arm. My father had already left for work and I was standing at the door, watching her. My mother was sitting upright on her bed, rubbing her left arm with her right hand. As I entered the room, she flicked her head up in surprise. She forced a smile. I smiled back at her. She asked what I wanted to wear, if we should dig out something bright and pretty for the park. Naively reassured, I gave myself a head-start by running out, back towards my bedroom. But no familiar laughter followed me. I stopped and looked over my shoulder. My mother was not behind me. Worry crawled up from my gut like hundreds of small insects, and I knew something was wrong.

I ran back to her bedroom. I saw my mother's long bare back, hanging to the floor. Her head was squashed into the tiles at her shoulders, twisted unnaturally to the side.

I didn't scream. I didn't make a sound. I stood rooted to the spot. Surely this inelegantly slumped figure could not be my mother? Surely, when I finally screamed so loudly that I thought I'd torn open my throat, my real mother wouldn't have just continued to lie there, sprawled crookedly on the cold floor?

My mother was taken to the hospital on the 152nd floor, but they didn't help so much as emphasise each horrific component of her new and mysterious condition. She regained consciousness, but there was no relief to be had in this development. Her head was capable of little more than a drugged swivel on her neck. Her eyes were no longer sparkling carnelian gemstones but a dull obsidian, permanently locked on some far-off thing. Over the course of two days, every one of her basic motor functions ceased. Her legs and her arms were the first to go. These were followed by the muscles in her neck and her face. Ultimately, she was incapable of blinking an eye or swallowing water.

The doctors conducted test after test. She was probed and prodded for days before a panel of experts confirmed she had been infected by a rare, non-contagious virus and there was nothing that could be done to help her.

This infuriated my father. He was not a man disposed to being told what could not be done, he needed to know what could. He spent all hours on finding a cure, and it was only later that I began to realise that his efforts were based more on the blow to his ego than anything else.

That sounds harsh, I know, but he offered her no comfort during that time—never sat at her side to hold her lifeless hand, never whispered words of love and hope in her ear.

The woman in the chair no longer looked like my mother. The colour and life was gone. Her skin hung on her face. Her hair was a mess. Finally, my father surrendered. He settled for an alternative to a cure. This alternative was so monstrous that he could only have decided on it as a means of resolving his own sense of powerlessness. There is no other reason for him to do what he did.

He had a robot avatar built for her, linked it directly to her brain, and gave her at least the illusion of mobility. From the chair, my shrunken shadow of a mother could control a six-foot human-oid machine, willing it to perform basic actions via thought alone.

No care had been taken with aesthetics—my father was more concerned with functionality than beauty. This mother was a metallic skeleton bursting with plugs and wires. No voice. No expressions. No heartbeat. Through the cold, mechanical effigy of a human being, however, my mother was once again able to prepare my lunch, to tend to the house and to walk with me through the park.

In my mind, she had been made into a monster.

I did try for a short while, mostly for my mother's sake, but holding those hard metal claws never came close to holding my mother's soft hands. Looking into its two milky, globular "eyeballs," I saw none of her familiar warmth—just the mirrored reflections of the environment bouncing off its polished body. It had no colours or textures of its own. Each movement it made was the will of my mother, and that offered a slight consolation, but I'm sure you can understand when I say it was impossible to accept it as any form of replacement.

I'd enter the kitchen and it would be standing over the counter, either chopping onions, preparing sandwiches, or doing something else one might call "motherly." The head would pivot mechanically to its side and tip to position me in its line of sight. It would edge towards me, one heavy foot in front of another, and I would take a fearful step or two back. Picking up on my apprehension, the robot would return to the counter to continue its chore, as if I had never entered the kitchen at all.

We'd go to the park, but as soon as the doors of the tube slid open, I would hurtle ahead. I'd turn to wave, a tight smile screwed on my face. When I had run far enough, I'd duck behind a bush and sit sobbing softly, all the while peeking through the leaves as the robot walked through the park by itself, cranking its head from left to right to find me.

In the evenings, while the machine was being recharged in its customised wall-unit, I would disappear into my mother's room and embrace the real her—throw my arms around her limp arms, burrow into her bony shoulder—and cry myself to sleep.

This went on for a few weeks.

One morning, on one of the days selected for a flushing (when the park was shut down for a session of light-dimming and programmed rainfall), I sat on my bed and observed what I could through the tiny square window in my room. I could see only the faintest outline of a distant mountain range, cloaked in mist. The two and a half peaks (all I had ever been able to see of the range) were at the end of a long horizontal stretch of land. My concept of travel was based mostly upon going up and down, and I had little understanding of exactly how far those mountains extended. I didn't know whether it would take a few hours or a few days to get to them.

A knock at my bedroom door drew me away from the window.

The expressionless robot was standing there, holding up a yellow dress. The dress had a white frill along the neckline and tiny blue flowers printed along the hem. It had been my mother's favourite (*was* my mother's favourite, I should probably say) and she wanted me to wear it that day. The robot left the dress on the edge of my bed and went out.

After showering and getting dressed, I walked into the kitchen. For the first time, I did not see the robot preparing my breakfast. I moved through the kitchen and entered the living room.

The robot was sitting at our dinner table, doing nothing. It was simply staring at the wall.

As I approached, the head revolved in my direction. It stood quickly from the chair and stiffened.

It walked towards me slowly, each of its heavy feet thumping on the floor, and its right arm extended out. It opened its hand. I stared at the hand for a moment and, sensing that the action was no simple plea for affection, rested my soft hand in the rippled rubber palm. The cold metal fingers closed gently over mine. Then it turned and led me towards the door.

I was being taken out of the house, although I had no idea where we could be going. I hadn't yet eaten breakfast. The park was closed. It was still early in the morning and nothing was open. Once out of the house, we walked along the smooth black walkway under the light of the low sunlight orb. It moved slowly from one end of the curved blue ceiling to the other. I looked down. With the orb low and behind, our shadows stretched out ahead of us, reducing the two of us to stick-shaped characters of similar appearance. No skin. No steel. Just two long, black stick people walking hand-in-hand.

We waited outside the glass doors at the tube stop among a small crowd of early commuters. I was the only child in the group and the adults towered around me, each looking lifeless and disgruntled, the sort of expression you'd expect at the end of a long day, not the start of one.

One of the long white vertical tubes raced towards us—thrust down by the water pressure that powered each of them through the building—coming to an almost soundless halt in front of the silent group. The doors opened and four people entered. They sat. Their seats were raised and the next four available seats rose in their place. Eventually the robot and I were able to enter and take a seat.

Sitting in the tube as it raced downwards from floor to floor, watching and waiting as people stepped on and off, I still had no idea where we were going. The park raced past. Then the floor with the restaurants and entertainment facilities. I looked at the robot sitting beside me, but there were no clues to be read off its empty metal face.

The tube cleared out until only the robot and I were left. Finally it stopped on the first floor of the scraper. I thought we would be getting out there, but the robot stayed in its seat. The nose of the vertical tube extended below ground, a space I had always assumed to be reserved for leftover track. This, as I was about to discover, was incorrect.

The robot stood, pushed a red button beside the door, and the carousel of seats began to move. We were lifted up, across the top of the tube, and began our descent on the opposite side. The chair-lift stopped and the bottom doors opened, revealing a floor I had not known existed until then.

A floor below ground level.

A thrill rushed through me.

My mother willed the robot to stand up and I did the same. We stepped off the tube and into a long white corridor. The door closed behind us and the tube raced upwards.

The robot walked and I followed. The lights above the corridor were warm and yellow. On both walls of the long corridor were rows of framed pictures: photographs of my father shaking the hands of suited men (looking as if they'd like to suck the powers out of each other), schematics of unknown machinery and devices, certificates, a map of some kind, as well as what I now reckon must have been architectural floor plans. At the time I had no clue about any of those sorts of things.

At the end of the corridor, a door came into view. My mother lifted the robot's arm to punch a code into a keypad. The door opened and we stepped inside. The lights inside buzzed to life, revealing one part of the large space at a time.

It was a house.

A living room with three chocolate coloured sofas, various ornaments, paintings and paraphernalia—even a piano in the corner. There was a kitchen with all the accessories and amenities, as well as a fully stocked pantry-hall with enough food to feed a family for years. At the top of a spiralling steel staircase, I could see a number of bedrooms. We wasted no time, bee-lining through it all, making our way to the large steel door behind the staircase. The robot opened it by punching the same code into a keypad, and we went into a new room. It was large and filled with things I had never seen before. Things that, quite frankly, scared me. Strange weapons hung on racks attached to the walls. Three sets of body armour were on exhibit behind three glass cubicles. There were oxygen tanks. Gas masks.

I've since realised that the entire house was a protective bunker of some sort. My father was either more paranoid than I had imagined, or expecting some war or catastrophe to occur— one that would force the three of us to vacate the city-scraper and take up residence in that large, furnished, underground house.

My mother's robot offered no tour of the house. We had come for a specific reason and she went straight to it. She opened a large drawer and pulled out a brown cardboard folder. She turned and held it out and I took it from her slowly. I was about to open it but my mother's robot extended its hand and shook its head. I was not supposed to open it straight away.

After that, the robot closed up the room, switched off the lights, and we left the house. The tube returned to our underground floor and took us back home.

There, my mother's robot prepared lunch and dinner and marched back to the recharge unit for the rest of the day. It was not like her to shut down so early, but I felt guiltily relieved that I would have a break from our increasingly awkward interactions.

The rest of the day proceeded normally. I received private instruction from my regular old tutor, as boring as ever. I had my lunch, and I managed to push thoughts of that unsettling morning trip from my mind until the evening.

As usual, my father and I ate dinner in silence. Afterwards, he mentioned he'd go for a swim upstairs and, once he'd left, I went to my bedroom.

I sat on the bed for a long time holding the dossier. Should I open it? Something inside me said I should wait, and I decided to heed the instinct. I put the dossier in my bottom dresser drawer and went to sleep.

The next morning, I awoke as usual, but the robot did not come by with anything particular for me to wear. I showered and dressed. I remembered the dossier, but a growing sense of unease had surpassed my curiosity. I was afraid of what I'd discover inside. There was no reason to believe it would be bad news, but I felt it. The moment I opened it, horrible things would be set free. They'd fly out into the world and I'd never be able to put them back in.

The robot wasn't in the kitchen, nor was it in the living room. Perhaps it was standing like a palace guard in its recharge unit? But when I opened the door, the unit stood empty. Finally, I entered my mother's bedroom.

The machine was standing beside my mother as she sat in her chair. The plasma-window behind them showed the wide digital image of a mist-draped lake in the valley of two green cliffs. Both the robot and my mother were standing on the rippling surface of the lake; they appeared to be part of the image. Then the image changed and they were on a grassy, wind-flattened plain beneath a cloudy blue sky.

At first I thought the robot was assisting my mother in some way. Feeding or cleaning her. But it wasn't doing anything. It was bent over her with its arms out. My mind ticked over slowly and the horrific truth of the situation became apparent. The robot wasn't helping her. It was stooped over her body and its metal claws were clasped firmly around her floppy neck.

My mother was dead, her face inert and blue. She had used her robot to strangle herself, and the robot, having disconnected as soon as my mother's brain had ceased to function, was still frozen in its final, merciful act.

I could do nothing but stand and gawk. I was in a strange and surreal place and I couldn't register anything. I remembered seeing my mother in the bed more than three months earlier, but this time there was no running for help. No scream.

Instead, a kind of strange thoughtlessness was promptly followed by grief. The grief entered and settled in my gut like a dark and slippery creature, living off my pain. For two days, I refused to leave my room. I hardly ate. I moved in and out of understanding her final act, feeling furious and broken-hearted at the same time. And underlying that, in the deepest part of me, guilt simmered steadily.

Perhaps I had created too great a divide between the machine and my mother. That's why she'd killed herself. I'd treated her avatar like an intruder and had grown to despise it. All she had wanted was to walk and explore the tower—to spend as much time with me as she could. I had never considered that. I had never adapted, as hard as she had tried for me. I had never truly considered her feelings. I had been a selfish child. She had taken her life because of me . . . Once I allowed these thoughts to surface, I couldn't escape them.

It was not long afterwards that I entertained my first serious thoughts about life outside. I was only able to see a fraction of the world through any of the windows in the tower—mostly the thick ribbons of mist partially cloaking the mountains—but still, I dreamed of faraway places. These thoughts were the only thing that could distract me from my grief.

As time passed, the dreams grew stronger. The need to be out in the world intensified. My heart ached for freedom. I tried to tell myself none of these dreams really mattered since I lacked the most important ingredient for such an escape: courage. Only later did I realise that it wasn't courage I needed. It was *hatred*.

Hatred of the life I had been given, as well as the one I had been denied. A hatred strong enough to strip me of my fears and insecurities. A hatred that filled me two weeks after her death—the morning I remembered the dossier still tucked in my dresser drawer.

I took it out of my drawer, sat on my bed, and cautiously flipped it open. I looked towards the bedroom door, knowing nobody would be coming anytime soon. I reached into the brown dossier and pulled out a thin stack of senso-sheets. Flipping through each page, I could not work out the gist of the subject matter, but tried to pick up what I could. There were walls of printed text and signatures on the bottom corners of each sheet. An application form had been filled in, by either my father or my mother; their names were scrawled all over it. From the letterhead I determined it had been issued by the hospital.

I laid the documents on the bed and looked inside the dossier again. There were a few other items I had missed: pages with letters and codes, the moving image of what appeared to be a brain, and a handwritten note on a folded scrap of digital paper.

My name was on it: Jai-Li.

I unfolded it hurriedly, leaned against the wall, and began to read my letter.

I have read my mother's letter so many times since that moment that the memory of each word is etched into my mind. It went as follows:

> Dear Jai-Li
>
> You are only a baby as I write this, but I have spent so many nights wondering about the right time to show you the contents of this dossier. Hopefully, you are now almost an adult. If you are only a young girl, it means I've had to give you this difficult news early. I can't imagine the reason for such a thing, but if it means I am no longer around, I hope you find the strength and courage to see yourself through your years. I am sure that you will.

I'm not sure there is a right time to read such a thing as this. Nor do I know if your father ever plans on telling you—indeed, I fear he may not. I must be the one.

Just after you were born, I made a terrible mistake, and agreed to something I shouldn't have. It wouldn't have been easy to disagree with what was planned, to go against your father, but I should have done more to resist him. I should have fled, found a way out of this place. There must have been *something* I could have done. I don't know. What I do know, though, is that you must be told what I did, what happened to me. Hopefully, one day, you will find it in yourself to forgive me, although I do not expect your forgiveness to come easily.

When I met your father he was not the man you probably believe him to be. In the very beginning, we were young and we were in love. We dreamed about leaving the Huang family, the company, about eloping to avoid the terrible trap of a life of laid plans. But those years of hopefulness were short-lived. Somewhere along the line, the pressure from our families became too great. Somewhere along the line, I lost your father.

His own father, the grandfather you never met, filled his head with fear. The world was a wasteland, he said, a place in which your father would stand no chance of surviving. Furthermore, he added, your father was a wretched disappointment of an heir, a *boy* who could never hope to satisfy a woman like me. (Yes, this is what he actually said to him.)

This went on and on. Never once did your grandmother stand up for him. Mostly she smiled behind her husband and kept her tongue.

I turned to my own parents for help, but they would hear nothing of it. They told me to do whatever the Huang family wished. They were meek people of modest origins, overwhelmed by the prospect of their daughter marrying into an empire of such power and repute. I don't know if they hoped some of that power would come trickling down their way, or if they were relieved I'd be protected from the world in a way they had never been, but they brushed off the thought of the psychological torment that accompanied such a "merger."

Eventually, it reached a point where your father felt he could do nothing *but* submit—and he has been submitting ever since.

Day by day, I watched him slip away from me. In the beginning he was furious about his father's cruel taunts and threats, and we promised we'd find a way to deal with it all together. But fury cannot be channelled as one might hope. We can harness a few rays of the sun to do what we need—power a building like the one we live in, for instance—but we cannot harness the sun itself. It will burn as it wishes. And so it is with fury. The rage your father held in his heart for his father began to burn for me. His fuse shortened. Everything I did became an annoyance to him. At first, after one of his explosions, he would apologise, but these moments of contrition were brief, showing the fading remnants of the man I once knew and loved, the final few wisps of smoke before the embers of his love and compassion turned to ash. As if by death or the devil, he was finally lost. To me, and to himself.

Then came the day when the blood clot in your grandfather's head finally ended him, as embittered and pitiless as he had always been. With his death, something changed in your father. A change that took him from me forever. On that day he truly became a Huang.

For a while he simply withdrew into himself, barely finding the energy to fight with me, let alone communicate his feelings. When this detachment was replaced by something else, it was not by love, anger or even indifference. It was by the work to be done. Your father was consumed by the need to feed the shackled monster in the basement that runs on its wheel to keep the company going. The family legacy. The empire of guilt and shame.

And so came the plans for expansion. Everything was to be heightened and widened. Blueprints were drawn to extend the tower in which you were later born, and in which you are probably reading this: a prison of steel and glass where the outside world would have no domain. A place where every son of a Huang would be able to play out the role of God, a sinister, bloated pantomime for a crowd of spectators held hostage.

When he was satisfied (as much as he could feel for a short period of time), your father decided it was time to get on with the business of producing his son.

Of course, instead of a son, you were born. Since he had never insisted on genetic preparations to ensure your gender, you must understand your father has always accepted you for who you are. Unfortunately, there was more to this acceptance than meets the eye. It was the decision that was later made that haunts me each and every day. This is what I must confess to you.

Your father was not that concerned when you were born because he already had another plan firmly in place. Since he is relatively young, having only recently been made the head of the company, his plan is to hold his position for a significant amount of time, perhaps even until he is a hundred years old, or more. He knows the baton of leadership must be passed on, but he is equally determined to have his own time to reign. He also knows I am getting older and the window for me to have more children is closing.

And so, he told me of his plan: You, his daughter, will provide him with the son he needs. One day you will give birth to a boy and this son of yours will be your father's heir. In order to ensure this, however, my darling, I'm afraid some choices were made that I can no longer keep to myself.

You must know what is to come.

Merely a few weeks after you were born, on your father's wishes, you were sent back to the hospital. You were isolated in a laboratory for just under a month, during which time certain preparations were put in place. Your genes were altered so that, using genes extracted from your father's own skin, your body was set like an alarm clock to fall pregnant on the day you turn twenty years old. Within your blood a genetic clock is ticking, counting down the days until your body begins to produce a child.

Your belly will swell as the months go on. As far as I know, the child you give birth to will look and behave exactly like one produced from normal conception, but it will not be the child of any man you meet and love. It will not be a child of your choice, or even of a chance meeting. In truth, it will not be *your* child. It will come as close to physical and intellectual perfection as your father has ordered. It will exist for one reason and one reason alone: to follow in your father's footsteps and take over at the end of his years of control. He anticipates being in power for a good sixty to seventy years.

This heir, the one you will incubate, will allow him two things: his long and selfish time at the helm, and *you*, a caretaker for the child in the early years, for I will be too old to be of any worth. Your father has no intention of ever releasing you from this tower, and this is why. You will remain here for the rest of your life, first as the daughter who will never be allowed to fall in love, or marry, or have children and a home of her own, and later as the guardian to his new son . . .

I do not know whether you understand what it is that I am trying to tell you. You may be too young to grasp all of these details, but take care of this letter and reread it at a later stage if it is too difficult to make sense of right now.

All I can say is that there are no words to express my regret for having allowed this to happen. Once you've read this, you may reject every good thought and memory you've ever had of me, drench it all in bitterness or hatred. And while I remain the coward who has given up on finding a way to save you from this fate, all I can do is tell you this and pray you have enough courage to find a way of fighting this cruel plot against you.

I love you, and have always loved you, but that has never been enough. I have never been able to tell you all the things I've wanted to. You have been fed lies your entire life. You've been separated from the other children in this tower so that you never find a partner and fall in love, but also so that you continue to believe this tower is all that remains of a deserted and inhospitable world. This is not true. It is a fear put into your head to contain you.

The world is not a desert. It is full of life and wonder. There are things out there far beyond what you have ever been allowed to imagine. Do not do what I did. Do not give up out of fear.

As I have said, if you are reading this letter, I am no longer with you. But no matter what has happened to me, do not spend a second weeping for me. Do not hold so tightly to your memory of me that I continue to hold you back. I deserve neither your sympathy nor your admiration. What I beg of you is that you do something for yourself. Find a way. Find love. See the world.

With hope and hurt,
Your mother

And that was it. That was the end of the letter. My mother's final words, scrawled on a few pages.

As she had predicted, I did not understand everything at once, but I understood enough: the tower was not my home. It was my incubator. I was not being kept as a daughter. More of an investment, I suppose.

As I folded the senso-sheets into a tight square, I noticed something else: crude drawings on the back of them. I moved my hand over the pages and thin green lines appeared. I pulled my hand away and the lines began to fade. Ghost print, they call it. Secret digital print that will appear on a page only if brought near a particular, intended hand.

My hand, as it turned out.

I unfolded the pages again, flipped them over on my bed, then smoothed out the creases. It was an image of a maze, like one of the ones my tutor had often made me do. But this wasn't some meaningless maze from a puzzle book. It was a map.

There were two drawings. The one was a vertical rectangle divided into smaller rectangular segments, with a horizontal line across the final segment. On the bottom right, there was a second square with corners, flaps, angles, and what looked to be a tunnel extending to the top right of the page.

The purpose of the sketch struck me in an instant: it was a map of the underground house. I could see the floor plan of the corridor, the living room and the room containing the weaponry, the oxygen tanks and the gasmasks. Loose words floated between the lines: "squat-hatch," "keypad," "air-pod— remember to speak your name," "Exit A-3," as well as "Code: 65388." As the instructions floated in, I remembered the robot's long, metal finger punching in that very code on the keypad.

My mother had drawn an escape route. For me.

My heart leaped in my chest. I could barely contain my surprise, my fear, my exhilaration. I flicked my head to the door, expecting my father to burst in and rip the pages from my hand. He never came to my room, and there was no reason for him to do so now, but I was filled with sickening fear. My father could never be allowed to see those plans. I folded my mother's letter and slipped it into the shallow back pocket of my dress. Then I hopped off the bed and left the bedroom.

The house was cold and lifeless, as it had been for months, the black furniture and grey walls a stubborn stand against a world of colour and life. I would never again see that place as my home, I knew that, and what I did next was an easy thing.

I opened the front door and walked out, into the wide boulevard. There was no one around at that hour of the day. With the sun-orb high above me, I made my way towards the tube stop. I watched air bubbles rise in the water within the glass rail-channels. They changed shape as they floated and quivered up and out of sight, a strange blob-like family of their own. The tube pulled up in front of me and the doors hissed open. I entered the empty tube and took a seat. Then I pushed the button I had not pushed often, but was always all too aware of. It would take me to the top floor of the tower: to my father's office.

Even now I can't say why I decided to go there, but I do remember feeling both fearless and composed as the magnetised doors came together. I had already decided I would not be staying, but perhaps I needed to look once more at that aloof and uncaring face.

I needed to see it. Remember it. Use it.

Each of the levels flashed by my window. I closed my eyes, but could still tell when a floor had passed by the rhythmic *whomp* of air against the side of the tube. Without needing to stop for other passengers, the tube was able to build great speed as it raced to the peak of Huang-345.

I opened my eyes. The stacked floors flickered before me in succession, a jittery film that showed the vertical world of my childhood: the halls, fields and suburbs, once designed and built as a testament to human ingenuity, now the cluttered shelves of a musty broom closet.

The tube began to slow. The high pitch of my rushing glass vestibule lowered and softened until it came to a complete stop. At the edge of the platform a long red carpet led to the enormous double-doors of my father's office. The walls of the lobby were lined with dark wood. The tube hissed open and I stepped out and onto the soft red carpet.

I approached the front door. It was an old-fashioned door: no blinking lights, glowing palm-plates, or numbered keypads. My father locked it with an old-fashioned key when he left the room. When he was inside, however, it was usually left unlocked.

I took a deep breath and realised: I had absolutely nothing to say to my father. Why had I even bothered going all the way up there? What was I hoping to accomplish? Besides, my father had never shown any interest in me. Why should this change now? My mind raced with indignant questions all trying to block the fear that was beginning to return. All I was looking for was a good reason for turning around, going back down the tube, and returning to my room for the next sixty to seventy years of my life.

I tucked my hand under the large brass handle and pulled.

The first thing I saw was the enormous glass wall. I saw the expansive blue of the sky, my eyes relishing the rare chance to flex out into infinity.

The door opened wider and the scent of the wooden panels in the lobby faded completely, replaced by stark marble floors and walls. At the end, I could just about see one lone desk in the distance.

But my father was not sitting there. He was standing in front of the wall of glass, his hands behind his back, staring at the endless rolling cloudscape before him.

I had never seen him simply stand and do nothing. Something was different. Something was wrong. He must have heard the doors open and the *pat-pat-pat* of my shoes as I walked along the hard floor towards him, but he did not turn around. He didn't move at all. I finally reached the far end of the room and stood alongside him. As always he was wearing his immaculate grey suit, the unwrinkled maroon tie around his neck. His head was like a concrete block, his thin hair slicked and combed to the side. His eyes were narrow, his lips tight on his mouth, as if he was biting them closed from the inside.

I squinted through the glass. Outside, the sun struck the surface of the clouds, casting restless shadows in its constantly moving nooks.

Then my father opened his tight lips to speak.

We were wrong, he said. *We were so wrong. How could we have been so wrong? And now, because of it—a miscalculation—everything's lost. Everything's finished.*

I couldn't tell if he was speaking to me or to himself. His head didn't move, his eyes didn't blink, but his lips were trembling a little. He went on:

Idiotic. Pathetic. That we thought we could control it. We thought we knew what we were doing. But we had no idea . . . have no idea what we're doing. We've never known. We're fools, and soon we'll be even greater fools. Everything . . . every last thing we've ever learned and acquired will be gone. And we'll be like animals again. Animals. Stupid, useless animals.

I had no idea what he was talking about; he was rambling.

Chang'e 11, he said. *Chang'e 11 came back . . . it came back to us. A Trojan horse. We thought it was a gift—our lost cat had found its way back home—but it came back with something else . . . and soon everything will be gone. Our memories. Our identities. Wiped away. He got inside my head and he showed me. He showed me his plan to end us all. Whispers in my dreams. Whispers and laughter. A picture of an empty world. Everything we've ever worked for will be gone, everything we've done, and we'll have to start again . . . like stupid, stupid animals . . .*

A tear oozed from his eye and ran over his cheek to the right corner of his mouth. *A man makes a life. He makes his choices. He lives with his choices. He paves his fate. He makes something of his life and all he wants is for his name to go on—to be remembered. That, above all. But now? This? A waste,* he said, softly, and then, louder, *a waste! A waste of time! It's all been a waste of time!*

His colourless face began to redden and tighten. I took one careful step back.

I needed to leave.

I wanted to say goodbye. *Goodbye father, I'm leaving.* But it wouldn't have mattered. He wouldn't have heard me. He was still screaming that *everything was lost* and that it had all been *a waste of time* when I turned and walked quickly towards the doors of the hall. With his voice booming behind me, I picked up speed until I was sprinting to the exit.

I slammed the doors shut behind me and fell to my knees. I was panting heavily and wanted to retch. I pressed my hands against the soft red carpet and closed my eyes. Then under my breath, I said it: *Goodbye.*

That was the last time I saw my father—and those were the last words I heard from him, those screams behind me: that we'd all go back to being *animals again. Animals. Stupid, useless animals.*

It was the last time I stepped into that ridiculously capacious room. I needed to leave immediately and I couldn't waste another minute. In my head and my heart, it was finished. I, the daughter of a Huang, was finished.

So I pushed myself up from the carpet and ran to the tube stop . . .

The smoking mirror

Jai-Li stopped speaking. Her eyes darted to the side as the malformed shadow of a person crawled across the wall of the tent. The zip of the tent buzzed down and you saw it was Theunis.

He poked his head inside and beckoned you out of the tent. You turned back to Jai-Li, told her you'd be back soon and that everything would be all right. She smiled in appreciation of your assurance, but it was clear you were less than convinced.

You stepped out, zipped up the tent behind you, and approached Theunis. He was pacing in circles and raking his fingers through his hair. The heat of the dying fire was losing its reach and the icy wind that edged your skin was like the breath of death. But you kept your composure to help Theunis keep calm. Something had gone wrong. His eyes were wide and wild. His skin was damp with sweat.

You asked him what it was, but he couldn't speak. There was the rustle of some nocturnal animal flitting about the trees above you, and Theunis jerked his head up in alarm. You shook him gently and said his name twice. *Theunis. Theunis, what is it?*

Finally he turned to look at you.

At first, everything had gone fine, he said, but hardly a few minutes after arriving at the commune, a young boy had summoned him up to the house on the hill.

He'd told himself it was a coincidence. They didn't know, he'd told himself; they *couldn't* have known. But then he'd walked into that white room with the large window and the pale moon swimming behind those shadowy shapes and found himself wired to that machine. The Body had fired off their questions—their weird, philosophical questions. Waited for the answers he was supposed to know by heart. Dreams. Numbers. God concepts. They had not asked about Jai-Li. So maybe it *had* been a mere fluke he'd been called to bear witness at that precise time. The problem was, he'd been unable to conceal his nervousness from the grey machine. The machine was hardly necessary, he added; he'd perspired and fidgeted like a boy. And, of course, the more nervous he felt, the more his anxiety grew. At one point, they'd had him sit for almost five minutes without saying a word. The longer he'd sat, the hungrier that thing had seemed to get, and the longer The Body had waited. After that, they'd sent him back down to the beach.

At that point you said it was okay, that maybe they still didn't know, but Theunis was adamant. They did. They knew he was guilty of *something*.

You took a moment to think about what to do next and then you said to him that the two of you could not do this alone; you needed someone else to help you. Someone you could trust.

Theunis wasn't sure there was anyone, but you said you knew somebody. Gideon. If anyone could be trusted, it was Gideon. You would have to do it in turns, rotate your shifts, otherwise there'd be no hope of securing the secret. And besides, you added, Gideon was one of the better carpenters on the beach. He'd be able to make the oar, quicker and better than either of you.

Your responsibilities were taking on new weight, new shape almost, and you were hit with a sudden sensation. Purpose. It was a feeling both familiar and anomalous to you. Before this, such feelings had only washed up occasionally, like rare and colourful shells on the bleak shore of your existence. When one arrived, and you picked it up and put it to your ear, you could still hear within its smooth folds the oceanic echo of the person you had once been. Now the feeling filled you, strengthening you, frightening you.

Theunis and you decided that he should go back down to the beach and stay there until morning. The Body would be watching him closely after his interrogation, so you'd have to be the one to stay with Jai-Li. The next day he would come back up the mountain and you'd go down to find Gideon. Jai-Li needed to stay out of sight and at least one of you needed to be constantly in sight. So that was the plan, for now. It wasn't a perfect plan, but it was the best you could think of. Theunis handed you the bag of food and two rolled-up blankets. He thanked you as if you had agreed to do all this for his sake only, and then he left.

You watched as he rushed away into the darkness, beyond the light of the glowing moon. Then you turned and took the bag and blankets back to the tent. Jai-Li was probably hungry; she hadn't eaten for at least a few hours. But when you pulled up the zip of her tent, you saw that she had already fallen asleep.

You reached up and curled your hand around the rough branch of the gigantic tree. You grabbed it tightly and hoisted yourself up. You slipped your right foot onto a woody protrusion, pushed down, and pulled yourself up some more. Your breath was misfiring, in and out of your lungs like a car battling to start. Your face pressed against the bark and you closed your eyes, willing yourself into a state of physical calm. You could not give up. Not yet. You'd seen the red shoe on the ground below and were convinced you'd find Andy at the top of that tree.

You looked down. The trunk of the tree ran downwards, vanishing to a pinpoint among the green canopy below. You gripped the tree harder. You had climbed for so long and you were terrified of being so high up. The fear throbbed in your throat and chest and stomach like a fat and unearthly slug.

You looked up. The top of the tree disappeared in thick clouds. Andy would be up there. He would be waiting for you. You were sure of it. So you decided not to look down again, and continued on, controlling your breathing all the way, gripping one branch at a time. The wind danced around the trunk, mocking you for your lack of dexterity. You ignored it, held tighter, and ascended.

Soon, the colours of the world began to fade. You realised you were entering the thick blankness of a cloud and you could barely see the next branch you were supposed to grab, let alone where the top of the tree ended. You stopped and lifted yourself onto a wide branch, taking a seat. Your head tilted up and around. There was nothing but the whiteness.

Had Andy come up so far? Could he have?

You were beginning to doubt it, but wouldn't let yourself give in to the doubt. You had felt so strongly that he'd climbed the tree, and you had come up so far in spite of the fear pounding in you. You could not lose faith now.

You called his name. Your voice barely penetrated the thick cloud. You called his name again, louder.

Andy . . . Andy!

Nothing came back but the haunting stillness. You arched your head up. Through the white shroud above, you could feel the sickly, dull warmth of what you thought was the sun. But the warmth did not comfort you. It was a humid thickness, the sort in which terrible, diseased things grow. You squinted at the cloud and now you could see the faint outline of a weak, glowing orb suspended somewhere far beyond. This must be the sun, you thought. The orb shone feebly, its shape barely distinguishable, like the intangible image cast on the back of your closed eyelids when you couldn't get to sleep. It was very near and yet very remote, like a faraway planet brought close by the lens of a powerful telescope. It shouldn't be called a sun. It was something else, an eye that could somehow see you more clearly than you could see it.

You were sitting there, still wondering what it could be, when a soft voice crept into your head. It seemed to be your voice, but it wasn't the voice of your normal thoughts. It was clear and direct and had come into your head from somewhere outside. Above all, you were certain of this.

I'm beginning to understand, *the voice said softly.* I'm beginning to remember.

You did not know what the voice meant. But as it came into your mind, a new realisation dawned upon you: the voice was coming from the orb. It was speaking its mind through you, using your voice, becoming clearer and more direct as it went on:

Do you remember Jack Turning, Kayle?

Remember Jack Turning. Remember his face. Remember him. Remember his fear and his guilt. I will help you to end this, Kayle. This silly daydream of an existence. Where are you climbing? Who do you think you will find up here? You will not find Andy here, Mr. Kayle. You will not find him because he is not here. Soon, *I'll* be there and I'll show you for myself. But the alp on your chest is getting bigger, my friend. And they say it takes a human body a variable amount of time to decompose properly. It all depends on the conditions, Kayle, for there to be nothing but bone. You can understand that, surely?

So a man makes a life. He makes his choices. He lives with his choices and he paves his fate. You'll all go back to being animals. Stupid, stupid animals . . .

The voice made no sense to you, although you somehow recalled each of its strange words. You had heard them before—in another place, another life, perhaps. You pushed yourself up and asked again about your son, Andy, and where you would find him. You needed to find him.

There was a hum of white noise, the echo of the Big Bang, the physical sound of beating light. And the voice of the orb again: And you'll be animals again. Animals. Stupid, useless animals . . . how do you get a fifty-ton beached whale to move, Kayle? You ask it *reeeally* nicely . . .

You collapsed against the trunk of the tree. The orb wouldn't tell you anything. The words coming from it were nonsensical, but you did understand one thing. Andy was not in the tree. You had made a mistake. You leaned over the edge of the branch and looked down. You were too high up. There was no way to climb back down. You wouldn't make it—up or down. You had put every thing into the climb up and had nothing left for the climb back down. You closed your eyes and rested your head against the side of the enormous tree and finally, you gave up. You would never find Andy.

It was over.

And so, with the orb still filling you with its meaningless words, you slid and tipped to the side, losing your seat on the branch. You felt the gravity of the earth as it wrenched you down. You were out of the tree, your legs flailing, your arms flapping at your sides as you went plummeting. The air wrestled with you; the force and speed of the earth's pull seemed to separate your internal organs from each other until you were no longer a person but a formless and powerless mass. Your body plunged and you forced your eyes open. The cloud above pulled away and suddenly you were in the brightness and clarity of a sunny day. The tree trunk raced up into the sky alongside you, becoming another pinpoint, this time in the cloud, as if it were growing upwards at a rapid and unnatural rate. You were calm, your mind was at rest. At peace. You surrendered to the whim of an uncompromising physical force, waiting to smash you to pieces on the ground below.

But then you saw him.

Andy.

And your body seemed to slow mid-fall. Your hair didn't flap madly on your head, but undulated gently as if you were now underwater. You turned your head to see him. The boy you had yearned to see for so long.

Your son was climbing up the tree trunk. He had been climbing up behind you all along, looking for you. If you had waited there, up in the tree, he would have reached you. You would have been reunited. But you'd given up. The orb had said you wouldn't find him, and you'd believed it. Now you were falling, and there was nothing that could be done.

Andy turned his face and saw you. His expression was one of surprise and horror.

Andy, is that you?

Dad!

You were now filled with a painful guilt, and the slowing of your fall gave you the time to feel the full throes of your remorse. It gave you the time to think you could do something about it—that perhaps *you could grab onto the tree and save yourself—but no, there was no hope. You had only appeared to slow, and your body was still on course with the hard ground below. You could do nothing, and when you turned again, you could see that the trunk beside you was changing; the rough texture of the bark was smoothing over, losing its brown colour and beginning to glimmer with a metallic sheen. The tree formed windows—windows and linear edges—and soon, it wasn't a tree at all. It was Jai-Li's tower, the Huang-345. You were falling alongside a vast city-scraper of steel and glass.*

Let me tell you a story, *the orb said, the voice having changed neither its tone nor its tranquillising tempo.* Would you indulge an old woman and her story?

You could still see Andy far above, and now he was clutching onto the side of the tower, but he was shrinking into the distance as you fell further and further from him. Your speed began to escalate, and your arms, legs and hair fluttered wildly as you raced breathlessly towards . . .

You blinked. Your eyes were open. At first you did not know where you were, but it came to you quickly. You were lying on the slope of the mountain beside Jai-Li's tent, next to a smoking pile of blackened wood.

The dream. It was the same moment that had played itself over and over in your mind, night upon night, week upon week. But this time it had been clearer than ever. It had been so clear that when you awoke, you could still feel the tingle of the rushing air on your skin, still feel the nauseating warmth of the orb. It left you feeling the agony of having lost your son for the first time more clearly than ever before.

Remember Jack Turning, the voice had said again, as it had said every night. *Remember his face. His fear.* But still, you couldn't. You did not know a Jack Turning, you had *never* known a Jack Turning. Maybe Jack Turning knew where your son was; maybe Jack Turning had taken him.

You rolled onto your back and looked up into the sky.

After your waking world steadied, you managed to clear the dream from your head. It was time to think about Jai-Li's story about her life in the tower. Her story had been interrupted, but she'd said enough to keep your mind ticking over—her father, her mother, the robot, her prearranged child . . .

Did this mean her newborn was the one she had been warned about? And if so, did that have something to do with the reason she so desperately needed to escape?

But there was something else on your mind, besides all of that: both Jai-Li and Moneta had told you their stories in such great detail. *You*. Jai-Li couldn't have told Theunis, and she must have trusted him, surely. And Moneta had purposely sought you to tell *her* story. She'd needed your help in the garden, but that was little more than an excuse.

So again, you mused, why *you*?

Bits of bark and leaves crackled under your weight. There was the strong fecund scent of soil and sap. You pulled the blanket Theunis had brought up to your neck and folded the end of it under your feet.

You forced your eyes shut and coiled into a foetal position and your last thought before slipping back off to sleep was what Jai-Li had said before she'd even begun her story. She'd *needed* to tell you. She'd believed it would "guide" you in some way. As absorbed as you had been by the tale that had proceeded, however, you could not see how it would direct you. Perhaps, if she finished her story, it would all become more obvious. But her last words, the ones that persisted, clinging delicately to the rest of your thoughts like a stubborn gossamer web, were more direct and more tenderly haunting: Find him. Never give up. *Find your boy and bring him back to you.*

You finally drifted off, and achieved a few more hours of sleep untroubled by dreams of any kind. In the early morning you awoke rested. The woods seemed a different place. In the light of dawn, there were new colours and textures; the world was green, brown and yellow, rough, smooth and prickly. The darkness that had constricted you the night before had broken like a fever.

Theunis was standing over you.

You rubbed your eyes and squinted up at him. He looked tired. His eyes were red. The stubble on his face was longer and darker.

The night, he said, had gone by without incident. You nodded and crossed to the tent to check on Jai-Li, but she was still asleep. You patted Theunis's shoulder to clock out of your shift and, within a few minutes, were making your way down to the beach.

When you stepped out of the woods and into the open white light, it seemed as if you hadn't been part of the commune in weeks. Something had changed over that time, but how? You had only been away for a night. Nothing could have changed. Perhaps it was you. You had changed.

Either way, the commune appeared even more hopeless and removed than it had before. You walked across the sand, between the fly-covered stalks of roasted brown kelp. Between and behind the tents were the usual faces, but nobody bothered to look at you. No one had missed you (*the boon of a being a loner, Kayle*). You headed straight for Gideon's tent.

He was sitting on a stump of wood outside his front entrance, reading a comic book. He craned his head up as you approached and bent back the folded pages. He held up the cover of the comic for you to see.

A large and muscular man wearing a tight blue suit and red cape was grabbing two dejected-looking criminal-types by the backs of their jackets. They were flying far above a densely compacted metropolis. You knew the fictitious character fairly well, although you couldn't recall having read a comic book in your life. He was Superman, the so-called Man of Steel.

This belonged to someone I knew, he said softly, cautiously. *I don't remember who, but it was someone close to me. I remember that.*

He thumbed through the book quickly, as if hoping to have some hidden significance spray out from between the pages. Then he rolled the comic book up and tapped it against his left hand.

This super man, he's an interesting character. Everyone else in the book is weak and helpless. But he flies around saving people from their own clumsiness—these others, these ordinary people, they're always falling off buildings or losing control of their aeroplanes. When there's a problem, this super man arrives and saves everyone. It's amusing, don't you think, Mr. Kayle? They would rather make a story about one man with all this strength and power, and then have him go around protecting everyone, instead of a story about people learning to save and protect themselves. Is this what people want? To stay weak and blundering and have someone else do the saving and protecting? Very anti-Darwinian. But it's a very interesting fable. Funny as well. I've read it a few times already. You should read it.

You huffed and took a seat on a second stump in front of him. Gideon sloped over and handed the book to you.

The expressions of the drawn men were charming and rudimentary. The one criminal was a bald man with a tattoo of a skull on his neck, the other a shaggy-haired young man in a leather jacket, evidently the more fretful of the two. Superman looked calm, collected, and unapologetically smug as he dragged them up to the clouds like bags of refuse. You handed the book back to Gideon.

Finally, he said: Something has happened, hasn't it?

A pang of uneasiness fired through you. Gideon glanced down at the comic book again, rubbing his thumbs over the page in circles.

How is the alp on your chest these days? he asked, and looked back up. Is it getting worse or getting better?

I don't know. Worse, I think.

He spoke again: I've been dreaming too, Mr. Kayle. Recently, I've been dreaming every night. I know we shouldn't speak about it, but it's true. I have not been sleeping very well.

It was the first time Gideon had spoken about his own experience on the beach.

You know, I don't remember much about my life before the beach. Not as much as everyone else. I don't even remember my real name. Gideon was not my name—I chose it for myself before I arrived here. Most of my memories didn't come back to me. I remember moments and flashes. Some things seem to trigger a feeling, like *this book—I seem to remember countless stories that aren't my own, that can't ever have been real: impossible creatures, gods, monsters, superstitions, the details of meaningless mythologies. But nothing about me, about my life. There are no names. I might have lost them along the way, perhaps even some time after Day Zero. Maybe they will still come to me. I don't know.*

There is, however, one clear thing. I need to tell you. Something tells me I am not the only one dreaming about this one thing, but there's no one besides you I feel comfortable asking. Tell me, Mr. Kayle, in your dreams, have you seen a glowing ball in the sky?

You shuddered, but played devil's advocate, saying, *You mean the sun?*

No, not the sun. Not exactly. But a ball. A sphere in the sky that sits like a planet. It is everywhere I go in my dreams. No matter where I am, it hangs in the sky above me. It is warm, this sphere, but the warmth sickens me. It makes me anxious. And it speaks, using my voice, but the voice is in my head, and it says peculiar things. It says it is coming. Coming for us. Every night this sphere grows larger and bolder in my mind and I'm starting to believe it. And fear it. Please, Mr. Kayle, I know I shouldn't ask, but tell me— have you dreamed of this also?

You forced a slow, heavy nod. Gideon sat upright. You couldn't tell whether he was feeling relieved or troubled by your admission.

You know, Gideon said, *it reminds me of a story I do still remember. A long time ago, sometime at the start of the Age of Self, the Aztec people worshipped a god named Tazcatlipoca. It's a mouthful to say. Tazcatlipoca. But this god, he was in charge of a great many things. The weather, the night, the universe, the earth, harmony, war, beauty . . . all of these things. And his name, translated from their language, meant "the smoking mirror" because of the obsidian glass he would use to see the entire cosmos at once. It was his looking glass, and through it, he could see everything that happened. He could peer into the corners of existence and change and engage with whatever he saw fit.*

The reason I'm telling you this, Mr. Kayle, is because I'm beginning to think such a smoking mirror exists today, with us. I have a feeling that not only you and I are having this dream, and that is why we have been told not to speak to each other about it. I am beginning to think we have become sitting-ducks, as they say. In my opinion, I do think something is coming for us. Something from far away—an orb, a force, I don't know—but in the meanwhile, it is observing us. Through our dreams. It's looking into us, and it's getting stronger. I cannot know for certain, but I believe that we have become its smoking mirror. And that is what they're not telling us. Because The Body knows this thing, knows what it is, and fears it.

This is what I fear, Mr. Kayle. This is what these dreams feel like to me.

It was astonishing that Gideon remembered these stories about mythological characters and old gods, but could not recall the real people in his past life, or even his real name. You couldn't help thinking perhaps those were the recollections that mattered most to him, but that didn't feel fair—you knew how unsystematic and fractured the memories were that eventually came back. But what he'd said seemed chillingly right. Perhaps you had become, as he'd put it, the smoking mirror through which you were being watched, even studied. The orb itself was definitely getting bigger, bolder—the voice, clearer and closer—and if Gideon was seeing this same strange ball in the sky, then others were, too.

So, what about The Renascence? you asked finally. *What is it then—some charade? What are we doing here? What are we really waiting for?*

I don't know, he said softly. *Maybe we aren't waiting for anything. Maybe they believe The Renascence is some kind of defence against this thing in our dreams. A way of hiding? I don't know. As I said, it is only a feeling, but this feeling is growing in me. I'm sorry, Mr. Kayle. We shouldn't talk about it, but I can't keep it to myself anymore.*

Gideon got up, took a few steps away from the tent and looked up at the sky. His face was bathed in the sharp morning light. The strengthening wind moved through his dreadlocks, causing them to swing a little. His square jaw was clenched tightly, his thick arms flexed and mapped in long descending loops of veins.

Gideon, does the name Jack Turning mean anything to you?

Gideon turned to you. *Who?*

Have you ever heard the name Jack Turning?

Jack Turning? Gideon shook his head. *I can't say that I have. Who is he?*

I'm not sure exactly. Never mind. It's probably not important.

You dusted the back of your pants and walked to Gideon's side. You told him then that, as he had guessed, something had happened and you needed to tell him all about it. But you couldn't do it there. Not in the middle of the commune. You insisted on going for a walk.

The two of you moved away from the commune and made your way to the water's edge. The waves were rough and foaming white, rolling thickly and rushing up the sand. A cool mist was thrown up and against your hot skin as you walked ankle deep in the icy froth. When you were far enough away, you told Gideon about the situation. You told him about Jai-Li, the child, the escape, and the oar that was still needed. He listened intently and didn't say a word. When you had finished, he said nothing. He stood and stared out over the ocean. His expression at that point was difficult to read; you couldn't tell what he was thinking. Then he turned to you and said *Come,* leading you away, back to the commune.

Gideon already had an oar that only needed to be repaired. You and he went together up the mountain to Jai-Li's tent. On the way up you thought about what Gideon had said about the smoking mirror and wondered whether it could be true: were you being watched by that thing in your dreams? Did it really exist? Was it coming for you, for all of you, and what did it want?

You led Gideon up through the crooked trunks of trees and the thick green underbrush, carrying the oar on your shoulder. Jai-Li's tent appeared in the clearing, beyond the rough thicket.

As you and Gideon emerged into it, Theunis sprang up from the forest floor, rattled. He eyed Gideon cautiously, but all Gideon did was bow to him before making his way to the tent.

You rapped twice on the canvas, Jai-Li told you to come in, and you unzipped the tent. You introduced her to Gideon. He assured her he'd do what he could to help, and the two of you stepped out and joined Theunis.

For the two days that followed, the three of you took turns bringing food and water and keeping watch.

One time when Theunis appeared, however, he was accompanied by another person: Angerona. Theunis explained that he'd been halfway up the mountain when he'd seen her behind him. She'd followed him from the commune; there had been nothing he could do.

There were four of you now, more than had initially been intended, but you'd do what you could. And Angerona, it turned out, proved to be far more useful than you had thought she would. She was small and quiet, the perfect member of your group to slip away and return with supplies when necessary.

And all this time, none of you was called up to the white house on the hill. There were no hints that anyone had a clue what you were up to. You were getting away with it. The plan was working.

On the third day, you were finally ready to get Jai-Li and her child off the beach. Gideon had fixed the oar and a long, safe route had been mapped to the cove.

On the morning of her departure, a perfectly dense, white mist had fallen. It was difficult not to see it as a sign—the cloak of a guiding force intending to ensure safe passage. A sign was just what you needed, so you took heart from it, and set off.

You walked down the mountain, one behind the other. Angerona led the group, moving nimbly between the small rocks and tricky dips. Gideon and Theunis carried the boat and you had the oars on your shoulder.

The bottom of the slope disappeared into a murky white mist. A nocturnal bird hooted its last for the night. Jai-Li checked on her baby. He was fastened to her back with a towel and sleeping soundly. She peeked over her shoulder at you and slowed the pace of her walking until she was beside you.

She said: *Kayle, I need to tell you the rest of my story.*

You looked at Theunis behind you and Gideon ahead. Nobody reacted to her words.

Jai-Li's face appeared older and paler, as if her blood had been drained out overnight. Her eyelids opened and closed slowly. She was exhausted, obviously. But she walked on, putting one foot in front of the other with dogged determination.

Kayle, I need to tell you what happened next.

The first escape

Stupid, stupid animals, ringing in my ears. My father's last words, screaming, thundering in my head. I was terrified. Excited. Frustrated. But still, from the cloudy chaos of my thoughts and emotions, one impulse shot out like a beam of light: *it's time to leave, right now.*

I ran from my father's office and never looked back. The tube took me back down the tower and I sat and watched the floors flicker before me. I was breathing so violently I thought I'd pass out. The faster the tube raced down the tower, though, the greater the distance created between my father and me, and the better I felt. My mind began to calm, my breathing steadied. My fear drained away and by the time I reached our floor, I was already thinking about what I needed to do.

I ran across the boulevard and burst into the house. I hurtled through the rooms, grabbing what I could, what I thought I'd need. I had no idea what that was, though; I hadn't a clue where I was going, what challenges would be waiting on the outside. So I filled my rucksack with nothing but warm clothing, a two-litre bottle of water, dehydrated food cubes, and the only printed photograph of my mother in the house. I double-checked that her letter was still in my back pocket, swung the rucksack onto my back, and took a brief moment to look about the cold and hollow house.

There had been life there once. I could still hear my mother's laughter as we chased each other through the rooms. I could still smell her perfume—a trick of memory; I had long been denied her scent. Honestly, I told myself, there truly is nothing left here of home, no echo off the walls. The glints of light off the metallic surfaces, the glowing neon of the visual-glass, the drone of the air conditioner—they would buzz and shine on forever, irrespective of whether anyone was there.

I ran from my childhood home. At the tube stop, a man was waiting for a ride. He was wearing a grey coat and hat, reading off his palm-plate. I slowed my run to a nonchalant walk. I waited next to him without looking up, but could see from the corner of my eye that he had dipped his head in my direction.

You're going to be in big trouble, young lady, he said.

My hand tightened on the strap of my rucksack, my face filled with heat, my breath lodged like a stone in my throat. He didn't know, I thought; he couldn't know! *Your teacher isn't going to be happy you're late for school*, he added, returning his gaze to his palm-plate.

I snapped up at him, saying that I didn't go to school. Of course, that made him realise he was speaking to the daughter of the CEO. I regretted having said anything. I should have tried to leave without being recognised, but even at that point I suppose there was a remnant of childish pride left, of loyalty to my family's name.

Ms. Huang! My apologies. He tipped his hat. *I didn't recognise you. Of course you don't. No, of course not. You have a lovely day.*

The tube doors hissed and parted. I smiled uneasily at him and went inside. He came in after me but I sat two rows above him, staring at the top of his head all the way down. I expected him to look up and ask me some question I couldn't answer, like *So where are you off to?* or *Does your father know you're here?* but a few floors later, he exited and I was taken by myself to the bottom of the tower.

I spotted the red button across from me, climbed on my seat, leaned across the tube, and stretched my arm out to push it. My chair clicked, whirred, and began its rise to the top of the tube, its descent on the opposite side.

The doors to the secret floor slid away from each other, and the corridor rolled out ahead. I stepped out cautiously and my small shoes clacked on the tiled floors. The doors closed behind me and the tube raced back up.

The sound of my breath was louder and harder in the narrow corridor. It seemed longer and wider, colder and more daunting, like one in a dream that would continue to lengthen no matter how quickly I ran along it. I wished my mother was with me. I dreaded having to continue all by myself.

I remembered being down in the corridor with my mother that first time.

But I *hadn't* been with my mother. The robot had been holding my hand that day. So why did my memory say her, and not *it*? I'd filled in the gap between the machine and my mother, something I hadn't been able to do at the time. The thought sickened me. How stupid I had been. The moment she'd taken her own life, that was when I had really lost her, when she had truly ceased to be. Before then she had been with me all the time and I hadn't appreciated her for what she was, for the huge effort she had made on my behalf. All I had now was her letter, but the words of the letter would never change . . . they would never show me some new way.

I pulled my rucksack up my shoulder and made my way along the corridor. I checked the paper for the number and punched it into the keypad. The door opened and I entered the underground house. Once again, light upon light flashed on in sequence, revealing each ornament and piece of furniture. It smelled musty down there, untouched by fresh air. There were probably fans and ventilators somewhere, but they weren't on, and the place stank.

I studied the map and keyed in the same code to enter the room behind the staircase. It was unnervingly cold and practical—a bunker, a panic room, a paranoid's dream suite.

Blue UV tubes lined the walls, saturating everything in their light: padded body-armour, large black guns slotted into metal brackets, holding out their many hands, insisting, *Go on, take one. You're going to need us where you're going, little girl.*

Droplets of sweat were beginning to form on my brow. I scoured the wall, searching for a suitable weapon.

What was I doing? As I tried to select a weapon I realised I had no clue—no idea of what lay ahead. All my life the outside world had been labelled a wilderness of nameless evils. There were predators out there, my father had once said to me, that's why the tower had been built in the first place. To protect us. To keep us safe. And so once again questions peppered my mind in a shower of hot sparks: Jai-Li, what *are* you doing?

I turned from the wall and studied the armour and the glass cubicles housing the gas masks.

I should grab one of those, I told myself. What if the air outside was bad? What if I was poisoned as soon as I stepped out into the open? Maybe my mother had been wrong, maybe she knew no better, bless her. Maybe my father knew the awful truth. But I couldn't go back.

No, Jai-Li, a second voice chimed. *You're leaving here. You're getting out of the tower. Don't lose your courage or your hatred now, Jai-Li; you'll need both for a while to come.*

I opened the cubicle door, quickly whipped the mask out, and gave it no more thought.

My eyes narrowed as I scanned the blue map. I proceeded to the hatch door at the far left corner of the room, grabbed the handle, lifted it and peeked through.

Beyond lay a short narrow tunnel, illuminated by a sequence of glowing glass floor tiles. I crawled through. My breathing began to quicken in that constricted space and my escalating heartbeat thudded in my ears. The hatch door closed behind me and after crawling a short distance I came to a large, dimly lit space.

Several bright white lights flared at once, and for a moment I thought I had been lured into some trap, but the lights revealed only a cube of a room without doors or windows. In the centre of the room something shone bright and new and astonishing. On the map it had been labelled "air-pod," but this was like nothing I had ever seen before.

It was bean-shaped, a vehicle of some kind—metallic, curved and immaculate—like a gigantic drop of mercury, with no windows or doors to break its smooth surface. The vehicle was inactive, but something was keeping it hovering off the grey tiled floor. Beneath, I could see no stand, no wheels, no platform. It was clearly sitting in a state of rest, as light as a cloud in the sky, as a bubble under water. This strange machine was, according to my mother's map, what I would be using to make my escape.

On the map, I had read *"air pod—speak your name."* So I did. I said my name out loud and the side of the pod opened along seams so fine I hadn't noticed them. The door rolled out and touched the ground, revealing the rungs of steel steps which led directly inside.

As I took my first step towards the pod, I was encouraged by the strong sense that my mother was still guiding me. The thought gave me strength, filled me with hope. I was charged up, ready to go up those rib-like steps. Ducking my head, I slid into the miniature cockpit. Four red chairs were positioned near a panel of instruments. I took the front seat. The outside of the vehicle was mirrored, but from my seat I could see the entire room.

The door rolled up and closed behind me. I surveyed the instrument panel. I had no idea what to push, what to pull, how to get the thing started and moving. I stopped my frantic thoughts, reassured myself. If it was that complicated, surely I'd have been given instructions? And sure enough, the door sealed of its own accord, securing me in the metallic bean. I heard the hum of a generator and steadily a vibration began to build in my seat . . .

The vehicle lifted—I could feel it in my gut before I could see it—and as the ceiling of the room slid apart I saw rays of light.

I tilted my head. I had never seen it or felt it before, but I knew what I was feeling and seeing.

The sun. Rays of natural light. The powerful, incomparable sun blessed my face and I ascended slowly into it. This was the real sun, the one that had lassoed the planets, wrenched trees from the dust, man from the oceans. It felt like the real sun. The tower engineers had designed and constructed the sun-orb to generate heat and light, but this sun did something more than all that. *It* had designed and constructed *us*, and inexplicably, I knew the difference.

Soon, the pod had emerged entirely from under the ground. I could see the boundless expanse of brown and orange desert sand. The sky was bluer than I had dreamed. The two peaks I had been able to see through my bedroom window were revealed as being two anonymous tips on a horizon of distant peaks . . . but the sand! The kilometres of flat sand! There was nothing out there. The desert stretched in every direction except one: directly behind me. There the glass and steel monolith that was Huang-345 sprang from the dirt, cementing itself just as firmly somewhere up in the clouds.

The pod stopped rising and was now only humming and hovering. I had risen like Lazarus but had not gone anywhere yet.

Yet.

Without warning, the pod accelerated from its spot, racing at full tilt across the sand. It blasted off horizontally, low to the ground, whipping the fine sands into clouds. Nonetheless, not a hair on my head moved; the internal atmosphere of the pod was perfect. Looking down, the world flashed by in a formless blur. Twisting back over my seat, I watched as the tower shrank in the rapidly increasing distance. In a mere minute that "glittering megalith of human ingenuity," that "city in the sky," had become a needle pulled back into the earth.

And I was alone.

I still had no clue where I was being taken, though. I had been so ready to leave that I'd given my destination almost no thought.

After a while I saw something else in that desert, far in the distance. At first I thought it was another mountain. It was an enormous machine of some kind. A machine or a ship, simply sitting in the desert as if it had crashed from the sky. I'd heard about such a thing. I'd overheard people in the tower talk about it. My father had mentioned it the moment I'd run from the office.

Only much later in my life, looking back and puzzling together small pieces of information, did I come to know what it was: Chang'e 11, a spaceship my father's company had once built.

The small screen on the panel in front of me lit up. I took my eyes off Chang'e 11 and sat back in my seat. The screen bleeped once and an image appeared. It was my mother, looking young and beautiful. No hanging skin. No untidy, entangled hair.

Hello Jai-Li, she said. For a moment I thought it was actually her, that she was alive and able to see me, but then she said, *I have made this recording for you. I hope, for the moment, that it will be enough. You may have some questions. I cannot guarantee I will be able to answer all of them, but perhaps you will find some of the answers to your questions in the same way as we all try to do: through experience, over time, and with unfailing hope.*

This pod was created for an emergency, a kind of life raft in the event that we ever had to make a quick escape from the tower. But by now I'm sure you know your father will never abandon his tower. Like the captain of a sinking ship, he will go down with it, if necessary.

And so, now, this vehicle is yours. Your life raft. Your quick escape. And if you are watching this, it is serving its precise purpose. This is the Silver Whisper, my dear. May it serve you well and take you far . . .

The voice continued as the vessel sped across the surface of the sand. The range of mountains rose high ahead of me. The sun beat down from a blue infinity. Time and space warped, boom by sonic boom.

Her words trickled out: *. . . you are probably wondering where this pod is taking you. Well, my child, there is a place, a very safe and special place, where you can stay as long as you need to. This destination has been programmed into the vessel. In this place, are people who can take care of you. It is a place I know well, and have known since I was a young child. It means a lot to me, has*

*changed me in ways I could not hope to expect. It has remained in
my dreams for as long as I can remember. Some may try to convince
you otherwise, say it is a mythical, imaginary place, but I can assure
you—it is real. It may even be the last real place on earth. It is a
place to which I have been indebted my entire life. You know this
place. I have told you about it. For certain reasons I feel I should not
record its exact location. That is a chance I cannot afford to take.
But I am sure, if you think hard enough, you will remember it.*

As soon as my mother said this, I was disappointed. I did not
remember it immediately. As the vessel raced across the land,
I trawled my memories for something my mother might once
have mentioned. I forced myself to relax, take a deep breath,
and all at once it came to me. A story. It was utterly obvious.
Not only a story, but the *one* story. The story she had told me
a few times, not onlybecause it was my favourite, but, as she
often reminded me, because it was true.

It was the story of something that had happened to my
mother when she was young. As I watched the world outside
roll itself out, the details of her story fell into place like a puzzle
I had done many times.

I remembered my mother sitting on the edge of my bed,
pulling my duvet up to my shoulders. I saw myself snuggling
into the warmth, listening . . .

It always began in the same way: with my mother reminding
me that, unlike my father, she had been born into a very poor
family, nothing like the tower in which I was born. Her concept
of luxury was having more than a single meal a day. Her concept
of power was watching her father—my grandfather—labour
continuously for the Chao-Bren Glass Factory. Sometimes he'd
get no more than three or four hours of sleep a night. Her family
lived in a shanty house in the village of Yihezhuang, deep in
the mountains between Hebei province and the city of Beijing.
She remembered the streets smelling like dust and burning
metal, how putrid the village was, drab and dilapidated, but
it was her home, and she knew no other. Her father worked
long and senseless hours for a meagre income. He would
often come home early in the morning, having walked a great

distance from the factory, and sometimes, she said, she'd lie awake listening to him as he sat in the dark room, dry-coughing and mending the soles of his shoes with wire thread. She never wanted to let him know she was awake, it would upset him, she thought. The time he worked—nineteen hours a day was his sacrifice to her and her mother. He wanted to know that they were well rested, strong, as healthy as he could never be.

It was around this time, she said, that people were becoming agitated about a particular problem. Old men talked about it in the streets, she read it on the communal news board. Later she learned that the problem was widespread, not restricted to their village alone. Scientists and doctors were noticing a sudden increase in cancers and nervous disorders. They all had different theories about the cause, but most surmised that the launch of a series of experimental military x-ray grid-satellites was generating dangerous levels of radiation. More than a thousand of these interlinked satellites were bombarding the earth with rays powerful enough to look through the rooftops of buildings and down into underground bunkers. This was all taking its toll on the earth's atmosphere. Babies were being born undeveloped or deformed. Tumours were sprouting in people's bodies like mushrooms on wet forest floors. The air was being poisoned, not only by chemical pollution, but electronic pollution too. Devastating physical effects were becoming more and more prevalent.

Around this time, my mother became sick. She wasn't sure whether it was connected to these rays, but her symptoms did present themselves as the stories began to go around. She awoke one morning with a headache, which became a migraine, which led to her having a violent seizure. Soon afterwards, she slipped into the first of a series of short comas. Her parents were, of course, devastated. It needn't be said that they could afford no treatment, no hospitalisation. Her father continued to work, her mother took care of her at home, but each day her condition worsened. She was young, she said, but not too young to understand that it would not be long before she died. It was something she now knew for certain.

The imminence of death is felt deep within one long before it occurs, just as someone who has been long at sea smells land before she sees it.

Then, one cold and rainy night, her father came home with a man she had never seen before. She was burning up, shivering in her bed, and the strange man standing over her in his sopping hooded raincoat seemed like a hallucination induced by her raging fever.

Her father stood behind him, holding his hat in his hands, twisting it round and round as if he was trying to open a tight jar. Her mother stepped aside and the man leaned over her. He put his hands under her thin body and lifted her into his arms easily.

It was a hazy memory—she said—being carried out of the house by that strange man. All she could recall was seeing her parents standing in the doorway, watching as she was taken away. She was placed gently on the back seat of a vehicle, a needle was plunged into her arm, the door was shut, and she passed out. She had terrible dreams that night, and she remembered waking intermittently only to realise she was still in the vehicle. Night turned to morning, and then to night, and then to morning again . . . and still she lay there in her sweat-drenched blanket.

On the third day, the vehicle stopped and the door opened. The large man leaned in and lifted her out. He carried her away from the vehicle, and though she could see little, she could smell the most incredible things. The air was clean, cold and fresh, teeming with the sweet fragrances of flowers, trees and soil. She heard water running over rocks and through crevices. She heard birds cheeping and insects twittering. The man carried her up a large number of steps. At last, he stopped and laid her down on a patch of the greenest and softest grass she had ever seen or felt. He stood, blocking the sun, and said, *You must be hungry.* That was all. Then he walked away.

She sat up and looked around—her curiosity superseded her physical pain and discomfort—and what she saw stunned her as she had never been stunned since.

A ragged sweep of enormous, snow-tipped mountains stretched below and ahead of her, like the resting place of old, forgotten gods. The green lawn was on the edge of a mountaintop of its own, the steep precipice rolling down to a deep, shadowy valley. On either side of her, trees lined the lawn, powdering the ground with light pink petals. Behind her, a grey temple sat firmly beneath the large rocks.

It was a paradise, she said. A beautiful shelter from the storm of clutter and chaos that had battered the rest of the world into diseased oblivion. And it was to be her new home for just under a year.

The stranger who had collected her from her parents' house was a man named Sun Zhang. He'd built the place himself and lived there with his three daughters, tall and slender women who welcomed her eagerly, gently stroking her soft hair, handling her as tenderly as a fragile doll that might shatter at any minute. When she had rested they took her on a tour of the temple. The inside of the temple was lit by a myriad of crooked candles. The halls were lined with stone pillars, and each of the few rooms contained nothing more than a mattress on the floor and a small table carrying several slim candles. She was given a room of her own, ate dinner with Sun Zhang and his bowed, respectful daughters each evening, and was encouraged to read various books during the day.

Mr. Zhang was a hard and unruffled man. In the evenings after dinner, he smoked a long wooden pipe by himself. During the day he did little but work in his garden and practice a form of t'ai chi ch'uan she did not recognise. At first she thought he was treating her with an almost resentful aloofness, but soon she realised that he treated her precisely as he did his own daughters, entertaining no idle conversation, with little humour, and demanding utter paternal respect.

He said nothing about her father and mother, or why he had come to collect her from her house inYihezhuang—and she didn't ask.

Most importantly, and strangely, every day that she stayed there, a bit of her strength returned, a morsel of her energy. She spent her mornings and evenings sitting on the lawn where he had first laid her down. She watched the clouds weave in and about the abundant peaks. She watched the sun move across the sky and thought about her parents, but never asked him to take her back. She couldn't say why, except that she knew the place was healing her and she trusted Mr. Zhang to return her if he thought it the right thing to do. But, she told me, this was no mere temple on the mountains. There was something else about the place that she only learned much later—something that transcended its beauty and purity.

She learned that Mr. Zhang had once been a very rich businessman. When his wife had died because of a brain tumour many years earlier, he'd left his business and had the temple built on top of the mountain using a special material that, ironically, had provided his wealth in the world of money and men. The temple and the foundation had been built out of a synthetic substance used to counter the negative effects of electromagnetic radiation near power plants, radio towers and pylons. It had once been bought and distributed around the world but funding was low, and most companies abandoned using it altogether, preferring to believe, or even disseminate data that said the harmful effects of electromagnetic frequency pollution had been proved to be negligible.

The result of this, Mr. Zhang explained to her, was that the true benefits of his material had been severely undermined and underutilised. He discovered that the material had other properties: it caused plants and vegetables to grow at alarming rates, to incredible sizes. His mountaintop garden bore the largest and most delicious plums, the reddest, juiciest tomatoes. His new substance could purify water, slow the ageing process, speed up self-healing. Increased altitude, where the air was pure and free, accentuated all of these properties.

This material, it just so happened, was the accidental harbinger of a new natural world, and his temple on the mountains a retreat like no other. A magic existed there. It was a place of life and energy. A true Shangri-La, and a carefully guarded secret. How Mr. Zhang had come to meet her father, and why she had been chosen to stay with him on the mountain with his three beautiful daughters, she never did find out.

One day, at the end of her year, once she had more than overcome her ailment and attained what can only be understood as a "resistance" to the fears and insecurities that had once beset her, he took her back to her parents. His final warning rang in her ears: *The world has not changed. While people can temporarily alleviate some of their problems, the real problem isn't in the air. It's in the mind. And the mind of Man is sick with rot. Though my home is a secret I urge you to keep, I will give you one final gift: you may, at any point in your life, send one person in need of healing to live with me at my home for a year. I promise you this now, as I once promised your father, and someone else before him. But only one person, and for one year only. I'll be waiting.*

He'd said it after my mother had climbed out of the vehicle and into the dusty streets of home. And then the door of the vehicle closed and he sped away, never to enter into her life again. She knocked on the door of her parents' shanty. They opened it and cried when they saw her. And her life, although forever changed in the deepest way, continued on as it once had—except that she was never sick. No colds, no flu, not even a migraine, she said. That year on the mountain had strengthened her body in some wonderfully strange and incomprehensible way . . .

And that's where the story she told me ended. And I'd go to bed and dream about that place, and wonder if I'd ever see it, if it truly was as real as I had hoped.

It was now obvious that the temple was the Silver Whisper's intended destination. Though I could only be there for a year, it had been her only option. Hopefully, when my year there was up there'd be somewhere for me to go. Perhaps, she said, Mr. Zhang would be willing to let me stay.

I stared back down at my mother's digital face. On top of everything, what really lingered now was the reminder that my mother had been sick as a child. She had come away believing she'd been cured for life. But even though cured, her life hadn't been a happy one. She worried about me, about my father, feared that something might happen and she would not be in a position to save me. Perhaps she saw that his dynasty was heading for some sort of cataclysmic collapse. And if that happened, would she be able to save me? She had to have a plan in place that would get me away, because my father would never put me before his precious dynasty. If anything, he'd keep me in captivity there, let me sink with him in the hopes that the heir I was programmed to deliver would provide some miraculous means of salvation.

Maybe my mother thought he would separate us, keep her from telling me what his plans for me were. Whatever the case, she had worked hard to have an escape plan in place, to save me, to make up for what she had allowed him to do to me. Of course, the one thing my mother *never* foresaw was the situation that had arisen, where the sickness came back to take her once more, like a devil who had returned to claim a soul bartered for a few untroubled years of good health.

I was filled with the deepest sympathy for her, reminded that she hadn't always been my mother. She'd once been a young girl. She had endured a childhood of poverty and sickness, an adulthood of loneliness and marital enslavement. She had done her best . . . until the day the world had become so unbearable she'd had no choice but to leave it . . .

Beauty. Grace. Wisdom. She'd had each, but life hadn't cared, hadn't shown her any favour. What were the rest of us supposed to live by, if anything at all? Tragedy, I learned that day, floats . . . And then it lands arbitrarily, like a feather from an indifferent bird high in the sky.

The pod left the flat plains of the desert, zigzagging between the gorges of the mountains, swinging around wide bends, gusting a rippling wake across the surface of a narrow lake, bending reeds and gliding slickly over stone slabs. I flattened my hands against the side and looked up to the tops of the rocky cliff-faces. The sun popped in and out of the cracks and gaps, my constant, protective companion.

It was then that an unexpected heaviness filled my head, the weight of a blanket soaked in water. I collapsed back into my seat. I felt nauseous. Outside, the walls of the valleys still raced rearward. The sun struck out, but now the rays were an expanding, blinding sheet that grew whiter and brighter. The heaviness intensified and became a sharp, piercing pain, followed by a penetrating noise.

My mother's face began to warp and distort. The pod that had whipped over the land so smoothly was now shuddering and shaking . . .

I'm sure you've already guessed. The growing pain, the shrill sound . . . all happened the moment our memories were wiped clean and humankind lost a link in the unending chain of advancement and accumulated knowledge.

Day Zero, we now call it.

Of course, I had no idea that at that very moment everyone else in the world was suffering in the same way. As that malfunctioning glass bubble spluttered through the rocky vales, I thought it was an environmental factor, some sort of karmic penance even, for daring to leave the tower. These thoughts lingered for a short, bewildered while and then everything ended in sudden, mind-blotting blackness.

Who knew how long I had been out?

It could have been hours, weeks, or months—there was no way to tell. When I came around, my memory was gone, drained like old water from a tub. Everything I've just told you has been dug up and pieced together over many years—detail by detail, word by word. I'm like an archaeologist, delicately picking rock from fossil. At that moment, though, when my eyes opened, there was nothing.

I was lying on a bed in a room. I had no memories of the tower, or the pod, or Sun Zhang's temple on the mountain. For all I knew, my life had begun right there, sprawled on those brown blankets.

The first thing I noticed was a damp patch on the ceiling. The centre of it was dark, bulging—water waiting for the opportunity to burst through. The air was warm and musty, the room small and unfamiliar. I climbed out of bed and walked unsteadily to the door. I turned down a dark corridor, and found myself in a quaint kitchen with sunflower-patterned curtains on the windows and an old refrigerator droning like a disgruntled house spirit. A man and a woman stood near the sink and gawked morosely back at me. They said nothing as I entered. The elderly man was thin and weathered with a balding crown, and he wore faded overalls and mud-caked blue worker boots. The woman was about the same age, her face hidden in a scrub of thick black hair. Rolls of fat swelled from the shoulder straps of her purple dress like baked bread. They didn't recognise me . . . no reaction, no change in expression. Then the man turned and left the kitchen as if he'd forgotten to do something out there. The woman sat down on a chair at a round table, fingering the petals of plastic pink flowers in a jar. She ignored me as I stepped to the door that led outside and swung it open.

I was on a farm. Fat, blotchy pigs snarled and fought to secure their places at a mucky food trough. A boy was leaning over the crude, wooden fence, watching them. As I descended the steps of the porch and planted my feet on the muddy earth, he looked at me over his shoulder. He pushed himself off the fence and approached me, took my hand, and led me back to the fence. I leaned against the post alongside him. The sty smelled like rotten vegetables and excrement. Beyond the sty, the few acres of farm were grey and neglected. Clouds tumbled in high winds, sliding patches of shadow across the land like a desperate, migrating herd.

I never did fully remember the three people I saw in the house that weird day, but as the weeks continued, there were more and more clues. I saw myself in photographs on the walls. If the pictures were to be trusted, I had spent my entire life with those strangers. I saw myself as a young child in the woman's arms. There was a picture of the boy and me bathing together in a steel tub. I saw each of these pictures, yet recalled nothing of the moments.

Over time, *their* memories slowly came back, but mine didn't. On several occasions, the man sat me down and tried to convince me that he was my father, the woman was my mother, and the boy, my brother, but I struggled to accept it. Not only did I experience an absence of connection between us, I had also begun to dream of other places and other people.

In my earliest dreams, I saw nothing but a long white elevator. I had flashes of a beautiful woman applying her make-up before the mirror of a large, elaborate dresser. I saw a gigantic room containing nothing but a window that spanned the length of a massive wall, and a small desk. I saw one room drenched in blue light, another containing a floating metallic vehicle.

Night by night, the dreams became clearer and more consuming. By day, I helped my alleged brother on the farm (a boy whose company I had grown to appreciate, although I could never see him as my brother), cooked with my "mother" in the kitchen, and sat at my "father's" side in the evenings while he watched a fire burn beneath the mantelpiece and drowsed on tumblers of whiskey. But all the while I felt that I was merely pretending to be a part of that rural family.

Sometimes, when everyone was sleeping, I would wake, climb out of my bed, sit by my window and stare off into the outlying mountains. My eyes were always drawn to the same spot—a valley I could just about make out in the obstinate mist that shrouded the land. It was not long before I decided I couldn't continue in such a way.

One crisp morning, a few months later, I met the boy in the barn beside the house and told him I needed to go. I was carrying nothing but a small bag filled with food, water and a sweater. He asked where I needed to go, and I said I didn't know. I was being drawn to some place in the mountains; some mysterious location was pulling on me like a magnet, and I knew I could no longer ignore it. He tried to convince me to stay, but when I told him I could not, he decided he'd come with me. He said he would return to the farm, to his mother and father, but he'd go with me as far as he could. I was relieved. I was terrified of what lay ahead and welcomed the thought of his company. I thanked him and we agreed to leave the following day.

We set off in the morning and walked for almost three days. The boy had brought a tent and essential supplies and we camped in bushes when we needed to rest. He tracked and killed small game and we cooked rabbits and pigeons over a fire. The boy said little to me; I knew he was worrying about his parents alone on the farm, but he did not complain, did not once suggest going back. He could see I needed to go on, to reach the place I sensed I needed to find, and he stayed to protect me. Perhaps he too was curious.

On the third day, filthy and exhausted, we saw something in the valley of the mountains—light, reflecting off the surface of an object partially hidden between the rocks. We hurried ahead to examine it further.

It was the pod, half-buried in the dirt, its mirrored exterior layered in rain-streaked dust. Behind it, trees and bushes had been ripped from the damaged soil. It had clearly come crashing down at a great speed . . .

I must have blacked out when it hit the ground, I said. *It's a good thing your parents found me when they did; I'm not sure I would have survived.*

We circled the object for a few minutes, and I could see him trying to make sense of its strange shape.

This is mine, I said. *The Silver Whisper. I was escaping the tower and on my way to the temple . . .* From the look on his face I could tell he did not understand a word.

As before, I spoke the word *Jai-Li* and, with a hiss, a door rolled out. I held my breath, gave the boy a last blank look, and climbed inside.

In the cockpit, the air was foul. I saw four red chairs, a bag and a gas mask, lying on the floor. Those few items didn't surprise me; I remembered them all.

No, what surprised me was the figure of a small person slumped over in the front seat, head against a shattered panel of instruments. At first I thought it was a loiterer, a sleeping wanderer who'd taken shelter in the wreck. But how could anyone get in? And what was that awful smell? I struggled to catch my breath. I leaned over and touched the stranger's shoulder. The body lolled back, exposing her face, and I drew back in horror.

It was a girl. A dead girl. Her face was cut and scratched and the blood had clotted and crusted. Her yellow dress was splattered in dark brown smears. Her arm had been broken and twisted in an unnatural position. It was her, Kayle. Her, and somehow, me.

I recalled that a letter had been written, and carefully reached into her dress pocket and pulled it out. I unfolded it, recognised the handwriting, the roughly drawn map . . .

I stumbled out of the pod and threw up on the ground outside. Tears ran down my face. *Wait. Wait a minute,* I muttered *No, no, no . . . it's not right. It doesn't make sense. It doesn't!*

The boy crouched down. What wasn't right, he wanted to know, what didn't make sense?

I answered: *It was me. It was supposed to be me.*

I couldn't speak for a few hours. I huddled in a corner reading and re-reading the shabby letter. The words were precisely as I had remembered them: the story of a young couple who had failed to resist a family empire, the programmed pregnancy, the need to escape . . .

But the girl.

She looked nothing like me, but I knew her face. I knew her face as well as I knew my own. It was one I'd somehow once *had*, but what did that mean? If I wasn't her, who was I? Who was she?

The boy camouflaged the pod with dirt and bushes. We set up camp, made a fire and ate another small animal, then went to sleep. At first light, I helped him pack up and he laid his hand on my shoulder, *Come on, Jun; let's go back. Let's go home.*

And so we did. We travelled back to the wooden house on the farm—to our parents, our pigs, our grey and neglected acres.

When I entered the house, the man and woman threw their arms around me and hugged my limp, exhausted body, but I felt nothing. No love. No connection. They were my real parents—I knew that now—but it didn't matter. Not at that point, anyway.

I lived out the rest of my childhood with a family I never entirely accepted as my own, even though they continued to love me. I never shook the feeling that I was supposed to be the girl in the pod, that my true mother had been the one who'd strangled herself with her own robot avatar, and that my father had been the man on the throne of a monstrous city-scraper. I remembered, too, that I despised it, but that didn't stop me from feeling as if some furtive injustice had been done to me— against my identity and my history. My mother hadn't loved me; she'd loved the girl in the pod. And that girl's escape had never been my own, the plan to live in the temple with Sun Zhang and his three daughters, never promised to me. I had lived her life—but only through the memories that had jumped from her to me at the point of her death. And while I did *try* to make a new life for myself in the years that followed—growing to genuinely love my brother, Huojin, meeting my one true love and husband—I have never been able to let go of what I remember of "my" childhood, of a young, hopeful girl named Jai-Li, and of her curious life in the sky.

Ice-cold water

Her story had stunned you. You could not entirely comprehend what she had confessed; it was a tale both spookily familiar and logically stupefying. There was no reason for her to have invented such a story, but how was it possible she'd adopted someone else's entire life?

So if you are not Jai-Li, why are you using her name?

You asked this as you walked down the mountain alongside the mother with her son. You could have asked a dozen other questions but that was the only one that came to mind.

She replied, *Because of where I'm going and who I'll have to be to get there. Jun may have been the name given at the point of my physical birth, but Jun is a stranger. I may have been her, but I know nothing about her. Nothing about what she wanted in this life. I am Jai-Li, or I'm nobody at all.*

The mist had withdrawn and the thick forest had thinned and at last the beach of the semi-circular cove came into view. The water was silvery grey, calm but chopping gently in a light breeze. The fronds of palm trees hung lifelessly over the dunes. The jagged faces of the cliff enclosed the beach, a pair of cupped hands around a butterfly whose wings could not be touched for fear it would never again be able to fly.

Angerona was the first to step onto the beach; Theunis and Gideon carefully manoeuvred the boat off the miry slope and onto the slanting belt of sand. You laid the oars down beside the boat and arched your back, rolling your shoulders to ease the burn in your muscles. There was no sun in the sky. The mist that had covered you on the mountain shifted low and thick above the water like a fleet of ghost ships hiding the horizon.

You're going to the temple, aren't you? you asked. *That's what this is all about.*

She lowered her head, tightening the blanket around her sleeping baby, and then said, *A promise was made to a little girl in need of help. It was a promise of sanctuary. That little girl is dead, but I am still here. Fulfilling that promise is now my duty. I've carried the burden of Jai-Li's past for long enough; it's only fair my own son be allowed to carry her hope.*

Gideon clenched his hands over the rough edge of the boat. Neither he nor Theunis had said anything at all. Had they heard what she had said? Perhaps her voice hadn't carried across the still air. Perhaps it hadn't made much sense without the first part of the story. Then again, they may have been smart and ignored it all. You shouldn't have been so willing to accept the information, Kayle. Would her story be used against you? Surely Gideon wouldn't have concerned himself with such a possibility. No, you were overthinking it. They had been ahead of you the entire way and probably heard nothing at all.

We shuffled the boat to the edge of the water, ripping a deep gash through the wet sand.

This is it, you said as Jai-Li clambered into the damp boat. *Are you sure you want to do this? You could wait.*

Angerona had begun packing extra blankets and bags of food into the boat. Jai-Li wrapped one of the thick blankets around herself, tying it around the front of her chest so that the baby was securely attached to her torso.

No, she said. *No more waiting. We'll be fine. We'll leave the water when we can, but we can do this. We must. Will you pass me that oar?*

You reached down, grabbed it, and gave it to her. She took it from you, smiling as she lifted it up and into the boat. *That's heavy,* she said, unable to disguise her obvious nervousness. You couldn't even try to hide your concern. You were worried about her and felt you had every right to be: the place she was talking about was thousands of kilometres away. She'd have to retrace her tracks, all the way back to the pod in the mountains, which, she was only *guessing,* would take her to the temple. But what if she was caught, or hurt along the way? What if the Silver Whisper was gone, or damaged beyond repair? Where would she go? If something happened to her, who would look after her child?

Gideon hauled on the front of her boat with both his hands, Theunis and you pushed from the back, and the boat finally splashed into the water, free from the support of the earth. It swayed gently as you moved away from it and Jai-Li adjusted the mismatched oars to suit her position. She thanked each of you individually, offering prayers of good fortune, and each of you offered the same in return.

Jai-Li, you added, as she dipped her oars into the water, *in the beginning you said you felt your story would guide me in some way. I'm sorry, but I still don't see how. What did you mean?*

Jai-Li tucked away a strand of hair. She turned to look into the thick mist—the mist into which she would soon make her way—and said, turning back: *You know, it's a funny thing. That young girl was once told she would fall pregnant on the day she turned twenty. It had been programmed into her blood. Although it was unplanned, my own child was conceived on the day I turned twenty.* She took a moment to consider her own words, concluding, *That would seem to some like quite the coincidence.*

And then she set off. She pushed away from the shore and rowed out into the ocean. The three of you stood and watched her disappear into the whiteness. The only sounds were water dribbling and oars creaking as she pulled them up and slid them back in. Her spectral figure lightened until there was merely the faintest shade of her, an almost imagined ashen hue, and then she and her child were gone—off the beach, away from the commune. Free.

When you got back to the commune they were waiting for you. Everybody knew what had happened. How they knew, none of you could say, but it didn't matter. They had left that blank white room in that white house at the top of the hill. They were standing on the beach and their many faces watched as you came down from the mountain. It was the most you had ever seen of them. Their faces were older than you had imagined, pale, rubbery, almost corpse-like, their lips thin and white.

As the four of you entered the commune, the communers stopped doing whatever they were doing and turned their faces in your direction. They said nothing. They simply stared and edged away from you, surprise and fear in their wide eyes. It was as if the four of you were now lepers. You could only guess that a whisper had spread among them. A whisper of your rebellion. You wondered who had told them. Had someone seen you? Had the body interrogated them all in an attempt to find you? Regardless, it was the first time you'd seen the communers act in any form of unison. In spite of their coldness, they were behaving as if your return was the moment they had been waiting for all along, the point of The Renascence, the moment of communalism that had been promised to them.

The Body watched it all with small beady eyes, set deep within dark sockets. They wasted no time, of course. Without a word, several communers surrounded you and took you up to the house on the hill. The Body separated your small group and brought you into the room one by one.

When it was your turn, two communers sat you in the large, padded seat and strapped you down. They had never used straps before. The bright light beamed over you brighter and stronger than ever, and sweat ran into your eyes, burning them. They attached their sensors to the sides of your head and your chest, and the wires ran out in all directions. The grey machine was fired up like an ancient boiler.

The silhouettes of their heads floated behind their long table at the end of the room and you did not know which was worse, knowing what they looked like or imagining it. The heads said nothing. They watched silently as you perspired and shifted, trying to get comfortable, though there was no real comfort to be had.

You knew you were in for a long and exhausting interrogation because they weren't going to get what they wanted. They couldn't get her back and they wouldn't be able to ferret any information out of you. All they would get, possibly, was why you had helped her, and how. And then, inevitably, you'd be given your sentence.

They bombarded you with questions. They used every psychological tactic in their arsenal. They told you Gideon and Theunis had already confessed, but that was blatantly untrue. They might have mentioned something about the second half of her story, if they'd even heard it, but not even you could wrap your head around the full version. So what else? That she'd rowed away in a boat? Of course she had. It was the only way off the beach.

When the questions did not work, they made you sit for an hour in silence and all the while the grey machine rumbled and leeched what it could from your mind. You asked for water but they wouldn't give you any. They said you'd get what you wanted when they got what they wanted. They expressed their disappointment in you. You had been so promising, they added, a member of the commune they'd once considered a role model for the newer members. You were tempted to smile at their efforts, exploiting the gap of meaninglessness they had created in the first place, telling you they saw you as a leader in a place that allowed no leaders. A role model in a place that actively eschewed the concepts of both roles and models.

At last, you were given your sentence: an *as yet undetermined* length of time on the raft. They said you wouldn't be allowed back into the commune until they were satisfied with the information you gave them and when there was a significant change in your attitude. You had to admit your insolence, realign yourself with The Renascence, and prove you'd be no threat to the commune.

You kept your mouth shut. You nodded.

And then the interrogation was over.

You slept in your tent under constant watch. In the morning, two communers entered your tent and gave you breakfast—a bowl of fruit and sourdough bread. You finished it all, knowing the next meal could be a while away. After you had eaten, they tied your wrists. The one communer was a man you hadn't seen before; the other was Daniel. He wouldn't look you in the eyes while he tied you up, but you understood.

Once they had tightened the ropes around your wrists, they led you down to the beach. A crowd had formed, just like the one that had encircled the whale before it had been burned. There was the same look on their faces, too. Curiosity. Fascination. Fear. Always fear on top of everything else. They muttered under their breath, but you couldn't make out what they were saying. You saw Gideon to your far left, also being led down from his tent, while on your right, Theunis and Angerona were already at the water. As far as you could recall, Angerona was the youngest ever to be put on the raft. No mercy. No exceptions. As communers, you were no longer individualised even by age.

Directly ahead of you, a wooden raft bobbed at the water's edge, waiting for you like a hungry living thing—a large, flat crocodile. Rough leather straps hung from the corners, lapping at the water like four grey tongues.

This was your raft. Your exile.

There were another two communers on either side of the raft, up to their knees in the cold morning sea, fixing four orange buoys to the corners so that the raft would be both anchored and prevented from capsising. The one communer was a muscular man with a hard, stubbly face, the other a teenage boy with long, matted hair and pale, thin arms. They turned to look at you as you approached, and then stepped away as your feet touched the water.

The iciness struck you to the bone. The ocean would not, it seemed, forgive you either. Daniel undid your bounds and you rubbed your freed wrists. Another tall communer approached you with a compact tablet of various herbs. You were made to swallow it. Then they brought a pouch of crushed leaves and a glass of water. They added the leaves to the water, stirred them in, and made you drink it. You gulped it down in one go, doing what you could to spare yourself the bitterness. This was the hallucinogen—you knew that—the catalyst for the alignment.

On the beach, your mind was all you had. Your composure and control. What would you see and hear out there on the sea? Who would come crashing into your thoughts? What would leak out? And once it was all done, once the hallucinogen wore off and your raft was pulled back in, what would be left of you?

You stepped up to the raft and climbed on. The wood was damp, cold and slimy. You stretched out on your back and the water swelled through the slats and licked your spine. You looked up at the sky. *Get used to it,* you told yourself; the sky would be all that you saw for the next few hours, or days, or however long it took for you to be brought back in for your second interrogation.

The communers leaned over. Their faces hung in the sky as they looked back down at you. They pulled your arms and legs outwards and strapped you down. Someone fastened another strap across your neck to prevent you from lifting your head. The strap was soft and clammy, like the fingers of a dead man, throttling you. All you could move were your fingers and toes. All you could control were the blinks of your eyes and movements of your mouth. You were utterly immobilised, as if your spine had been broken and you'd fallen into paralysis.

The sun shone warm and bright over your body, a gentle introduction that would prove to be a long and cruel relationship. The wind also said hello, rolling over your face and chest. The water lapped and nipped with sharp cold teeth.

Two communers fastened a long rope to the front of the raft; the other end had been connected to the pier a short distance away from you.

And then they pushed you out.

The raft drifted further and further from the shore, burst through the first few waves, and jerked to a stop as the length of rope tightened. Your breathing was loud and ragged, misfiring in your lungs. Your heart pummelled the wall of your chest.

All you could think about at that moment was Jai-Li and her child, out on the sea in a flimsy vessel of their own. You felt you had done the right thing by helping her, but had she even left the misty cove? Perhaps she'd toppled over and drowned, crashed into the rocks. Anything could have happened. How far had she made it? Had she made it anywhere at all?

After all, convictions and good intentions mean nothing. The ocean makes no promises. The sun makes no deals. The wind never listens to your pleas, your screams, or your prayers. And the world does not care if you belong in it. There is no forgiveness in nature. Only a gauntlet. A hurricane. An explosion of particles and a fluke of order. Right and wrong will never be as hard as stone or as wet as water.

Not for Jai-Li, and not for you, Kayle. Not here. Forget it all. Forget your sense of *belonging*. Life has given you nothing but one, unpractised shot at it—nothing more and nothing less. So do what you must. Hold on to your mind and your body for as long as you can, let go of your silly hopes, your futile fears, and your inapt questions.

You have nothing.

Now you have nothing but your raft.

The burned man

I am walking alongside my mother in the street in Tulbagh. I'm nine years old. We've just come back from the supermarket and she's carrying a small bag of groceries. I'm hauling a larger bag with two hands and trying my best to keep up. It's just a normal Saturday. The sun is bright and the sky is a pure and cloudless blue. Cars pass by, pedestrians go about their Saturday morning business—getting their hair cut in barbershops, window-shopping for clothing they can't afford, compulsively checking the time as they stand in their queues at the bank.

I'm walking on the steaming pavement and I see an old man walking towards me. He's wearing a large green trench coat with the collars thrown up. His thin strands of hair are combed to the side, drooping like dead tentacles, revealing pink scalp. He passes me, and the unpleasant secret that lies behind his upturned collar is exposed: his face is a mess of burned skin, a large patch of knots and cracks and swirls stretching from the neck to the forehead, a sludge of skin stirred with a spoon and allowed to set. He shifts his eyes down and looks at me as he goes by, dragging the long, mephitic tail feathers of a strong aftershave behind him—but he doesn't move his head.

His eyes seem to say, *You see me, but I see you too.*

The man's face repulses me, but for some reason I also want to touch it—that canyon of scarred tissue—maybe even poke it to see if my finger will push through.

My mother says, "Don't stare. It's rude to stare," and I snap out of my trance. I look back over my shoulder and see only the normal back of his coat, hunched over as he makes his way to wherever it is that burned people make their way. A cave, I think, or a lair. Some dank and lightless hole, no doubt. Not a regular house like ours, certainly.

Don't stare. It's rude to stare.

Stare at the stars. Stare at a sunset. Stare into the eyes of someone you love. Stare at your teacher droning on about the fall of apartheid. Stare at your grandfather's pale face in his open casket.

But do not stare at the burned man.

I study my mother's wide and ordinary face. She's scanning the lot, looking for her car, one of the many ovular autovehicles glistening beside each other, but this time she looks different. I've seen her every day of my life and now she seems a stranger, her car-searching routine a mere impersonation of the woman who did the same thing last Saturday, and the Saturday before that.

I glimpse behind me. The burned man is gone, and all I can think is that I want to meet him. I want to stare at his face for as long as it takes to satisfy me. Maybe even ask him how it happened. Instead, I climb into the back of my mother's car as she locks the doors and starts the engine.

I'm going home but I don't want to; I don't want to go home with my mother. I want to see the other side of this pure and cloudless world. I want to see the dark places, hang in the shadows, mingle with the grotesque.

I gaze through the window as the car pulls out—at ordinary people, walking, talking, laughing—and suddenly feel that everything is *wrong*. I can't help sensing, for the first time in my life, that something is being hidden from me. Some difficult, scarred truth. I can't help feeling I've been told not to stare at the burned man all my life.

Jack Turning can't get enough of it. He's finding my thoughts hilarious; he's laughing maniacally. Strapped to my raft, I feel like a patient in a hospital for the criminally insane. Jack's some twisted orderly who revels in mocking me, knowing there's nobody who'll believe a word of my implausible rants. A part of me knows it's not possible he's actually there—out on the ocean at night—but the manipulated part of me wins out and accepts that he is. He's been there a while now, but I can't see him. My head's facing upwards and all my eyes can see is the night sky, peppered in bright white stars. I've been here almost a full day, bobbing and rolling in a drugged daze. The water beneath is completely still, as if the novelty of my arrival has worn thin. Directly above, a big white ball hangs in the sky. On any other day I might mistake it for the common moon, this beating planetary *thing*—but tonight I know better; this is not the moon. It's a masquerader. A fake moon, the throbbing, sickly orb that's been hanging in our dreams. It knows our secrets and has promised a few more of its own.

"The burned man's a good one," Jack says. "You've held on to that little bauble of a memory for a while now, haven't you? Kept it all bundled up in the back of your head somewhere. Ja. I like it. Really. I do."

I hear him kicking his feet in the water like a bored child. He's there, my mind tells me, sitting on the end of my raft, but I feel no extra weight there. I wonder what it must be like to exist in a state lighter than air. Surely it's easier than carrying the extra luggage of heavy bones, organs and flesh? Maybe that's life's big problem—its obsession with matter, weighing everything down, making everything just a little harder for us all.

Jack says, "You, Mr. Kayle, *if you please*. Tell me something about yourself I don't know."

"You don't know anything about me."

"Don't I?"

My raft rolls over the water. I turn my wrists in their straps, trying to relieve my irritated skin. Overhead, the moon-like orb is a fat yellow blister against the black rind of the night, waiting to burst and spill its pus. When it does I'll be here under it. I'll be drenched in its infected discharge. Drenched and helpless. And Jack Turning will probably laugh his non-existent head off.

"I know that you think you've done some good thing, helping that woman," Jack says. "And that's why you've accepted this whole raft business. Like some kind of martyr. Ha! I'd go so far as to say you're even proud of yourself. But here's the kicker." He pauses and cackles. "The kicker is you're *not* a good man. And you know it. All the helping everyone, listening to everyone's stories . . . you're not doing it because you give a shit at all. You're doing it because you know what *I* know."

"And what's that?" I say. My voice is hoarse, my throat dry with thirst.

"That you're trying to make up for something. You're trying so hard to be this shoulder to lean on, this sympathetic ear, but the truth is, good men never worry about doing good things. They just do them. You're doing it because you *know* you're not a good man. Not a good man at all. Only bad men have to work hard at being good. No. You did something terrible, didn't you? You don't remember what it is, I'll give you that, but you know it deep inside of you. You know there is something dark and horrific lurking in the basement of your past, and all this being-a-good-listener, protecting these people's silly little secrets, is not driven by love, or sympathy, or all that other nonsense, is it? You, Mr. Kayle, are driven by guilt. And the reality is, you've accepted your fate on the raft, not because you're willing to nobly pay the price for helping that woman and her child, but because you know, you know, oh *you* know that *you deserve it.*"

"What do you know?" I blurt, defensively. "You're not even real."

"Not even real?" he roars out hysterically. "Not. Even. Real. That's great. Just great. Not even *real.*" The water babbles and slaps against the sides of the raft. "Let me tell you what else I know, Mr. Kayle. After helping Jai-Li, you've already decided the beach just isn't good enough anymore, is it? All this waiting, dreaming, moping. You won't let yourself waste away on the sand with the rest of them. Nope. So what are you to do? You're going to get out of here. You're going to look for your son. Your love will guide you, won't it?" He chortles again. "A father's love will guide like the stars in the sky. But here's where you're wrong, Mr. Kayle. You will find Andy. I can feel it. I have a kind of sixth sense about these things. But you will not be guided by love. It'll be by guilt."

"Guilt?"

"Guilt is strong, Mr. Kayle. Powerful stuff. Love nests. It's an undisturbed ecosystem, like all the little bugs and slugs that live happily together in an everglade. You can sit in one place and wallow with all the love in your heart, but it won't get you anywhere. You'll never evolve. You'll never crash through walls. Love doesn't change the world. The real driving forces in this world are guilt and fear. Guilt and fear. And you, my friend, have oodles of both. So you'll find him. Oh, trust me, you'll find him. Eventually."

I scrutinise the surface of the moon orb and it's moving, swirling like sour custard, bubbling, beginning to ferment. The warm wind rushes across my body and there's a terrible smell in the air. It's the smell of cooked meat. It doesn't belong out here on the ocean. I know this even as the drugs do their work and as Jack Turning rattles on.

Suddenly, Jack Turning is right there, leaning over me, but I do not recognise him. His face is burned. He has no hair. His lips are taut and shiny, his teeth bared in a wide and unnatural grin. His left eyelid is folded over crookedly. His ears are tucked into his head like folded pairs of socks, and he smells like seared meat.

"But," he says, "but, but, but . . . will Andy want to see you? That's the real question. Will Andy really want to reunite with a *murderer* like you?"

Murderer.

The word swipes at me like the swift talons of a dangerous animal. I don't know what he means. No, he's lying this time.

He *must* be, I tell myself. I have never murdered anyone. I don't know everything but I know what I'm capable of doing and not doing. Some things we don't have to remember because once they've happened they form a part of our constitution forever, like a deep scar that will never fade completely. If anything, I need to believe that, at *least*. I would know if I'd done such a thing, *surely*.

Jack says: "Oh yes, Mr. Kayle. You *murderer*."

My head is strapped down and I can do nothing but look directly back into his face. He squats, perched above me. He will not go away. I want the drug to wear off, to turn to my side, to run and hide, but I can't, and the saccharine smell of his cooked face sickens me. I cannot turn in the other direction. Because of the raft, I have no choice but to keep staring at the burned man.

Extracts

(Excerpt from the *The Age of Self Primary*)

There were attempts to restore society, of course. Humankind had lost its memories but little of its instincts. Over time, individuals stepped forward proclaiming they recalled how various systems had once worked—currencies, industries, hierarchies—but their recollections were limited. It was as if each of them recalled the purpose of an arm, or a foot, or an ear, but had no concept of the body as a whole. More importantly, a greater number of people were less than convinced by these declared systems, or interested. Most could barely remember who they were, let alone comprehend the part they were expected to play in the dead trends that had governed modern industries. The factory conveyor belts that had once produced thousands of identical must-have curios produced nothing but dust and webs. The latest fashion trends hung on mannequins in shop windows, enticing nobody. Who could tell the difference between the older model electronic palm-plates and the newer ones? Who had once had authority and who had followed? Who could be trusted to perform a surgery or educate a child? Who were the rightful heirs and what good were class structures without an understanding of status?

It was soon evident that trying to put together the complex labyrinth of civilisation would be impossible. Nobody knew where to start. The class structure collapsed at the same time as the economy. There were a few sporadic acts of violence and destructive behaviour from a small group of frustrated individuals, but on the whole, the amnesiac populace knew too little of their predicament to build up sufficient rage, let alone sustain it for long enough to act. In the months succeeding Day Zero, most people behaved like harmless, curious babies enamoured by the simple forms of the world.

It was not long after that a structured group did arise within the broken collective. Established by a man named Diet Coke, this group quickly became known as the New Past. It was the philosophy of Diet Coke and the New Past that the re-establishing of a society was no longer an option. According to the New Past, the extent to which they had found themselves disabled post-Zero had been precisely because of their reliance on external attachments. It had been their superficial regard for the material things that had inhibited them, many centuries before Day Zero had even occurred.

This pre-Zero period came to be known as the Age of Self, and was denounced as a time of conceit and hollow consumerism. It was "attachment" itself that had crippled the people of the world. It was suggested that the only way to advance was to embrace their disconnection. Materialism was an archaic construct, and only with "detachment" could they hope to prosper.

Word of the new model spread. Most adopted the model with the sense of hope that had once evaded them. They were given meaning like manna from the sky. Within months, several factions of the New Past sprang up around the world. Electronic technology was rebuked, and forbidden. Land ownership was abandoned. Money was forsaken. It was not long before the New Past proposed its most ambitious policy: the separation of the members of biological families. The family nucleus was the seed of tribal culture, and tribal culture had accounted for most of pre-Zero's afflictions.

It was suggested that in order to attain absolute "detachment," these self-absorbed, outdated nucleuses would need to give way to Diet Coke's "One Family" proposal, and the timing couldn't be better. Most members of families did not remember each other well enough to fully resist, and the factions responded with gusto. Protocols were put in place. Locations were selected. Children were removed from their parents, husbands from their wives, and brothers from their sisters. Like the brave passengers of a boat that floats upon an ocean without the labours of unsynchronised oars, they cast out to the remotest corners of the earth with fellow exiles in the belief that their absolute detachment would propel Humankind into its new evolutionary era, the Age of The Renascence.

III

Gideon

K Jenner sat on the porch of his house and drank the last of his beer while he watched the rain. The grey clouds were thickly woven together without a single thinning patch of hope. It had been raining for hours now. K took another sip of his beer and stared out across the dull, mushy land. To the side of the house the two horses stood drenched and motionless in their paddock, blinking their eyes.

Thunder grumbled in the distance.

Behind K the front door of the house hung open. Somewhere inside, his son was keeping himself occupied. Andy was good in that way. He didn't need much to keep himself busy, and K was grateful for that, if nothing else. He no longer knew what to do for the boy. It was hard enough for K to get himself out of bed in the morning without having to worry about how he'd entertain his only child. Recently, the days had been long, silent and uneventful for them both.

And still, the rain. The hard rain kept coming.

Months had passed since he had stumbled from his AV on that bright morning without a memory in his head. Months since he had begun to rediscover his wife, and his house, and his life. But now his wife was gone and it was just the two of them. K and Andy. The memories that came back to each of them day by weird day did not arrive in any hurry, or any particular order. The day he and his wife had walked back into the house to find Andy curled up on his bed had been a day of hope. Hope that soon everything would make sense and a semblance of the lives they'd once lived could go on. But it hadn't happened that way. K had remembered Andy as soon as he'd seen him in the photograph, but his wife had not. To her, the boy on the bed, the boy that she had carried in her body for nine months and had taken care of for twelve years, was a stranger, and seemed likely to remain so.

K had tried to convince her that Andy was her son, but in the end it had become clear to the woman she'd never remember. Nor would she remember the young girl who'd been her daughter. After some time, perhaps because of frustration or shame, it had become too much for her to handle; one morning K had awoken to discover the woman he'd vaguely recalled as his wife had left. No note. No goodbye. One unremarkable day she had simply vanished, and K and the boy were left to themselves in that big wooden house on the hill.

K's own memories were far from complete. In fact, among all the small unrelated fragments that came floating in, it was really only the recollection of having loved his son and dead daughter that returned to him somewhat intact. He did not remember his children as the complex individuals they had undoubtedly once been to him. He knew his son and daughter's names, that they were indeed his own children, but recalled nothing of the precious stories of their lives that must have once been stitched into his love for them like the patterns that adorn a handmade quilt. The boy was still a stranger. A stranger whom he should continue to love. That's what something in him said he should do. That was all.

Besides the boy, K couldn't remember much of own life. In the days that followed the resetting, he scrambled to piece together the puzzle of himself. He studied the objects and artifacts in his home as if they were pieces of evidence left by trickster elves—house spirits that sat in the cracks of the walls and enjoyed the ensuing mayhem and confusion from afar. A picture on the wall. The smell of a cologne. The feel of a soft sweater. But even though these trivial memories came back to him like a few loose coins between the cushions of a couch— worth little but heartening nonetheless—he was not able to put any of it together. His ability to read returned but he struggled to use appliances and technologies in the house. Digital screens hung dead on the walls. Whatever information those machines held within their chips and wires, he hadn't a clue about how to retrieve it. And even if he knew how to operate them, the passwords and numbered codes that would grant access were gone forever.

The only reason he knew his surname and his initial was because of a plastic card he'd found with his face beside the abbreviated "K Jenner." Otherwise he'd probably still be nameless. Perhaps it would all come back to him. He hoped he'd wake up one day to find his life restored, but all each new day brought was a meaningless fragment of new knowledge or nothing at all.

K crushed the beer can in his hand and got up from his chair to go inside the house. Dim shadows of rain fell across the walls of his kitchen as he stood at the counter preparing bowls of noodles for his son and himself. After he was done, he took one of the bowls to his son who was lying on the bedroom floor, reading a comic book. He said nothing to the boy. He grabbed another beer from the fridge and returned to the porch to continue watching the rain as he ate. He had no idea how much of the day was left. The sky was too dark to give away the position of the sun. It didn't matter anyhow. He slurped at his noodles and followed it with a sip of his beer. When he looked back up from his bowl, he was startled to see an old man dressed entirely in black, standing in the rain, staring at him.

"Hello!" the man yelled over the sound of the rain. He tugged at his black jacket and trotted towards the porch.

K stood and fixed his eyes on the man.

The man waved a hand, looked up at the sky, and smiled. "I'm sorry to bother you!" he continued. "But you wouldn't mind if an old traveller took a moment to get out of this terrible weather, would you?"

K turned back to the open house door behind him, and then back to the man, beckoning him with a hand to step onto the porch. The old man nodded and hurried up the steps. He shook out his jacket and ran his hand through his thin white hair. He smiled and rubbed his shoulders. He had a strong, hard face and bright blue eyes rolled up in layers of wrinkled skin. Thin tufts of white hair grew from his ears and a big brown mole on his left eyebrow sprouted a small white tuft of its own, like smoke from a miniature volcano.

K took another sip of his beer.

"I've been out there for days," the man said. "Hierdie weer. This rain just won't let up, will it? At first you can handle it, but you can take just so much before it starts to drive you a little mad."

"Let me get you a towel," K said, and the man nodded. K went inside the house and grabbed a big red towel from the cupboard. As he passed along the corridor he looked in on his son, still on the floor, still reading his comic. He closed the boy's bedroom door and returned to the porch.

"O, dankie, meneer. That's perfect," the old man said, rubbing it hard against his head. He threw it over his shoulders. "So sorry to have bothered you."

"It's no bother at all."

The old man smiled again and looked around for somewhere to sit. K gestured towards a wooden chair and the man took a seat. For a while they simply sat in silence.

K turned and studied the old man again. "Where were you going?" he asked.

"Oh, here and there. I'm a walker, you know. God gave me two feet and I intend to use them till they're ready to pack in."

God. K thought about the word. It was a new memory for the day, the idea of God. He hadn't had a thought about the notion of God until then.

"Where are your things?" K asked. The man carried nothing on him, not even a water bottle, or a plastic bag with a few supplies in it. It may have been a blunt question, but the stranger had asked to share K's one and only sacred space in the world.

"I don't need anything. I carry and spread the word of God, and that seems to do me just fine."

K refrained from saying that at the very least an umbrella would have been a good idea. The word of God wouldn't keep you dry.

"You see," the man said, as if reading K's mind, "I could have packed myself a raincoat or umbrella, but then I wouldn't have had this wonderful opportunity to meet you. That's how it works, the way I see it anyway. And when someone like you invites me to take shelter from the inclement weather, the view is sometimes better. I can step out of the storm completely and observe it objectively. I get a chance to think about what a storm is and where it comes from, instead of only *dealing* with it. Dealing with it has its place, and I've done that to the bone. Now it's time to dry off and look back on it. This is the time to acknowledge the storm as a holy thing without begrudging it. Without the lies of despair."

"You think despair is a lie?"

"It is in God's country."

K didn't respond. He drank his beer.

"You know," the old man said, "When I came around from the day—the day I forgot everything—God was the one thing I remembered. I actually had a Bible in my hand at the time. Even though I couldn't read a word of it, even though I recalled nothing of myself or where I had come from, God's truth was still in me, like the low heat at the centre of a cold stone. Because, you see, God doesn't need our memories to be real. God exists regardless. Whether we're asleep. Whether we're dead. And whether we're thinking about something else entirely. The truth doesn't go away when we close our eyes, you know.

"God's stories came back to me bit by bit. Each time they did it sounded to me precisely the way it must have sounded to the first of the saved: incredible, mind-blowing revelations from a big booming voice in the sky. They were miracles, you know. These slow recollections. And they did not stop coming until I was left with no choice but to get up and share them with the world. And so I started walking. Going from empty head to empty head, telling them the truth. People need that."

"Do they?"

"Indeed. For instance, you're here on the hill by yourself, but do you know what's going on down there below?"

"Where below?"

"In the towns."

"No, what's going on?"

"There is a group of people visiting families in your very town. Going into people's homes and asking them questions. This group call themselves the New Past. They're keen to know how much people remember of their lives before the resetting. I've been told that the group in this particular town is actually one small part of a bigger movement taking place all over the world. They're very interested in what people are thinking and doing with their lives now that we've all been set to zero.

"And on my travels I've seen things. Big trucks being filled with men, women and children. You can see their faces through the windows of the trucks, no expression on them at all, they look just like dumb cattle. There are others in the street watching them being driven out of town, and those people don't have any expressions either, bless them.

"I met a man once while walking and tried to share the word of God with him. But he wouldn't have any of it. He said my beliefs were archaic. He said my truth was not the truth at all. He said the only memories that had returned to me were the memories of old lies. And then he proceeded to tell me about the real truth, according to him. The truth of the New Past. How we were lost, not because of what we failed to remember, but because we'd been denied the habit of lying to ourselves. Day Zero, he called it, the day we went "cold turkey" on the elaborate lies of our old lives. It was a purging, he said. A means of coming clean of ourselves. He was a very interesting man. I explained to him that the Bible was about the very same principles, really. I said that what he was talking about was what I believed also. We realised after time that we were really talking about the same thing, his beliefs and my own. And then we went our separate ways. It was a beautiful meeting of married minds, really. Him with his side and mine with my own, but realising that our ideas were really one and the same. And the more I thought about it, the more of what he said made sense to me. The old habits of the old lies. The subsequent purging, or as I like to put it, the baptism by amnesia. The same truth, it seems, appears to all in one form or another. Don't you think?"

K raised his can to take a sip but realised it was empty. He looked ahead and saw the faint yellow light of the sun finally breaking through the constant grey.

"I mean," the old man said, "sooner or later the truth will be apparent to all. Even you. I can tell you're a sceptic. You're not one for trusting, are you?"

"No one's ever given me a reason to expect my trust."

"I'm sorry to hear that," the old man said. "Because you'll be denying yourself the truth if you don't open your mind. Denying yourself, and denying your son."

K nodded and placed the empty can at his feet next to his last one. He cleared his throat and stared into the distance. Beside him, the old man was folding his red towel into a square.

K turned his head. "I didn't tell you I had a son."

The old man was smiling. He handed the towel back to K and stood. He fluffed out his jacket and slicked his damp hair back over his head. Then he descended the steps of the porch.

"Looks like the rain is about to stop," he said finally. He looked back at K. "Thank you for your hospitality. You're a good man. I can tell you're not someone who knows how to make things easy for himself. You may not remember much, but what you do remember you hold tight and close to you. It's understandable. Short-sighted, but understandable."

The old man walked away, across the soggy earth. Weak drops of rain glittered in the light of the sunshine. K got up from his chair and watched as he headed down the road, gradually disappearing.

K swayed on his feet, suddenly dizzy. The beer rose in his throat and he swallowed hard. He was unnerved by the strange man's brief visitation. Whatever the man had been talking about while he'd dried himself with K's towel, one thing was for certain: something was off kilter. Something was wrong. K didn't know what exactly, but as the rain stopped falling and the clouds broke slowly apart, allowing long angled rays of light to fall across the land, he sensed this above all else.

K could not stop thinking about the old man. At night he closed the windows, locked the doors and made a fire in the living room fireplace. (The quickest memory to return after Day Zero had been the memory of fear itself—irrational and intangible fear—and in a world of strangers, it didn't take K long to figure out the locks.) He pulled the sofa closer to the fire and poured himself a whiskey. Andy sat on the sofa beside him and they both watched the fire. All the while they said nothing to each other. K had prepared a small, ill-conceived dinner for them both—tuna, beans in tomato sauce and baked potato. It was Andy who had first remembered how to use the can-opener, and a good thing too; the pantry was full of canned foods.

Once they had eaten, they'd changed into more comfortable clothing and made their way to the living room. The rain was intermittent now, falling in short fits and starts. The air was cold and the fire took a while to extend any real warmth. The rest of the house hung in darkness. All that could be seen was the orange glow of the fire on their faces and the dim blue radiance of the moon through the window. All that could be heard was the crackle of burning wood and the clink of whiskey and ice.

K looked at his son lying on the sofa beside him, hugging a purple pillow. He drank his whiskey. He wondered whether the boy had always been so quiet. Perhaps it was a characteristic he had recently acquired. A lack of confidence. A new sadness. Or, simply, Andy as he had always been. Silent and undemanding. K would never know.

The image of the old man in the rain entered his head and a ripple of fear ran through him, setting the hairs on his arms and the back of his neck on end. The man had known he had a son. What else did he know? Who was he really, and, above all, what were his intentions?

Eventually, K's eyelids grew heavy, weighted by the warm and hypnotic fire and the warm and hypnotic alcohol. He fell asleep on the couch and dreamed, and in his dream the old man was standing in front of the house and K was yelling at him. Saying that he wasn't welcome, that there was no one else in the house. The man simply ignored the yelling, thanked K for his kindness, and proceeded up the steps of the house. K tried to hold him back but the man moved forward effortlessly, ignoring K's ineffectually outstretched palms.

Behind him, Andy was standing in the doorway of the house. K shouted for Andy to get back in and close the door, but the boy wouldn't move, and the old man kept pressing on—impossibly wet (so wet he seemed made of water) and grinning and pushing forward against K's body with supernatural ease. K's feet simply slid back on the wooden boards as the drenched stranger walked ever closer to the doorway. Ever closer to K's son. And in this dream K knew his efforts to hold him back were futile. The old man had the strength of an army at his back. The joy of the devil in his eyes. And K had nothing. No power at all. It was his dream but not his world.

And then he woke up and discovered that it was morning. He was still on the couch. The light of a clear day had spilled into the house and the shadowy atmosphere of the night had given way to the bland details of a cluttered room. The logs of scorching wood were now a warm mound of smoking ash. The glass tumbler was lying on the floor beside a small puddle of stinking whiskey.

Andy was not on the sofa. He must have gone to bed at some point, K thought as he pulled himself upright. He yawned and pushed himself up from the couch.

K called for Andy but there was no response. He walked through the corridor into the empty kitchen. The dirty dishes from their dinner were still sitting on the edge of the sink. K poured himself a glass of water and drank it quickly. Then he grabbed a mandarin from the fruit basket and peeled it as he walked through the rest of the house. He ate each segment slowly, savouring the sweet and natural juices. Finally he opened his son's bedroom door.

Andy was not on the bed. Instead, K saw a black book placed neatly in the centre of the bed. He grabbed it.

It was a Bible.

Terror struck him instantaneously. The worst possible scenarios stacked up in his mind, layer upon layer, all laced with the gravity of cold fact. He left the room with the book in his hand and ran to the front door. The door was unlocked. Beyond the shadow of a doubt K knew he'd locked it the night before. He swung open the door and found himself on an empty porch. Ahead of him, the green and ordinary land stretched on. The horses in the paddock fanned their tails and huffed. Trees shook lightly in the morning breeze. Nothing was out of place, as far as he could tell. Nothing, except that Andy was not in the house. Not on the property. K was certain of it.

Someone had come into the house in the middle of the night and now Andy was gone.

K glanced down at the black laminated book and opened it. On the first blank page there was a handwritten note.

This has been done for your own sake. This is what is best for your son and for yourself. You are a good man but you remember too much. You would not have let him go willingly, and so this had to be done. It is the only way. There are bigger forces at work. We all have a role to play. Do not look for your son. You will not find him. But he is well and safe, and it is in all of our best interests that he remains well and safe for as long as possible. Trust this and you can go on to live a life of your own. If you do not trust in this you will live in the lie of your own despair.

It is your choice.

Beneath the note there was a handwritten reference: *Judges 8:23*, a passage somewhere in the Bible. K did not know his Bible well but paged furiously through the book until he found it. On the page the sentence had been underlined in pencil.

And Gideon said unto them, I will not rule over you, neither shall my son rule over you: the LORD will rule over you.

Upside down

I opened my eyes and saw the stars against the thick, black night. A distant satellite moved slowly through them like an impostor trying to make a stealthy escape.

I was still on the raft, bound and powerless, but now everything was silent. I could barely hear the ocean beneath me. If there was life in the ocean, I saw and heard no signs of it. If there was life somewhere up in the stars, they were keeping it to themselves.

I had no idea how long I'd been out there, and no idea how long I was supposed to remain. Had I been there for two days already? Was I into my third day? I could honestly not remember. I remembered a time of clear and sunny weather and a time of grey, overcast sky, but had that occurred in one day or two? I'd blacked in and out several times. I hadn't even needed to relieve myself, but couldn't be sure I hadn't already done so in my affected state.

Apart from the shifting of the stars, I had nothing to orientate me. My ability to distinguish between the ocean beneath and the sky above was slipping; they had become one and the same with their dark depths and shapeless textures. My raft was no longer a sea vessel but an extension of my body. I could barely tell where the surface of my skin ended and the bark of the raft began. We had been fused, the raft and I, and I was no longer attached to the earth by gravity but hovering in a midpoint. She'ol. A limbo. It felt as if I was now the only conscious thing in the universe. The centre and the source of perception. And though I had recently gone through the pains of physical hunger and thirst, the pains were now gone.

At an earlier point, the water had washed over me and run into my nose, burning the back of my throat and causing me to cough frantically. After that it had been so cold my teeth had chattered like glass ornaments quivering on a table in a tremor. But the chattering, too, had stopped. The feeling of cold had faded. Instead, there seemed to be nothing. Nothing but my thoughts.

The satellite moved out of my peripherals. I closed my eyes again. The darkness behind my closed lids was now my only refuge. Maybe, when I opened them, they'd have pulled me back in. Maybe when I awoke, I'd be back on the beach.

The next time I opened my eyes I thought that a few more hours had passed; it was still dark but the constellations appeared to be different. The dark, treacly ocean murmured beneath me, but the night sky . . .

As the night had worn on, the world had turned and the sky had moved with it, but this wasn't a simple shifting of stars. This was the same night I'd seen earlier, but there was something different. The layout of the stars had been changed in some inexplicable way. Had I been looking wrongly at them before, or was I looking at them wrongly now? And how much of this night could possibly be left? What had happened to the sun; where was the morning?

The sounds of the ocean returned. I pulled in my fingers and clenched them tightly into fists, embracing the sense of pain caused by my untrimmed fingernails in the clammy and wrinkled meat of my palms. There was no breeze. The air was still, but warm now. I blinked my dry eyes hard, and studied the stars more closely.

It took me a few minutes to grasp what I was seeing.

It *was* the same sky. That was for sure. But somehow, I was looking at everything upside down.

But that's not possible.

I wouldn't be able to see the sky from that position because my raft was attached to the shore and anchored by the buoys.

A terrifying notion struck me.

The raft was no longer attached to the shore.

And I was floating freely across the ocean.

Somehow, the rope had snapped and the buoys had failed, but how far had I drifted out? Had I been free from the shore for minutes, hours, or more than a day?

Panic descended. My chest heaved as I fought to catch my breath. The pulse on the side of my head pounded like a small and impatient fist on a door to my mind. I willed myself to think clearly, to regulate my breathing and steady my mind. I closed my eyes and took in a deep breath, held it, and then slowly released the thin and empty air.

Okay, Kayle. Think. Think. Think.

I mustered the last energy in my body and tugged my arms as hard as I could. My wrists burned as I strained to free them from the shackles. The straps would hardly move. I tried to kick my legs free of the straps below, hoping the seawater had somehow weakened the restraints. All I managed to do was exhaust myself and, judging by the sensation on my ankles, scrape my skin. Seawater stung as it poured over the fresh grazes. I wondered if Gideon, Theunis and Angerona were still alongside me, and tried to shout their names. My raspy voice was like the first, broken bleats of a newborn animal. Hardly anything escaped my lips. I swallowed air and tried again.

"Gideon! Theunis! Can you hear me! *Gideon!*"

I closed my eyes and focused on hearing—something, anything. I waited but there was no sound other than the near and distant purr of endless water. Either my voice was too shallow or they were incapable of answering. Or . . . I was too far away from them. The raft continued to dip and roll over the surface of the black ocean. And then it moved. It was *rotating*. The stars spun on the axis of my line of sight, and I was now certain: I was far from the shore, out on the vast black ocean, alone.

Dad?

Hm?

Why do we have a moon?

What do you mean?

I know why we have a sun, but why do we have a moon?

Well, if we didn't have a moon the tides wouldn't go in and out.

Is that important?

Pretty important.

Why?

If the tides didn't go in and out, life wouldn't have come out of the ocean. And humans wouldn't be here today. We'd probably still be jellyfish.

That's funny. So if we found another planet like ours, that had people on it, like ours, it would have to have a moon too, right?

I guess so.

A moon like ours?

Or one that was similar.

Another earth and another moon.

That's right.

Like a mother and a father.

Sure, Andy, like a mother and a father.

The ocean moved like a blanket being flapped out beneath me, carrying me across the surface of the earth. The raft drifted beneath the sun and the moon, and I passed through the darkness of the night and the light of the day as if they were the rooms of a strange old house. After a while, I lost track of the time and stopped counting the hours and days.

When I did manage to get some sleep I had dreams of flying. I'd dream of being as light as a mote of ash and of rising ever upwards into the sky. I'd rise through the clouds and the sun would touch my face. I'd look down and see the ocean glittering far below, and there, like a miniature cartoon, the raft where my body lay open and taut like a torture victim on a medieval stretching rack. But then I'd awaken to remember that I *was* that man on the rack and that I wasn't rising anywhere. And I'd wish I could fall asleep again. I'd wish I were still dreaming of being light as ash . . . rising . . .

Now and again I thought about the beach and the commune, about my son, but when I tried to hold onto the thoughts they became jumbled and senseless. My memories were distant relics, fragile artifacts covered in dust and time. If I blew too hard, tried to see them more clearly, I was afraid they'd simply disintegrate like ancient paper.

The sun baked my skin by day; icy winds froze my blood at night. At times, I felt as if I was expanding and contracting like an alloy that would crack, and that's when I tried my best to meditate. I remembered reading about monks who could alter the beat of the heart with only their minds and tried desperately to tap into that sacred and elusive ability. Occasionally I could blot it all out, and think of absolutely nothing, but my meditative abilities were unexceptional, and wandering thoughts intruded upon the stillness of my mind like loud-mouthed heathens in a mountaintop temple.

The raft continued for two days, or was it three? I had no idea. It sailed on and on, until one day the sun rose to an ominously dull morning. The sky lightened but there was no colour, no streaks of yellow and red. Not long after, the first few drips of rain landed on my face. I opened my mouth and swallowed as much of it as I could. The clouds darkened. The droplets came down harder, faster and furious. The wind howled like a warrior psyching itself up for battle.

And then the storm arrived. The raft rocked wildly. The sky closed in like the walls of a womb, birthing an abomination of thunder, lightning, wind and rain. For hours I was beaten by the rain. The raft tipped up as the sea rose beneath it. I was passed over the waves and rushed feet-first back into the ocean, struggling to catch my breath as the grey water crashed over me. The raft plunged into the ocean like a diving bird making a catch, before bobbing violently to the surface, returning me to the blistering barrage of rain.

I took deep breaths when I could, not knowing when and for how long I'd have to be under the water again. Sometimes I mistimed it and submerged just upon exhaling. Water rushed through my mouth and nose into my lungs and stomach. I returned to the surface gagging and vomiting, choking and drowning.

One particular wave knocked the wind out of me completely, and I fought to catch a breath. Lightning flashed and I caught a glimpse of a wave rising beside me like a giant hand. It came down over me, shoving me under the icy sea. The raft descended into the darkness before catapulting to the surface. It sprang from the ocean, flinging me into the air. I came down body first and upside down. I was now in the water but strapped to the underside of the raft.

This is the end. For the first time I fully believed that I wouldn't make it. I peered into the depths, holding my breath and wrenching my limbs on their tight straps. The raft would never turn back over. Soon I would have to breathe out, and that would be it. My lungs would fill with water and I would die.

Lightning must have struck the ocean at that point because blue light filled the darkness beneath me, flashing it into a jagged byzantine of deep-sea caverns and crevices. I felt like an alien pinned to the ceiling of a strange and inhospitable underworld. Lightning struck again. As it shot into the abyss below, throwing twisted new shapes onto those walls of shadows, something else appeared: a large mass, moving of its own accord. Something very big and very much alive. A drawled and sonorous song soon filled my submerged ears: the song of a whale. Even as the waves crashed and the thunder boomed somewhere overhead, even as the fear of my pathetic death took hold, the song of the whale was stunningly beautiful. Lightning flashed a third time, and I saw the mass rising up quickly towards me. I felt the impact of the whale's back against my spread body as I was hurled into the open air. The raft landed right side up and I was once again exposed to the sky. Old air rushed from my lungs and I sucked in the rain and the wind. I reached for my throat without thinking, and only after my right hand sank to my side did I realise that it was no longer bound. I grabbed hold of the strap that had once shackled me.

I coughed and spat the water from my lungs. One of the planks of the raft snapped under me and the splintered wood grazed my back. As my raft lifted and dipped over another big wave, I saw—in the flash of yet another bolt of lightning—a large tail and fin elegantly rising from the ocean. The fin hung suspended in the air for a moment, waving like the hand of a gracious royal, and then it went back down, vanishing into the black and angry ocean.

Time slowed to a gentle crawl, but now there was no fear in me. Instead, my mind lost all contact with my body. All I was aware of was a sense of depleting energy and consciousness. I saw nothing, heard nothing. I became a constituent of the chaos itself. I was eroding, the way a jagged rock is whittled to a smooth pebble.

Finally the sun came up and the waves died. The clouds separated, thinned to impotent wisps. The wind moved on and the air warmed. Within a few hours the fickle world was an oven again, and I was the overcooked order of the day.

My senses reconnected with my body—I was a person again—and with sensation came the full throes of pain and exhaustion. I was beyond thirsty. I had been dried out like a slab of meat on a hook in the desert sun. The salt had crusted on my skin and every inch of me burned. I had no idea how far I was from the beach—the safe and predictable beach—but was sure I'd been ushered out as far as was possible by the most powerful and wilful forces on earth.

The raft continued across the surface of the ocean. There were no sounds other than the gentle slapping of water at my sides and the whistling breeze overhead. Another ordinary day in the world, nothing of any consequence noted down or remembered. No, in spite of everything, I knew that above much else. It was another ordinary day in a very old world, and as always I moved through it, tired and alone on my broken raft.

Fruit

Mr. Kayle. Mr. Kayyyyyyle . . . it's your old friend Jack Turning here.
Wake. Up.

The first thing I became aware of when I came around was the pinch of a crab's claw on my nose. It had a firm grip and was trying to clamber up my face with its many pointed legs. I plucked it off and opened my eyes. The light of the sun cut through my retinas. The tall silhouettes of trees swayed against the sun and from somewhere nearby came the sound of the ocean washing softly ashore.

I was on a beach.

The raft had washed up on an embankment, quite a distance from the shore. The front end of it was buried in white sand. I quickly realised this was somewhere new. Somewhere new and somewhere deserted. There were no signs of life.

I wiped the sand off my face and my skin burned at the lightest touch. Carefully, I undid the strap across my neck then gingerly lifted my head from the raft and proceeded to undo the rest of my straps. My body ached as I stretched to my side to undo my left arm and then forward to undo my feet. Eventually, painfully, I managed to free myself entirely.

I got to my feet and studied my surroundings again. At the edge of the beach began a wilderness of trees and bushes, running the length of coastline as far as I could see. They were like no plant life I had ever seen. The trunks were thick towers, stretching far into the sky, aligned alongside each other like perfectly positioned pylons. Beyond the wall of oversized trees was what looked like a dense jungle running up a large green hill in the distance. This was not mainland. This was an island.

But the tide . . .

I turned to examine the sea.

There was something uncannily unnatural about the way the waves washed up the shore. The water didn't foam at all but ran clearly, with a slightly greater speed than waves usually do—more in the way water laps cleanly and forcefully against the edges of a lake on a windy day. Nothing about it seemed right.

I stepped off the raft and lurched onto the sand. The sand didn't feel right, either. It didn't even look right. I bent to pick up a handful and opened my palm.

It was like no sand I'd even seen—soft flakes instead of grains and almost metallic in the way they shimmered in the sun. They could have been finely crushed shells but that seemed unlikely; each gleaming flake seemed identical to the next one, almost synthetic. I dusted my hand on my pants and rubbed off the last bits between my fingers.

"Hellooo!" I shouted into the jungle, but there was no response. The trees caught the wind and they swayed and shrilled in their fixed spots. I looked back over the ocean and noticed something else, far off in the distance.

There was another small island out there, ten maybe twenty kilometres away. I wondered what it was, whether it had been there all along. But never mind that island; I still hadn't explored the one I was on. I turned to look into the jungle again. I knew I should go into it, explore, get a better idea of where I was and what was on offer. For a while, though, I'd stay on the beach and get my strength back. Find some food, drink some water. The last thing I needed was to be in a weakened state, being chased down by a wild cat or bitten by a venomous spider.

But my instincts were telling me something else. It wasn't the treachery of nature, the natural hazards of an untamed world that had me unsettled and scared. This place had been tamed. Arranged. Manufactured to look and feel like an island. And all the while I stood there, staring into the thick jungle, I felt I was being watched.

I found a bowl-shaped rock filled with rainwater and drank it dry. The water filled my shrunken stomach and I didn't feel like eating, even though I knew I should look for food, something solid. I put off foraging and instead pulled the raft up against a tree and slept there that night. The night was warm and accommodating, but I slept fitfully. I had nightmares of being bound and on the ocean. When I finally awoke, I was briefly unsure about where I was, but the shiny sand and the uncharacteristically tall and smooth-trunked trees soon reminded me.

My energy was drained. I lay in the rising sun for hours, trying to regain my strength. Eventually, I managed to get up and make my way to the shoreline. When I looked up, I noticed something peculiar about the other island—it seemed closer than it had been the day before. It was a small island—more of a ship-sized islet than an island—but now I could make out the volcanic shape of it, the faint hue of green undergrowth and the rise of the central peak. I walked down to the water's edge and peered out at the floating island. It could have been a trick of light or trick of the mind (I hadn't exactly been in the clearest and most perceptive state the moment I'd awoken), but I could have sworn it *was* closer than it had been. By three or four kilometres, at a guess.

Even stranger, when I looked down into the water, it seemed my own shore did not stretch out gradually beneath the tide, the way it would on any normal beach. There was a sudden drop, as if I was standing on a cliff. Less than a foot from the edge of the dry sand I could look directly down into the dark abyss of the ocean. It was like peering over the side of a boat.

A large fish fluttered a metre down into the ocean, and then, to my surprise, disappeared *under* the shore.

I didn't have the strength to dwell on these observations: I was suddenly ravenous. I found a large branch near the fringe of the jungle, took off my shirt and created a kind of net, which I then attached to the branch. I leaned over the edge of the island, dipped the branch and shirt under the water, and spent at least an hour scooping water until eventually I was able to catch a fish.

I hoisted the thrashing fish to the shore and killed it. I had no way of making a fire, but decided to skin and gut it, tear off the head and tail, and eat it raw. Each salty sliver slipped uneasily down my throat. When I was done, I stretched out on the beach under the harshening sun. The sky was perfectly blue. At a great height, birds crossed overhead. I didn't know where I was, but no longer cared. I was simply relieved to be off the sea.

I spent some time thinking about what had happened, how my raft had come free at all (Had the rope broken? Had it been cut?), but even these thoughts seemed irrelevant to my situation. Whatever the reason, I was here now. Stranded on the strange new beach of a strange new island. It was time to focus on surviving—and on finding my way to my son, because the truth was, whether the rope had been deliberately cut or had snapped on its own, I was free from the commune.

Starving. Exhausted. Free.

I closed my eyes, settled my mind, and sailed once more to sleep.

The next day I woke up feeling better. It was time to go into the jungle. I tied the raft to a young tree further up the beach and headed inland, beyond the wall of impeccable trees—smooth and identical, standing like ancient warriors on eternal watch.

The jungle was thick and wet. The canopy overhead had knitted together so that only a few shafts of light managed to cut through. They ran into the undergrowth at angles like rungless ladders. Each beam revealed wispy floating strands, like human hair, dancing in the warm, dank air.

One of the first things I noticed was the lack of any wildlife—no birds, no creatures scuttling through the trees. If not for the occasional spider web strung like necklaces of wobbly water droplets, I would have thought the jungle devoid of animal life. I stepped carefully through the undergrowth, keeping my wits about me. This was not a normal place. Not a normal jungle.

I walked for what must have been ten minutes before an astonishing new part of the jungle revealed itself.

Fruit.

The trees were now garlanded in clusters of bright and luscious fruit. This new vegetation didn't make sense either. The variety of fruit was contradictory to what I remembered about where and how fruit was grown. In the orchard beyond the paddock in the house I had left behind me, apples grew next to apples, and oranges nowhere near those at all. Bananas were tropical fruits, that fact floated in as I looked at the trees. So maybe they belonged here, in this clammy, humid forest. But here an orange tree grew beside an apple tree beside a banana tree, all hanging thick with the largest and most colourful fruits, big enough to feed two or three people. And that wasn't all. I saw pineapples the size of watermelons, watermelons scattered like boulders. There were unusual fruits too. Mulberries and pomegranates. Jujubes and kumquats. Quinces and lychees and kiwi fruit.

But still, there were no animals.

No flies or butterflies or monkeys or lizards. Just the fruit, perfectly and conveniently arranged, ready for a traveller's banquet.

As appealing as each fruit was to me—who had hardly had a thing to eat in days now—I was sceptical. They were simply too perfect. They had been put there to be eaten, but that instilled no faith in the motives of the caterer. There were many ways to ensnare an animal, and a sumptuous bowl of food left out in the open was one of them. I resisted the urge to pick one and carried on walking.

As I walked, however, the sweet fragrances of the fruits began to fill my nose. The smell of them was deliciously potent, far more tantalising than anything I had ever encountered. I found myself struggling to compose myself. Struggling to resist.

Nothing this wonderful can possibly be bad for you, I told myself as I trudged through the bushes beneath the hanging garden of fruit. *Why are you denying yourself these fruits? Because they're too inviting, too delicious and fragrant? For God's sake, stop being so paranoid! You're starving!*

My stomach gurgled loudly and that sound decided me. I'd walked almost a kilometre through the fruit trees and I could contain myself no longer.

I reached up to a conveniently low treetop to pluck a football-sized pear. The surface of its smooth and perfect skin shone in the light. I wiped the dew on it and plunged it into my mouth, taking as big a bite as I could.

My sense of taste had never done me so proud. The juices ran into my mouth and down my throat like the liquid essence of life itself. The sweetness ripened in my mouth, developing complexity as it lingered, filling each small space and gap, nursing and refreshing. Almost instantly, my eyes widened and my body came alive. I was sure nothing had tasted, or ever would taste, as good in my life.

I took another bite and walked on, reinvigorated. And now I felt something else, a pleasant tingling and warmth expanding within me.

I looked up.

The jungle, I realised in that moment, was a *paradise*. A place of pure and painstaking beauty, bathed in a golden aura. Each leaf glistened before me. Each shaft of light through the leaves was a passage to a divine tier above the known world, one that had always been there, sheltering me. The trunks of the trees glowed. The fatigue in my muscles and joints began to lift. My skin prickled. My head cleared. Every fear I'd had about these unknown surroundings was flushed away by the juices of the fruit.

The *fruit*. Was this all because of the fruit?

I didn't know and didn't care. I was overwhelmed by the sense that I was complete in every way. Nothing more was needed. How could I have not realised this? How much time had I wasted trying to figure out the world when the world had already figured itself out?

I am alive! I am free! Time is an illusion!

The past and the future vanished and I floated across the land in the euphoric glory of *now*, seamlessly at one with myself and the cosmos. I no longer cared about where I was going, what I was expecting to find. I was where I was and that was all that mattered. Destination was a cruel misconception posed as a plan and purpose. *Fear is a fabrication! Loneliness is a lie! How can any of us be lonely when we're surrounded by so much life?*

It was not long before my stomach was full.

I stopped eating and kept walking.

It was about then—a while after having taken my last bite—that the sense of enlightenment began to slip away.

It began with the jungle.

It was changing . . .

The glistening leaves grew dull and grey, decaying on the ends of their stalks. The bright colours of the world faded, leached by some terrible, chemical agent. Shadows flickered in their corners, stretching and reaching with twisted black hands.

Paradise? This wasn't paradise. What had I been thinking? This was a dungeon. A dungeon constructed of dying things. Fear and anxiety leaped back. The world began to take on strange and menacing undertones . . .

But this is the real world, Kayle. Everything choking, struggling and gasping for a chance to live out a painful and exhausting life— one that inevitably comes to nothing. Cruelty! Deterioration! Death! This is how things truly are.

How lost I really was. How alone. What if I didn't find anything here? Or anyone? What if my son was being abused or tortured or enslaved? What could I possibly do about that? I could barely keep myself alive, let alone save him. Besides which, I had no idea where I was.

I stared down at the remnants of the pear in my hand. It wasn't juicy and succulent. It was bloated and tumorous, the red and green streaks patterning the skin like the hard veins of a dead thing. The juices on my hands felt like the gummy secretions of some abominable creature's saliva.

My head began to spin. I could no longer tell which direction I had come from, or where I had planned on going. Light and darkness were mixing and forming bizarre new shapes. My heartbeat accelerated and my face spat sweat. Absolute fear filled me like hot acid.

The last thing I saw was a young man's face staring down at me. And then I lost the strength in my legs and disappeared into unconsciousness.

Cartoon elephants

Oh man. Oh man oh man. Here's yet another fine mess you've gotten yourself into, Mr. Kayle.

I thought I was on the raft but I was on a bed in a room. The lights were dim and there was the strong smell of food being cooked somewhere. I tried to lift my head but felt nauseous and wanted to throw up. I turned to my side and my wrist tightened and burned, tugging me back. I'd been tied to the bedposts with rough but effective rope. My eyes adjusted to the light slowly, to the dark blur of a person approaching my bedside.

"Well, look. You've made it," came the jubilant voice of what I figured to be a young man. "Congratulations," he said as he took form before me. "I have to say, I wouldn't have *buh*-bet on it, but you never know. People can be tough ol' bastards. And you're clearly tough, that's for sure. Still gotta figure out whether you're a *b-b-bastard.*"

The person sat down on a chair beside my bed. I blinked hard to better see him. He was a young man in his early twenties, at a guess. Lean. Handsome. Harmless-looking, but for the long white scar running from the bottom of his left ear to his nose.

In his hand he was holding a large blade. It gleamed in the light of a candle on my bedside table.

"Where am I?" I asked.

"In my bed. I don't usually give up my bed but you were in luck, sir. The sheets were in need of a clean and I hadn't *gurguh*-gotten around to it. So now my sheets are all yours, Columbus."

"Who—"

"Okay. I'm no good at answering questions. Really. Not my thing. But I'll ask a couple questions and make a big red cross next to all the ones you get wrong." He held up his knife. "All out of pens."

"Look—"

"Look? No, *you* look. You're on *my* island. It may look like your island, I don't know, but it's definitely mine. And you see, I don't get to keep an island like this with complimentary slippers and by serving breakfast in the morning. I hold on to it the old fashioned way. So let me lay it down. You turned up on a raft, right? That's your raft out there?"

"Yes."

"Hm. And you came here for a reason?"

"No—"

"No? So why *are* you here? That fruit did a number on you, didn't it? One minute you were in your own *mur-muh*-mountain-top musical and the next you were drooling in my dirt."

"Water."

"What?"

"I need water."

"Of course you do."

The man got up and grabbed a mug at my bedside. He held it to my lips and I drank the lukewarm water messily, spilling it on my chin. I sighed with relief and closed my eyes. The man snapped his fingers at me and put the mug back on the table.

"Talk," he said. "Explain."

"I was on a raft. It washed up. I had no control. I'm sorry."

He paused to consider my words, his finger running over the edge of the bedside table, pressing against the splintered corners.

"I see. Where are you from?"

"A beach."

"A beach? A commune?"

I nodded.

The man paused again and wiped his mouth with the sleeve of his shirt. "I've seen what they do," he said. "The people in the communes. They put people on the raft . . . leave you all out like laundry. It's a *puh-puh*-pun-ish-ment, am I right?" He stopped again, sighed and rested his palms on his knees. "You were punished for something, is *that* right?"

"Right."

"Why were you punished?"

I said nothing.

The man continued: "Did you kill someone?"

"No," I said. My throat was still burning. "I helped a woman."

"A woman?"

"A woman on the beach. She was pregnant, had her baby. She needed to escape. I helped her escape."

The man didn't say anything again for a while. He got up from his chair and circled the bedroom floor, flicking the sharp edge of the knife blade with his thumb.

"You helped a woman escape," he repeated.

"Yes."

"Her name?"

"What?"

"What was her name?"

"Jai-Li."

"Huh. And have you got a plan, or were you planning on bobbing across the seas on crime patrol, Raft Man?"

"My son."

"Speak up."

"I need to find my son. He's somewhere. In another commune, I think."

"How old is he?"

I took a moment to respond. "I'm not even sure any more. Things have been . . . confusing."

The man nodded then. He rubbed his face and turned to look out the window. From the bed I could see nothing out there except the stars of a clear night sky.

"Okay," he said. "Okay."

Then, without a word, he left the room. I expected him to return soon, but he didn't. I closed my eyes and thought about my son's face. How could I not remember how old he was? I'd thought about him every day, dreamed about him almost every night, but the specifics of time had been lost along the way. For as long as I could recall, time had been reduced to the rise and set of a sun, the wax and wane of a moon.

At that point I passed out again, pulled into a deep and lucid dream.

I'm standing in a room. I'm sweating even though I can see through the windows that it's night. Standing in front of me is a young boy in a yellow t-shirt. He's looking back at me without expression. All I can think of saying to him is, Your father was a hero today. I'm not sure why I say that.

His lips stretch from side to side and become a thin and devious smirk. I'm trying to comfort a child but this child does not need comforting. His sneering grin reveals that I'm the one in need of comfort; I'm the one sweating and trembling and filling with fear. Then the boy slides into the shadows behind him, his feet not moving, his smile growing and growing. There's more heat now, a dull heat that draws the oxygen from the room, and the sweat keeps coming.

My eyes opened heavily. I was drenched with perspiration, burning up. The young man with the scar was standing over me, the same leer on his face as the boy in my dream. He raised a rag and laid it on my forehead. The rag was cold and wet.

"Raft Man," he said. "You're alive, in case you're wondering."

I passed out again, falling into a place too cold and deep to permit even a dream.

I came around some time later, but there was no way to tell how long I'd been out. I turned my head and saw a blurry figure standing in the corner of the room, wiping his hands with a cloth.

"Your son," the man said. He folded the cloth and threw it neatly over the back of a wooden chair beside him. "I take it you plan on finding him." My head was spinning, my throat dry. He was speaking as if we had kept the previous conversation going without interruption, but for all I knew, it was hours later. "That is what you're going to do, yes?"

"Yes."

"And what will you do after you find him? T-*tuh*-take him back to the commune?"

"No."

"Haven't really thought this through, have you, Raft Man?"

"My name's Kayle."

"And your son, what's his name then?"

"Andy."

"Andy. That's a nice name. Friendly. Easy to remember. So, you find Andy. Lovely. What then? Where do you go?"

"I don't know."

"You don't know. Well, maybe he's better off where he is right now. Have you thought of that? After all, look where *you* are. Doesn't exactly instil a great deal of faith in your capacity to protect anyone, does it?"

The man reached towards a desk and took the same large knife into his hand. He wiped the blade on the cloth hanging over the chair. First the one side, then the other. He spun it in his hand and approached the bed, blade towards me, the metal sparkling in the dim light.

He smiled at me, the white scar on his face crinkling like a thin skin of boiled milk on the surface of a mug. He stepped to the bed, leaned over, hacked my wrists free, and slid the blade to my throat.

"This is my home, Kayle. You're in my home," he said, "and there are rules. Disrespect my island and m-muh-*my* rules and I'll feed you to the trees. You understand?"

Despite the knife, I was hardly intimidated. His threats seemed hollow; his attempts at some kind of menace were puerile. Contrary to what he thought, his stuttering words and actions made him seem anything but tough. He reminded me of a character in a comic book. He was emulating someone he'd seen somewhere—someone he'd told himself was intimidating—and doing a poor job of it.

"I understand," I said, a line in a script I was expected to say next.

"Fantastic. Come," he said. "Get some food." He whipped the blade from my neck and left the room. Cautiously, I climbed out of bed and rubbed my wrists. The blood rushed from my head and I grabbed the post of the bed. I took a moment to find the strength in my legs, and was finally able to stand and walk slowly across the room. I made my way through the door leading to the kitchen.

It looked more like a wizard's laboratory than a kitchen. Shelves of spices and dried roots and leaves were crammed into various, mismatched jars and tins like mystic potions. The walls were wallpapered yellow and a big grandfather clock with a shattered glass face stood in the corner. The hands of the clock were still moving, but the time was wrong. Unless the stars were still bright in the sky at five thirty-six in the morning. The smells from the bubbling pot were overwhelming, delicious and impossible to distinguish.

"Have a seat there, Kayle. Take a load off."

I sat down slowly at a small steel table covered in a ragged plastic tablecloth. The cloth was patterned in cartoon elephants marching behind each other, each trunk curled around the tail of the one in front.

"I hope you like Giant Squid with Kraken sauce. Just like Mother used to make it."

He grabbed two bowls, dished up the meat and broth with a wooden ladle and brought them steaming to the steel table. I lifted my bronze spoon and dipped it into the bowl of food. It was chicken and potatoes. He smiled at me and wasted no time, slurping and chewing his meal. At least it was edible then. Safe. Good to know. I ate slowly anyway, my stomach still turning slightly after my last disagreeable meal.

"I see you admiring my grandfather clock over there. It's a beautiful piece. The k-k-kitchen's the only place on the island where time matters, Kayle. If you want that chicken done just right, that is. You've got a splash on your chin there."

I wiped my chin and licked the sauce off the back of my hand.

The young man turned back to his bowl. My eyes scanned the room again, and then the door through which I'd entered.

"What is this place?" I asked.

"This is my house. Well, our house. On *our* island."

"Our?"

"My father's in the next room. My brother's downstairs."

"There are only the three of you?"

The man grabbed a chicken leg with both hands and bit into it.

"I was impressed, Kayle. I really was," he said, putting the stripped bone back in his bowl and licking his fingers one by one. "You know, the only reason you made it is because I was down in the jungle. You do know that, right? But also, the reason you m-*muh*-managed to get all the way to me was because you resisted. You walked almost a kilometre inland before taking a bite of that pear, and that's the furthest I've seen anyone get in a while. Most can barely make a few feet before they're c-*cuh*-climbing up trees and stuffing their faces.

"It's not easy resisting those fruits, is it? All that time at sea and suddenly you've got this incredible buffet, this orgy of fruity goodness there just for you. The smells are hard enough. And I should know. They were designed that way. Designed to be irresistible. So congratulations, Kayle. It was impressive. That, and the f-f-fact your stomach was so shrivelled you hardly had any fruit at all. That probably saved your life too."

"Those fruits were put there on purpose?"

"That's right."

"And they're all . . . ?"

"Yes," he said, understanding. "The ones in the jungle, yes. We've got our own fruit up here at the house. And not just fruit. Some livestock, vegetables, grain. The really guh-*good* stuff. But out there . . . well, it's a jungle out there."

"Why?"

"Because you're not on a real island, Kayle. It's more of a ship, really. And if you've ever read a book or seen a movie, you'll know, where there are ships there are pirates."

The young man finished off the broth with his spoon. After he was done he took his bowl to a blue plastic tub filled with water and soap.

"What do you mean *ship*?"

"This all *looks* like an island, but you aren't on some exotic getaway. This island is made of the real shit of the human world, Kayle. Refuse. Bottles. Machinery. Plastic. Ground down, tied up. Squashed and compacted into bricks. Whatever can be used. And it turns out, most of it can be used."

The young man rinsed his hands in another bowl of water and dried them on a tea towel hanging from the dark mahogany clock.

"What's your name?" I asked.

"My name?"

It was as if nobody had ever asked him.

"Anubis. M-mm-*muh-my* name's Anubis. Now, Kayle," he said. "Finish up my culinary delights and come with me."

Anubis led me through the house and out onto a wooden deck. There was no moon and it was too dark to see much of my environment. We were at the top of a thick black patch of the oval island. He leaned on the rail.

"You want to know where you are, I can tell you," he said. "Why not? You're here now and you have a right to know, I suppose." He stared out towards the ocean. "There are only the three of us here. My father, my brother and me. But I deal with the running of this island by myself. I have no choice. My brother and my father have certain conditions that don't allow them to be out here, managing the ins-and-outs. You'll never see my brother rigging up pulleys, repairing the house, raising stock, cooking and doing meet-'n'-greets with people like you. He *does* help me, in ways I probably need to explain, ways even

I don't fully understand . . . but nevertheless trust and depend upon. I guess you could say we're kind of a *tuh-tuh*-team." He turned around and put his back to the rail, resting his elbows behind him. He turned his head up to a sky splashed with countless stars and continued to speak . . .

*

The mirror man

My brother and I were born twenty-three years ago, five minutes apart. We're identical twins—and when I say we're identical, I mean *identical*. With most twins, there are always small differences upon close inspection. Slightly larger eyes. Smaller hands. Wider nostrils. Something! But not us. Nope. We're identical in every way you can imagine, as if the same p-puh-*person* came into this world twice.

My parents were what you'd call extreme environmentalists. Protesters. Anti-establishment people. Always going on about the corporate overseers, you know, those evil bigwigs who twirl their moustaches over some new profitable way to poison our bodies, our minds and our homes. I'm sure you know the sort. One thing was for certain, however: whether bound by their political passion or perhaps even something more, my parents were truly in *love* with each other. My father wuh-wuh-worshipped my mother, my mother put all of her faith and trust in my father, and together, the two of them became Bonnie-'n'-Clyde-Gone-Green.

He was an English teacher and she was a secretary, but after only a few years of living together, they left their jobs to join an aggressive, growing movement of outraged people called The Borrowed Gun.

It was the accidental dropping of the "Gas Giant" Bio-bomb in Maputo in '55 that really sparked The Borrowed Gun, I reckon. I mean, everyone saw it on the news. A city of corpses. Dead fish floating on the surfaces of the lakes. Acidic rain riddling crops and p-p-people's hair falling out. All of those suits in court, shrugging and *oopsing* and cutting deals to dodge the blame bullet . . .

And it was right about then that my parents came off the leashes of society like two wild dogs. It wasn't charity work on their minds, though, it was vengeance.

My brother and I were sheltered from most of their undertakings in the early years. People would come to our house in the evenings and my mother would bring out trays of tea and coffee for these strangers. They would talk about things I couldn't understand and the same few words would g-g-go back and forth: "government," "tactics," "infiltrate," "liberate." Words like that.

Sometimes discussions would get heated, at which point my mother would enter our room to tell us a story. She made them up as she went along, which meant they'd only ever be as good as her mood. Her stories were full of make-believe creatures and farfetched adventures, which often bored me, but my b-b-b-brother seemed to appreciate them.

No. I wanted to know what the adults were talking about. I didn't want to lie in my room and listen to fables about monsters and dragons. I wanted to hear about the monsters that scared my parents. The dragons they were trying to defeat. And I wanted in.

It was around this time, on an ordinary trip to the seaside with my parents, that we found out about my brother's unusual skin problem. That was a particularly strange day. One day you think you know how the world works and the next you don't, as if over the course of a night somebody went and changed a rule somewhere.

My brother and I were eight years old. My father was lying on a towel, wearing big sunglasses and drying off from a swim.

My mother was reading a book. The rest of the beach was full of the regular Sunday crowd. I was sitting next to my parents, trying to make a sandcastle, and my brother was playing d-d-down by the water.

That's when we heard the scream. Blood-chilling, unearthly. I remember people on the beach turning their heads at the same time. I remember thinking someone had been eaten by a shark, the way that scream rippled across the beach. It was only when I stood that I realised it was my brother making that sound. He was running back up the beach towards us.

I'll never forget that first time I saw him standing there, veins of ocean water running over his, his b-b-b-body. He was covered from head to toe in the biggest, reddest blisters you can imagine. His face was twisted and pulpy, his eyelids almost completely closed. His arms looked like a string of onions in a tight red sack. There wasn't a part of him that wasn't bulging and burning—and he just kept screaming and screaming. A sound I'd never heard before, but recognised anyway.

It was like it was me screaming.

EPP, they call it. My brother's an extreme case. It means he suffers from a photosensitivity to light, and any prolonged exposure makes the poor guy look like he's been tossed in a lobster pot. In an instant, my Mirror Man—as I still like to call him—was more my shadow than a brother, a familiar figure trapped in constant darkness.

He was given medication, but his body reacted badly, and it didn't seem to help much anyway. So my mother decided it was best he stayed inside while I got to play outside with friends. Curious kids often asked about him and I'd just shrug and say he was sick. He'd get better, I told them, but he was sick. I can only imagine the b-b-b-bullshit stories they spread about the boy who lived in the darkness—the boy who could do nothing but stand at his upstairs bedroom window and watch us kick a soccer ball about in the street.

Some days my brother did come out of the room, but he looked like a ghost wrapped in those black sheets. The look did him no favours. It only mmm-muh-made him even stranger to the other kids. I'd spend time with him in the dark room, of course, and we'd chat and joke and talk nonsense. That lasted for a while, but eventually he lost interest in what I had d-d-done with my light-filled day. He lost interest in our favourite TV shows. TV and video games and comics. He stopped laughing at my jokes too. Don't get me wrong. It wasn't like he was sad or depressed, it was more that, while he lost interest in some things, others interested him more. He began to talk about strange dreams he was having—things he was seeing in the darkness. People's faces, places he'd never been to. His words became more and more puh-puh-puzzling, and after a few months he was barely stringing together a sentence that made any sense, kinda the way people talk to you in dreams. I'd listen to him, patiently, you know, maybe I could figure something out, but sometimes I felt like running away and never seeing him again.

Adults think their problems are so bloody big, but they're equipped to deal with them, and that makes all the difference. For a kid, everything's the most incredible thing ever, or it's the end of the world. Nothing's just fine. And that's how it felt, dealing with him. I couldn't handle it, and couldn't handle that I couldn't handle it, you know?

One morning, I woke up in my bed and he was standing over me, his skin white as cream cheese, his eyes . . . We were both born with dark guh-guh-*green* eyes, but now his were like new leaves on a tree. He had no expression on his face. He was sleepwalking. I asked him what he wanted—why he was out of bed so early—but he only leaned and said, *Bang! Crash! Bang! Don't look right. Look left.*

That was it. That's what he said.

And then he went to bed.

I thought nothing much of it, went about my day as normal, met up with Joey Sinclair and Ben Beatty, two friends from school. We went skateboarding through the city. We were about to cross a road, but as we came off the pavement, we heard a loud crashing sound on our right. We turned to see some poor guy drop a television he'd been carrying from his car. Joey and Ben laughed and pointed, and I would have probably joined those losers, but something in me clicked without thinking. For some reason, I looked the other way. That's when I saw the big red van spuh-sp-*speeding* down the road. No time to shout. The van ended up hitting Joey and Ben both. They rolled over the bonnet, landed in the road like boneless chickens. Joey pulled through but lost a leg, Ben Beatty dud-duh-d-d-died right then and there, and I went on to skate another day.

Later, once I was able to think back on it (*Bang! Crash! Bang! Don't look right. Look left*), I knew my brother had given me a warning of some kind. I asked how he knew. He said he didn't know what I meant. He didn't remember saying anything, and we never brought up that weird, shitty day ever again. It took me a while to work my way through the events of that day—reach any kind of firm resolution—but I found myself listening to my brother all the time. The more I listened, the more *sense* he started to make. He'd still babble and digress, but I never thought of wuh-wanting to run away. I'd play all day in the sun, and later, after meeting with my brother, would talk about my day a little differently, fill him in, make him part of it. I was no longer smug about it. We became a team. I became his eyes and ears in the world, giving him reports on the working world—what I had seen and heard and figured out about life in the light—and he'd report back on what he'd seen and heard and figured out about life in the dark. In that way, as was always meant to be, we got the whole gig covered.

The world was a funny place around that time. There were the riots. The bank bombings. Six hundred angry people crashed through the front doors of the Gausen Telecommunication Tower and trashed the offices one floor at a time until they reached the top floor, burst through the CEO's office door and threw that old Carl Gausen guy off the rooftop of his own empire.

My father was brought home late that night by one of his friends. His head was bleeding and he was hobbling like he'd been in a fight. I tried to find out what had huh-*huh*-happened but my mother told me to go to my room while she grabbed the med-kit and cleaned his cuts in the bathroom.

Later, when the footage came out, I thought I saw my father between those tower-stormers, but I told myself it wasn't, that it was just someone who looked like him. To this day I'm not really sure. My brother, on the other hand, had nothing to say about it. He didn't even watch. All he said when I came back to my bed that night were two words: *Bad fruit.*

Then he turned over and went to sleep.

After that, more people came to our house, and I watched them from the door of my room. My mother sat on my father's lap in his armchair, listening to what these strangers had to say, but something was different about these later meetings. My father was less vocal, let others do the talking. One night he and my mother came into our bedroom to talk to us about something important. My brother and I just sat in our beds and listened. My father said that we'd be leaving. It was buh-*buh*-buh-best for us all if we didn't live in our house anymore. My mother was rubbing his back, nodding and smiling at us.

There are people who want to own us, he said. *They're everywhere. Sometimes they're even people we think we like. But we have to be careful, because they're really trying to control us, and the best way to control someone is to first get them to like you. We see these people on TV and in magazines. Sometimes we meet them in the street. But we need to leave because we believe in something better, don't we, boys? We believe in freedom.*

He said we'd be on a ship for a few weeks. We'd be there with our closest friends and family. I asked where we'd be going and he said, *An island. There's a beautiful island owned by one of these bad people. It's a floating island. One of our dearest friends saw it, and he knows where it's going. So we're going to find it and we're going to take it from him. That's where we'll live.*

I could barely contain my excitement. An island! Juh-juh-just like in the movies! But when I turned to share the moment with my brother, I saw he was looking back at my parents with these scared, scared eyes. At the time, I didn't get it. I mean, we'd live with our friends and float around the world, going wherever we wanted and doing whatever we wanted. No stupid school. No pollution. No problems.

My father saw his alarmed look. *Don't worry kiddo,* he said. *There's plenty of shade on the island.*

Then my parents left the bedroom arm-in-arm and closed the door behind them.

Two weeks later we were on the ship. It was an old ship, but enormous. My parents were excited that day. I ran on board to find our cabin, and as always, bagged the top bunk. The lights of the cabin were kept dim, the curtains of our little window remained drawn and the door stood only slightly open. The first night, everyone ate dinner in the Mess Hall. (Except my brother—he ate his meals in the cabin. He could tolerate electric light, but he'd become kinda solitary.) I recognised a few people from our neighbourhood. Kids from our street, a coupla teachers. A local security guard, my father's mechanic, the Indian from the corner shop. And a few others I only knew by face. Anyway, everyone seemed optimistic. Friendly. Helpful.

Everyone but the captain.

The captain was a raggedy old man, built like a German Panzer, and he never smiled at anyone. I'd pass him in the c-c-*cuh*-corridors and he'd look at me as if he was planning on putting me between two slices of bread. I asked my mother about him and she said he was one of the most respected men in the group; I should always do what he said. Not that he told me to do anything—didn't speak to me at all, actually—but still, he knew I was there. I reckoned he didn't like me too much, which didn't bother me. He was just this beat-up old bastard with knives in his belt (he always had knives on him), and when I asked my father about those knives, my father only said, *When you're out in the wild, knives have all kinds of purposes. Cutting ropes and gutting a fish or peeling an apple. A knife's like an explorer's palm-plate, son.*

Well, that ship sailed the ocean for three weeks, and by then, you can imagine, people were getting impatient. *Where's this island?* everyone was asking. The excitement was gone, the thrill—and then there was this one night when my friend's father's tiles slipped off his ol' roof—if you know what I mean—and he began flinging tables and saying we'd run out of food, which scared the shit outta everyone. A bunch of guys had to take him into another room, calm him down.

It rained a lot, so we were stuck in our cabins, with nothing to do. Sometimes we'd get into a storm and everything would fall this way and that, and we'd have to pinball ourselves against walls just to get to the bathroom.

But then, one morning, we heard someone shouting from the deck. I was on my bed, peeling an apple with a knife I'd nicked from the kitchen. I saw this group of people rushing past our cabin doorway. I hopped off my bed, told my brother to come see. He was on his bunk below, saying it was too b-b-bright out there. I said that was fine, I'd tell him everything when I got back.

By the time I got to the deck there was this crowd of people leaning over the rails, whistling and shouting and cheering. I pushed my way through them and grabbed the rail.

The island.

My first thought was that it was unusual-looking, protruding from the ocean like a gigantic green nose. Someone yelled they could see the wake in the water, and that the island was moving, definitely moving, and everyone cheered.

It wasn't just any island. It was our island.

We'd made it.

It was just in time too, because that table-flinging father hadn't been far off course; we'd almost completely run out of provisions. That night everyone got a small portion of the last remaining food and we simply trailed behind the island at a fixed distance.

Father said he and my mother had to have a meeting with the others. The island was owned by a member of the most powerful company in the world. We'd have to approach carefully. These big shots wouldn't give up their toys without a fight, father said, but luckily we were in the business of fighting too.

The next day the ship pulled up behind the island. The men brought out the secret stash of guns and weapons we'd had on board all along. They lined up along the rail as the ship came in. The rest of us watched through the murky windows of our cabins. The closer we got, though, the stranger the place appeared. The trees were perfectly straight and evenly lined up like an oversized fence. Behind the trees we could mmm-muh-make out a mess of dark and thick jungle, and on top of the hill, there were a couple of house-like structures.

I gotta say, even then it didn't look as formidable as we had been expecting, but nobody said a thing. Nobody cared. Nobody gave a shit what it looked like. We were all silent now, just the s-s-s-sound of the waves crashing against the sides and the steady drone of the engine, like a big sleeping thing. Then the engine was shut down, and we drifted closer, guns pointed and aimed. We honestly believed we were ready for anything.

We pulled right up to beach without a hitch. That was the easy part. The ship touched the back of the island and the anchors were thrown on shore. A bridge was unscrewed, lowered onto the sand, and the men with the guns went down first, though they were hardly trained soldiers. Most of them could barely hold a gun. There was my English teacher, Mr. Harris. He couldn't seem to decide whether to keep pushing up his glasses or keep his finger on the trigger. Another was my neighbour, Mr. Caldwell, clutching a big black handgun like it was a kid's water pistol. In front of them all was Captain Knife-Pants, a cigarette hanging from the corner of his mouth, walking ashore with the anxious toddle of a man looking for the nearest bar.

The rest of us began to leave our cabins. We moved onto the deck. My brother was wrapped in his black hood, fully clothed and gloved, even though it must have been about ninety d-d-duh-duh-degrees out there. My mother held him close. We made our way to the bridge and down onto the beach—the white strip where the men were already standing in a huddle, throwing their barrels up in every direction, ready for action. But nothing happened. No cannons, no armed guards running out of the jungle.

For a while everyone simply stood together, wondering what to do next. We ventured forward and saw signs on the trees warning if we trespassed we'd be putting ourselves in extreme danger, but this lot took it as a bloody invitation to go hunting.

So into the jungle we went.

The women and children were told to wait on the beach but none of us wanted to be separated. I suppose they could have gone back on the ship, but no one did. Instead, we walked into the jungle together, gun barrels pointing the way. I was walking next to my brother and he didn't say a thing all the way. My mother and father stayed out in front.

We walked for about ten minutes, and then, as you've most likely guessed, we saw the fruit. Bur-bur-*big* juicy fruits hanging from the trees like colourful lanterns. Something for every taste.

Needless to say, everyone dove right in. Everyone that is except my father, he wasn't ready to relax. He had his gun aimed into the dark crannies of the jungle, still cautious, still worried about being ambushed by a hidden enemy.

I was about to grab an enormous orange when I felt my brother's hand on my shoulder. I turned to him and his earlier words clanged into my brain, the way they had on the street with Joey and Ben: *bad fruit.*

I nodded, trusting my other half, my eyes in the dark, and watched the rest of it unfold. I felt some concern, but mainly I was curious. People clambered up trees and stuffed the fruit in their mouths. It was the first fresh food they'd had in weeks and nobody wasted a moment. Everyone began chewing and mashing it down, and juice ran like small waterfalls from their chins. Eating and grinning and looking like a bunch of loons. Guns fell to the ground, people were laughing, hugging and kissing each other, saying they were home, they were *home!*

Everyone was eating except for my brother, my father and me. I asked what was happening, why everyone was so happy, and for the first time my father had an uncertain look on his face, as if he too didn't know. I mean, there's a cuh-cuh-cuh-craving, and then there's *craving!* Even my mother was eating and laughing and bouncing around. The three of us who hadn't touched the fruits expected the group to come to their senses at any minute, but they wouldn't. Even after they'd finished gorging out, they were still duh-dancing and lifting each other in the air, singing praises and hallelujahs.

My father told them to keep their voices down, *We have to be careful*, but nobody took notice of him. He grabbed my mother's arm. *What on earth's gotten into you, sweetheart?* She threw her arms around him and planted kisses across his face. He pulled her head back and told her to snap out of it, *What the bloody hell, Jane?* but she wouldn't. Then my mother turned and kuh-k-kissed some other man, full-mouthed kissing with tongues, and then another man. My father tried to pull her away, yelling for her to stop.

This went on for a few minutes before everyone *did* calm down. The laughter died, the kissing and hugging, and now puh-puh-people were ambling slowly in small circles with blank looks on their faces as if a thick mist had come down, shrouding them.

I remember my father panting, resting his hands on his knees, saying at least it was all over, *whatever the hell it was*. He took the opportunity to tell the men to pick up their guns and keep moving, but they still wouldn't listen. He shouted at them and slapped a few of them in the faces; they stood frozen in some self-induced trance, haunting the little clearing.

That's when things went from bad to worse.

Everyone did come out of the trance—Mr. Harris, the captain, my mother, the soccer kids and rest of them—but now there was a different look in their eyes. It wasn't joy or relief. Nope. Now they all looked duh-duh-deranged. That's probably the right word. *Deranged.* My father shook my muh-*muh*, my *mother,* and told her to come around, *Come around baby,* but her gaze turned on him and all he could see in her eyes was fear. Fear like he'd never seen in anyone before, and it sent him reeling backwards in shock. A deep, deep panic grew and grew in her until she was screaming and she held up her hands and her hands were like gnarled claws. The vein on the side of her head began to throb and throb. Her neck tightened, her teeth began to grind. Each person began to turn on the other, snatching, screaming. I grabbed my brother and we jumped into a bush. My father fumbled for his gun and didn't know where to point: his neighours, his friends, his *wife?*

What we saw next is something I'll never forget.

Friend attacked friend, parent leaped on child. Jumping on each other, wrenching the hair from scalps. Biting. Scratching out eyes. The captain, looking even crazier than normal, had one of his knives out, but he wasn't peeling apples or gutting fish; he was peeling and gutting people. One or two managed to get hold of the guns and fired blindly into anyone who came close, murdering the people they'd once trusted.

Right about then my father grabbed me by the arm and shouted for my brother and me to run . . . to keep running and not look back. So we did. The three of us ran deeper into jungle, cutting ourselves on the branches and leaves and bushes. But even though I knew I shouldn't, I did look back one last time, and all I could see was the shuffle of blood-soaked bushes and gut-smeared trunks. Eventually we had run so far we couldn't see any of it.

But the screaming . . .

Boy, oh boy. Tuh-tuh-tuh-*trust* me when I say the screaming didn't stop for ages.

Burt

Over the course of the story we'd moved back inside and now Anubis was sitting on a tattered sofa in the centre of a living room. "We ran until we got all the way to the top of the hill," he said. "And we found this house. This house, and the laboratory, and the small farm out back. But there was no one here. It had been abandoned. So we tuh-*tuh*-took it—my father, my brother and I—and we've been living here ever since."

I walked around the living room, inspecting books in the shelves. There was a metronome sitting on a wooden table beside an unusual assortment of collectibles: a doll, a broken watch, a knife and a pair of glasses with cracked lenses. The rest of the room was surprisingly homely: a furry rug under an oval wooden table, a brown paper globe of the earth acting as a shade on the light hanging from the ceiling.

"We realised this was once some kind of lab and the plants and fruits had been made to protect it. Turn people crazy before they could get up here. Pretty effective. You wanna stop people from busting in your home? Make something that makes them forget why they bothered in the first place. Have them turn on themselves."

"With fruit that makes you psychotic."

"Ha! The fruit doesn't *make* you do anything. It's more of a catalyst for who you already are. Some enlightened monk makes his way into that jungle, all he'll do is forget why he bothered coming up. And that's enough of a defence. The rest of it, the *levels* of crazy, that's all you, man. Your worst fears, right out there, ugly and awful. All the stuff we've pushed down deep. We think we're happy, Raft Man, in control, but there are mean things in the basement of our s-suh-*suh*-souls. Like sewage floating under a super city. The fruit just buh-*buh*-brings it all out. Smart, huh?"

"Hm," I said noncommittally, examining the old, dusty books on the shelves and reading the unfamiliar titles: *Thirty-Minute Meals with Jamie Oliver. Peter Pan. Where's Waldo? Conquistadors of the Useless. The Decameron. The Silver Brumby.*

"We kinda like it here now. My father built this cabin for my brother, down in the woods—a little cabin with one window and hardly any light—and I think he prefers it down there, you know? I mean, he comes up here for dinner sometimes, but mostly I take something down to him. My father . . . well, he was okay for a while, but I think he really missed my mother. We fought, you know. A lot. I reckon he began to lose it, lose his muh-m-*muh* . . . his muh-*mind*. And now he's sick, stuck in bed in the other room. Can barely walk these days, but I've got him on some good drugs. Turns out this place had some decent medical supplies and equipment too."

I sat down on the couch beside him. "So everyone died out there that day?"

"Almost everyone."

"I don't understand. Why did they attack each other?"

"Because the best thing you can do to keep this world going is not be born at all. To not exist. Consume nothing. Waste nothing. Use nothing and leave nothing behind. Sounds kinda extreme, right? But that's the reality, whether we like it or not."

Despite his logic, I wasn't sure that had been the reason. It didn't satisfy my need for answers, the idea that they'd torn each other apart as an act of environmental conviction.

"And the bodies—they're still down there?" I went on.

He watched me carefully as he answered. "All part of the design. That jungle down there—it just *loves* flesh! Takes those bodies right up, and after a couple weeks—nothing."

A memory snapped back to me. *The trees, it seems, will take the body of a dead thing as quickly as they* want *it, or want to get rid of it.*

"Nothing left?" I probed.

"Even if you don't eat the fruit, other parts of the jungle have other kinds of biological defence systems. Wild stuff. Fringe genetic programming. It took everyone in the juh-juh-*jungle* that day. Apart from us."

"You said *almost* everyone."

The young man smiled.

"That's right," he began, sitting forward. "You got me. Not quite everyone." He paused for a moment, and I wondered if he was going to continue. "I went back out there, into the jungle, many months later, and I ran into this man, standing there, near a river. I knew him once . . . but not well. He came around to our house a couple of times. Buh-buh-*Burt*. I think that was his name, he used to live on our street. Tall guy, in a black coat. Anyway, I saw him out there and . . . I don't know, I reckon he must have got away from the group like we did. Not sure how he survived so long down there in the jungle by himself, but there he was. I tried to ask him about it, but he wouldn't answer. He didn't smile, didn't even move. He just stood there. I don't know if he remembered who he was, or even *how* to speak—"

"He chased you," I cut in.

"Yes."

"And the trees, they stopped him. Attacked him."

Anubis frowned and leaned back, the scar on his face creasing.

"How did you know that?"

I shook my head. I had to tell Anubis about Moneta, as much as I had promised myself I wouldn't tell anyone. The decision didn't seem to come from me, though. I felt as if I was being directed to speak—a whisper from a faraway place, as if from the orb in my dream.

"There was an old woman," I said slowly. I sat forward on my chair and rubbed my hands together. "Part of my commune on the beach. She told me a story, about a man in the woods, like the one you've just told me. The only thing is, she said it happened to *her*. Her story happened a long time ago and in a different place. But it was the same story. Same man. I'm sure of it. Burt."

Anubis said nothing, but the look on his face had changed— back to that conceited, plotting look from before. I wasn't certain whether he believed me. He said nothing, waiting for me to continue. "A few days later she took her life," I continued. "She left a letter explaining everything: that she knew the story didn't belong to her. It wasn't her memory."

"Me," Anubis said, possessively. "It belonged to *mm*-me."

He seemed agitated by my remark, peeved that for the first time he'd been put on the back foot of our exchange. He got to his feet and walked to the bookshelf. "Here," he said, grabbing a book from the shelf. He handed the small notebook to me. "I drew a picture of him. A picture of Burt and me. I was young and liked drawing. Crappy drawings now, if you ask me."

I paged through the notebook. There was a crude drawing of Burt and of the young man. Burt was tall, lanky, with a narrow, pale face. He was wearing a big black coat.

I handed the book back. "I don't know," I said. "I can't explain this. I wish I could but I can't. She couldn't understand it either. But the coincidence . . . her telling me all of this, me somehow ending up here, meeting you, the real owner of that memory . . ."

Anubis took the book from me and put it back in his shelf. He seemed relieved that I had decided it was *his* true memory and not hers and this seemed to allow him to probe the matter further. "What was her name?" he asked.

"Moneta."

"Moneta."

"Hm."

"You know, my brother," he continued. He paced the room in circles, tapping his finger to his lips as he stared at the ceiling. *Another cliched charade*, I couldn't help thinking. Gone was the comic-book villain. *And now, ladies and gentleman, I'll be playing the part of the contemplative man.* Was anything about his behaviour genuine, or was it all some kind of act?

"He used to talk about these dreams he had. He'd dream he was a very old woman living in a glass house. A g-g-glass house overlooking a beach. He could never explain it, but he'd dream of her often."

I rubbed the back of my neck and closed my eyes. "That's her. I don't know how, but that's her." I shook my head and took a breath. "It doesn't make sense. It makes no sense. No *sense* . . ."

"Are you okay?"

"My head hurts."

"I don't usually invite strangers to meet my brother," Anubis said, "but I get the feeling you need to speak to him. He understands this sort of thing. I don't know how else to put it. He may even be able to help you find your son—what's his name again?"

"Andy."

"Andy, Andy. Right." He nodded, as if agreeing with himself. "Okay. Here's what you have to do. Go down to the cabin tomorrow, after the sun comes up. Have a ch-*chuh*-chat. Like I said, he might be able to help you. Sorry, but that's all I can say. It's difficult to tell you what to expect. But you'll see what I mean."

I stood slowly. I didn't feel like seeing anyone, least of all the man's reclusive brother. I wanted to get off the island. That was it.

Anubis went on: "My advice, grab some biltong in the kitchen. He *loves* dried meat. There's not much biltong up here but every now and again I make some out of one of the older goats. It holds for longer than cooking it. Not as good as ku-ku-kudu or ostrich, of course, but he likes it. That'll soften him up."

"Look," I said, standing. "Thank you. For . . . taking care of me. Bringing me in. I'm grateful. But—"

As I got to my feet, the room began to spin. The sound of a choppy ocean crashed into my head. I felt myself losing my balance, felt the chicken dinner rising in my gut. I grabbed the arm of the couch and hunched over. For a moment it felt as if

I was back on the raft, a violent body memory. Anubis grabbed me and held me up.

"You okay?" he asked.

I nodded because I knew I'd throw up if I said a word. I took a deep breath.

"I'm fine. I need to rest," I managed. "Lie down somewhere."

"Okay. Come on, Raft Man," he said, making his way to the door. "Let's get you out before you're s-s-sick on my floor."

We waited until my seasickness lessened, then walked down the corridor to my room. I noticed the door of another room was standing slightly ajar. I could hear a faint and rhythmic breathing coming from within.

"That's my father's room," he said. "You shouldn't go in there, he needs his rest."

I could just make out the ghostly shape of an old man lying in a bed in the darkened room. He was covered in a white sheet and attached to an IV drip on a long steel pole. I felt my stomach lurch and steadied myself on the door frame, Anubis right behind me. I could see the man better now. He looked older than I'd imagined from the story, by at least fifteen or twenty years, but then I knew nothing about the father or how sick he really was.

"What's wrong with him?"

"An acute case of shitty luck," Anubis said.

I turned from the door, following the young man back along the corridor. He took me to a new bedroom, not the one in which I had been bound. It was neat, clean and basic, with a window overlooking the ocean.

"Sleep tight, Raft Man," he said. "I'll wake you in the morning. You've got a baa-*baa-bathroom* through that door there." Then he closed the door. I stood and listened to the discomfiting sound of a key turning as he locked me in.

Before I finally got to sleep, I thought about Anubis's story (that was Moneta's story) and wondered how such "sharing" could occur at all. His brother knew about Moneta; she'd had Anubis's memory. There was the incredible unlikelihood of having actually *met* both owners of that one memory. Was that in itself a coincidence, or had I been told the one precisely *because* I'd soon hear the other? Had Moneta known, either consciously or subconsciously, that I'd find myself on Anubis's island?

Nothing added up.

In the morning, I was awakened by Anubis shaking my shoulders. When I opened my eyes, he was already at the door, encouraging me to get up and join him outside.

I climbed out of bed and bent over to put on my shoes. A warm beam of early morning light filtered in through the windows. I pulled the blanket back over the bed and headed back along the corridor.

The door to the father's room was open and I glanced inside. This time he was awake, staring back at me with glassy eyes. I closed his door and continued to the end of the corridor.

As I stepped out onto the wooden deck, the fresh morning air hit me like an icy wave. The house was higher above sea level than I'd imagined, truly at the summit of the island, looking down on the thick green jungle stretched out like a tattered rug, the thin outlying lip of white beach, and, all around, the infinite blue ocean.

I slid my hand over the wooden rail and walked along the deck towards a narrow footbridge. The roughly constructed bridge hung over a twenty-foot drop into dark undergrowth before connecting with a second wooden deck surrounding another wooden house. On the roof of the second house there was an archaic satellite dish strangled by thick vines. I couldn't tell if it was working. The entire house was draped in vines embellished with bright pink flowers, each like a pair of pouting lips poised for a deadly kiss. The sight of these plants unsettled me. They crawled along the gutter, under the window frames and through the gaps in the wood, ensuring a firm stranglehold before consuming all.

Anubis was standing at the other end, gripping the rail and breathing deeply and dramatically.

I crossed the bridge and joined him.

"This view," he said. "This view. Makes you just wanna break into song, doesn't it?"

I leaned over the rail. The support beams of the deck vanished into the tangled canopy of trees below. Staring down onto the top of the jungle reminded me of my recurring dream: following the trail of a red shoe into that tree in the clouds . . .

"And to think," he said, "all this is one big floating pile of shit. You know how many plastic bottles it takes to keep an island afloat? Millions of the bastards. And that beach sand, that soft sand right there . . ." He pointed and I looked up. "Millions of shards of finely shredded electronics, my friend. Yesterday's must-haves. Computers, palm-plates, puh-puh-*plasma* TVs and tablets and Senso-sheeting and thinkscreens and smartphones—all the toys people *buh*-buh-bought and threw out and bought and threw out."

"But hey." He shrugged. "Now it's home. Home-sweet-home-on-a-mound-of-crap. And she may be one tempestuous bitch if you ever get your grubby paws down in her bush, but she floats just fine."

A cold wind rushed over the deck. A set of hanging metal chimes jingled and an old-fashioned cockerel weather vane perched on a wooden post spun clockwise, then back again.

"That's why we need to defend her," he said.

"From what?"

"From them," he added, and pointed into the distance. He was pointing at the smaller island I had seen the day I arrived. It was much closer now—only a kilometre or two from the beach, by my guess.

"I saw that from the beach," I said. "Getting closer all the time. Are we going to them or are they coming to us?"

"They're coming. They're coming and they want this island."

"Who are they?"

"Pirates."

"*Pirates?*"

"There are a number of these islands, Raft Man. People living off the map. Off the grid—I mean, if there still *was* a grid. But we're out on the high seas now, Captain! And this is the prize. They'll be here soon, probably by to-tomorrow. But boy, they're gonna be in for a big surprise. *Nobody* gets very far up the jungle, and neither will they."

"If they do?"

"If they do! If they do, well . . ." Anubis turned and smirked. "Let's just say the surprises don't stop at the plant life. But I can see you're a man who understands what it means to pruh-pro*tect* the thing you love, don't you? You know what a man has to do to stake his claim, to fight and defend the thing he values most. I mean, helping that woman escape the island, that must have taken a couple of cuh-cuh-*cannon*balls, am I right? But you did what you had to. Just like we will."

He slapped my shoulder. "But we've got time before the show. And you should see my brother. I insist. Go down to the cabin and hear what he's got to say. He's a lot easier to understand these days—most days, anyway. He'll welcome a visit. I've had lots less time to chat with him recently."

"I see."

"Take this."

Anubis gave me a small plastic bag filled with sticks of dried meat. I didn't understand the sense of urgency. My body was still recovering and I was in no mood for introductions. I wondered if I was being called on to pay some kind of debt for my accommodation.

"I'm still not feeling very well," I began to excuse myself. "I'm not sure now is a good time."

"I get it. But it's worth it. You'll wanna hear him out. Believe me."

I looked back out to the approaching island, reluctantly agreed, and asked where his brother's cabin was located.

"Down in the jungle. Not far from here. Take the st-stairs at the end of the deck. Follow the path until you reach a fork. At the fork, go right. You'll see his cabin. Knock. Go in. It's okay. He's expecting you."

"Expecting me?"

"I mentioned you and he said he knows you," Anubis said. "How's that for a strange twist of fate? He saw you talking to

Moneta. He remembers you sitting there and drinking tea while she told you her story. You had no idea what you were guh-guh-*getting* yourself into, did you? It was all over your face. He said that too. You didn't realise you'd been selected for something more than moving a few pots around. So whaddya know, Raft Man, you washed up here for some reason after all."

Anubis said I should leave before the sun rose any higher. He assured me it would take no longer than two or three minutes to get there. I wouldn't have to contend with killer vines and malicious plant life either. Those flesh-eating plants were making their way to the top of the hill—that was a fact, according to Anubis—and getting closer every day, but they were not near enough to present any immediate threat. One day, they would. One day they'd grow up the hill and weave through the windows and doors of the house, drawn by hot human blood. But that could take months—or years, even; he didn't know. He made it sound inevitable, and, bizarrely, as if he was open to the idea—of being suffocated in his sleep by a creeper and then promptly consumed. Almost as if it would be an honour.

But for now, the route between the deck and the cabin was a manageable one. I wasn't certain whether he could be believed, but I also refused to accept that I might be trapped in that house. If I didn't have the courage to walk at least a few paces, I wouldn't have the courage to go anywhere at all.

He gave me the directions and I walked past him to the stairs. The stairs descended into the trees and finally rested on uneven ground, webbed by the thick, exposed roots of the jungle trees. I glanced back at Anubis standing on the deck. He was eyeing the approaching island the way a vulture eyes a crawling, starving animal.

The jungle was dark, nearly all light blocked out by the foliage. I made my way through the thick trees and over puddles of stagnant water. I ventured deeper into the jungle until I was surrounded by a wall of wet, densely green plant life. A soft breeze whistled through the jungle as if each leaf was the string of a large musical instrument.

I could no longer see the stairs behind me, but I followed the directions Anubis had given me. I reached the fork and turned right, but after ten minutes of walking I feared I had taken a wrong turn somewhere.

I was lost.

I circled back and tried another route, but couldn't recognise the twisted and tortuous space behind me. The ground held none of my tracks. I should have left markers—coloured rags, stones, a trail of breadcrumbs. I wiped my forehead and looked up, but the weak light straining through the leaves did nothing to help.

And then, as if it had been slipped into the jungle while my back was turned, the cabin was suddenly there—tucked between the trees, hidden by the green blanket that snaked over its walls and its rooftop. It was a wooden cabin with a flat roof and a yellow paint-flaked door, greenery woven into the neat logs of its walls. A single square window sat beside the door, and beyond that the house was filled with darkness so thick that if I were to open that yellow door, I imagined it would spill like a crude oil—spill out and drown everything.

I walked to the door and knocked. The door was hollow and rickety, sagging loose from its hinges. On the third knock it creaked gently open.

Still, there was no sound.

"Hello?"

I stepped inside. The floor and walls had been painted black. This wasn't just darkness. It was blackness. A place not simply devoid of light, but repellent of it.

I closed the door behind me and stood for a moment, hoping my eyes would adjust. They didn't. My other senses took charge. There was a strong smell of mildew and wet wood. At first I thought the cabin was empty, but then I heard a slight shuffle and the soft huff of shallow breathing.

"I've brought you biltong," I said. I heard something scuttle across the floor—a lizard, a large spider, or something else—and took a step back. Warily, I held out the biltong, and felt it get snatched from my grip. I felt nothing else: no touch of skin, no warmth of a body's presence.

"I can chew a piece for ages," a slow and wispy voice came from the dark. "Until I've gotten every last bit of flavour out of it. And then I spit it out—or swallow it."

I heard him tear off a piece of biltong with his teeth, and then I heard him begin to chew, and I imagined him working his jaws, coating the hard meat with saliva. He crunched and snapped his way through the biltong. The grunt of his chewing slowly dwindled to a soft, wet mashing until finally there was the sound of noisy swallowing.

"I had a dream last night," the whispery voice floated towards me. "Nothing special. I dream every night. But I'll tell you anyway, since you're here, and the memory of a dream only has the lifespan of the day that follows. Did you know that? After that it's gone for good. You may remember the events of it two or three days later—sort of—but it's almost impossible to relive it in your mind. So, if you'll permit, I'll pay my respects to last night's dream before tonight comes by, *chew the flavour* out of it, so to speak."

"Okay."

The brother in darkness paused a moment and then spoke:

"I saw a thin naked man with a big beard dancing barefoot on a bed of hot coals. He had two big eyes and two rows of large white teeth, grinding into each other. I asked why he was dancing on those coals, and he said, *Dance. Dance like a drunken orangutan. But whatever you do, do not mistake the tolerance of your moving feet as a reason to stop . . . because you'll burn, brother. You'll scream and you'll burn in the agony of your arrogance. And brother, he says to me . . . he says, brother, have these feet been* burned."

There was pause. I didn't think it was a joke, but it had ended with some kind of a punch line. A bit like a lit firecracker that hadn't gone off. I waited for something to be added, but when nothing came, said, "I see."

The darkness hung just as thick and I knew how powerless I was, sure he could see me with eyes that had grown accustomed to that blackness. I wanted to turn and leave, but I had to relax. I wasn't going anywhere in a hurry, it seemed, and these were my dubious hosts.

"It doesn't really have to be this dark, does it?" I asked. "Surely you can handle more light than this."

"Yes. I probably can," he whispered. "But who's content to spend a life *tolerating*? At least this way I feel I've made a choice. If the light won't have me, let the dark. It's proven to be a far more giving medium, anyway. The light, you learn, is happier to whore itself."

"Your brother said I should speak to you. He said you might have something to tell me."

"In a minute. Tell *me* something first."

"Like what?"

"When you're in your darkness, what do *you* see?"

The wind had picked up outside, and I could hear it beating against the sides of the cabin.

"I don't understand."

"When the lights go out, what do you see?"

"I don't know, less than I used to, I suppose," I replied. "But there's always my son. I see his face."

"Andy."

Anubis must have told him.

"Yes," I said. "I'm looking for him."

"And Andy's been gone a long time."

"Yes."

"And you have no idea where he could be?"

"No."

"That's unfortunate for you," the ghostly voice sighed. "An idea would help."

There was a silence at that point, drawn out by the heavy darkness, as if it could last forever.

"Do *you* have an idea?" I asked, entertaining the notion that this man could somehow help me.

There was a faint patter of footsteps and I wondered if the twin was walking the floor in circles, tapping his finger on his chin. What else was in the room? Was it empty? Was there a bed, a toilet? A shelf of unreadable books and a vase of dead flowers? Could this place really be his home?

"I have a few," he replied. "But ideas are funny things. They're not trinkets. You can't hold one in your hand or bottle it. They're like atoms. Atoms are always moving, vibrating, giving an object the illusion of solidity, of forming a single object at all. But the truth is, they vibrate against every other atom in the universe. Ideas vibrate against each other too. To give an idea its due, you have to understand that one idea is connected to all the others. No one idea stands alone. So all I can give you . . . are some vibrating atoms of an idea. But to understand what it is I'm going to tell you, you're going to need to see the bigger picture. I'm going to explore my options of explaining it to you and you're going to explore your options of understanding. And there *are* options. An idea, after all, is not a simple thing." He paused, then said: "Come back tomorrow. At the same time. I'll tell you what I know, and maybe by tomorrow I'll know a little more. In the meantime, you have to think long and hard about how much you're willing to hear.

"And thank my brother for the biltong," he added. "It's our favourite, you know."

The voice stopped. As did any sounds of movement.

I turned and felt for the front door. The light of day slipped into the room, but still, nothing was revealed. The darkness of the cabin ran deep within, and I could see no back wall—only a vast amount of empty space.

I left the cabin and walked back in a strange daze. I turned to get one last look at the little wooden structure with its lone occupant. The door of the cabin banged softly on its crude frame. The darkness hung densely behind the tiny window.

I walked slowly along the crooked path, to the point where the path had forked, finding my way to the stairs between the trunks of trees with unconscious ease.

I held the rail and ascended through the leaves, and stepped back on the wooden deck with the bright and sunny view.

Anubis was no longer there, but the weather vane spun on its post. The vines along the walls of the house shook their many pink and impatient lips. I looked out to the ocean. The island was even closer than before, its sliver of beach almost touching our own. I stood at the rail and watched it for a while. From where I was I could see no signs of anyone.

Pirates. What kind of pirates were these people? A large family? A band of businessmen? A tribe of some kind? A rugged crew and a whip-cracking captain with a hook for a hand? And just how much did they know of the botanical death trap they were about to enter?

I crossed over the narrow hanging bridge and hopped onto the deck of the first house. Beneath the deck, the vast blanket of the trees swayed in the wind. All I could think of was the *strangeness* of my visit to the cabin. It hung in my mind, insistent and urgent.

I could not shake the sense I was being manipulated, one moment being shepherded by one bizarre brother and the next by the other, a prop passed between deranged performers in a type of twisted theatre I didn't understand.

I shook myself free from the thought and stared into the distance. Clouds were pulling together on the horizon, the thin dark line at their base foretelling rain. I left the deck and went inside. There was still no sign of Anubis. I passed along the corridor and made my way to the tiny bathroom at the far corner of my bedroom.

The bathroom was cramped but sufficient. Light slipped in through the gaps in its wooden walls. A grubby tub stood in the corner, a brown puddle of undrained water at the centre. A dying hornet floated on its back in the puddle, kicking its crooked black legs in the air, its misshapen wings hanging drenched and torn and useless at its sides. It was the only other creature I had seen on the island . . .

(*The hornet landed on his face and stung him,* Moneta's voice drifted into my head, delicate and feathery. *He shuddered, froze in his spot, and shrieked. I looked up. A second hornet was spiralling down from above towards him, and a third. Soon there were hundreds, literally hundreds of them, descending from the trees and engulfing him as he flung his arms out madly and let off a high and unearthly screech)*

I rinsed my face under the tap. I looked into the cracked and spotty mirror against the wall and rubbed the baggy skin beneath my eyes. I could hardly recognise myself. I couldn't remember the last time I'd seen my face. I looked older. Craggy. Exhausted. My eyes were set deep in their sockets. My beard climbed high up the sides of my cheeks, dark and rough. Deep lines scored my forehead. There was a cut beside my nose, already dried and scabbed, and the insides of my ears were thick with grime. I ran my hands through my hair, pulling the long brown strands behind my ears, and dried my hands on a grimy hand towel hanging over the pipe that looped beneath the basin.

I left the bathroom and made my way back down the corridor.

The father's door was open, and once again I looked inside. He was awake, staring off into the far corner of the room. He didn't seem so much in a state of serenity as surrender—a man who had, in some indeterminable way, given up on a long fight. He turned his head and stared at me without blinking.

"Who are you?" he asked.

"My name's Kayle."

He looked me up and down.

"How'd you get here?"

"I—"

"Well, hey-hey." A cheerful voice came from the corridor. Startled, I turned to see Anubis standing at the entrance to the kitchen, smiling at me.

"Hey," I said, and when I looked back at the old man, his head was turned again, his gaze on the opposite corner of the dim room, as if we hadn't conversed at all.

Anubis approached me, slid between me and the door and pulled it shut.

"He needs his rest," he said. "Come on. Give me a hand."

At the back of the house there was a surprisingly large stretch of flat, grazed land. The perimeter of the land had been fenced with rough logs of wood. Wire-mesh divided a cordoned area into small squares. In one square were chickens and hens, stomping their thin, reptilian feet, clucking and putting on a show for each other. In another section, there were a few goats. The rest of the closed land had been reserved for vegetables—rows of onions, carrots, beets, beans, potatoes, pumpkins and tomatoes—as well as tufts of herbs. Rusted tools hung on nails against the back wall of the house, dented metal buckets hid in uncut grass. A rough lean-to kept a stack of firewood and bags of seed dry. Everything, it seemed, ticked at a cool and languid pace.

It was an impressive subsistence farm, certainly, and Anubis seemed to be the only one on the island capable of attending to it. We were standing in the chicken coop. I'd passed him the large sack of seed I'd carried from the wooden shelter and was now watching as he fed them. They jerked their heads towards the food and then turned away, and then back, almost as if they didn't believe it was real.

"So you went to see my buh-bub-brother," Anubis said, folding the top of the thick woven bag and tucking it into itself. "He tell you anything worthwhile?"

"He told me to come around tomorrow," I replied. "He mentioned a dream he had, but I'm not sure why."

"Mm. Dreams. He likes his dreams."

He stood, arched his back and twisted his neck to loosen his muscles. He grabbed the seed and carried it to the side of the fence, and dusted his hands together.

"It was really dark," I said. "And he's not blind, is he? Does he really live there?"

"Pretty much. He knows his way around in there, and I ruh-ruh-reckon he can see way more than either of us ever could. But he's not scared of the light—"

"He's resentful of it," I finished his sentence, and he nodded. He ushered me out of the coop and closed the warped wire gate behind him.

"So you gonna go?" he asked.

"Go where?"

"Back to the cabin."

"I think so."

"He intrigued you," he said. It may have been a question, but it came across as a statement.

"He did."

"Me too, sometimes. But intrigue doesn't keep you fed. Muddying it out on a mound of chicken shit, that keeps you fed. I'm not sure he always gets that."

We walked together back to the house. He rinsed his hands in a trough of water at the back door and patted them down on his pants.

"They're gonna be here," Anubis added. "The pirates. They'll probably make their way into the jungle by noon tomorrow, if I were to guess. An hour later there'll be a mound of well-fed corpses down there. You'll never see anything like it in your life, Raft Man. And that," he said, opening the door and waving me in, "is what intrigues *me*."

For the rest of the day I could not shake the feeling there was something I was not being told. There was Anubis, seemingly taking care of the workings of the island, and then there were the other two, content to only haunt it. The question was why any of them were there at all. Were the three estranged occupants content to simply drift purposelessly across the ocean, until the trees grew into the windows and under their doors, impatient to appease their appetite for fresh flesh? What had happened to the ship that had brought them there? Had Anubis never made his way back down to the shore to look for it, to try to get away?

That night, I had dinner with Anubis at the kitchen table, but we said almost nothing to each other. After dinner I went straight to bed. My curiosity about the brother in the cabin had grown. Although I wasn't convinced it would be worth returning (regardless of what I had told Anubis), I felt once again the pull to decide, a strange persuasion of whispers and voices from an external source.

When I awoke the next morning, my door was unlocked. I came out onto the deck but Anubis was not there. The other island, however, was right against the beach. It was too far away to see any detail; no people yet. But they had arrived—for better or for worse.

Finally, I made my way back down the stairs and into the jungle. The cabin was easier to find this time, but still as mystically odd as it had been the day before.

I knocked on the yellow door, it creaked open, and I stepped back into darkness.

The door swung closed behind me. Eventually the soft voice said: "There's an armchair to your left. Please. Have a seat."

I felt my way to the armchair and settled into it. It was surprisingly comfortable.

"There was once a king," said the same voice from the day before. "A mortal king who had been cursed by the gods with an insatiable hunger. One day, fed up with his curse, he raised his fist to the heavens in anger. As he did, he noticed how delicious and plump his own fist was, and, giving in to his hunger, proceeded to eat himself, including his own mouth, which, of course, he had to leave for last."

"Your brother says you can see the future."

"Does he?"

There was another drawn out silence, and then, as I sat comfortably in the dark before that unseen man, the unearthly voice went on . . .

Becoming God

My brother doesn't really understand what it is I can do. He has an idea, but he doesn't really know. I can see the future sometimes. There is no limit to what I can see and no control over when I see it. Sometimes I see billions of years into the future. Sometimes only three or four minutes. There is no period in the future that is any more or less available to me. Time doesn't work like that.

The future is always only the future, whether it's thirty seconds away or thirty million years, but I'm able to form an insightful if somewhat incomplete model of what I see. I'm not sure, though, from whose perspective it is that I see these future happenings. I've seen the earth once the sun has burned itself out and this planet has become nothing but a cold and barren graveyard, so these can't be my revelations, but they feel guided, focused in some way, as if this consistent perception of events is coming from somewhere.

But that's too far and too much to think about. There's no need to go into it right now, because it is a futile exercise for both of us. We are people in the present, with problems of the present. So what can I tell you? To give you your "idea," the idea that has been promised, I should mention that over my travels I have seen the outcome of human evolution. I've gone to enough points in the future to have quite a clear picture of how we turn out, and it is fascinating. This picture is not only of the end of Man, but of the birth of God.

God, you see, has always been the benchmark. Every endeavour we've undertaken has been to acquire the characteristics and abilities of God—or rather, the concept of God that we conveniently created for ourselves like a kind of beautified self-portrait.

Well, there's no need for further conjecture, no guesswork needed. I have seen how it happens. I have looked into the future and I have seen how it turns out for us. How we become God. If you are interested, I can do my best to explain what I have managed to puzzle together.

I cannot guarantee this is information you should be allowed to know but I think you *should* know it because of someone you will meet one day soon. Someone who will put you to the test in order to find your son. He may try to deceive you, as he does all people of the indomitable *now*, and you should be prepared for that meeting, when it comes.

So I'll tell you.

Based on what I have seen, as we evolve, the first thing to occur will be the merging of our senses. Humans of the future look very different from us, and it took me a while to understand why. After enough trips into the years ahead, meeting a few of these future humans, I ended up formulating a hypothesis of my own.

It goes as follows: for now we see with our eyes, hear with our ears, and so on—and this is sufficient for our most basic needs. Sufficient, but not perfect. Our brains need to build bridges between these separate organs to form a coherent "picture." Since we hear and see with different organs, there are still limitations to the complexity of the "picture" we can see.

Over time, however, as our processing abilities increase, so will the demands made of our senses. The bridges between our senses will shorten and vanish altogether. One day it will be harder to distinguish between the eye and the ear. We will see and hear with the same organ, and this will make perception more accurate. The same will apply to the rest of our senses.

Our separate organs will evolve into a single sensory organ that sees, hears, tastes, touches and smells at once. Perception will be amplified. The need for the compartmentalisation of the body will be diminished. Eventually, the organs of our body will unify to become a single, shapeless mass of intellect and consciousness, capable of absorbing information, processing and communicating on multiple levels and in all directions.

We will then close the gap between our own individual being and the beings of others. Communication, after all, is a form of connection, and as with the bridges between the eye and ear, the spaces between ourselves must shorten too, before vanishing altogether. Two minds will merge into one body, and then three in one. And then four, and five, and so on, until all of humankind is a meta-entity—an Argos of supreme consciousness. Later, we will evolve out of the prison of matter itself, like the stem from a buried seed, until we become a matter-less, all-powerful, all-knowing consciousness.

After all, life is the will to connect.

And this will is all life has over chaos. If you offer nothing to life you will be trimmed like the fat from a piece of meat. Similarly, if you choose to sit on a throne—to monopolise—you are doomed to stagnation, to collapse back into chaos.

This is obvious, isn't it?

And yet this remains the simplest and most misunderstood truth of all.

Yes and no

"**A**nd I have seen this. In here. In the darkness and in my dreams. This process has happened before in previous universes and this will happen again. I've seen how this will happen. Or rather, how this is *supposed* to happen. I say 'supposed to' because something else has happened. Something I could not foresee. There's been an intervention."

"Day Zero."

"Precisely," the voice returned. "The process was stunted. We're being held back from evolving."

I sat up in my seat and leaned forward. I could now make out the faintest silhouette of a man before me. "But why?" I asked.

"Why?" the figure said. "I cannot say. I do not know the motives of the forces that exist, only what I see of our future. You've seen it in your dreams as a large glowing ball in the sky. Others have too. But for whatever reason, this glowing orb is wilful. Why Day Zero occurred, I cannot tell you, because I do not know. Remember, my visions are fragmented and what I know has been pieced together from mere glimpses of what is to come. But there is someone who *does* know. A man. I've seen him once or twice in my visions and he sees me. It is the only time someone in my visions has been aware of my presence—

watching me watch him at various points in the future. I don't know how he is capable of doing this, but he is."

"A man? What man?"

"He is a man who scares me, I must admit. It is also worth mentioning that I know he is here, on earth with us right now, in *our* time, and he has the answers to questions few of us have bothered even asking."

"Do you know who he is?"

"I know who he is, but I do not know exactly where he is. I have no reason to actively seek him out. I don't care enough to be bothered. But you do, don't you? Oh yes. You have a reason to find this man. Because if anyone knows, he will know how you may find Andy. Whether he's willing to tell you where the boy is, I don't know, but he does know. And there's enough courage and will in your heart to at least try."

"So who is he?"

The voice stopped. Outside, the jungle was sounding strangely disturbed. Without my sight, I could hear the slightest of sounds: the rhythmic drip of water on the wooden floor, the scuttling of a small *something*, the moaning of the wood being pushed and pulled by the wind.

"Our story starts many years ago, Kayle," the voice continued. "With the disappearance and reappearance of Chang'e 11. The crew of that ship returned from a place they could not explain. Nine of them came back. Not long after that, one passed, and there were eight. And seven. And six . . . until finally there were only two. Their names were Shen and Quon. The last two survivors of an ill-fated mission to the stars.

"One of them knows the whereabouts of your son and his name is Quon. He is the one who sees me in my dreams. Will he help you? Who can say? He won't let me know. But to find this man, you must find the family of his old friend, Shen. They are the only ones who can lead you to Quon.

"To find Shen's family—and remember this is a vision that was passed on to me—sail through a sea of rooftops until you come across a burning house. Follow the road along this burning house. At the end of the road you'll find the nicest family ever made. They will point the way."

He paused.

"That's it?"

"I'm afraid for now that's all I can tell you. I wish I could tell you more. I am still in the dark, you know. But sometimes I think it's no darker in here than it is out there. That is what my brother understands the least, although the truth is he doesn't need to know what I know to do what he does. He knows only what he needs to know. The habit of selective forgetting and living by convenient truths, Kayle. It is a dangerous habit. One we have all entertained for far too long. But on your journey, remember this always and above all: the thing you see and know is not the true nature of the thing. You are but a dream of yourself, a dreamer in a dog's reality.

"I really do look forward to meeting again when we are one, Mr. Jenner. When we're free, and in the light."

At that point, the brother of the darkness stopped talking. I took it as my cue to stand and exit. As I did, however, his voice shot out again.

"There is one other thing," he said to me. "Before you go."

I had my hand on the door handle. Through the window I could see the shaking leaves, the filtered light of the sun, and the black cut-out of a seated man.

He went on: "You don't have to fear what it is you secretly fear the most, because you have no need to fear it."

"And what fear would that be?"

"That your memories are deceiving you. And that your son is not really your son."

My stomach lurched. It was as if he had reached his pale hands down my throat and pulled some true and terrible thing from the depths of me. He was right. After everything I had heard, this was the very possibility that was tormenting me. What if everything I thought I knew was a lie, as it had been for Moneta and Jai-Li? What if Andy wasn't my son at all?

"Like I said," he went on. "You have nothing to worry about. Trust me, on this above all else, I've been told. Andy is waiting for your arrival. But now that I've told you all of this, I'd very much appreciate it if you'd do one thing for me."

"What's that?"

"Would you tell my brother I am sorry."

"For what?"

The voice sighed.

"I do love my brother. He's taken good care of me. But as I once overheard in a conversation between two men sitting inside a beached whale: *If you come to the realisation you are a mistake in this world—will you have the courage to go willingly, to remove yourself of your own accord, or will you stubbornly remain, in stupid denial and against the will of nature?'* Very interesting thought, from a very interesting dream."

I remembered those words. I remembered that dream. It had been *my* dream, the one in which I had spoken with Jack Turning.

"Please remember that," he said. "Tell him I'm so sorry; there are some things I can no longer permit in good conscience. That's just the way things are."

"I'll tell him."

There was another sigh. "Very kind of you. Very kind of a very kind man. Now, if you'll excuse me. You have your idea. Your few vibrating atoms. And I need my sleep."

And then there was nothing. No sound at all. He had returned to the darkness, and the darkness to him.

I opened the door and stepped back into a bright and baffling world.

I sat on the wooden deck by myself and watched the other island in the distance. All around, the jungle moved with the wind like an animal slowly waking from some long and dreamless sleep. The grey cloud was still growing far out over the ocean but overhead the sun was beating down. There was still no activity down below, no sign of anyone from the other island.

I thought about the man in the cabin's words: his prophecy, I told myself, as difficult as it was to accept that it could be a prophecy at all.

A sea of rooftops. A burning house. Shen. Quon. And the nicest family ever made. With nothing else to guide me, I wanted to believe him, wanted to accept his advice, but beneath the mantle of my hopes stirred the molten rock of dread. I had washed up on the shore of that place bound on a raft, but the relief of my arrival was gone. All I could think was that on this new "raft," something terrible had been allowed to grow. The carnivorous trees. These people, marking time until the trees grew wild and uncontrollable enough to take them . . .

Finally, I shook my head and stood up. The brother of light was nowhere to be seen. I supposed he was getting himself prepared for these "pirates."

I turned from the deck and went into the house. I grabbed a cup from the kitchen and poured myself a glass of water, which I drank quickly. Then I walked back along the corridor towards my bedroom. I needed to lie down for a while, close my eyes and give my mind a chance to rest.

Coughing.

I stopped. The sound was coming from the father's room. The door was standing slightly ajar and I peered in. The father was awake, twisting his shoulders, hawking hoarsely.

I glanced down the corridor, checked the narrow window that revealed a part of the deck, and turned back to push open the door.

The man was still on the bed beneath the white sheets, head on a flat pillow. He was a gaunt skeleton of a man with skin like leather.

In the corner of the room an old television showed nothing but static. There hadn't been a signal in years now, not since Day Zero, and I wondered whether the television had ever shown anything besides those chaotic speckles of snow fuzzing in and out of existence.

The father's cough went on, an endless wheezing. I approached his bedside and propped his pillow up behind his head. His thin grey hair was glued to his forehead by a film of thick sweat.

There was a glass of water on a table next to his bed. I held up his head and put it to his lips. He took a sip and released a foul sigh. He closed his eyes, taking a moment to calm his laboured breathing, then he turned his head and looked at me.

Without warning, his hand snapped out from under the sheet and grabbed my wrist. He tightened his grip and pulled, urging me to lean in. Cautiously, I did. He lifted his head off the pillow and brought his face nearer to mine.

His cracked lips opened to speak: *"Run."*

Startled, I pulled back. He held his grip, but with the jerk of his arm came a new sound. The rattle of metal on metal.

I looked down at his pale and spotted hand and carefully lifted the sheet.

I shuddered. His wrist was shackled by an enormous rusted handcuff. It was attached to a rusted chain which in turn was attached to the frame of the bed.

Suddenly there was a great distance between me and every other object in the room. It was as if my mind was fleeing the scene before my body could take the chance. He wasn't bedbound because he was dying; he was a prisoner.

"You don't know," he said in a crackling whisper, "you don't know where you really are. You don't have a clue what's going on here."

I wrenched my hand from his grip, began to back up slowly towards the door. He lay limp on his bed, coughing, exhausted, frustrated. All the time I could hear his chains clanging beneath the sheets.

"He can't know you're in here." Desperate gasps escaped as he spoke.

"Why are you chained?"

"Leave. *Run . . .*"

The man began to cough again, waving his hand weakly for me to go. I hurried from the room.

Bouncing back into the bright corridor, I was suddenly aware that everything I thought I knew was wrong. I was dizzy and the walls and the door leaned in on me, the way an image on a page warps one last time before flames burn it to ash.

I forced myself to stand upright, slowed my pace to a casual walk. My eyes remained wide and alert—I was on the lookout now—but my heart! My heart hammered in my chest.

I closed my eyes, breathed in deeply, then stepped out onto the wooden deck.

Anubis was standing at the rail with his back to me, holding a large dark object. He looked over his shoulder and smiled.

"Hey," he said.

"Hey," I replied.

As I approached, the object in his hand became alarmingly clear. He was holding a firearm of some sort—a big, black machine connected to a strap over his shoulder.

"Take a look," he said. "It's an ingenious piece of machinery, really. A thousand years ago it would only have tuh-tuh-taken one of these to win a war. It would have seemed like dark magic. The enemy would have simply surrendered out of fear. And respect. They would have bowed on their knees. They would have thought me a god."

"And they wouldn't have known any better," I said. My heart was still beating madly but I kept my voice cool and even, as un-flustered as I could manage.

He held the weapon up over the rail. "You ever use one of these before?" he asked chirpily.

I shook my head. "No . . . You?"

"*No-ope,*" he said, one eye against the sight attached at the top of the weapon. He was poised for a kill, swivelling it on the rail, on the lookout for something moving in that jungle. "Always wanted to though. Always wanted to know how it would feel. Th-*th-thun*-der and lightning in the palms of my hands."

I nodded.

"You see my brother?"

"I did."

"What did he have to say?"

"Not much," I said, a small and unnecessary lie I regretted immediately.

"Really?" Anubis said. He pulled back from the sight and glanced up at me. "That's too bad. Sometimes he's a real help."

"Where'd you get that gun?"

"Where do you think?"

"Left in the jungle after your friends and family were taken?"

"Taken. Good one. I like to th-think of it as an inheritance."

"Is it necessary?"

"Necessary?" he said, and then once more, as if he was still deciding, "Necessary. Well, take a look." Still supporting the weapon on the edge of the rail, he moved his head away, giving me space to look through the telescopic sight. I leaned in. The sight had incredible range. It was pointed at a group of people in the distance—the so-called pirates had landed.

"I thought you said they wouldn't get through the jungle," I said, my eye darting from one distant person to the next. "Why the gun?"

They didn't look like pirates. Just regular people: a couple of women, a slightly overweight man, a younger man carrying sling bags. But then, what were real pirates supposed to look like?

"Well, yes, I did say that. Yes. Except . . ." He turned the gun on the rail. "Look left."

The people on the beach were opening a small crate. Somebody was pulling out what appeared to be black gas masks.

"See what I mean?" Anubis said. "I don't know how, but they know about our island. They've come prepared. And it looks as if they have no intention of *stuh*-stuh-*stopping* for a bit of lunch. Which means, if they push right through the jungle, they'll be here in less than an hour."

"So what's your plan?"

"You mean *our* plan. You're a good man, Kayle. I feel that you understand me. This place. And I'd be honoured to have you at my side when those b-b-bah-bastards come crawling up the hill." He whipped the gun off the rail and held it upright, the barrel resting on his shoulder. "We're gonna come down on them with thunder and lightning, my friend. Light up their little lives in a hail of bullets. But first, we've gotta get you one of these. There's a whole stash in the shed at the back. You can take your pick."

I looked out towards the beach. I needed to go along with this for as long as I could before choosing the moment to make a move.

"Okay."

The man patted me on the shoulder.

"Oh-kay! Okay, Raft Man," he chuckled. "It's a bit of a walk out back, but we'll need ammunition. I've got bullets for Africa but damned if I know which go where. One thing's for sure, they're gonna think we've got an army at our backs!"

I looked back at the house.

"You go ahead. Grab one for me," I said. "I don't know anything about guns. Really. I'll stand post. Keep an eye in case they've brought any surprises of their own."

Anubis thought about it a bit, glanced towards the people on the beach, and grinned.

"Suit yourself," he said.

I said nothing. He smiled, barely noticing the fear creeping beneath my flapping facade. He was clearly too excited to care. He hoisted his gun up and walked over the hanging bridge towards the second deck.

I waited for him to be completely out of sight before darting back into the house. As I ran I thought about what Moneta had said about Burt chasing her in the woods—how she'd feared that his large hand would land on her shoulder at any moment. I glanced behind me. There was no sign of Anubis.

I sprinted down the corridor to the old man's room, gave one last look through the window to make sure Anubis hadn't returned, and went inside. The old man was on his back, eyes closed, breathing loudly.

I rushed to the bedside and shook him by the shoulders.

"Hey," I said. "Wake up."

He opened his eyes.

"Where is he?" he asked.

"Out back. Is there a key?"

The old man shook his head. "I don't know. Maybe. I don't know."

I glanced around the room. There was nothing else in there—at least nothing I could use to help me. The television on a wheeled trolley. A pile of magazines against the wall. A portable electric fan, unplugged, its cord wrapped around the base. Nothing else.

"Talk to me," I said. "Tell me what's going on. Did your son do this?"

"He's not—"

I moved closer. "Not what?"

"He's not my son."

"I don't understand."

His eyes were deep in his narrow skull, a sheen of mucous rimmed his nostrils. A terrible, foetid smell came from his mouth.

"How did you get here?" he asked.

"I washed up on the beach. I was on a raft."

"Did he tell you about his brother?"

"Yes. His twin. I met him in the cabin."

The man sighed and closed his eyes.

"Listen to me," he said, his voice a panicked whisper. "Listen carefully, and when I'm done, leave. Leave immediately." His dark eyes burned. "There is no twin brother."

"What?"

"It's him. Only him."

It wasn't as if his words confirmed something I already knew, but as soon as he spoke I knew he was telling the truth. It was an outrageous notion, but it explained my unease since arriving on the island, slotted neatly into the many discomfiting gaps in the twins' stories. But still I needed to test it. Make sure.

"He told me a story," I said. "A story about his parents. His life. His brother's condition. I *met* the man in the cabin. Why would he go through the trouble? Why would he lie?"

"He isn't lying," the old man said. "He just doesn't know it. He doesn't know and doesn't care to know."

"This isn't making any sense."

"Please, *listen*,' the old man groaned. "*Parts* of what he says are true. His parents . . . the ship. That's what happened. But no one survived that day they came through the jungle. No one survived but him. I found him down there and I took him in. Because this is my island, not his. Always has been."

The man lifted his head and coughed loudly.

"Who are you?" I asked.

He lay back on the pillow and took a deep, calming breath.

"I used to work for Huang Enterprises. A plant geneticist . . . we were weaponising organic environments for . . . for the military . . . but I *left* . . . I left the corporation a long time ago . . . escaped it . . . and I had this island made. A place to get away from a world I didn't understand anymore! That was the idea. All I . . . I wanted, was somewhere safe . . . no fear of anyone disturbing me again. Dear God. I had no intention of deliberately harming anyone. You must believe me! I had signs . . . signs put up on the beach—warning signs about the fruit, the trees, the—"

"I believe you. Go on."

He cleared his throat. "No one came further than the beach . . . and for a while I lived in peace up here . . . with my wife . . . my darling wife . . . There was no trouble at all."

"Your wife?"

"My wife passed away . . . and I was left alone, resigned to living out . . . the remainder of my days here . . . that is, until that day *his* family came to the island—those Borrowed Gun activists on their corporate witch-hunt, looking to find and destroy people like me . . ."

I felt myself slide out of reality. I could see everything—the old man in bed, the walls and the television—but everything was out of sync. Unstable. Ready to spin off into space.

"But the boy. He didn't die. He survived, and I took him in. What could I do? I had no choice. He was by himself. I was all alone. I thought I could raise him. Teach him to take care of this island . . . *Water.*"

I grabbed his mug again and held it to his lips while he took another sloppy sip. When he was done I returned the mug to the table.

"One day something happened—there was a terrible screeching sound in the air—and after that we struggled to remember who we were. Where we were. Any of it. We heard reports—people on the radio. People calling themselves . . . the

New Past, telling us not to worry if we didn't remember. There were answers waiting for us. All we needed to do was make our way to the communes. I tried to steer the island to one of these communes but the boy wouldn't let me. He said . . . he said the voice on the radio was telling lies."

"What made him say that?"

"I don't know," the old man said, and then again, "I don't know. By that time my memories were beginning to return . . . as were his. Only, for him, new memories came back—ones I was sure he hadn't had before."

"The brother."

"Yes. He began to talk about a brother he hadn't mentioned before. I thought he was telling me about a brother from back home somewhere. I didn't realise the brother was now here. With him. In him. Until the night I saw them switch before my eyes."

I rubbed my eyes with the palms of both my hands, struggling to grasp what I was being told. I thought about every moment I'd had with both Anubis and his alleged brother. How long had I been lost in the jungle while trying to find that cabin? Had it been long enough for him to get down there before me?

"It wasn't long before this brother was completely real to him," the man went on. "And then . . . and then things moved from bad to worse. He began to believe I . . . I was his father. I wouldn't let him believe such a thing, of course—I couldn't! That only worsened the situation. He moved between these characters more often. He saw me as a threat . . . I tried to explain that his brother didn't exist . . . and he became paranoid. He cuffed me to the bed . . . took down the warning signs from the beach."

The man coughed again. I put my head around the door and peered through the window. The young man had not yet come back. I moved back to the old man's bedside.

"Please," the old man said. "Turn off that television. It's been playing constantly. It goes on and on . . ."

I went to the corner of the room and shut off the incessant static.

"Sometimes he thinks he was born here," he continued. "Other times he recalls the truth. It's all mixed up in his head."

"What about the pirates?"

"Pirates?" The man looked me straight in the eye. "You are in his fantasy, sir. There are no pirates. You are playing a game with a very sick and dangerous boy . . ."

"So who are they, then?"

"They?"

"There are people making their way into the jungle as we speak. People from another island."

The old man stared at me and his eyes brightened. "They came. Oh God, they came," he said. "They're trying to find me. They *must* find me."

"I don't understand."

"I sent a message on my radio a while ago . . . a plea for someone to find me. But no . . . he won't let them. No, sir. They're a threat. And he'll do whatever it takes . . . with violence if necessary. This is his world now. His rules. And he'll never let it go."

I stepped away from the bed and paced the floor. I had to think. I had to make sense of my predicament and gauge the precise level of threat. I didn't know the island; Anubis did. For all I knew, he was watching us. I had to play the fool for a while longer or I might not have a hope of getting away. I had to be patient—calm and exacting—or I'd never get the upper hand. I'd probably find myself drugged and chained like the man in the bed.

"You must be careful!" the man said, louder than was warranted. "You must!"

I put my hand swiftly across his lips then moved it away. "Keep your voice down," I said. I grabbed the tip of the duvet and wiped his perspiring forehead. I couldn't leave any sign that he and I had been talking. I went back to the television and switched it on. "Just for now," I assured him, studying the rest of the room for signs that I had been there. "A little bit longer. Breathe slowly. Settle down. I'll be back. But you stay quiet. Stay calm."

Then I left the room.

The cloud on the horizon had grown into a grey wall. The wind had picked up over the ocean and the colossal grey wall tucked and tumbled into itself with speed, edging closer to the island like the ominous chariot of Zeus himself. From somewhere far away we heard the first boom of thunder.

"There they go," Anubis said, pointing to the beach below. The group were visible now, small black specks making their journey inland, moving slowly towards us before disappearing beneath the canopies of the jungle.

Anubis stroked the chunky barrel of his weapon. "Poor sods. No idea of the shit-storm to come."

He gave me a shotgun and I held it anxiously. He raised his own weapon, cocked it, and then laid it down on the rail carefully, stretching out his arms and finding his stance. I imagined he'd learned to hold a gun from a movie he'd once seen. It was a dramatic showing of technical flair that didn't ring true, elbows prodding out and the stock not quite aligned with his shoulder, which was surely supposed to absorb the force of a recoil.

The most disconcerting part was his utter conviction. He knew what he needed to do and there were no conflicting voices advising him otherwise. When those people came out on our end of the jungle, having survived its strange tricks, he wouldn't hesitate to finish them off. I could already tell.

"You know," he said, eye against the sight, "I went down to speak to my brother and he told me that he's seen this, all of this, in one of his d-d-dreams." He pulled his head back from the gun and straightened his back. "He's seen how this ends."

And then he turned and smiled assuredly, devilishly, back at me.

"Tell me about your suh-*suh*-son," he said. We'd been waiting on the deck for over an hour. The visitors had gone into the jungle but hadn't yet come out.

All the while Anubis and I had been patiently waiting, mostly in silence, but now cracks were beginning to show in his once cool character. He was becoming impatient. Each time something rustled down in the jungle, he'd whip up his gun to take aim. Realising it was nothing, he'd drop it back on the rail and huff to himself, disappointed and frustrated.

"Tell me about Andy."

I didn't want to tell him about my son. I did want to disarm him, but convinced myself I was waiting for the right moment, uncertain when or if the moment would come. He was clutching his weapon too tightly, itching to squeeze that trigger. I couldn't underestimate that; I couldn't risk having the barrel swing my way.

"I don't know what you want to know," I said.

"I want to know about your son, Kayle."

I rested my own gun on the rail, but only because it was getting heavy.

"I don't remember much about my son."

"You don't?"

"No."

"But you love him."

"Yes."

"And thuh-that's enough."

"It's enough."

I wanted to say nothing at all but that might make him suspicious. He'd know something was wrong. As I thought about what I could tell him, however, I became lost in a dream of finding Andy, what that might be like. For a moment I forgot about the island, the man in the bed, the unsuspecting guests in the jungle. For a moment I wasn't even talking to Anubis.

"I have to believe he can be found," I said. "I don't remember the details of who he is or was, but none of that matters. I love him. I've loved him since the day he was born. I love him *because* he was born. That's why it's enough."

"Yes," Anubis said, nodding. "Perfect. F-f-antastic! That's what I'm talking about."

I resented his reaction. The last thing I needed was his approval, his pat on the back.

"And you really remember nothing about his life?" he asked.

"Like I said. No."

"Huh. So do you . . . duh-*duh*-do you remember anything about *yourself*?"

"Not really."

"Your childhood?"

"I have flashes. But no."

"Heavy," he said, scratching the crown of his scalp. "So really, you don't know what kind of a father you were at all, do you? You go around telling yourself you've guh-guh-got to find him, you *have* to find him, he *needs* to be found . . . but, for all you know, you were the worst father in the world, because you can't remember anyway."

"I suppose."

"But maybe *he* can remember. He could remember all too well. Which begs the question, Raft Man: how can you be sure your son wants to be found by you anyway?"

"I can't."

"What about the rest of your family?"

"I had a daughter."

"What happened to her?"

"She died. A long time ago."

"I'm sorry," he said, sounding sincere. "How?"

"She was hit by a speeding car."

"On purpose?"

"No, but he was speeding. And he didn't slow down. Didn't even stop. Just kept going."

"Bastard! You ever find the driver?"

"No."

"Doesn't that cut you up? That would cut me up."

"Hm."

"And what about their mother? You remember anything about her?"

"No."

"You don't want to find her?"

"No."

"Why not?"

"I just don't."

"Why?"

I sighed. "Because she left us. After Day Zero she . . ."

I paused, fed up with the conversation.

He leered knowingly. "She couldn't remember, could she?"

"No. She wouldn't."

"I didn't say 'wouldn't', Kayle," he added, bending to look through the sight again. "I said 'couldn't'."

I hadn't thought about Sarah in months. Perhaps his insinuation had been right: I *did* resent her—resented her for not being able to remember us. So she'd left that house of strangers, as I supposed anyone eventually would. I'd jumped to the defence of my children so quickly, without allowing that I hadn't given her the proper consideration. I recalled nothing of our early lives, hers and mine. What had we been like together, before the children? What promises had we made and what kind of life had we once dreamt of sharing? What had we known of each other that we later did not even know of ourselves? Were we once in love . . . and how had that felt? The day she left I shut her out of my heart and mind—cancelled my caring—but now, all this time later, there was finally the dimmest sense of remorse. The sense that I had somehow wronged her.

"Don't beat yourself up. That day we forgot everything, that day we went blank, no one came away c-c-clean, did they? But there's no reason to think we're any more f-fuh-*fucked* up now than we've always been. Or any less."

The first few drips of rain began to fall. The sunshine had gone and the world turned grey and gloomy.

I said nothing. With every moment, my patience with him grew thinner. He thought he knew it all. He thought he knew me. I wanted to grab that gun and invert that sneer on his face, remind him he was just a boy and that the world was not a game. It was a starving dog in the corner of a cage. If you prodded it with a stick enough times it would forget you were once its master and make you its meal. I wanted to do all these things, but I didn't. I couldn't. Instead, I kept my eyes on the wall of cloud and prayed that the small group making its way up to the house through the jungle was just as prepared as he was—just as ready for battle.

Another hour passed and still no one had emerged. The rain was falling lightly and steadily. Anubis was pacing the deck now, raking his hands through his hair, wiping the rain and sweat from his face. He slammed the gun back on the rail and pushed his eye against the lens.

"They sh-shuh-*shuh*-should have come out by now," he moaned, staring through the sight, desperate for action. His stutter was thickening and protracting with his growing agitation. "They sh-shuh . . . they *should* be here."

I stood alongside him, on the lookout. The trees of the jungle stood motionless, with only the rain patting on their leaves.

"Something's not right," he said, twitching restlessly. "Maybe they ate the fruit. Maybe not even their stupid gasmasks could help them."

He stood up and slid his gun back off the rail. "They're down there. They're in the jungle. Come. Change of plan. Grab your gun."

He grabbed my arm and pulled me across the deck. He sprinted quickly over the bridge and towards the stairs that spiralled down to the jungle floor. I lifted my shotgun and followed him. He landed on the soil, gun already raised and ready.

We began our walk through the jungle, over the protruding roots and across the muddy patches. The trees hung thickly overhead and the dim light of the day was all but gone. Water trickled down between the leaves—big drops, splashing heavily. Anubis held his gun and stepped carefully forward. I followed alongside him.

"You know," he said, as if he'd been thinking carefully before choosing to speak. "My brother and I have got each other's backs. Always have done, always will. And I don't know what he told you out there in the cabin, but we don't always agree on everything. He has his dreams and his future-telling, but he doesn't know how to live in the-the-the here and now. He doesn't know what it takes to muh-muh-*make* that future he dreams about. His perfect world. He doesn't know how to make the big decisions, get his hands dirty for something he b-believes. Part of me thinks *he* believes my parents got what was coming to them, bringing us all here, but I don't think he realises what they were trying to do. For him. For us. For everyone. Hey, he's my brother. He can see the outcome, but he can't see the way of getting there. I mean, he appreciates what I can do that he can't. Tend to this place. Fix it up. Protect it. And I can't see the things he sees, but if I were you I'd take some of the things he says with a pinch of salt. Just some. Though I can't tell you what, exactly. That's never been as easy."

I walked silently with my shotgun pointed down. I thought about his supposed "brother" in the cabin, and everything that he'd said. Was I still supposed to believe him, even though I now knew everything, all along, had come from this reckless man with his big gun?

"This one time, when we were children," Anubis said, lifting his feet and stepping carefully over the uneven ground, eyes ahead and focused intensely on the dense greenery, "I was walking with my brother down the street. We were coming back from school together. This was before his skin thing. He was always a quiet kid—in his own little world—but he had me, at least. I was the one on lookout, y'know. Scoping for that crazy neighbourhood dog that loved terrorising the local kids. Keeping his pocket money in my pocket in case it fell out of his own. Making sure he didn't walk into an open man-hole or something . . ."

We were now deep into the jungle, the stairs and house long gone, swallowed by the trees. I thought about the old man in the bed. I had to get back there sometime and let him loose.

"But this one afternoon, we were passing the little stretch of road with the shops and bakeries . . . and he said he wanted something to drink. He was thirsty. So I stopped and counted our money. We'd spent our pocket money at school and didn't have enough, and it was at least another ten minutes 'til we reached our house. That's when I told him to wuh-wait outside

Tony's cafe. He stayed on the pavement outside while I went in by myself and pretended to be choosing something to buy. When Tony was looking the other way, I grabbed a coke and slipped it into my blazer pocket.

"I turned to head out the door, and that's when I saw a couple of kids standing outside, talking to my brother. Except they weren't talking. They were hassling him. Circling him like hyenas with these stupid grins on their faces. One of them pushed him, but he didn't budge. I hid behind one of the shelves and decided I wanted to see what would happen next. I kinda needed to know how my twin would handle himself. But he wasn't handling himself. He was being pushed, being called these names. The kids were yelling that our father was a kook, a weirdo, and their fathers had told them he couldn't be trusted.

"For a while, I just stood there, watching this. I wanted my brother to lift a fist, hit one of those bastards back . . . but the guy just wouldn't, y'know? He just took it. He didn't cry or anything. He just hung there like a dumb punching bag. Hung there while I hung *back*.

"I think about it now and I realise maybe I wuh-wuh-*wanted* one of them to hit him. Hit him really hard. Even break his nose. Anything to make him snap and defend himself. And then one kid *did* hit him—a mean blow to the stomach, and he reeled, and I watched him reel back as these jokers kept laughing and pointing and calling our family the neighbourhood freak-show.

"Anyway, when I realised my brother wasn't going to do anything but put himself in the bloody hospital, I finally came running. Beat the hell out of all three of them. Went nuts really. Kicking, hitting, kneeing. And then they scrambled away, and I asked if my brother was okay, if he needed anything.

"And he said he didn't. He wasn't even thirsty anymore. He just wanted to go home. So I drank my stolen coke myself, and we went on walking. We didn't talk about that day again, and those kids, they never again tried their luck. But now, what I remember most about the whole thing was me, watching him from behind the shelf. Just watching. Waiting. Funny, huh?"

Anubis said nothing else and neither did I. I watched him as he spoke. He wore an expression I hadn't yet seen on him— the one of the man who looks back at himself in the past and wonders, *Why on earth did I do what I did? What could have been going through my head at the time?*

We walked for a few minutes more. He stopped and held up his hand, signalling that I too should stop. Then he put his finger to his lips and stepped lightly through the bushes before us. I could hear a rustling from somewhere ahead. I ducked my head and entered the bushes as quietly as I could.

Finally, he sprang forward.

There was a group of people standing in the middle of a clearing. They all looked the same with their matching black gas masks. Anubis thrust forward his gun, lined it with his face, and aimed the barrel at each of them.

The masked men and women held up their hands slowly, not quite surrendering, but showing they had no weapons of their own. Anubis flicked his barrel left to right. He was jittery. Agitated.

One of the masked men approached us.

"We're not here to harm you," he said, his voice muffled by his headgear. "There's no need for that, son. Put it down."

"I've gah-gah-got you now," Anubis said. "All in a row. Seven little ducks."

The masked man took his time to respond.

"We're here for the owner of the island," he said, extending his empty hand. His voice was relaxed. His movements were slow and restrained. "You know who we're talking about. So you can hand over the weapon now, son."

"Fuck you, I'm not your son," Anubis replied. "I'm not your son. Stay right where you are. I'm not k-*kuh*-k-kidding. I'm all outta' kidding." The gun shook in his hand. "You people. The nerve. The *nerve!* Coming here. You really do want everything. All of it. You wanna buh-buh-brand me too? Control us, make us do what you want and act the way you want us to act . . . wuh-*wuh*-with your rules and your lies . . . well, you *won't.* We won't let you own it. We'll never stop fighting. We'll never g-g-give it up. How's that! So you can turn around, turn around and go back to wherever you came from, back to sleeping on a b-b-bed of your own bullshit . . . but this is *my* place. This is where *I* was born. My home. My feet are deeper than the trees. And I'll throw you off the roof of your own bah-bah-bloody *tower* before I let you take this away from me. Oh man. Oh man, oh man. I was right. I was right all along." He swung his gun nervously. "Right all along!"

The entire scene slowed down before me. The raft had passed through a storm, crossed some indeterminable stretch of ocean, and now here I was, between a man with two faces and a group of people with no faces at all—all of them desperate to be understood, to lay claim to a piece of this island of *yesterday's must-haves*.

I raised my gun and pointed it at Anubis. As I pumped the action, he turned to me. His face contorted with the shock of my betrayal.

"It's over," I said, my weapon raised to his chest. "It's over now."

I watched as his faith in me drained away. He stood there despondent, incredulous.

"You?" he said. "Why?"

"This isn't right. You know that."

"Right?" He shook his head. "*Right*? How c-c-can you . . . how can yah-yah-you say that? Look at them. Look! They want it all. They want to take it away from us. Look at everything they've done to the world. They've ruh-ruh-ruined it. They've ruined it! That's what you always said. That's why we came here in the first bloody place!"

"Put your gun down."

"You're so blind. So blind. What did they promise you? They pah-pah . . . they pah-promised you something, am I right? Bought your soul." I felt my heavy gun sagging in my arms and I pulled it back up to take aim. Anubis went on: "I didn't mean that. I didn't mean what I said. But . . . I'm confused. I duh-duh-duh . . . "He looked at me with wide and rage-filled eyes. "We were supposed to save it! We were supposed to take it back. To make the world ours again. Isn't that what you always wanted? No . . . no, no, *no*. We've come too far. We can't let them win!"

"You're right," I said. "We shouldn't. We won't. But it isn't them. And this isn't the way. Put the gun down."

"You left me here!" he shouted, thrusting his finger at me. "You left me in this place to take care of myself. All those nights of sitting in my room listening to you t-t-talk about fighting, fighting, *fighting* . . . you two wanted to save the world, but what about me?"

He tipped up his head and let out a long and furious scream. If there had been birds in the trees they would have flown from their perches. But there were no birds in that jungle. There were no creatures at all in that undesirable place. No foolish creatures but ourselves.

"Your brother," I said. "Your eyes in the dark, remember? He knows. And you know. You've always known. We can do better."

"I was your son!" he cried, and then said again, overcome with anguish, "I was your *son*. And you left me here. You for-gah-gah . . . you *forgot* me. Why?"

I juddered, lowering my gun slowly. My son. Alone. Lost in the world. The words came out before I allowed myself to even consider them: "I'm sorry. I'm so sorry."

Anubis closed his eyes and lowered his head. He was breathing hard. He wiped his runny nose with the back of his hand and sniffed. "And now? Wuh-what now? What! We throw it all in?" he said. "We let them win?"

"No. I don't know what we do. I really don't, Anubis. But maybe the world isn't a place to be *won*."

Anubis eyed me one last time, his face red with rage and wet with tears. He appeared ready to surrender his gun, but instead swung the barrel up swiftly. One of the masked visitors launched himself forward to grab the weapon, but he was too late. Anubis pulled the trigger and released the thunder and lightning he had always hoped for.

Except that something had gone wrong. At the instant he fired, there was an incredible roar and flash of light, and

Anubis fell backwards to the dirt. The group screamed and spun away. I stumbled against a tree. When I looked again, I saw no bullet had been fired. No one had been shot. The gun, the one Anubis had commandeered from the jungle, had been faulty. That doomed machine had come apart like the shell of a detonated bomb. It had torn through his torso, bursting a large red patch of blood and bone from his chest.

He was on the ground, on his knees. The expression on his face was tragic and confused. He looked at me as I edged towards him and knelt next to him. I reached for his hands and gently pried his fingers free of the decimated weapon. The game was over. Anubis looked at me again, expectant, waiting for me to do something. I was supposed to have his back, as any "brother" should.

At that point I remembered: the brother of the dark had asked me to apologise for him. I'd been asked to say sorry for something and I hadn't understood what he'd meant. Now, standing before him—he who had asked me to apologise in the first place—I couldn't bring myself to say the words. Anubis had said his brother had seen how this would end. He'd told me with a big confident smile on his face. Now here he was, on his knees on the ground, dying.

"Is this what your brother saw?" I asked. I had to know. I had to know for the prophecy that been imparted to me: The sea of rooftops. The burning house. A man named Shen. A man named Quon. And the nicest family ever made.

I had to know for Andy.

He lolled his head clumsily, looking down, fascinated by his own bleeding chest. Confusion filled his face, then terror, then disbelief. Then all expression faded and he looked like a boy again, young and ignorant. The stuttering crusader was gone: the calm and enlightened Holy Man too.

He looked up at me slowly and he held out his blood-red palms for me to see, the way a child might after messing with paints. As his hands came up, I was reminded of the story he'd told me himself: the story of the king cursed with insatiable hunger, wagging his fist at the gods before choosing to eat himself into oblivion.

"Yes," he said. "No."

And then he collapsed in the dirt, fresh bloody kill for the trees.

Extracts

(Excerpt from *The Age of Self Primary*)

After the "One Family" proposal was implemented, and family members were separated in the hopes of deterring tribal culture, it was later agreed by the New Past that information itself had been the means of mankind's spiritual and intellectual undoing. Where once it was believed that knowledge would set them free, they now learned that a traditional information-based education only denied them the inheritance of a more profound communal connection. In the same way the Agricultural Revolution had only taught them to distrust that the world would continue to provide for them, thus perpetuating a culture of fear that consequently distanced them from the natural world, a questioning mind only served to separate them from the one and only answer that was: they were already complete by simply existing at all. The blind addiction to questioning had been the true inhibitor during the Age of Self. A question, after all, only leads to more questions. And a dream—whether of the past or the future, beautiful or nightmarish, aspiring or sentimental—only robbed them of the perfect present, the one true medium in which they were capable of evolving into something interminably greater than themselves.

Chang'e 11

S hen Wu woke up to the sound of the phone ringing
beside his bed. It whined like a sick animal, flashing blue,
projecting twisted shadows against the walls of the dark room.

His wife shifted beside him, and he turned to see if she
had been disturbed by the electronic intrusion. She was lying
with her back to him. Her shoulder blades slid beneath her
smooth skin. She groaned and pulled the blanket up around
her small shoulders. Beyond her, long arteries of rain streaked
the window, each drop holding the green and red neons of the
city lights.

"Shen. Private call," he said, clearing his throat. The ringing
stopped. A man's ragged breath reverberated in his inner-ear
receptanode.

"*Wéi* . . . *nǐhǎo,*" Shen said softly, rubbing his eyes and
looking at the time on the phone. It was 1:34 am. "Who is this?"

"Shen? It's Quon," a voice replied.

"Quon?" Shen slid up against the cold wall at the head of his
bed. "It's one-thirty in the morning."

"Can you sleep?" Quon asked.

Can you sleep? Shen thought. *What kind of a question is that,
can you sleep?*

"I was sleeping, if that's what you mean."

"Were you?" Quon said, his voice nervy. "So you can then. That's good. That's good. I can't. Not like I used to, anyway . . . "

"Quon? What is it? What's this all about?"

"I need to talk to you, Shen," Quon said, his tone passive, panicked, as if he had been asked to make the call at gunpoint but didn't want to give away the gravity of his situation. "I need to talk to you right now."

"Okay, well. We are. We're talking."

"No," Quon cut in. "No. No phone-nodes. I have to see you in person. Meet me at The Glimmer Room in twenty minutes. I'll be there."

"What? Wait—"

But Quon had already hung up, severing any chance of making an excuse not to go.

Shen frowned in the darkness. He looked to his side and touched the small exposed patch of his wife's shoulder. Hua moaned softly again but went on sleeping. Her skin was soft and firm—softer and firmer than he remembered it ever being in the eighteen years they'd been married. He knew she was a woman who took care of herself, but ever since his return to earth his wife had seemed younger and more beautiful than ever. At the time of his arrival, he had attributed it to having spent such a long time away from her—drifting through the loveless, inhuman chaos of the universe and staring at the cold, geometric machinery—but it had been weeks since his return, and the novelty of her suddenly-realised beauty had not worn thin. If anything, every day he found himself more impressed by her, more baffled by her ageless body.

"I'm going out for a bit," he whispered, and kissed her on the cheek. The skin on her cheek was cold. She murmured something—a lazy semblance of words. Shen covered her with the blanket and got out of bed. He went to the bathroom and stood in front of the mirror, turning his face from side to side.

He was getting older. There was no escaping that fact. His eyes were buried in satchels of skin. The lines that connected the sides of his nose to the edges of his mouth were deeper and longer. His hair was thinning, just as his father's had done, and his earlobes were wide now, and dangling.

Perhaps, he thought, it was because of everything he had seen. Perhaps we were not yet ready to behold those nebulae in the furthest reaches, those spiralling vortexes of ancient matter, that vast raw core of existence. Out there, from the windows of his vessel, he had seen the birthplace of time. They all had: Quon and the seven other astrominers aboard Chang'e 11. And perhaps now it was time to pay back all those free trips through time with a few extra wrinkles, thinning crowns, and enlarged ear lobes . . .

Quon.

Something was wrong. He had never known Quon to be a skittish man with a flair for such cloak-'n'-dagger dramatics. Quon had always been reserved and composed. A straight arrow and a sharp shooter, as they used to say in those old American movies. The space program didn't choose paranoiacs and unstable neurotics, especially when they were going to be restricted to the claustrophobic confines of a lone space vessel, and Quon had been no exception. Also, Shen had spent almost nine years with Quon up in that contraption; if ever there was a place to get to know someone, it was there.

So was he now suffering some kind of agoraphobia? It wasn't impossible. Even Shen had had to get used to being back on earth. He too had felt uneasy about this place he called his home. It wasn't that everything had changed too much in the time he'd been away, but rather that too *little* had changed. All the expectations he'd had aboard Chang'e 11 of feeling left behind by a new world had not come to pass.

An unsettling feeling, and he didn't think it was all in his head.

After all, time shouldn't stand still for anything or anyone. We expect cities to expand, oceans to rise, the human body to get older—but none of that had happened on the earth he had come back to. Too much was the same: The same people. The same technologies. The same problems. In some cases, even the same goddamn hairstyles. The same but not the same—

like a deeply loved song overplayed until it becomes almost impossible to stomach listening to it.

That's exactly it, he thought, looking at his reflection. *Nothing has changed—nothing but you. You've changed, Shen. You've definitely gained a wrinkle or two.*

Even so, had he really grown as old as he thought, or had the eerie stagnancy of the world around him simply emphasised the otherwise ordinary marks of ageing?

Shen rubbed his eyes and looked at his bleary reflection again. Time to wake up, be alert for Quon. He ran the water into the basin and splashed it into his face, then dabbed his face dry with a towel. He dressed quickly and quietly left the apartment. The hallway was empty, dimly lit by mustard-tinted lamps. Identical wooden doors stood alongside each other, just as they had done before he left, but as Shen passed along them, he felt the hallway was longer than he had imagined, with a few more doors at the end. *That can't be true*, he told himself. It was evidently his brain kick-starting itself from the deep sleep Quon had disturbed. A forty-seven-year-old wife with unusually youthful skin was one thing, a lengthened hallway in a fifty-storey apartment block was another.

He took the elevator to the bottom and stepped out into the cold, wet street. The Glimmer Room was a good twenty-minute walk from where he stood. He could grab a taxi, he thought, but he could do with some fresh air, a bit of time to prepare himself for whatever it was Quon was so eager to tell him. So he pulled up his collar and took to the street.

Shen hadn't seen Quon for at least two months. Not since the last round of interviews, when everyone had finally lost interest in the crew's dramatic return from their voyage. The last time he'd seen Quon had been at that awkward dinner with the executives. Quon had been there with his wife, a quiet woman who'd attached herself to her husband like a pretty little cufflink and smiled carefully at all the right lines. Conversation hadn't exactly flowed that night (most of the astrominers had difficulty talking freely about their nine isolated years), but Quon had not seemed particularly out of place. His wife had selected his meals for him, with no thanks from him. No surprises there. On Chang'e 11, his nickname had been Mr. Droid because of his stony and mechanical nature. When their meals had finally arrived he'd dismantled and ingested each course like he was performing an important task. Once again, nothing unusual for Quon.

At the end of the night, Quon bowed, shook hands all round, then left with his wife in a taxi.

That was all Shen remembered of the last time he'd seen him, so what had happened since then? What had led to that rock-headed man falling to pieces?

As Shen walked along the damp street to The Glimmer Room, he studied the world and its people like an undercover anthropologist. Neon lights reflected in the puddles and windscreens of cars. Flashing arrows brought brothels and clubs to the attention of passers-by. Shen slowed to look across the street. Thin, vampiric teenagers were standing out on the pavement, draped over the takeout counter of a small roadside diner, hassling a plump teenage clerk. A blob-like autovehicle *whooshed* through the water that had flooded the centre of the street.

This was the world Shen knew, he was certain. There was no mistaking these few details. But still, something was wrong with it all. He couldn't say what, except that once again the details were too precise . . . too familiar. Surely those wasted kids at the counter had been there the night before when Shen had walked along that same street with his wife? Not kids who looked like them either, but those self-same kids.

Okay, he thought, perhaps they had. So what?

He had to concede that that alone would be nothing extraordinary; it might have been their second, third or fourth night out for all Shen knew. They might have made an unfortunate habit out of harassing that fat, pimple-faced clerk in the silly white hairnet and the stained white butcher's coat.

But still.

The way that one with the bad teeth and electrically charged hairstyle mocked the clerk while the rest of the squad cackled— hadn't he made the same dumb gag the night before? The way that skinny girl with the smeared eye make-up leaned over the counter to wrench the clerk forward and kiss him on the lips— how many nights in a row would she tease the poor boy with the same cruel gesture?

Shen was thinking all of these things when, prompted by some sort of collective thought, they all turned to look at him. Shen's heart skipped a beat as their animated expressions fell away, and they swivelled their heads to eye him as he passed. Even the clerk was now staring, as if he had suddenly been accepted into their fraternity by their shared captivation. In Shen's mind, there was no explaining it; he was on the other side of the street. He couldn't imagine why he'd caught their attention, or how they'd all known he'd been watching them in the first place.

Shen ducked his head and hurried along the street. He hailed a passing taxi and told the driver to take him to The Glimmer Room. *Those staring teenagers,* he told himself, *figments of my imagination. You're getting paranoid in your old age, Shen.* They'd probably either mistaken him for someone else or hadn't been looking at him at all. Had there been someone walking behind him perhaps? Someone they would have known? He didn't know and he didn't have time to think much more about them. All he wanted was get to The Glimmer Room, figure out the business with Quon, and get back to his warm bed.

He watched the streets through the window of the taxi. Dark, drenched and hopeless, he didn't feel as if he was moving through them as much as they were moving past *him*—as if the hawkers, prostitutes, the drunks and the homeless were standing on the open platforms of a gigantic train going in the other direction, all of them casually unaware they were being led to a place of execution: a death camp, a slaughterhouse, to plunge off the edge of an unfinished bridge.

Shen sighed, sat back in his seat, and looked ahead. A pair of plastic black cue balls dangled from the rear-view mirror. The back of the driver's big head was set square on his shoulders as if it had little need of a neck.

"Miserable night, huh?" Shen said.

The driver said nothing, and the car kept cruising down the street. *And let's all just make it a little more miserable, shall we?* Shen thought. He abandoned any attempt at chitchat and sat back in his seat. The vehicle turned a corner and finally came to a stop outside The Glimmer Room. On the dashboard, the fee flashed on an LED display and Shen placed his thumb on the square glass plate beside it. His print was fed into the machine and the amount was deducted from his account. Then the door opened and he got out.

"Thanks for the—" he tried to say, but the door shut instantly and the car pulled back onto the street, vanishing silently into the night.

Shen looked up at the flashing sign for The Glimmer Room. He nodded at the bouncer perched on his stool like an overfed parrot and went through the doorway.

The ramshackle bar was quiet. The barman was behind the counter with a clipboard, lining up half-bottles of hard liquor and taking stock. In the corner, two men played an unhurried game of pool, dense clouds of cigarette smoke hanging over their heads as if they'd been playing for days already.

Quon was sitting at the end of the bar, nursing a short drink. Shen walked up to him, took off his coat and pulled out a stool.

"Quon," he said.

Quon turned, snapping out of a daze. Shen was shocked. Quon looked like a terrible effigy of the conservative, mathematical, military man he had once been: his hair was shaggy and dishevelled, his eyes sunken, his skin creased. This was not the unemotional, disciplined scientist Shen had come to respect aboard Chang'e 11 . . . Quon smiled drunkenly and put his hand on Shen's shoulder.

"Shen. My friend," he slurred.

"What's going on Quon?" Shen asked, wasting little time. "What's this all about?"

"How are you, my friend?"

"I'm okay. How are you?"

Quon shrugged and tapped his empty glass on the counter. The barman turned to top it up, but Shen put his hand over the rim of the glass, pulling it away.

"How about we keep things simple for the time being," Shen said, and then told the barman to bring them a couple of Cokes. "So we're both on the right level. What do you think?"

"On the right level. Sure," Quon said, waving his hand. "I'm glad you made it out. Glad you could come."

"Of course."

Quon must be getting a divorce. That's what it was. Quon and his wife were splitting and Shen was the only person he could call. That was his best guess. "How's the wife?" he asked.

"The wife?" Quon replied. "Wouldn't know. Haven't seen her."

Divorce. Shen was almost certain.

"Is she not at home?"

"Oh, yes, she's at home. She's *all* the way back there, at home. But how can I know with this place, hm? Tell me."

"Well, maybe you should go home, Quon. Go home to Fang. You'll feel better in the mor—"

"Go home? Go home! And how do you expect me to do that?"

"C'mon, I'll get you a taxi."

"Yes!" Quon laughed. "A taxi! Let's get a taxi, all the way back home. What do you think the fare will be for a few billion kilometres? How much you got on you?"

Shen frowned. "What's that supposed to mean?"

"Let me ask you something, Shen. Let me ask you this." Quon leaned forward. His breath stank of alcohol and an empty stomach. "How's *your* wife?"

"She's fine."

"Is she? Is she ab-so-lute-ly *fine*, Shen? Just the way you left her nine years ago?"

"Okay, that's enough, Quon. Come on. We'll talk about this in the morning, when you're—"

"All right! If you won't tell me about your wife, let me tell you about mine."

"Fine. What about her?" Shen said, relaxing into his seat.

The Cokes arrived and Shen passed one of them to Quon and told him to drink it all quickly.

"Two weeks ago," Quon began, "I woke up at six in the morning. Fang was up and in the kitchen, making something to eat. And you know what? She looked beautiful to me. Just beautiful. You know when a woman just glows? She was glowing. She made me my breakfast and it was the most delicious breakfast ever. Exactly what I like. When I was done, I grabbed my case and walked to the door. She came to see me off. She stood at the door in her pink and yellow pyjamas and she had this smile on her face. Empty. Like she was being controlled by a little man in her head who was making her smile against her will. She had a bit of ketchup on her thumb. She was licking it off as she waved goodbye. I got in the car, pulled out of the driveway, and she was still standing there. Waving and sucking her thumb.

"I was away for four or five hours—went to the gym, did some errands—and then I came back, right? Except, you know what, guess who was still there in the doorway when I pulled the car in? Fang. Standing in the doorway in her pink and yellow pyjamas, sucking her thumb, smiling like a mannequin."

"Okay . . ."

"She'd been standing there the entire time I was gone, Shen. Standing in the doorway for five hours!"

"How do you know?"

"How do I know? Christ!" Quon slammed his glass on the counter. "I don't *know*. But I do. I do know. Her hair was exactly the same as when I left. She was still in those goddamn pyjamas. She was still sucking her thumb, and not a single thing had changed in the house. The dishes were still all out. The egg shells were still on the counter. The bed was unmade. Nothing had been done. And I know my wife, Shen. *You* know my wife. That would never pass. No. Whoever or whatever was at the house, that was *not* my wife."

Shen swigged his Coke. Maybe he should have ordered something harder, he thought. Quon was staring him down, waiting for a reaction.

"I don't know, Quon," Shen said, finally.

"Don't do that. Don't pretend you don't know what I'm talking about. I know you do. Now. Do you want to tell me about *your* wife?"

Shen rubbed his hand around the glass, gathering the condensation on his fingers. "She's younger," he said finally. "She's younger than I remember."

"Younger. Ha! Yes. Not the woman you left behind, is she? Okay. How about this—what do you remember about us being up there?"

"Up where?"

"In Chang'e 11, Captain. What's the last thing you remember about our mission?"

"The last thing? What do you mean?"

"Anything," Quon said. "Do you really remember anything? Anything specific? Re-entry? Do you actually remember the day we landed?"

"Of course I do. It was only a couple of months ago."

"Was it really? So you remember it. Great. Give me one memory of it. One story. Detail. Anything."

Shen smiled. Quon was having him on. The entire conversation was some kind of weird wind-up. Of course he could remember it.

"Okay, well—" he began, playing along. "The day we landed. Let's see. We . . . uh . . ." He paused. He trawled through his memories, but where there should have been facts and feelings about the event, there was nothing, a void. He could not even access the next available memory. A black hole had materialised in his head and it was sucking in the weak light of what he should have known.

"Forget the arrival," Quon said. "What about this place? Home. Hell, let's talk about this very bar. Do me a favour. Close your eyes."

"Quon . . ."

"Close your eyes."

Shen did as he was told.

"When you stepped into this bar, ten minutes ago, what did you notice first?" Quon asked.

"Um. The bar counter."

"What else?"

"Two men playing pool."

"Right. Go on."

"And—I don't know, Quon—you. Sitting on the stool."

"Who was behind the bar?"

"A barman."

"Barman. Okay. What was *he* doing?"

"Taking stock."

"Hm. Open your eyes."

Shen blinked hard. At first he could not tell what he was expected to see. As he looked around, however, he noticed certain details had changed. The barman was not a barman, but a young and beautiful woman. She was fidgeting at the till. The two men playing pool weren't behind him as he was sure they had been a moment earlier; they were wearing expensive suits and halfway through a card game at a small table. There wasn't even a pool table.

"What's going on?" Shen asked. "How did—"

"What I saw when I came in here," Quon said, "is probably what you're seeing right now. Once you told me what you saw, I projected my environment onto you, as if your mind was a screen. Don't ask me how."

"This doesn't make any sense."

"It's as if there's something, someone maybe, trying to rectify the discrepancies between us. To balance our perceptions and create a synchronicity between our conscious minds. It's failing. But it's trying. Trying to make us believe the same lie."

"What lie?"

"Captain Shen. You know what I think?" Quon asked. He ran his finger over the counter. "I think this isn't home at all. It looks like home. It *feels* like home. But we're not on earth. We haven't returned from our mission. We're still out there, and whatever, or wherever, this place is, it's trying to make us *think* we've returned."

"That's ridiculous. No. We landed. Two months ago."

Quon turned back to the bar. "No. No. These environments have been downloaded from our memories. Everything we see here we've seen before. Perhaps we're being shown a world that we *want* to see. Our beautiful, ageless wives, for example. But there are glitches. This place is full of them. Look," he held up his glass. It was a tumbler with a few last drips of whiskey sloshing at the bottom. "You ordered two Cokes. I wanted another whiskey. So mine's a whiskey. Has been all along."

Shen took a moment to process what he was being told. He watched as the stunning young lady behind the counter diced a lemon. She looked up at him, thinking he needed to be served, but he waved his hand gently, and she turned back to her task. "There must be an explanation for all of this," he said.

"I've just given you one."

"Have you spoken to the others?"

"The others? The crew. They're not here."

"Where are they?"

Quon shrugged and tapped his glass on the counter, signalling the barmaid to fill it up. He smacked his lips.

"Living in their own projections, I suppose. Stuck in their own lies. Who knows?"

The barmaid filled the glass and Quon beckoned her closer with his finger. She leaned over the counter and Quon whispered something in her ear. Once he had spoken, she headed back to her lemon. Shen thought it was odd, *What secret could Quon have with a barmaid?* but did not consider it for long. He was studying the bar for clues. The missing pool table. The card players.

His mind played over the events of the past two months— if it had been two months at all. Was it a dream? Was he dreaming right then? Had he really just walked back from his apartment or had he simply been in the same *nowhere* Quon had postulated, fabricating a past for himself as he went along?

He thought about his wife's face. Her unnaturally young face. He thought about the extra rooms in the corridor. He thought about those wasted kids in the diner, eyeing him as he went by. He even thought about the taxi driver whose face he had not seen. Did the man even *have* a face, or was he only a back that could not be turned? There had been two black cue balls hanging from the driver's rear-view mirror, but even though Shen knew he'd seen them, the mental image of what he'd really seen was different. In his mind, the totems hanging from the mirror were two playing cards, twisting on a string: a king of hearts and a joker.

Christ.

Where were they? Were they still in Chang'e 11? Was this a kind of simulation, and if so, who was controlling it? Who was controlling *them*? Shen rubbed his temples with his fingers and told himself to breathe. *Quon's drunk. This is a joke. A prank. We're home. On earth. We returned.*

"Okay . . ." Shen continued the discussion, pulling himself together. "All right. I'll play along, and then how about you and I hit the road? If what you're saying is true, and this is all some kind of a trick, where are we, Quon? And how do you suppose we get out?"

Quon smiled wryly and added, "I think I might know, Captain. After all, I'm the scientist. But as Heisenberg himself proposed, a good scientist must be completely removed from the equation in order to yield accurate results."

As he completed his final statement, the barmaid lunged towards Quon with the knife in her hand, extended her arm over the counter, and slit his throat cleanly from side to side.

A sea of rooftops

"You had a nightmare," said the owner's son. He was lying on the bunk bed beneath me. I pulled out my pillow, squeezed it into shape and put it back behind my head.

"I suppose so," I said, coming back to waking reality after plummeting from an impossibly tall tree.

"I think you were falling," the boy said. "It seemed like you were falling. You were saying your son's name."

"I was?"

I pressed the palms of my hands against my eyes. I had a headache. More than likely, I was dehydrated. For more than a week I had been ill, running a fever and sweating in my sleep. I was only just beginning to feel vaguely normal. We had been at sea for almost three weeks and I'd spent most of it in bed. I'd been struck by spells of delirium and disorientation. I once found myself waking up in the bathroom after a somnambulistic stroll in the night, throat dry and head pounding. Members of the island took me back to bed and did their best to settle me. Another time, the owner of the island, a tall bearded man who always wore a ragged old red baseball cap and smoked brown hand-rolled cigarettes, was sitting at my bedside after a particularly troubling night. He said we'd had a conversation but I didn't remember it. He said I thought he was a man named Jack Turning.

(*"Whoever that fellow is or was to you, friend,"* he said. *"You sure didn't like him much."*)

On better nights, as I lay there weak but awake, I could do nothing but work my way through the memories of recent events—memories culminating with the sound of a gun exploding in the hands of a young man who'd mistaken me for his father. The sound still rang in my ears, his words echoes in the crooked halls of my mind: *I was your son. And you left me here. You forgot me. You forgot me.*

Sometimes, I thought I was still trapped in that dark and menacing jungle. I imagined the ceiling of the room was covered in fruit—sweating, bulbous fruits that looked scarcely as appetising as I had once thought them. For at least a week after being welcomed onto this new island I struggled to keep food down after meals and had an almost rabid aversion to drinking water. The mornings were clearer, and I'd remember that we'd long left that island of mind-altering fruits and carnivorous trees, and were now on another island altogether. An island that, by comparison, was a kind of secular monastery.

Both the bed-bound geneticist and I had been offered passage on the second smaller island with its community of nomadic seafarers. We had taken them up on their offer—left that overgrown island to drift unmanned across the sea—and become their welcomed guests. They were a hardy and upbeat group who believed in a simple way of living, and I liked them instantly. When I told them where I had come from, how I had been set adrift on a raft, they said they knew about the communes. They'd heard about the New Past and The Renascence, but had decided that until they were caught and dragged off they would never readily submit themselves to a cause they didn't completely understand. Whatever the purpose of the communes might be, they insisted, they didn't care. That was where the discussion ended before the generous food and strong alcoholic malts were served to celebrate our arrival.

The inhabitants of the island also assured us, with no real plan or destination of their own, that they would gladly take us wherever we wished to go. The old geneticist later asked if he could stay with them—his agricultural know-how was certainly of prodigious value—and they welcomed him as a permanent addition to their community. I, on the other hand, decided I could not stay.

I had to find Andy, my son, I explained.

I had to go on.

I climbed down from the bunk bed and grabbed a mug of water off the boy's desk. He was lying on his stomach and reading some kind of magazine. It was yellowed and tattered, but I could still see the faded images of beautiful houses with their landscape gardens. Dining-table sets and exquisitely crafted furniture. Polished silverware and extravagant crystal chandeliers. Matching drapes and duvet covers. It had been years since I'd seen any of those things.

The captain's son was no older than thirteen or fourteen years old. I wondered what he imagined as he turned the pages, looking at the trappings of what must have seemed like a fantastical place, the paraphernalia of an extinct alien world, once populated by aliens with extinct alien interests. He'd probably never seen anything as indulgently decorative in his life.

"Did people actually have all of these things?" he asked.

"I guess they tried," I said.

I left the room and the house and walked onto the balcony outside. The day was hot and sunny, the sky blue and cloudless. The old geneticist, his name was Klaus I learned later, was sitting on a chair, surveying the ocean. A hundred-metre stretch of plant-life circled the balcony—patches of low shrubs and bushes. A low stone wall surrounded the island, and stretching in all directions beyond that was the ocean—the endless, inconstant ocean. There were three rain-stained villas behind us, built on a mound in the centre of the island. A few palm trees hung over the villas, more for shade than anything else. The entire island was only a fraction of the size of the geneticist's abandoned one (it took me less than twenty minutes to walk all the way around), but there were no devious tricks up its synthetic sleeves, and it seemed to be all the community of twelve needed to call a home.

"I'm glad to see you're feeling better," Klaus said as I stood alongside him. Since the first time we'd met, the colour had returned to his face, he'd put on a healthy amount of weight, and there was a pleasant lightness to his character. A far cry from the frantic man I had found chained to his bed.

"I am," I said, and cleared my throat.

I stood there silently, sharing his view of the open water.

"The world is an unforgiving place," he said. "The only real commitment we can make is to spend our lives trying to make sense of it. The only real problem is that it doesn't. Are you sure you won't stay?"

A few days after we'd boarded the second island, I had mentioned the prophecy of the sea of rooftops. It turned out the captain had once seen a place matching the description. He even had an idea of how to get there. That alone was enough for me. Perhaps I was a desperate fool, putting stock in some weird words uttered in a dark cabin by a man of questionable sanity, but I had nothing else to go on. Without those words, I didn't know where to begin. I asked the captain if he'd take me to that place, and he said he would.

"I can't stay," I said to Klaus. "This is a good home. But this is not my home."

"Do you have a home, Kayle?" he asked.

"I believe so," I replied. I sucked in the cold sea air. "My son is my home."

Klaus looked at the ocean.

After a while, he said, "There's something I should tell you. Before we left my island, I had a very strange thought. A very strange thought, indeed. It came to me out of nowhere, as if it had been put in my head by someone. I'm not sure if that makes sense?"

"I know that feeling," I said.

"Something prompted me to take something from the island. A kind of souvenir, perhaps, or possibly more important than that. But the idea was to give it to you. It's something I believe you should have. I'm not sure why."

Klaus took an object wrapped in a plastic bag from his lap. He unfolded the plastic carefully and withdrew a large, shiny apple. I took the apple from him and studied it. It was smooth and green. A perfect specimen.

"It's from the jungle. Of course, I don't have to tell you not to eat it. You know that. But trust me when I say I think you should keep it. It won't go bad. It won't rot. It'll last for as long as you need it. And somehow I know you *will* need it."

He handed the plastic bag to me and I took it gingerly and wrapped it up. Even then I could smell its venomous sweetness.

"It's the most peculiar thing," Klaus said. "The thought to give you this. You might think it cruel, after everything you've already been through—to burden you with this. But I feel like I'm doing the only right thing I've ever done in my life. I have not been a man of clear judgement in the past. Now, I hope that I am being wise."

I laid my hand on his shoulder.

"I'll take care of it," I said.

The island sailed on for another week before I was finally called from my room. At the time, I was playing chess with the owner's son. Somebody came to the room and said I should go down to the wall at the edge of the island. I toppled my king, explaining to the boy that he'd checkmated me with his last move, shook his hand gravely, and left.

I didn't need to reach the wall. As soon as I stepped outside I saw it, passed to me from a stranger's dream: a sea of rooftops.

The man in the cabin had been right.

Houses and buildings rose above the surface of the ocean. It had once been a residential suburb of some kind, now it was a deep watery graveyard revealing nothing but an assortment of sloping rooftop tombstones. There were hundreds of them.

Our island drifted between the contorted, leafless tops of soggy trees. A pair of rugby poles jutted from a submerged field. Wooden boxes bobbed beside a headless mannequin in the attic of a big house. Chairs and desks floated in water-filled offices. A peeled and faded plastic billboard warned that driving under the influence of alcohol made you a murderer.

It was hard to say whether the suburb had once dipped into the ocean or the ocean had risen to claim it. We passed slowly between the roofs of derelict buildings, many metres above where people had once driven their cars and walked their dogs and met their friends and done their business, and what struck me hardest was the deathly stillness. The ocean was flat, with not the faintest breath of wind. And reaching from it, the rotting top of a sunken ghost town stretching bleakly for the sky. Further along, the water became shallower and the island had drifted as far as it could go. A strip of marshy shore lay in the distance, long and straight, extending in both directions.

Behind us, the sun was beginning to set. The temperature started to drop as the darkening sky welcomed its first few stars for the night.

The islanders had suggested I stay with them until morning, but I'd told them I would be okay; I needed to keep moving.

I was sitting at the front end of a rowboat, holding a black bag of food and supplies prepared by two kind women. The captain's son sat at the back of the boat and rowed me to shore, like Charon, the Greek ferryman of the dead. The wooden boat moved silently over blackening waters. I watched as the island shrunk away, dimming to a silhouette in the setting sun. Ahead of us rose the land, no mountains or hills of any kind, only swampy coastline and an expanse of flatness lurking in the darkness beyond. No people. No houses. No signs pointing the way. Nothing but reeds and mud.

The boat pulled to the shore and I climbed out into the sickly warmth of the marsh. My feet sank into the mud, releasing a strong smell of decay. The eldest son shook my hand and wished me well, and then pushed off into the water again. He rowed back to his island as I tramped my way up the marsh to solid ground. I beat the mud off the sides of my shoes and buttoned my jacket to the neck. I didn't know which way to go, but began to walk anyway, across a grim and barren new land.

It was a world without colour. After turning inland, I found myself walking the ashen streets of an abandoned ashen town, studying each worn and weathered remainder. Dead trees hung on the sides of the street, tall skeletons clutching thick white sheets of spider web between their leafless branches. There was an empty school with broken windows and grassless fields, enclosed by rusted fences. Nothing but memories existed inside the houses, once quaint but now rundown and forbidding. A red bus lay overturned across the road, like a big bloodied animal, its wheels missing and seats long since removed. Crows squawked from a hanging rooftop gutter, eyeing me as I walked past.

I had no idea where the people of the town had gone. Perhaps they had been relocated to communes. Perhaps the town had been struck by disease. I wondered with every breath whether some deadly bacteria had already begun to incubate in my warm, living lungs. If so, there was nothing I could do about it.

I kept walking.

I passed a faded poster on a lamppost advertising a rock show (HOMESICK WHORES—DEAD IN CONCERT!) and a billboard reminder to vote in the "upcoming" municipal elections. A spinach quiche was on special at the local deli, on Sundays there were free orchestral performances in the park. A number of cars had been abandoned in the middle of the street, their doors open as if the drivers had chosen to get out and make a run for it.

I stopped to look through the window of a corner shop, the interior lit by nothing but the moon. The shelves were not entirely cleared—some cans and boxes had fallen to floor. Whatever had occurred there in the final moments had been quick and chaotic, I decided—an act of horrific desperation.

I knew I should not stay long.

I walked for some time before noticing a pillar of smoke coiling up into the moonlit sky—smoke and yellow light and the smell of burning. I turned off the street and walked in the direction of the smoke.

I passed through alleys and crossed wildly overrun yards and finally arrived at the source of the smoke and light: a house on fire. Flames lashed ferociously at the air and I felt the intense warmth even though I was on the opposite side of the street. The fire was almost too bright to watch, magnificent in its complete consumption of the house. Above, the sparks and smoke twisted upwards like a stairway into the sky. I could not tear my eyes away.

It was then that I noticed a dark figure standing in front of the house. A man. He stood motionless. His lone presence alarmed me and I wondered if he'd started the fire and was now relishing in his own doing. I crossed the street towards him. The fire rumbled and crackled, and the flaming bar of a window frame came loose, crashing to the ground.

The man stood with his back to me and all I could tell was that he was tall and hefty. He was carrying nothing with him and his muscular arms hung loosely at his sides. His hair looked wild and bushy, and the light from the fire played in it, creating a nimbus around his head.

I approached him cautiously.

"Hello," I said.

The man turned his big head. His face was shaped by the brilliant light. He was the last person I had expected to see in that forsaken place.

It was Gideon.

The Blue Caribou

The day I was picked up to be taken to the commune on the beach, I was staying at the Blue Caribou Motel, a highway ramshackle for tired night drivers and cheapskate holidaymakers. I'd been there for months. I didn't remember booking myself into the room, but at some point after my son had been taken, I must have left the house with a kind of delirious plan to get away from the world.

I was the only person staying at the Blue Caribou. There weren't even owners on the premises. Perhaps after Day Zero they didn't remember they *were* the owners, and took off without bothering to lock up. So I must have grabbed one of the keys hanging on a sheet of chipboard behind the counter (a key to Room 73, to be precise) and let myself in. I don't remember, but that's what I must have done.

While the rest of the amnesiacs wandered the world, I wandered the halls and yard of the motel. When I felt like it, I went behind the bar in the dining room and poured myself drinks. There was a freezer of food at the back of the kitchen and I helped myself when I wanted. In the outside area, a bean-shaped pool full of green water was encircled by a selection of white plastic deckchairs, warped by the sun. I'd make use of all of these, and at the end of my motel-loitering day, would return to my room. This went on until the morning I woke up and the man with no expression was standing in my room.

The room was a mess, strewn with empty bottles, unwashed dishes and cutlery. I had taken towels from a number of other rooms and they were hanging over the electric heater, the bathroom basin and the shower rail. The curtains had been drawn and a long strip of daylight shone through the gap where they hadn't quite closed.

The man looming over me was that uncommon combination of very old and very tall, wearing a long coat and a pair of roundframed sunglasses. He told me to take a shower and get dressed. I didn't argue. I put up no resistance, believing that perhaps the jig was up—my long, free use of the motel had come to an end. I slid out of bed and showered and shaved and dressed myself, and then met back up with him at the pool area. The sun was already scorching the earth, and though I'd showered I could smell the alcohol seeping from my pores. The man in his absurdly heavy coat was standing at the edge of the swampy pool and staring at a lone brown hill in the centre of the surrounding desert.

He asked how long I'd been staying there and I said I didn't remember. He asked my name and I said, "Kayle Jenner." He then told me that no Kayle Jenner had signed himself into the motel (he'd checked the books).

I said maybe I'd just walked in after discovering there was nobody there. The thought didn't seem to surprise him. The world had already gone mad. Nobody knew who they were and where they belonged, anyway. At least I had been resourceful.

He asked where I was from and I said I'd had a house, and a family, but now the daughter was dead, the wife had run away, and the son had been taken. After all of that, the house had become too big—or was it too small?—so I'd left it and moved into the Blue Caribou.

I said these things to the man in the brown coat but wasn't sure if I believed my own words . . . I'd done so much drinking at the motel bar I could barely hold a thought in the searing midday sun.

He asked who had taken my son and I said I didn't know; I'd just woken up one morning and he was gone. He must have believed me because he said he had a way of helping me. These were confusing times for us all, he said, but his people had the answer. His people had figured a way of bringing the world together once more.

I asked what he meant and he told me that in order for me to reconnect with my son, I'd have to go with him. He wouldn't take me to my son, not exactly, but he'd help set in motion a sequence of events that would lead to us being . . . "reunited, if you will."

That's when I asked his name, and he said his name didn't matter. What mattered was he belonged to a group called the New Past. The New Past, he explained, had the answer. We didn't need to be lost anymore. There was a way of being found—a way for us all. To make it work, however, we'd need to commit to the cause. We couldn't be afraid of a few new rules.

Only much later did I realise it had been the perfect pitch and plan, designed to recruit more than enough willing participants: in that post-contextual world, rules were *exactly* what we desired.

He told me to get my things together and go with him. There was no reason for me to stay at the motel (on some level I'd probably expected to die in room 73, of either booze or old age), so I packed almost nothing and ended up doing as he said. I grabbed a seat on a bus full of strangers and was taken to the coast, where we were each shown a list of random boat names. We could choose the boat of our choice, and wherever that boat went, that's where we would go too. We went along with it, hoping there was a grand reason for all the fuss. On the boat, we were given the first volume of a script called *The Age of Self Primary.* If we remembered how to read, we were told we had to study it.

It was there, on that same boat, that I first met Gideon.

There was something both different and familiar about the man the first time I saw him. Gideon didn't read the scripts. He wasn't interested. He sat on the side of the boat and chose to take in the view. I walked over and grabbed a seat beside him;

the sky was showing off a striking arrangement of red and grey clouds, like hot ash. Everyone else was spread out over the boat, cramming the scripts, knowing they'd be tested as soon as they arrived on the beach. Gideon preferred the scenery. I remember him saying, "There's a fine line between hope and delusion. Like that last strip of light on the horizon before the sun goes down."

He said nothing else. But I knew from that moment, having already picked that same boat to ensure our parallel fates, we were bound by something greater than what we both no longer knew.

Gideon sat near the window of a dark and empty house, eating from a container of roasted vegetables I'd taken out of my bag of provisions. Through the window we could both observe as the house outside toppled to a flaming heap. Gideon explained that he'd set the house on fire in the hope of drawing someone's attention. He'd had no reason to expect it would be me.

"I washed up here on my raft," Gideon explained. "Less than a day ago. I don't know how the rope came undone, but one moment I was attached to the beach and the next I was drifting on the ocean. I thought it was only me. I was terrified at first, thought I was lost forever, that no one would ever find me and I'd die out there, alone and helpless. But then I passed out. When I woke up, I was here. In truth, I have no idea how I really got here."

"What about your restraints?"

"They were loose when I washed up."

Gideon had decided to stay the night in the house beside the one on fire. We'd thrown a brick through the glass back door and searched the rooms, but found very little: no food in the kitchen and any blankets, pillows and sheets had been taken. We'd turned on the taps in the bathroom and waited as the groaning pipes spluttered nothing but cold and undrinkable brown water. Expecting no further favours of our appropriated home, we sat on the carpeted floor of the main bedroom. The closet was empty but for a few mismatched hangers. The mattress on the bed was missing, revealing a skeleton of wood and springs. Framed pictures of a family still hung on the walls (they seemed happy enough, young and doing their best), which meant they hadn't cleared those closets and taken that mattress themselves; the house had been raided after they'd hastily left.

"How can this be . . . *possible?*" I said, struggling with the logistics of his story. "I've been away for weeks and we're nowhere near the commune. There's no way you could have survived such a trip . . . The coincidence is too great. It doesn't make any sense. None of it."

"It seems," Gideon said calmly, "that I have."

". . . and there's no way we would have run into each other in this place," I said, watching as the house next door came furiously undone. I thought about Moneta's Burt in the woods and Anubis's Burt on the island. I thought about the unlikely timing of Jai-Li's pregnancy. So many astonishing coincidences . . . and now this. "I'm not sure how, or even why, but this has been arranged," I said.

Gideon picked out a slice of potato and handed the container back to me. I put the lid on and slipped it back in my bag.

"Let's get some sleep," Gideon said. "And if we wake and we're both still here, still in this town, we'll at least have enough to make a plan."

"And if we're not here? If we wake up and we're somewhere else . . ."

Gideon lay on his back and released a long, expired breath. "Then we are only dreaming. And none of it matters."

Those were his last words for the night. The burning house crackled and smoked. It had drawn the attention of no one else—the place was truly abandoned. Nothing there but the crows and the spiders. For a brief moment, it felt as if the entire world had ended during the blink of an eye, and no one had let us know.

We awoke the next morning in the cold and empty house and did one final search for anything we could take with us. I grabbed a knife and can-opener, a few boxes of matches, a solar-powered flashlight, a bar of pink soap and a clean dishcloth. Gideon found bandages and antiseptic oils in the bathroom cabinet. After our rummage, we took to the streets. I smashed through the front window of the corner store and gathered what food I could (cereal bars, biscuits, crackers, cans of pilchards, mixed veggies and biryani), and met up with Gideon outside. He'd found a rucksack of his own and two rolled-up blankets, which he'd held in place with leather belts. We tried to take one of the many vehicles with no luck. Even if we'd fully recalled how to operate them, the solar cells were dead and beyond resumption.

By day, the town had revealed no saving graces. A cloak of thin dull clouds hung overhead, blotting the sun and making everything bleaker. Emptier. The crows on the roof of a library watched us go by, and one squawked loudly, mockingly, and it was easy to put words to his raucous tone: *Good luck out there, walkers. Nothing to eat but dirt and shit where you're going.*

And then we made our way down the road beside the burning house, and started walking as I had been advised, out of the town and along a long and vacant highway.

The town was far behind us, and on either side of the highway there was nothing but desert and dry pastures. We'd been walking for hours. The flat landscape extended forever in all directions, offering nothing.

We saw the crumbling husk of a brick house long since stripped of its roof, windows and doors. It squatted near a meadow where two black cows and a few grey sheep still ambled and grazed. Somebody had lived in that husk once, I thought. Someone had called that shell a home. As we passed, I imagined the place restored: a neatly-tiled roof, glimmering windows, the walls plastered and painted, the garden green and trimmed and bursting with flowers, the chimney exhaling smoke from a well-tended fire on a winter's night. I imagined someone daydreaming out the window, the life that once occupied that crumbly remainder.

We walked until we reached the boom of a five-lane toll (jammed by a line of empty trucks and cars). A little further on a dark concrete tunnel sliced into a rugged mountain. The beam of my flashlight offered little as we made our way in, but we stuck to the centre of the musty throughway. After two-point-seven kilometres (or so the green sign board at the entrance had promised), we walked out into the full force of a brightening day. We wandered through soundless valleys, shadowed by high mountain peaks. A flock of birds soared far above, circled, and vanished.

Before the sun began to set, we turned off the road and found a hollow in the side of a mountain. We unrolled our blankets, gathered wood, and made a fire. Gideon opened a can of mixed vegetables, heated it over the fire, and we worked our way through it. It was a rich and tasty concoction, sopping in a spicy juice, and it went down well. I thought about the apple. I could smell it. I wanted to eat it too. The thought of its delicious juices seized me. I could feel them trickling down my chin, feel my mouth opening to bite into delicious sweetness. Klaus meant it for when we had nothing else to eat, I argued with myself. I was wrong, of course. That wasn't why he had given it to me. I reached deeper into myself and somehow found the strength to repel the urge. I pushed all thoughts of the apple away and took another helping of the canned food.

Several small milky-white scorpions scampered through the dust and we kicked them away. A blue half-moon glowed over the edge of a rocky cliff and leaves rustled in a warm wind. We heard dogs snarling in the distance, probably fighting over the flesh of some dead thing.

"Let's make a bigger fire," Gideon said, and we did. We each grabbed a sharp wooden stick and kept it at our sides. We spoke about nothing, but I was glad he was there. I was grateful for the strange stroke of fate that had brought us together again. I probably wouldn't have managed the journey alone, I realised. Earlier in the day I had explained what I was hoping to do; he'd had no objections to the idea and since he had no plans of his own he'd agreed to come along. "You're lucky you remember your son so well," he'd said. "You feel pain. You feel hope. Doubt. Love. You feel all these things, simply because you recall him. You are lucky, Mr. Kayle."

My stomach was pleasantly fed and I was tired after a day of walking. I leaned back on the blanket and was asleep before my head hit the dust.

I woke to the sound of grunting and growling. I opened my eyes and took a second to remember where I was: the cave. The fire was already dead, smoking limply. Behind it, three lean dogs with matted black fur were tugging viciously on the ends of some object.

I grabbed my stick and sprang to my feet. Gideon opened his eyes and sat bolt upright. Three long black heads snapped our way. They lowered their shoulders, baring fangs and lashing out long purple tongues. Against the dark backdrop they looked like one big dog with three ghastly heads.

Our food. They'd ripped open our bags and torn apart the goods. Packets and bags were shredded and the contents scattered across the dirt. One of the cans had been crushed and punctured, leaking in the sand. I held my stick above my head and Gideon grabbed his own. The dogs took a step back but did not relinquish their threatening stance. I grabbed a rock and hurled it at one of them, striking it on the side of its head. It yelped and cringed back and then they spun slickly on their paws and slipped behind the veil of night.

Gideon inspected the strewn food. He picked up wrappers and shook out the crumbs. A plastic bottle had been mangled and the water had seeped into the earth. We had one good can of biryani, a few roasted vegetables from the island, and that was it. I checked to see whether the apple that Klaus had given me had been eaten too, but it was lying in the dirt, still in its wrapper.

I picked it up.

"What's that?" Gideon asked.

"An apple," I said. "I was given it. But we can't eat it. No matter how hungry we get. No matter how much we might want to eat it. Trust me."

Gideon asked nothing more.

There was no food in Gideon's bag. It hadn't been touched and I put what was left of our provisions into it. Gideon grabbed a handful of kindling, threw it on the fire, and added another few logs. He got on his knees and blew fiery life into it once more.

The moon was gone. The air was warm, but in a nauseating, ominous way, as if it had spent the best of itself hanging over some putrid bog. We were out of food. I was out of ideas. All I had been told to do was walk, and now I wondered what that meant. Would I have to walk for days, weeks or months? What desert creatures would we have to eat to survive, now that our rations were gone?

"This isn't the last time we'll be tested," Gideon said, closing his eyes and picking up on his sleep where he had left off.

We woke at sunrise, gathered our things, and continued on. We felt the first prickly drops of rain only a few minutes after we'd left our site. Not long after that, it began to pour hard. It hadn't rained for some time and the water didn't soak away. It flooded the surface of the desert, spilling across the highway. We couldn't allow ourselves to be bothered by it. If we did, we'd be doomed to failure. So we filled a container with rain and pushed on.

An hour later we sat under a lone oak tree on the side of the highway, ate a few cubes of vegetables, and drank some water. We waited to see whether the rain would stop. Finally, it did, and we made our way back to the road. I was losing my strength and, I noticed, Gideon was too. I didn't think we could go much further, but I kept my concerns to myself.

The clouds still hovered above, the sun was going down quickly; the night promised to be more challenging than the night before and I was worried.

"Look," Gideon said.

In the distance, at the end of a gravel path, there was a house. It was a small stone house with a thatched roof, draped in vines, surrounded by a short white picket fence. We stepped though a rustic wooden archway and onto a neatly gravelled path. The grass in front of the house had been trimmed, faint puffs of smoke rose from the chimney, and a warm yellow light glowed beyond one of the windows. Next to the house was a rickety gazebo sheltering some sort of van or truck, covered by a big brown tarp. Against the side of the gazebo, pink and yellow flowers bloomed from a rusted wheelbarrow.

Drenched and battered, Gideon and I walked up the gravel pathway, and up to the front door.

On the door there was a sign—a handwritten message on a white, wooden plaque: IF IT WERE NOT FOR GUESTS, ALL HOUSES WOULD BE GRAVES.

I knocked twice.

I looked back at Gideon, dripping and exhausted behind me. He smiled. We heard the fidgeting of the lock, and then the door creaked open.

At first, I thought I was looking at a boy, perhaps nine or ten years of age. He had a blue cap and t-shirt with a picture of a cartoon mouse wearing roller-skates. But it wasn't a boy; its face had a metallic sheen and its eyes were two milky balls. There was no nose, no ears, only a perfect little smile on silver rubber lips. The boy at the door was a machine.

A robot child.

The nicest family ever made

My hair was dirty and tangled. There were still smudges of grime on the backs of my hands, even though I'd done my best to wash them in the bathroom. My clothes had dried but my feet were still squishing in my soaked shoes. I was tired and my knees hurt, but more than anything, I was hungry.

Gideon sat beside me at the dinner table, looking no better groomed. He sat with perfect posture on his chair, hands on his lap, and smiled sheepishly as Mother—the robot designed to look like a middle-aged woman—leaned over and served him steamed peas from a bowl in her metal hand. The hair on her head was red, cut in a neat bob and she was wearing a flattering floral dress.

"Just say when," she said.

"That's fine, thank you."

She smiled at him and Gideon smiled awkwardly back. She crossed to my side of the table and I arched back in my chair to give her room.

Father sat at the end of the table, a robot man wearing a shirt and tie. His sleeves were rolled back to his elbows and his tie loosened—the look of a man who'd finally had the chance to get comfortable after a long day at the office. He rested his elbows on the table and put his hands together, as if about to say grace. Thankfully, he didn't.

From across the white table (a long, immaculate table lavish with chicken roast, pickled beetroot, yellow rice, cauliflower cheese), two robot children sat staring at us: Daughter and Son. Son was the one who'd answered the door, and he was eyeing us sceptically, probably wondering if we could be trusted. Daughter was a little taller, with a narrow "pretty" face, short brown hair curling where her ears should have been. She was staring at me dreamily—a teenager with her first fluttery crush.

I gulped and thanked Mother for the peas.

The house itself was warm and pleasant. A fire crackled in a large hearth, a few lamps bathed the rooms in a soft homely glow. Outside, the rain pattered the murky earth. Inside, it was like another world.

We were the humans, yet it was we who were the creatures of the night. In that house full of charming human touches, sitting before that dinner table topped with delicious human food, and hosted by the most "human" family I had encountered in years (perhaps even, the last of its kind on this shattered planet), we were the uncivilised outsiders. We were the grubby pieces that didn't fit. I'd been pawing my food for so long I could barely recall how to use a fork and knife. I grabbed each and held them uneasily, like the ends of live wires.

"It couldn't have been easy getting here," Father said. "You gentlemen seem to have managed well. Very few make it this far up the road."

"*Nobody* makes it up this road," Son cut in.

"It's not right to interrupt your father," Mother said. "That isn't polite."

"Sorry, Mother," Son said. "Sorry, Father."

"Thank you, sweetheart," Father said to his wife. "And apology accepted, Son." Father turned back to us. "But yes, Son is correct. Nobody's been here in a long time. Either the world's become too busy with its own business, or there's no business at all. These are challenging times, but I'm sure I don't have to remind gentlemen such as yourselves."

Father picked up his fork and knife and proceeded to eat. He sliced up his chicken, loaded his fork, and put it in his metal mouth. He chewed it comfortably. I watched him, wondering whether he could even taste it. As he swallowed, I was curious to know whether the food nourished him in any way, or simply dropped into a big steel tank in his stomach.

I realised I was staring, and turned to begin my meal.

"You're right," I said, cutting my food into neat bite-sized pieces. "The world has grown stranger. I'm not even sure it's our world anymore."

"That's an interesting remark," Father said. "Do you think it's ever been *our* world?"

Well, not *yours*, I would have said if I hadn't been wary of offence. But then, with a depth of awareness that astounded me, he added, "Actually, to be more accurate, *your* world?"

I loaded another forkful. The meal was remarkable. Perfectly cooked, perfectly seasoned. It tasted like home, a home I wasn't sure I'd ever had. Gideon seemed to agree. His attention was firmly on his plate and he was already halfway through the meal.

"Maybe not," I replied. "Maybe you're right."

"And maybe I'm wrong." Father looked at his robotic wife. "Honey, this is absolutely delicious! Thank you so much, my love."

Gideon and I added our thanks at that point, and Son and Daughter mumbled something to the same effect. Mother patted her mouth with a serviette, hiding a shy smile of gratitude.

"Well, if I don't feed this lot they'll eat the shoes off their feet," she said, deflecting attention.

"I love a good shoe every now and again," Father joked, and the kids giggled. "A good, hearty shoe stew. Next on the menu on Dad's dinner night."

"Ew!" Daughter said. She pulled a face, but was obviously amused.

"Okay, okay," Mother said. "Let's keep the shoe-stew talk down until our guests have at least finished their meals."

Father ducked his head to the kids and widened his mouth in a comically worried frown, as if to say, *I'm gonna get it in the neck now—but she started!*

He ended the gag there and continued eating, looking quite pleased with himself. The kids tucked in again. Mother ate slowly and delicately.

We enjoyed the meal in silence for a while. When Gideon had finished, Mother insisted, "Please, have more."

Gideon bowed. "I'm fine, thank you. Your cooking was delicious. I'm very grateful for your hospitality."

"Your house is beautiful," I said. "How long have you been living here?"

"Thank you," Mother said. "What is it,"—she looked at Father—"a few years now?"

"That's right," Father confirmed. "A few years."

"It's very inviting."

"Why thank you! We try," Mother added. She pointed to the rest of the food. "You sure?"

I waved my hand and smiled to assure her that I'd had plenty.

"Unfortunately," Father said, and then paused to consider his next few words, "we did lose a family member some time back, and it's been difficult on us all."

"I'm sorry for your loss," Gideon said.

"A tragedy," Mother said. "It was no way for anyone to go, let alone someone so dear to us all."

"What happened?" I asked, and then, realising my question might have been inconsiderate, added, "I'm sorry."

"No! No, it's quite all right," said Father. "I brought it up. Perhaps after dinner you'll join me for a drink in the conservatory and I'll tell you all about it. I've got a drop of single malt both of you will probably enjoy."

"Wonderful," I said. "Thank you."

"No, Kayle," he said, his milky eyes flitting between Gideon and me. "We should be thanking you."

We helped carry the dishes to the kitchen then joined Father in the conservatory, as he had suggested.

The two children retreated to their rooms to do their homework, maths problems that Father had set for them, Son said. Mother was in the kitchen (we had offered to help her, but she would have none of it) and Gideon, Father and I were now sitting in red armchairs in a glass-walled room full of hanging ferns, spiky succulents and a few herbs and vegetables. The rain struck and streaked the glass, revealing nothing of the black night beyond.

Father leaned forward from his red chair and poured us each a tumbler of the single malt. He put the bottle back on the unvarnished wooden table that sat between us, stained with the rings of previous drinks. He picked ice cubes out of a steel bucket, pushed our glasses towards us, grabbed his own, and sat back.

"Cheers," he said, and we tapped our glasses together. Gideon and I sipped our whiskeys and watched as Father threw back his silver ribbed neck to take a big sip. He leaned back in his chair and sighed.

"I'm well aware how odd this must all be for you," he said. "We are not without our insecurities either. Whether we were programmed to feel this way, or learned to be, our self-awareness comes with all the familiar drawbacks." The ice clinked as he swirled his whiskey in his hand. "In my particular case, my fears and insecurities are predominantly related to my family's capacity to cope with trying times."

"I don't know much," I said, "but your wife and children seem as if they're doing fine. Or they hide it well."

Father smiled genially. "Thank you for saying that. That's all I need to know. All I need to *ever* know. Mother and I have little more than fifteen to twenty years left of battery power. Then we'll be gone. Dead and rusting. And my children . . . they'll be left in this strange world, where nothing seems to mature with age. Not like this malt, anyway." He sighed and took another sip.

"I don't know," I said. "Losing our memories may have been the best thing to happen to this world. No industry. No pillaging. We may have given the natural world the break it deserves."

"The natural world. That is interesting." Father smiled. "Humans have interesting ideas about their relationship to the world. Yes. Truly polarised ideas. Some believe humans own the world and can do whatever they want with it . . . and some believe humans are worthless as a species, that they are not what was intended. This latter group tries not to affect anything, resenting their own existence. But they are just as guilty of making a distinction between man and nature. Because you *are* of the world, aren't you? As much as the oceans and the animals and trees. You are just as natural, as are your acts and intentions—as devastating as they can often be. Am I incorrect?"

"No," I said. "Technically, you're right, I suppose. We are a natural part of the world. That doesn't count for much, though. Not any longer, when we've made such a concerted effort to destroy our own home. If we're natural, what does that say about us, or the world, for that matter?"

"Hm. Yes. Well, perhaps then it would be better to classify you as natural *disasters*." Father laughed at his own joke. I wondered then how many humans he had ever met. Had these ideas been programmed into him or had he somehow been able to reach his own conclusions? How much experience could he have had on the subject?

"It does seem to be the case, though, doesn't it? Some humans treat their own intellect with such antipathy," he went on, "as if it is an alien thing. Intellect is treated like a dirty foreign object brought into the world on the underside of your boots! They seem to think it is noble to be dumb and ambling, without self-awareness, that you should all be possums and sunflowers and three-toed sloths." He paused and sipped again. "But never mind all that. We could go on about it all night. Most importantly, the two of you are here. And that gives me hope."

"Hope?" Gideon asked. "Hope for what?"

"You have no idea, do you?" Father said, jingling his ice. "He said you wouldn't."

"Who did?" I asked. I rolled my tumbler in my hands. The rain came down harder, clattering on the windows like a thousand fingernails.

"I know you're looking for your son," Father continued. "I also know you are not here by chance. You've been led here," he looked at me closely, "but something tells me you know that already."

"What makes you say that?"

"I was told by a departed member of my family, who was also my best friend."

"Shen," I said.

"Ah, so you do know," Father said, raising his glass.

"That's *all* I know," I said. "I was given a name and nothing else."

"Well, it's enough for me. Enough for me to tell you . . ."

He sat up and grabbed the bottle of whiskey, tilting the neck towards us in offering. We held out our glasses. He smiled and topped us up. "It goes down smoothly, doesn't it?" he said. "Much more than most things these days."

Other earth

I take it you gentlemen have heard of Chang'e 11?

If you haven't, it's important to know the story starts right there. It all goes back to that fateful ship. The day it took off and the day it came back. Perhaps one day, with a bit of luck, the story will end there too. For now, however, it is crucial that I tell you everything I know about Chang'e 11 . . . It is a story you may choose not to believe, but I'll leave that to you. At this juncture, what matters is I give you a chance to at least *make* that choice.

You see, no matter what anyone says, Chang'e 11 was one of a kind. It was the largest astromining vessel ever created, sent into the furthest reaches of space in the hope of extracting mineral resources from asteroids, spent comets, moons and planets. It was also the answer to a specific problem: the shortage of resources here on earth. But these kinds of answers are always the same, aren't they? They are considered just as far as solving the problem concerned, but seldom as far as the problems that invariably follow.

After Africa—the flagship of earth's resource supply—ran dry, the developed nations (having spent their time and money building up Africa's infrastructure in exchange for access) were faced with a conundrum. They realised they'd put their stock in a land of holes. So Africa was promptly abandoned, creating a vacuum of promises to be filled by new generations of dictators and enraged citizens. This is what led to the rise of The Borrowed Gun, the aggressive multinational African faction. The movement was not so much a revolution as a form of lionised pillaging. I don't imagine you remember this, but it was all over the news. The details have been lost in time with everything else.

The Borrowed Gun infiltrated several major international cities and plundered on a mass scale. Skyscrapers and airports were stripped bare. Factories were cleaned out. Department stores in popular shopping destinations were ransacked or bombed. Most attacks seemed to come from inside and there were few options to resist the sheer number of internal aggressors.

In the end, there was only one major corporation that remained immune to the onslaught of The Borrowed Gun. Conveniently, the centre for this corporation was located in the desert—out of the targeted cities—and had the foresight to anticipate the backlash of a group who'd been empowered by the very nations that had once forsaken them. It was a corporation that had long since disowned its national affiliation, knowing all too well governments were weak and disorganised bagholders, the perfect Straw Men for a misinformed, overzealous faction such as The Borrowed Gun. The name of the corporation? Huang Enterprises.

All they really had to do was do what they did best—cut a deal. So that's what they did. The deal was that The Borrowed Gun would continue to cripple the competitors and Huang Enterprises would supply The Borrowed Gun with resources and weaponry, like feeding bloody raw meat to a vicious junkyard dog.

Now, around about this time it just so happened that Huang Enterprises announced the return of Chang'e 11.

Forty years earlier, Chang'e 11 had been built on the dark side of the moon. It was built for that very problem, the limited supply of resources on earth. It took seven years to build and although it was the size of a small town it only required a crew of nine astronauts for a nine-year mission period. The selection process was rigorous but covert. No applications were submitted. The members were scouted: nine of the finest engineering and scientific minds in the world.

Chang'e 11 remained a secret right up until a week before the launch. The world, of course, was stunned by the knowledge of its existence. They watched as it was launched into the cosmos, this titan of a ship manned by a mere handful of pilots. They watched as it made its way to 4660 Nereus, tagging its first asteroid with a self-replicating refinery. They watched as it ventured further, to the moons of Jupiter, as it made its way towards the edge of the Solar System, and then . . . they stopped watching altogether.

In an instant, there was nothing to watch.

Chang'e 11 was gone.

Off the radios. Out of range.

No reason could be found. There was no distress signal. No messages. No readings on the earth-based warning systems. It simply vanished, as if it had never existed at all, and with it, the nine astronauts who had been selected for the mission.

This is probably as much as you know; this is what *everyone* knows, apart from the fact that it did eventually return, even though not much was publicised. For one, the news was that one day there'd been a sudden blip on a screen and the ship had been found drifting near Saturn. The news was also that, despite numerous attempts, no radio contact could be made with the crew. Auto-piloting systems had been reinstated and Chang'e 11 brought safely back to earth. The last two pieces of news shared with the world were that the crewmembers were the same age as when they'd left and that they had no memory of where they had been. That was it. That was what people were allowed to know. But what *nobody* knew—and never did find out—was where Chang'e 11 had been for all those years.

And that, gentlemen, is where the real story lies.

It was Shen who told me all of this. He was one of the nine astronauts. An exceptional mechanical engineer and the captain of Chang'e 11. We'd often sit together in this house and he'd explain what had happened, where they had been, what it had meant . . . because, of the few things the world thought they knew, one supposed fact turned out to be untrue: the nine did remember where they had been. They remembered all too well. The problem, you see—the reason it was covered up—was because of *what* they remembered.

At first Shen didn't say much about the voyage, but over time the details of his extraordinary experience were revealed. We sat in this very conservatory and he told me everything. The truth of a ship that had disappeared not only from our Solar System, but from our universe.

This had apparently happened without their knowing. Everything was going according to plan, Shen said. One moment they were on course to a mining destination and the next moment the instruments on Chang'e 11 were telling them they'd returned to the geospace of earth. They thought they had been brought back. They thought the mission was complete.

Chang'e 11 made contact with ground control and landed. Upon landing, they went through the standard decompression procedures and were welcomed by their friends and their family. For a while, he said, everything seemed normal. It was the earth they knew and remembered. They were initially quite happy to be home. However, it wasn't long before irregularities began to surface. Shen said that, though none of them could put their finger on it, they were struck by the sense everything on "earth" was off kilter. The number of steps outside a building would be different on different days. Sometimes an object in the sun wouldn't cast a shadow. People would say and do unusual things: strangers would often stare at them or not talk to them at all. There were only a handful of weather variations: sunny, cloudy, rainy. The astronauts recognised their homes, their wives, husbands, children and friends, but even these people did not seem themselves. They always talked about the same thing or repeated the same actions.

It was the world the astronauts had left behind, but somehow it was a world incapable of *changing* in any way. He said it was as if every day was simply replaying itself, and they were participants, actors in a contrived theatre of elaborate props.

It was his once-friend and colleague Quon who noticed it first. It was also Quon who came up with a theory. His theory was as outrageous as it was reasonable: they weren't on earth at all. Wherever they were, their memories had been downloaded and re-uploaded to give the impression of them having arrived at home. A simulation of some kind. Quon was also the one who proposed that the only way of escaping this manufactured reality was to commit suicide. If they killed themselves, he theorised, they'd be pulled from the program, the way one wakes before falling to a death in a dream.

It was clear to Shen that Quon struggled with that pseudo-reality. Perhaps more so than himself. It was no place for a man committed to a life of logic, he said. In a world where basic math no longer functioned and physics was subjective, Quon strained to stay his normal, composed self. This led to Quon being the first to test this theory. He killed himself. Shen was there when it happened, but he did not immediately follow suit. He still had his doubts. He continued to examine the world by himself, to investigate Quon's claim about it being a simulated world—but it was the event of Quon's suicide that ended up providing Shen with the most striking evidence to support the theory.

After Quon took his life, there was no funeral. No one recalled him having ever having existed. More than that, any connections to Quon vanished at the same time he did. His wife was abruptly non-existent. His house. His friends and family. Any footprint he'd left was gone. And it was this incontrovertible peculiarity that led Shen to finally do as Quon had done, and take his life. He rode an elevator to the rooftop of a tall building and leaped over the edge. Upon hitting the ground, he awoke in his hyper-sleep chamber in Chang'e 11. The rest of the crew was there. Quon and the other seven. They'd been waiting for him.

On Chang'e 11, each of them had an incredible story to tell. A story of a life they thought they'd had on that earth. Each crew-member spoke of limited landscapes, two-dimensional characters, and their occasional ability to manipulate that environment by will alone. It chilled them to think they had been so easily fooled. However, one thing stayed with them from that bizarre other reality: not one of them had an idea of what had really happened, of where they had been. The only two things they could agree on were that they had certainly been *somewhere*—a place not as tangible as reality and not as shapeless as a dream—and that they had all been in the *same* place.

For a while, Chang'e 11 continued to drift through the vast darkness of space. The crew went about the normal business of running the ship. They learned that they were somewhere near Saturn. At last, a message came through to them from earth, and Chang'e 11 was escorted by remote control back home.

So they landed. For a second time.

Here.

This time, no friends and family were awaiting their arrival. After landing, Huang Enterprises had the crew separated from each other and put into quarantine. They were probed. Interrogated. Tested. The military officials, scientists and psychologists who conducted these sessions gave them no information. The crew begged to see their wives, husbands and children. Their pleas fell on deaf bureaucratic ears.

They were asked about the events of their absence. The astronauts told their interrogators about the other landing—the first landing on what they thought was earth. They retold their anecdotes. They answered all of the many questions, completed all of the tests, but they received no further information or privileges. They were treated as if they were carrying some contagious disease.

Ultimately, the truth was broken to them by a public relations officer: though they believed they had only been away for nine years, it had actually been more than forty.

The astronauts were shocked by this revelation and found the news difficult to digest. For some of them it meant that their wives and husbands were now dead. Their children had grown up and had children of their own. They had been officially declared deceased many years back and their families had held memorial services for them.

This landing was far less forgiving than the first, the people colder and less sympathetic, the truths they had been made to face harsher and no easier to process and accept—but at least it felt real. As far as Shen and most of the crew were concerned, they were home, as unwelcoming as home was.

The only person who struggled to accept what had happened was Quon. He became increasingly detached. Erratic, even. Initially he was convinced they were still in a simulation. He said he had evidence to prove that this was so.

For some reason, who knows how or why, Quon could now hear what people were thinking. He could read minds. Shen disbelieved this claim at first, of course, until he discovered that he too had the ability. Possibly, they deduced, the result of a new capacity to manipulate quantum entanglement. They knew what the officials and scientists had planned for them. They could hear every conversation, not only when they were in the same room as others, but behind every closed door too. At first, Shen said, it was difficult to control their listening— whisper would stack upon whisper—but in the end they became better at it. They could select the mind they wished to read. They could even read each other's minds. And that was how they learned what was in store for them. They would never be released from the compound. Huang Enterprises had no intention of allowing them back into the world. They would never have normal lives. They would continue to be tested, probed and dissected, until—as with anything stripped of its worth—they were ultimately discarded.

Their nights in confinement were long and sleepless. Their days were filled with endless examinations, though they mentioned nothing to the scientists of their new abilities. The astronauts had occasional contact with each other, but soon that too was taken from them. They'd once imagined returning to earth as heroes, pioneers, idols; instead they were kept in solitary confinement like prisoners, or specimens trapped under glass.

One night, Shen was lying on his bed in his small room, thinking about his wife, when a voice slipped into his head. It was Quon, communicating telepathically with him from the room next door. Quon said something had come to him in a dream. He'd figured out the purpose of their arrival back at earth. He said that somehow there were new ideas being channelled into his mind from somewhere far away, and that everything was now clear to him.

They were destined for something greater, Quon said. They were part of a plan. It didn't take much for Shen to understand what Quon meant, because he too had begun to feel the same way: they were part of something bigger than themselves, something impossibly grand. They had to fulfil this plan, but in order to do so they had to find a way out of their holding cells. Break out.

There was something else they had learned in snippets of thought gleaned from the scientists' minds. At some point Chang'e 11 hadn't been lost within *this* universe, but had passed through a wormhole into another universe. A universe very similar to our own. This universe had topographical familiarities, planetary systems and constellations, but earth in this second universe was very different. It was precisely like our earth, except, they figured out, at an advanced stage of its own evolution. This second reality had once been the same as our own, but over time, life there had evolved to a point of collective consciousness. A noosphere. Simply put, the earth had evolved to become a single, sentient thing. Floating on its orbit around the sun but operating as one massive brain.

This sentient earth had extraordinary abilities, Shen explained. It had thoughts and a will of its own. As Chang'e 11 had passed through the event horizon—that point of no return—and into the universe of this sentient planet, the planet became aware of its existence. It drew Chang'e 11 towards it. This second sentient earth had created the simulation, to lure Chang'e 11 and the crew. It wanted to know what they were, to learn from them. It learned they had come from another earth in another universe—a less developed earth, but earth none the less. Despite everything this advanced planet was capable of now doing—manipulating matter as well as its own trajectory, downloading memories and playing them back—it had never encountered life from a parallel universe. It was fascinated by the astronauts' arrival, intrigued by their existence.

And that was why their host decided to send them back—to *this* primitive and divided earth. It had a task for them. It sent them back with a package which was to be delivered to mankind, a package of enormous importance. The package, buried within the minds of the astronauts, consisted of nothing but a single, powerful thought. A thought that could be passed from person to person like a virus.

Shen deduced that their new ability to read peoples' minds was the delivery system of this viral thought. The plan, it turned out, was for the astronauts to arrive here, spread the thought into the minds of men, women and children—every conscious soul on the planet, really—and by so doing accelerate human evolution.

This might be a lot for you to take in.

It was for me. Perhaps we should have another whiskey. I'm not even human and I can understand the gravity of such an idea. This is what Shen knew—what Quon and the other members knew. But of course it's not how things turned out.

Shen and Quon

The robot father took a moment to ease himself into the next part of the story. He drank his whiskey and looked out into the dark wet night.

"Quon," he said finally. "Quon was the one who realised he could steal people's memories. Not only that, but he could claim those memories for himself. He could use someone's own memory against him. The first time he tried this was on a guard who came into his holding cell. Quon took the guard's thoughts, memories—his entire identity, really—and walked right out while the man stood there in a zombified stupor. Quon did this to everyone he saw—anyone who attempted to approach him. He sucked their minds dry. Then he went to the rest of the astronauts, unlocked their doors, and set them free. Shen left the cell with Quon and the rest of the crew and escaped the compound. A clean and simple getaway. Not a single soul was able to stop them. Quon manipulated a man into driving them away from the site, and they got as far they could."

The robot sat forward in his seat. Gideon and I leaned forward too, entranced by the tale we were being told. As he spoke, all my unanswered questions played through my mind.

The glowing ball in the sky—the one in our dreams—had that been that second earth, trying to make contact with us?

"They tried to find their way to their homes," Father continued, "but they had no homes. Their families had either died or moved on. Earth was a relic, forty years out of time, the museum of a place they used to know. Upsetting, as you can well imagine. Some of them handled it better than others, but Quon was entirely indifferent to the news of his dead wife. He felt nothing, Shen said. Quon no longer entertained what he called 'infantile emotions'. Instead, he became obsessed with taking memories, saying that they empowered him. He acquired an incredible wealth of new knowledge because of his ability. New ideas. Feelings. Dreams. Secrets. The complex identities of total strangers became his to do with what he wished. Though the rest of the crew could do the same thing, they knew how inherently dangerous it was to indulge in such parasitism. They tried to talk him out of taking any more memories, but Quon wouldn't listen. He didn't see it that way. To him, this was no longer the world he'd once cared about. Everyone had moved on without him, so why should he care?"

There was a rap on the conservatory door. Mother was standing there, smiling, holding a tray.

"Sorry to disturb you gentlemen," she said. "I'm shutting down for the day, and I thought I'd bring some tea to flush out all that awful whiskey before bed."

Father smiled warmly at Mother as she put the tray on the table between us.

"Tea's the horrible stuff," Father said. "It'll rust your insides."

Mother kissed him on the cheek, wished him goodnight, and turned to us.

"There are clothes on the beds in the spare room. They used to belong to Shen. I don't know if they'll fit, but see what you can do. Good night, Gideon. Goodnight, Kayle."

We thanked her, wished her goodnight, and she left the room. Father sighed as he watched her go, then settled back in his chair.

"Shen went back to his old apartment but there were other people living there," he continued. They knew nothing of his wife, Hua. He tried to find her telepathically, but came up with nothing. She was dead. Buried somewhere, probably. He was alone. So he left that city and travelled a great distance before coming here. He found this house abandoned and fixed it up. After that, he made us. He made me first. He used his engineering skills to build me, and his new knowledge of the mechanics of the mind to infuse my molecules and matter with . . . well, consciousness. He gave me a wife and then my children. I suppose we became the family he always wished he could have had. I've been under no illusions. I've known that since the beginning."

I finally understood why it was these robots behaved like humans. The fact that they wore clothes and ate regular food was all part of Shen's plan. A plan to live as normal a life as he could with as normal a family as he could create. These robots were designed to love and be loved. We'd only been there a night and I was already forgetting they were machines at all.

"Shen and I were brothers, I've always believed," Father said. "He was a human, I'm a machine, but those are trivial details. We were family." He gestured at the table. "Please, help yourself to tea."

I poured a cup and handed it to Gideon, and then poured one for myself.

"My wife and I were designed to exist as is. We can't grow old, or change . . . or evolve, but Shen was kind enough to give my children those capabilities. They're self-replicants, you see. The first two of a kind, I believe. They'll learn and grow and one day, they'll become adults. They'll have to choose their own paths. Many parents believe their children are unique, but I'm proud to be able to say mine truly are. One day they'll make their way into the world on their own. They'll have to fight to be accepted and respected, I suppose. Just like everyone else. In the meantime, we're doing our best to prepare them for that day. You can understand," he said.

"I can," I replied.

"For a time," Father said, "we were happy. Shen was happy. We lived here together and we did our best. But this didn't last. Things changed. Shen began to wake from terrible nightmares, screaming, increasingly disturbed by something he was seeing. My wife and I tried our best to find out what was wrong. And for a while he wouldn't tell us."

The rain had stopped but there was low, faraway thunder. My tea was growing cold and I took a sip before putting the cup back on the table.

"One night he told us. He was shaking. My wife wrapped him in a blanket and seated him in that very chair. After he had calmed down, he told us that he had seen Quon in his dreams, what he was doing. Quon was plotting something terrible, he said. Quon had realised that the nine astronauts had each been given a portion of this ability to read and steal thoughts. They had come back to earth connected. And, this is the truly frightening part, Quon had learned that by taking their lives, he could assimilate that part of them. Quon was hunting down the astronauts, murdering them and acquiring their portion of the power. Shen said that he'd seen Quon do it, go from one astronaut's home to the next, kill them each off. Shen could see it all, from Quon's perspective and the victim's.

"With every death Quon was becoming more powerful. So powerful, so impatient, so hungry for more knowledge, more memories, more feelings and secrets and identities, that he could no longer contain himself. In one dreadful sweep Quon took it all. Every memory of every human soul on this planet. It happened in a single wave, stretching across every corner of the globe. Instead of sharing the one viral thought that would have bound men, women and children to each other, he did the exact opposite—he stole it all for himself. The accumulated wealth of knowledge and skills and memories and abilities of the human race. In the end, it was Quon who caused the event you have come to know as Day Zero."

I sat back in my seat. Father said nothing, waiting for us to digest his words. I could barely comprehend what I was hearing.

Billions of memories. Billions of lives.

One man. *One man had them all.*

"But there's something else," Father said. "Something I don't want to tell you. It wouldn't be right. I *could* tell you, but I think it would be better if you simply saw it for yourselves."

"What?"

Father looked anxiously towards the door and sat forward. "I can show one of you," he said, "if you wish to see it. It will not be easy, I must tell you outright, but I think it would be better." He looked at me directly. "You have a mission, yes? A mission to find your son. But after I show you this, you will realise there is more to your mission than you know. Are you prepared to see it?"

I looked at Gideon, and he nodded.

"All right," I said. "Show me."

"Lean forward."

The robot lifted his arm in the air above the table. His palm opened and his fingers became rigid claws.

"Are you ready?" he asked.

"Ready for what?"

"I must apologise in advance if my perceptions and opinions of the events were . . . rudimentary. I wasn't quite as, well, mentally developed at the time. I assure you, however, the record of events is entirely accurate."

"I don't follow," I said. Father didn't explain himself. His hand came down over the top of my head and clamped on my temples and forehead. A charge rippled through my brain and a bright white light emptied the world.

Father

I wish I could do more for Shen. He's sitting at his desk. When last did he eat something? When last did he sleep? He is worried about something terrible happening. I know it.

"Father."

I look down. Son.

"Hm?"

"May we watch a movie?" he asks.

"Have you done your chores?" I say.

"Yes," he says.

"Very well. Watch something your sister will also want to watch."

"Aw," he moans. I give him my serious eyes. He understands and smiles. I pat him on the shoulder and he leaves my side. I walk into the study room. Shen is sitting and staring out the window. I wonder what he is staring at. There is nothing out there but mountains and road. The sun is going down. It will be night in less than one hour.

"Shen?" I say.

He turns to me. There is fear in his eyes.

"What's going on? What are you doing here?"

Shen says nothing. He turns back to the window.

"I don't know what to do," Shen says.

"What do you mean?"

"He's coming. I tried to block my mind," Shen says. "I tried to not let him in, not let him find us. I couldn't. He's too powerful now. He knows where I am. He's walking down the road."

He is talking about Quon. I look out the window. I know Quon is not there but I stare at the landscape anyway. There is nothing out there but slow moving clouds. The flowers on the arch are flapping in the wind. A set of bells jingles. Everything looks normal.

"Why is he coming?" I ask.

"You know why he's coming," he says.

He is right. I do, but I do not want to think about it.

"How long will it be until he gets here?"

"He'll be here by tonight," Shen says. "He's walking down the highway."

Mother enters the room.

"Is everything all right?" she asks.

I turn and force a smile. "Fine, my love," I lie. "Everything is fine."

"Okay," she says. "Dinner will be ready in twenty minutes."

She leaves. I am glad she has left. I do not like lying to her, but I have no choice. It would not help to scare her.

"When he comes," Shen says, "I want you to take Mother and the children to the back room. I want you to lock it. Don't open the door for any reason. Do you understand? Not for anything, no matter what you hear."

I put my hand on his shoulder.

"I compute," I say, and he smiles. "What about you?"

Shen sighs and gets up to draw the curtains.

"Just promise me," he says. "Promise you'll do as I say."

I promise.

Fast-forward
Stop
Play

I have no appetite. I look at my family sitting around the table. Wife is eating her food as carefully as she always does. My children fight over the parts of the meal they like and those they dislike. Shen sits at the other end. He has not eaten anything. He is pushing his food around with his fork, daydreaming into the plate.

"Shen," Wife says. "You should try to get something down. Even a little."

Shen looks up at her and smiles.

"You're right," he replies. He spears a potato and puts it in his mouth. He pretends to enjoy it, for the family's sake. He is a good man. I want to help him but I feel powerless. I hope he knows how much we care about him.

His pretence helps me to eat my own meal. It is a cut of beef, some rice and baby potatoes in garlic butter. My wife is a good cook. She takes good care of us all. Tonight, I fear for her. I fear for us all. I am trying to remember when last I told her I loved her. Whenever it was, it was too long ago.

"I love you, my darling," I say to her. She looks surprised. My words have come out of nowhere.

"I love you too. Now eat up. I have made dessert."

I feel better. Everything will be all right. Tomorrow will come, and everything will be all right.

Shen jerks up in his chair. His eyes are wide. Fear floods through me. The rest of the family are as startled by his action as I am. He looks at the front door and then he looks at me.

I know what this means.

I do not want to know, but I do.

Knock. Knock. Knock.

"He's here," Shen says. He signals to me and I get up from my chair.

"What is going on?" Wife says. She is rightfully alarmed. "Who is that?"

"Come on. Everyone, leave the table. Come with me," I say. The family does not respond immediately. My children look scared. I raise the volume of my voice. I make it as hard as I can. "Everyone! Come with me." Still my family looks at me.

"Go!" Shen yells and finally they spring up. Wife's chair crashes to the floor behind her.

Knock. Knock. Knock.

I wave my arms, ushering them out of the dining room. I turn to glance at Shen. He looks back at me, and then I hurry towards the rear end of the house. I enter the back room with my family and close the door behind us. I put my finger to my lips. My wife and children are sitting on the floor. She is holding the two of them in her arms. They are confused. They are very frightened.

I look through the small window in the centre of the door. Shen approaches the front door of the house. He waits in front of the door for a moment, composing himself.

He slowly opens the door.

Quon is standing outside. I cannot see him properly. It is too dark.

"Hello Shen."

"Hello Quon."

There is a pause.

"Aren't you going to invite me in?" Quon says. Shen is silent. He steps away from the door. Quon enters. He is a tall man. He's wearing a long black coat, black boots, a black hat and black leather gloves. Shen closes the door behind him.

Quon stands near the door and looks around. "So this is where the esteemed captain now lives," he says. "It's quaint."

Shen walks past him and goes to the coffee station in the corner of our small sitting room. "So you're a murderer now, are you?" he says.

I begin to feel an increased amount of fear.

"Don't be so sensitive." Quon pulls off each of his leather gloves slowly. "Death's overrated. We've all done it." He steps slowly towards Shen. His black boots clap on the wooden floor. "They've probably all woken up in Chang'e 11. On their way to somewhere better. Some place better than *this* hole."

"You know they haven't gone anywhere. They're dead. And you killed them."

"Are you making coffee? I'd love a coffee."

"So you've come to take me too. I'm surprised you haven't sent one of your 'subjects' to kill me for you. It would have saved you the walk."

"Hm. I still like doing some of the dirty work myself. It keeps me humble."

"It keeps you interested. Because you're bored."

Quon walks slowly around the room. He looks at pictures of our family hanging on the walls.

"This is your family now," Quon says. "Shen, you outdid yourself. They look very loving. Fine craftsmanship, old friend. Oh! Are they here? They're here, aren't they?" He looks in our direction. "You have a lovely home!" he shouts.

"We *were* friends, Quon. Do you remember that?" Shen says.

"*Friends*," Quon says. He is grinning. "Grow up, Shen. There's no such thing. We used each other because we were insecure and powerless. That's all. That's all a friendship is— prostitution. But yes, you're right. We have gone our separate ways, haven't we? We could have gone the *same* way, but then you'd be my competition, and I'd be here anyway. How's that coffee coming?"

Shen switches on the kettle and turns over two cups sitting on a silver tray. He looks calm. I wonder if he has a plan. I hope he has a plan.

"Sugar?" Shen says.

"One," Quon says.

"Milk?"

"Black."

They say nothing for almost a minute. I look back at my family. They look as afraid as they looked five minutes ago. I turn back to the small window in the door.

Shen gives a cup to Quon.

Quon takes it and sips. "Mind if I . . . ?" he says, pointing to the couch.

Shen says and does nothing. Quon sits down. He puts one hand over the back of the couch and crosses his legs. He sips his coffee again.

"But they weren't your only little project, were they, old chap?" Quon says. "I know what you've been doing, Shen. And frankly, I disapprove. Taking memories from me and trying to give them back to the good folk of earth. You're making a real mess of it too, aren't you? Memories all over the place. Seriously. What were you hoping to accomplish with all that? We've got people thinking they're all kinds of other people! It's quite hilarious to watch, actually."

Quon drinks his coffee. "You know what I've learned," he says. "People are so well-acquainted with suffering they build nests in it. They eat their suffering like food. They drink it. They breathe it. And they wouldn't have the slightest idea of what to do with Utopia. Does that sound like a bunch who deserve such a thing?

"I've seen their minds. I've swum through their dreams and their fears and their self-sabotaging desires. There's nothing there worth fighting for, believe me. They're egotistical enough to think natural selection is unfair. Humans intrinsically believe life is cruel. Every wreck wants a chance to stick around longer than he's meant to—clog the world with his ineptitude. So why should life pander to a breed that cannot get it into their heads that the strong *need* to survive and the weak *need* to perish? I've seen their selfish little plans for a better world. I mean, this is a bunch who think you can cure famine by feeding people! It's absurd. You cure famine by letting them starve to death. It's basic maths. Something you've never been particularly exceptional at, have you, Shen? More of a handyman, really. A hired wrench."

"It's funny you should talk about selfish plans," Shen says.

"Oh, I didn't say I wasn't selfish! That would be a lie. I'm just your average man. Regular Joe with a few inside tips. But if those are the rules—and it's seems they've always been the rules—I'm just saying it's hypocritical to make such a fuss."

"They'll figure you out. You can't sustain it." Shen pauses and adds, "Mathematically. The numbers don't add up."

"They don't, do they? You're right. I've got all these . . . people under my control, I know everything there is to know, and there's still something missing. Something *not quite* . . . right. Hm. Well, maybe that's why I'm here. Why I made this trek into the nowhere to find you. Because *you're* the piece,

Shen. You're that thing I'm missing. Maybe *you* can help an old friend out."

Quon puts his cup down on the table beside his couch. He stands up. Shen doesn't move. "I should have been the captain of Chang'e 11, *Captain*. That's why you were the last to come out of the simulation. You were the weakest. Didn't have the guts to take your life. Or maybe it's because you've always been so self-righteous."

Shen smiles slightly. "Well, that's at least encouraging," he says.

"What?"

"That you still have no idea what I'm thinking."

Quon guffaws.

Shen grins and says, "You know what's even funnier?"

"Oh, go on."

"That you'll *never* know what I know, Quon. Even if you kill me."

"And why's that?"

"Because I'm erasing my memories . . . as we speak."

Quon whips a hand inside his pocket, pulls out a knife, and stabs Shen in the chest. He holds the knife in the chest and twists the blade. Shen gasps.

A powerful surge of energy passes through my brain. My mind floods with new memories. Shen's memories. His entire life fills me up. I see him when he was a boy. I see him marrying his wife. I see the interior of Chang'e 11. I see his plan. I see everything.

I lose my balance and stumble backwards from the door. I panic. I struggle to control my thoughts. My wife and children scream.

I hear Quon's boots clapping on the floor. He is walking around the room. I do not hear Shen. I want to run out. I should try to save him. I should do something. My wife is holding me in her arms. She is holding me down so that I do not go out there.

Quon's voice: "Thank you so much for having me! I'd better be on my way! Sorry about the mess! And if you're ever in the area, please, stop by!"

The boots clap again. He is moving away. I hear the front door of the house open and then the door shuts. The house is silent. All I can see is my wife and children. They are sobbing. Shen is dead. I struggle to believe, but I know it. I have his memories but there are no more. His memories ended with the twist of that knife.

Shen is dead.

Stop

A ride

There was another white flash of light and I was back in the conservatory. The metal hand on my head unclamped. I looked down at my hands. They were shaking. Gideon was hunched in front of me. The robot father was still in his armchair.

"Mr. Kayle," Gideon asked. "Are you all right?"

I put a hand on my forehead to quell the images still spinning in my mind.

"Have some more tea, Kayle," Father said. "It will soothe you. I'm terribly sorry. Really. I know that wasn't easy. I know from my own experience. It is a tragic memory. One I have had to keep all this time, just for you."

I stood up and felt the blood rush to my head. Gideon urged me to sit back down, and I did.

"So you see," Father said. "You see now."

"What did you see, Mr. Kayle?"

I had no way of explaining it to Gideon. I struggled to find the words. He handed me the cup of tea, I gulped it back, and then he took it and returned it to the table.

"Quon is a dangerous man. Dangerous and very, very powerful," Father said. "I know this because Shen told me, but

I also know this because, before he was killed, he uploaded his memories to me. Everything he had in the deepest recesses of his mind. I have been keeping them safe. Quon doesn't know I have them, and because I am not human, hasn't thought to take them from me."

I finally regained myself. As soon I did, I began to rummage through everything else I remembered. The Blue Caribou. The commune. The New Past. Moneta and Jai-Li and Anubis.

"The New Past," I said. "The Bodies that control the communes—they're all being controlled by Quon."

"I imagine so."

It made sense. Until then, I had always been suspicious of the speed and efficiency with which the New Past had orchestrated their regime. Within months of Day Zero, there had been groups all over the world, collecting people and separating them from each other.

"Quon separated us from each other to prevent us from rising up," I said.

"Correct."

I thought about those nights of interrogation. The plugs on our heads, the rumbling grey machine that formed its reports, the Age of Self scripts we'd been forced to learn.

"But I don't understand. In the communes, we were told our separation would initiate The Renascence. The Age of Self scripts were instructions for us to acquire collective consciousness . . . but they were really doing the opposite. They were *preventing* us."

"Hm. With all the memories, the wants and desires of mankind at Quon's disposal, he knew how enticing such a premise remained, in spite of the fact he had no intention of allowing such a thing. He prepared the scripts himself. He sold people an idea he knew they wanted—the idea of being united. The idea of humans evolving into something singular and cohesive and powerful . . . but then he did the opposite of what he'd promised under the guise of following through. Simple and malevolently brilliant. People didn't know any better. Who could argue? Desire trumps reason, it seems. And after everything was lost on Day Zero, humans were offered the promise of *exactly* what they desired. To be led. To be taught. To evolve. Evidently, however, somebody forgot to pay the piper."

I got up from my chair again and walked to the glass wall. I looked out over the murky countryside. Lightning flashed in the mountains somewhere far away, the finger of God pointing at some significant and remote destination.

"And we were brought here," I said. "Everything that happened before brought us to your house. To you."

"Shen did his best. Quon's arrogance led him to believe the mismatched memories were the result of mere incompetence on Shen's behalf, but he forgot about Shen's own brilliance and resourcefulness. The captain of Chang'e 11 . . . The architect of my family. Shen led you here in the only way he could—through a proverbial back entrance. A maze of other people's stories. Or a jigsaw if you will, of other people's journeys and memories. Given to you. Guiding you. Theirs, and those of your own."

I turned around. "Why us? Of all people."

"Why *not* you? You are guided by a father's love, no? Is there any more powerful reason?"

"Quon knows where my son is."

Father nodded solemnly. "He does."

"Then we have to find him," I said. I glanced once again at my outstretched hand. I was still trembling, the weak aftershock of a mighty quake of knowledge that had shaken me from my bearings. "How do we do that?"

Father put his glass on the table in front of him and stood from his chair. He dusted his pants and began to walk to the door that led into the rest of the warm house. His hand extended to suggest we should lead the way. Gideon got up from his haunches, and we followed.

"I have one last thing to show you gentlemen," Father said. "But please. After you."

We stood in the front garden of the house. The earth was muddy and the air was dry but cold. Thick black clouds hung overhead, brooding between the peaks of neighbouring mountains. Father led us under the wooden gazebo beside the house. A large object was resting under a thick tarp. I presumed it was an autovehicle—the solar-powered car ordinary people had once bought and used to conduct their ordinary business. Father moved to the back and gripped the tarp.

"If you wouldn't mind, Gideon. Would you grab that end and pull this off? My back is not what it used to be."

Gideon did as Father had requested, and in a second, the tarp slipped off, exposing a large ovular object.

I knew instantly what sat before us.

Metallic and seamless—like a massive and perfect drop of mercury, hovering off the ground in a state of rest.

The Silver Whisper.

This was the gleaming pod Jai-Li had used to escape that tower in the clouds. An immaculate display of engineering perfection, exactly as she had described it. I put my palms flat against the curved metal side. The surface was smooth and cold.

"I know this vehicle," I said.

"I'm sure you do. Shen insisted it be brought back here. No easy feat, I can assure you. Especially since it was broken. It was found between two mountains near Chang'e 11. Shen brought it here to repair it, and now I can say it's good as new. I didn't understand his interest in it at the time, but he said he'd brought it back because of two men who would be looking for a ride." Father smiled quickly. He rolled on the heels of his feet, his hands behind his back. "I'd know if they were the right men, he said, because one would know how to open it. That was the only advice given."

I backed away from the vehicle and put my hand to Gideon's chest, a warning to stand back.

Another memory: "Jai-Li."

At that, seams appeared on the side of the pod and a door rolled out to the ground, exposing its internal rungs. I felt the stirrings of hope, a faint tempting sense of elation, emotions I hadn't experienced in longer than I could remember. I looked to Father to see if he'd object to me entering and he waved his hand happily towards the entrance. I went in and saw exactly what I had envisaged. The red seats. The panel of instruments. The outside of the house through the one-way walls. I was humbled by the reminder that a young girl had died in there. A young girl with a will and a dream powerful enough to go on after she could carry it no further. The memories of the mother's story washed over me. I was once again alongside her in that monolithic tower. Once again at her side on the days of her mother's collapse and eventual death.

"There's a problem," I said, exiting. "There's a mother and a child looking for this pod. They're going back to the crash site to find it. They're expecting it to be there."

"Then you'll have to take it back there, Kayle. You'll put it back where it belongs. It's in far better condition than she'd left it, that's for sure! But for now, it's yours. Your ticket to that side of the world, to the site of Chang'e 11. Remember, you know she's going to find it only because she told you she was. The question you have to ask is *why* she told you."

I stepped out of the pod and back onto the muddy earth. The arched door pulled up behind me and sealed shut, leaving no seams.

"By now you should realise you are part of something more than what you know, my friend," Father said. "And a little mutualism goes a long way."

Feeding us had been Mother's primary concern when we arrived, passing on Shen's story had been Father's. Now our hosts did everything else in their power to make us as comfortable as they could. Gideon and I each took a warm shower and changed into new clothes that had been laid out for us by Mother. Shen's clothes fit me almost perfectly but Gideon could only wear a large jacket and a pair of tracksuit pants; everything else was too small. We were offered two single beds in the spare room. Father told us he hoped we'd stay for breakfast in the morning. He assumed we were eager to be on our way, but said he would be honoured to have us at his table one last time. We assured him we would and then retired to our beds.

I couldn't sleep. Gideon made no sound, and I wondered whether he too was struggling to cast his mind off from the shores of thought. I stared at the ceiling and retraced my journey back from that charming home tucked between those quiet, ageless mountains. The dizzying echo of Shen's death bounced off the revitalised memory of Jai-Li's escape and consequent crash. I thought about the Silver Whisper, how it brought the detail of a stranger's tale into my own vivid reality, how it completed a circle of fate that held us in orbit around some immense, radiating truth.

I could hear Gideon breathing softly now, and guessed that he'd finally fallen asleep. He hadn't said much all night and I wondered what he thought of everything we'd heard. Perhaps he was not interested. He did not remember any family that he'd had, or perhaps even *did* have. There were so many people who recalled nothing at all. I had one son to remember and that one memory had offered me everything there was to be offered by this world.

The weather had calmed. The house was black and still. Gideon's rhythmic breathing finally coaxed me out of wakefulness and into a deep and needed sleep.

I thought that I'd awoken in the middle of the night, but I was only dreaming that I was awake. I was lying on my back on the same bed, in the room I shared with Gideon, but none of it was real. This was a dream bed and a dream room, and I was only my dream self.

The room was dark and soundless. I tried to get up from the bed but I couldn't move. My neck was held down, my wrists and feet buckled to the bed with leather straps. I could smell the ocean. I could feel it moving beneath my bed. I could hear it slapping the sides. The bed was the raft.

A horrifying new impulse fired through me: the family, Gideon, the house and the Silver Whisper had been a dream, and *this* was reality. I was still floating across the ocean. I hadn't gone anywhere or accomplished anything. My existence was as meaningless as it had always been . . .

I tugged my limbs but to no avail. My head was still on the pillow, the floral blanket was tucked up to my chest, the mattress still supported my weight, but this was definitely the raft, I told myself.

"Don't bother," a crackling voice came out of the dark. "Save your tugging for a dream that cares."

Jack Turning.

I managed to see him, from the corner of my eye. Jack Turning, sitting on a chair at the window of the room, smoking a cigarette in the darkness. Threads of smoke twisted and curled from the glowing tip of his cigarette, becoming more shapeless the higher they rose. Jack was looking out the window, his face hidden in the shadows. He did not turn to look at me.

"You think you've got it all figured out, don't you? Mr. Kayle's cracked the code." He tapped his ash on the floor. "You're a bigger idiot than I thought."

The bed rocked gently on the unseen ocean that filled the room, but Jack sat fixed in his spot, unaffected by the elements.

"You think Quon's the one to worry about?" Jack said. "You just wait till you find me. I'm waiting for you, *Dad*. I'm the one you really want. And you can forget about your pathetic little *drip, drip, drip* of optimism, trickling in there—I *know* you feel it. You'll take any hand-out of hope you can get, won't you?"

Jack pulled on his cigarette and exhaled a cloud of grey smoke. Through the misty window of the room, a neon sign lit up the dark: the yellow trunk and green leaves of a drooping neon palm tree. A neon-blue word wired in cursive buzzed beside it. The whole thing was tacky—tacky and unmistakable.

The Blue Caribou.

The lights of the sign drew a faint line of colour on Jack's profile as he stared out the window. The water beneath my bed began to rise over the top of the mattress. I yanked my legs and wrists again. Jack Turning didn't bother to look back at me. He went on smoking, calmly, taking in deep, leisurely drags. Outside, the sign continued flickering.

"Who knows? Maybe you *will* find Andy. Maybe you'll even save the world. Stranger things have happened." He dropped his cigarette to the ground and crushed it out with his shoe. "But who's going to bother saving you, big hero?"

The water rose over the sides of the bed and washed against me. I screamed. I wrenched my limbs. Jack did nothing. He just sat there. Lit up another cigarette. In a moment the water was over my face, sliding through my nose and down my throat. I was filling up with the ocean, and no sound could escape my mouth. The water rose quickly, over my body, to the ceiling of the room, pulling everything under just as it had with that suburb against the marshy shore. I wasn't just drowning. I was disappearing, another forgotten part of that sunken graveyard, unworthy of the breathing world.

I was vanishing into oblivion.

We had breakfast with the family the following morning but I barely said a word. Father had made the breakfast— scrambled eggs and toasted bread. He waddled around the table in his purple apron, pouring each of us a glass of cold clementine juice. Then he whipped off his apron and sat down to join us—playing the role of the fool for his ever-amused children. I appreciated his effort at lightness but my mind was elsewhere.

The dream from the night before had robbed me of my few scraps of budding enthusiasm. I'd awoken sweating and in a disconcerted state. I knew I had to find Quon—that was a must—but now there was the pressing urge to find Jack Turning. He was out there somewhere, waiting for me, and nothing would be resolved until I met him face-to-face to settle some unknown debt.

After breakfast, Gideon and I collected our things. Mother gave us more food parcels and the whole family came outside to see us off. The weather was beautiful; the spiteful storm clouds were long gone, and we stood under a dome of bright blue sky. The mountains were clear and textured; every crack and bump could be seen from afar. Tufts of low-lying shrubs trembled in a tender breeze.

"Are you ready?" I asked Gideon as we approached the Silver Whisper, hovering beneath the gazebo.

"Yes. I'm ready."

We turned and thanked the family for their hospitality. Father shook my hand and held it firmly as he spoke:

"Remember, Kayle. Victory isn't getting what we want. It's getting what's owed to us. And what's owed is balance. Balance between right and wrong, the guilty and the innocent, the saved and the damned. We mightn't ever have Utopia—I'm not even sure it's what we really want—but *balance*: that's the first step towards retrieving Man's stolen destiny. Towards peace."

I nodded in agreement.

"Thank you," I said. "For everything." I glanced from one family member's face to the next, thanking them all. They were all smiling back at me. "We can only hope that one day people will have again what you have now."

Father lifted his arm around his wife's shoulders. Son and Daughter stood in front of them. The nicest family ever made waved their hands as I climbed into the pod after Gideon. There was only one place up front and he moved into the second row. I took the helm. The door rolled up behind us and we took our seats on the red chairs.

"Say goodbye, children!" Father shouted.

"Goodbye children!" Son and Daughter yelled in unison, and laughed. Mother smiled.

I sat before the panel of instruments. Several lights began to flash before I had pressed anything or given any command. There was the hum of the engine, the sound of the oxygen generator warming up. Gideon placed our bags under the chairs and leaned over to help make sense of the screens in front of me. I held my palm over a display screen, and dragged a list of its most recent logged-in coordinates. One of the coordinates was followed by letters and numbers: K49L3 J3NN3R. It did not take long to realise it was a crafty little code version of my name. I was overcome with anticipation. It was all true. Shen knew about Jai-Li. He had known this very moment would happen, and that it would involve me. And this code, this wink of Shen's eye, served two functions: to confirm my place in that seat and to preserve my anonymity should an intruder get there before me. I selected the co-ordinates by twisting my wrist in the air above the monitor. The words lit up. Our destination was set.

"That must be it then," Gideon said.

"Must be."

We were now at the whim of a plan that hadn't been revealed. And all we had to do was sit back and let the Silver Whisper take us wherever we needed to be. We could see everything through the shell: the family nucleus, waving and smiling, the rugged stone house Shen had built as a retreat from a broken world, the long unused road, the mountains, the desert land and the untarnished sky.

The pod floated forward slowly, from under the shelter of the gazebo. As it moved, the vines shook on their arch and the flowers trembled in their wheelbarrow. The sound of the engine grew from a low drone into a high-pitched hum, and then all sound stopped; we could hear nothing. It was the silence of a vacuum. I could hear my own heart beating and Gideon's calm, metrical breath.

I was just about to say that something was wrong when the pod rose rapidly in the sky, suspending us high above the land, then raced forward at a perfect right-angle to its ascension.

In a second, the house and the family were far behind us. The Silver Whisper blistered through the valleys at an unthinkably high speed. Inside our bubble, we felt nothing. We might just as well have been sitting in the red armchairs in Father's conservatory. I looked back at Gideon, seated in the row of chairs behind me. He was looking through the transparent floor at his feet. Far below, within the stone gullies of the mountains, bush willow trees looked like tufts of moss.

Narrow rivulets split into tributaries that ended in marshy green or continued winding along the ravine. Above, the full sun beamed through the tinted ceiling. The horizon showed no hint of what else lay ahead. If I hadn't known any better, I'd think that what lay below was all that was left, that mankind had already been wiped off the face of a tired and frustrated world.

I did not know how long our journey would take, but I was left with no choice but to trust in the vessel, to trust in the plan. I was too exhausted to dwell on any dire alternatives. I rested my head against the chair, closed my eyes, and thought about what I would say to my son the moment I saw him. I'd hold him close. I'd tell him I loved him, in case he'd forgotten. And then I'd show him a better world than the one he'd been forced to accept. I didn't know how—or if there was a better world left to be had—but I'd try.

The Whisper sped effortlessly across the unending blue sky, towards a long and impossibly distant horizon.

Andy, don't tease your sister.

But Dad—

Hey big guy. You're the older brother. That means you should know better.

I really need to pee, though.

I know. There's a recharge station up the road. We'll stop there. Just hold it.

But if I hold it I'll get a bladder infection.

Who told you that?

I read it.

Uh-huh. Well, I'm sure you'll be fine. Just a little longer. Why don't we sing a song?

What song?

I don't know. Don't you know a good song?

Da-aad, I'm dying here.

Don't be so dramatic, Andy.

What's dramatic?

Okay, okay. There it is.

Where?

You see that light up there? That's the auto-recharge station. See? I knew we were close. It's just around the corner. Just a little bit further, big guy . . .

Gideon tapped me on the arm and I opened my eyes. The Silver Whisper had left the land behind and was flying over the ocean. Away from the mountains, it had come down from its great height, and was now no more than thirty feet above the water. I squeezed the back of my neck and turned to my side. Gideon was pointing at something he'd seen in the water: the rounded black backs of a pod of whales moving together, tumbling and rolling through the silvery-blue surf. They moved serenely as one, migrating to warmer waters, I assumed. One of them sprayed water from its blowhole as it keeled over.

I thought about the stranded whale on the beach. The one we'd burned because there'd been no other option. I wondered whether we could have done something else for it, something we hadn't considered because we too had been stranded, without the provision of hope in our hearts.

The Whisper passed the whales, and we arched back to watch as they slid into the distance behind us.

Ahead, there was new land. Our pod raced towards it, and the nearer we got, the easier it was to discern the many tall buildings that fledged the coastline—a city rising from a remote mist.

The Silver Whisper passed over the shore where waves crashed and foamed against enormous concrete blocks. An empty highway ran beside the barricade. Beyond, Gideon and I saw no people at all. We entered the airspace of the city and passed between the skyscrapers, along a main road lined with twenty-foot high billboards advertising products long unavailable. One of these depicted the gigantic head of a handsome man, leering out at us, shaving off his facial hair with a Laser-Razor. Another was an enthusiastic group-shot of the cast of a theatre musical. The grass of a local park had grown long and wild, swallowing benches and swing-sets.

We zipped through the rest of the business district until the skyscrapers gave way to an expansive, wildly overgrown suburb of houses—another ghost town of swampy green swimming pools and untended yards. Then the dense settlement thinned into a few lone houses on the outskirts of the city and the land was once again countryside.

Beyond the rolling hilltops we saw what we knew to be a commune, the high fence enclosing a number of familiar tents. Communers ambled between these tents—people of all ages and ethnicities. As we soared over, they craned their heads and followed our pod with shaded eyes. They were less than twenty or thirty kilometres from a city, but would never have known it. The New Past had done its job:

The renouncement of civilisation.

The desertion of consumer culture.

The crooked proposition of enlightenment.

I'd once chosen to go along with The Renascence (or thought I had), but wondered if there was still any choice left in the matter.

The commune was soon out of sight and our vessel continued over the low green hills and snaking dirt roads of the pastoral landscape.

"You know," Gideon said. His deep voice was calm and unhurried. "I had a dream last night, in that house. Perhaps it was only a dream, perhaps it was a memory. I don't know. Either way, it was entirely new to me. It seemed to arrive out of nowhere, as if it had found *me* rather than I had found *it*. Does that make sense to you?"

I nodded. He stopped for a moment and looked out at the world through the wall of the pod.

"In my dream," he continued, "I am very young. I know this. I'm not sure how I can know such a thing, but perhaps that is the difference between a dream and a memory. In a dream we believe we're the age we're dreaming we are, with all the insecurities and . . . ignorance of that age, yes? In a memory, we see the past with our present eyes. Can either be trusted? I don't know. Perhaps I've got this all wrong. Regardless, in my dream, I am a student living in a big house with other students. The walls are plastered with movie posters and reprints of famous paintings. There's always music playing from one of the bedrooms.

"Most importantly, there's a young woman who lives in the room across from mine. She's the only female living in that house, but she gets on with every other housemate. They treat her like one of them. They joke with her and she jokes with them. They aren't afraid to be themselves—to be crude or absurd. I know all of these things in this dream. I also know I am not like them. I struggle to see her as just another housemate. Her beauty intimidates me.

"She's standing in the kitchen near the kettle, preparing a coffee. I slip by her to get myself something to drink from the refrigerator. When I close the refrigerator, she's standing behind it, holding her cup of coffee, smiling. I'm holding a bottle of tomato sauce instead of the orange juice, which is not what I planned on grabbing. She asks, 'Why don't you ever speak to me? Did I do something wrong?'

"In my dream, I shake my head. I say, 'No, you've haven't done anything.'

"She says, 'You're not like them, are you? You're interested in different things.'

"I say, 'Maybe.' Then she kisses the palm of her hand and puts it on my cheek, before walking past me. As she goes, she says, 'I'm interested in different things too,' and I think to myself, maybe if I'm lucky, I'll marry a woman like that. Then I wake up."

Gideon took a second, and added, "And I am sleeping next to you."

I laughed and Gideon's mouth lifted in a shy smile I hadn't seen before—the smile of a perfect thought. "That was a good dream. And if it is a memory . . . that would be even better."

"Maybe you did marry her."

"Maybe," Gideon said. "Nevertheless, it is always a good sign to have a good dream before a journey. After a good dream you know everything will be all right."

I sat back in my seat. I stared at the sweeping terrain before us and brought to mind *my* dream, the one I'd had at the same time Gideon had had his own.

I thought about being tied to the bed and drowning in the darkness. Screaming and straining and watching as Jack Turning sat by the window, uncaring, smoking his cigarette. I thought about how I'd awoken in the morning, sweating and shaking and filled with terror.

"A good sign, indeed," said Gideon.

Extracts

(Excerpt from the *The Age of Self Primary*)

1. *A questioning mind hampers spiritual and metaphysical acceptance.*
2. *Detachment displaces desire.*
3. *Knowledge corrupts the self.*
4. *The self serves no purpose unto itself.*
5. *A calm and patient disposition will ensure a prompt and prosperous ascension.*
6. *Every effort must be taken to disown the fraudulent values, traditions and habits of the Age of Self.*
7. *The members of the overlooking Body assigned to each commune are your metaphysical equals, but must be respected and obeyed as the facilitators of The Renascence.*
8. *Each commune will make no use of previous towns and cities.*
9. *There will be no significance placed on biological kinships; the family nucleus must be recognised as both destructive and elitist.*
10. *Any communer who dishonours the commune, and thus The Renascence, will be required to commit to a period of forced detachment.*

11. *The rewards of the willing participant are boundless; the unwilling participant selfishly impedes the process, and betrays us all.*

Two lights

Kayle was looking forward to a weekend away. It had been Sarah's idea—she was full of those kinds of ideas—but as the weekend neared he'd found himself increasingly pleased at the prospect of a break from the humdrum of regular life. At the university, students and faculty had had to contend with the administrative and preparatory nightmare of examinations, but now it was done. No more lectures for a few more weeks. No more papers to mark and submit, no more nagging students rapping on his office door every five minutes "wondering" whether there was anything else they could do to boost their average.

Sarah needed it too. Her physiotherapy practice was finally taking off and she had more new clients than she could have hoped for, but even a pair of healing hands needed a session or two to massage out the knots and kinks of hard work.

"Okay, okay. There it is," Kayle said as he drove the AV along the dark mountain pass. It was a two-hour drive to the lodge Sarah had booked for the family's weekend, and the juice they'd given Andy and Maggie in the backseat was back with a vengeance; Andy was in desperate need of a toilet.

"Where?" Andy asked. He'd been griping for ten minutes.

"You see that light up there? That's the auto-recharge station. See? I knew we were close. It's just around the corner. Just a little bit further, big guy . . ."

Sarah sat in the passenger seat and stared out into the dark woods that walled the road. Kayle looked at her and placed his hand on her thigh, and she turned to smile at him—wide and warm and dashed with two adorable dimples. He loved his wife, he'd always loved her, but their house had recently seemed more of an office than a home, with each of them running around to administer their children's busy little lives. But now the lodge was waiting—two rooms, a pool, a trampoline and various other activities to entertain the kids while Mom and Dad enjoyed some alone time.

"Dad!" Andy whined.

Sarah turned her head to her side. "Andy. We can't go any faster, and we can't stop here. Two minutes, my boy."

Maggie giggled beside her brother. She'd always been a laughing baby, and now at five, she still saw the lighter side of almost everything. She was tiny, even for her age, and the seat belt just about held her in. She clapped her hands and giggled again. Her brother was an animated sufferer, and his many jittery attempts to hold his bladder must have made him look like a silly, broken robot.

To Andy, the lights of the recharge station were brighter than the golden glow of the Pearly Gates. Kayle took one more bend around the mountain and then they were there, finally. He pulled the autovehicle off the road and parked in one of the empty bays beside two big rigs. The AV shut down and the seat belts retracted from their bodies.

Kayle looked out the window. There was nobody at the station. The lights of the signs beamed above the four big recharge cylinders. There was a small convenience store behind them, no one there but a lone woman at the counter, sluggishly paging through a tabloid magazine.

Andy opened the back door and was just about to dart off, when Kayle yelled, "Whoa, kiddo! Easy."

Sarah told him she'd wait in the car with Maggie. The last thing they needed was for Maggie to catch sight of the sugary junk food that lined the shelves.

Kayle got out and walked behind Andy as he hurtled across the concrete towards the lavatory. The country air was bitterly cold, but Andy wasn't outside long enough to feel it. He had rushed through the door, out of sight. Kayle opened the door to the lavatory to check if there was anyone else in there, and could already hear the steady stream of pee in one of the stalls.

"Meet me in the shop as soon as you're done," Kayle called out. "Andy?"

"Yes, Dad," Andy replied.

Kayle went into the clinically lit warmth of the convenience store. The girl behind the counter was no older than eighteen or nineteen, and Kayle wondered how safe it was for her to be holding fort after dark. She lifted her head from her magazine, acknowledged Kayle's arrival with a nod, but offered nothing else. He walked to the fridges at the back and grabbed two small bottles of still water and a can of Vintage Elixir, some organic energy drink he'd heard someone at work talking about. He was reading the incomprehensible ingredients on the side of the can when the door chimed and his son entered the store.

"Feeling better?" Kayle asked. "Mission accomplished?"

"Ja."

"Did you wash your hands?"

"There wasn't any soap but I used hot water."

"Come on. Let's get back to the ladies."

Andy smiled and Kayle guided him back through the shelves towards the counter. He looked up at the clock on the wall. About another thirty minutes of driving, he guessed, and then they'd be at the lodge. He'd tucked that good Pinotage in the boot when he was packing—Sarah's favourite. Just right for what he had planned: make a big fire, throw the blankets off the bed and onto the floor. The kids would go to bed and the two of them could curl up in front of the fire and catch up on each other's lives—all the deep, silly, sexy things they'd been too distracted to share in the last few weeks.

On the way to the front of the store, he grabbed a box of imported dark chocolates and two small chocolate bars for the kids. He put it all down on the counter and the girl scanned and slid each item over the thumbprint reader. She looked pale, almost sickly, as if she'd been sentenced to that convenient store indefinitely.

"Dad?"

"Hm?"

Kayle glanced down. Andy was standing with his back to the counter, staring through the glass doors. Kayle turned to see what was holding his son's attention. Beyond the recharge pumps and across the concrete, he saw the car—his car. The back door was open.

"I forgot to close it," Andy said guiltily. "Maggie."

Kayle spun around.

Maggie was out there. By herself. She'd climbed out and was walking up the grassy embankment that hugged the road. Sarah was in the passenger seat, completely oblivious.

Kayle burst through the door into the cold night. His eyes flitted from Sarah in the front seat, occupied by something on her lap, to their daughter, now climbing towards the dark mountain road . . .

"Sarah!" Kayle shouted, picking up speed. "*Jesus!* Sarah!"

Sarah's head jerked up. She turned and saw the backdoor. Open. Realisation hit: *Maggie. Where's Maggie?* She sprang from the passenger seat, stood for a fraction of a second. *Maggie. Where's she gone?*

That's when Kayle saw the lights.

Two yellow lights beaming in the darkness, two yellow flaming eyes, a hulking creature waiting for just that split second—just that terrible moment—to awaken from its slumber. A car, racing around the bends, screaming from its tyres.

"Maggie!" Kayle yelled as he ran. "Maggie!"

His daughter was in the road, far from their parked car, far from her mother tumbling through the bushes towards her. The eyes grew larger, brighter, the creature screamed louder and higher, it spun around the final bend, and then there they were on that fateful stretch, on a collision course towards a moment: one that would alter their lives forever. A moment that would delete a timeline.

Thump. A small sound. Almost no sound at all.

The car struck Maggie and she flew into the darkness. The two yellow lights flashed past, and then they were red and then they were gone. Vanished. Hidden by another bend in the road. The car hadn't even slowed down. But Kayle wasn't thinking about the car. Kayle thought nothing at all. Fear was erupting from the top of his head, spilling everything he was and would ever be into the world, leaving no remainder. Fear. Hot and blinding and cold and deadening. Destruction. No name. No place. No memory. Just destruction—and horror.

Kayle hurtled towards the embankment. But he could not move fast enough. He could not see over the rise of the embankment. He wanted to fly over it, into the wall of the night that was hiding an unimaginable truth from him.

But he didn't fly, he fell. His foot struck a corner of a concrete curb and he went hurtling down to the ground. His jaw struck the surface and he tasted blood from his tongue.

Kayle raised his hands in the direction of the road. His ears were ringing. His pants were ripped where his knees had met the hard earth.

And as he saw his shrieking wife emerge from the darkness, running through the bushes with their limp daughter flapping in her arms, flapping and lolling and bleeding, there was *knowledge*, sudden and immediate. She was gone. His daughter was no more. Maggie was dead.

Dust and skeletons

The Silver Whisper showed us the world.

As the sun and moon rolled overhead, we soared across every kind of terrain. We sped across a range of snowy peaks where two continents crashed into each other, over an ancient city, long silvery seascapes, patches of steaming marshland. We looked down on shambolic blankets of houses tossed in heaps around large cities, trailing into thin clusters as the countryside took over. We slipped through wrinkled canyons, over gushing rivers, and across grasslands bowed by the wind. We saw woods, cracked deserts, salt flats, twisted jungles and neat bays lined with the glittering towers of expired super-cities.

Each landscape could have been the surface of its own planet. Over every horizon a new face of the earth was revealed—broken and beautiful, peaceful and perilous—and I realised then the many outlandish faces of Man were but miniature reflections of those very outlands.

The final horizon of our journey had arrived and we were approaching the ragged valley where the Silver Whisper had first come crashing down. Gideon was the one who noticed the reading on the screen. The number of kilometres left to travel clicked to less than thirty, a short stretch from our destination.

There was a small farmhouse on a square of pasture to the left of us, which might have been the house of Jai-Li's unremembered family. I saw the route the young girl must have taken back to the pod. As I tried to imagine her down there, I felt something well within me—a sense that Gideon and I had become a part of that lore, of everything we'd heard. We were flying among the words of a story, into the realm of myth, a modest Holy Land only we had been allowed to know.

As the kilometres on the screen dropped to zero the Silver Whisper floated down and circled in the air above the rocky earth. We were hovering directly above the spot where the pod had once crashed, the only detail of interest in an otherwise unremarkable location. The pod lowered slowly, setting up a gentle rustling in the nearby brush and scattered trees. Small rocks and pebbles clattered in their places. We touched the ground and the whirring of the engine subsided and then stopped completely.

On either side, jagged cliff-faces extended upwards. The arid land was hot and unforgiving, and the trusses of dull green plants crawling up through the gaps between the rocks alluded to a long, waterless history.

Gideon grabbed our bags from under the seats as the side of the pod opened. The warm desert air rushed into the cool interior. I shouldered my rucksack and stepped out. I scrambled down a pile of dusty rocks with Gideon close behind me. When we were about twenty metres from the pod the door retreated into the body of the pod, closing seamlessly.

"Where do we go from here?" Gideon asked. I stopped and looked up and down the valley. I'd seen the farmhouse as we'd flown in, which meant the tower was most likely in the opposite direction. That was as much as I could deduce.

"There. I think," I said, pointing towards the narrowing walls of steep mountainside before us. "I want to say I'm sure, but . . . "

Gideon did not hesitate, and began to walk in the direction I had suggested, placing one careful foot in front of the next on the bed of loose rocks.

"There isn't a sure thing left, Mr. Kayle," he said, pushing on confidently as if he'd seen a large arrow painted on the side of the mountain. "I'm quite sure about that."

I followed him, over rocks that crackled and clapped beneath our feet. As we walked away, I looked back over my shoulder once more to pay my last respects to the vessel. The metallic bubble had served us well. It sat easily in its spot, catching the blue sky and orange cliffs, as if holding on to a memory of its own. It was finally ready to take Jai-Li and her child to the temple. It was her story that had allowed us to get to where we were. I would never forget that. But it was Shen—the one who had ingeniously intertwined our paths—who deserved more than our gratitude.

We owed it to him to go on.

He deserved an ending.

We hiked our way through the rocky gorge, along the flat, winding scar of a long-dried river. We'd been walking for a couple of hours and the scorching weather was doing us no favours. We drank small quantities of water frequently, to stave off dehydration. We passed the skulls and skeletons of small and large animals, reminding us of an all too likely outcome. Gideon's face was impassive. Either he was feeling no fear or he was able to control his emotions perfectly. I was faring less well. Each hot breath and sip of warm water did nothing to replenish me. I said nothing but could not help feeling we were marching towards our deaths. Any time now and we'd fall to our knees beneath the blue sky, defeated by the heat. We'd become two more fossils—two more dusty warnings for anyone foolish enough to pass.

"Gideon, I need to rest a moment."

Gideon stopped. He tilted his face to the sky and blinked at the sun. I took a seat on a rock and pulled up my shirt to wipe the sweat from my face. Gideon grabbed a bottle of water and gave it to me. I threw back my neck and sipped, but held back from drinking more than I should. The water barely seemed to touch my throat, vaporising at the back of my mouth.

Big black birds circled overhead, waiting for our bottles to empty and our bodies to collapse under us—waiting to feast on the soft meat of our sunken eyes and swollen tongues. They'd seen this before. They knew how it ended, and perhaps even how long it would take to end. They circled in front of the sun, speckling the earth in moving shadows.

Gideon sat down next to me and had a sip of water. He dragged his forearm over his face and put the bottle back in the bag.

"I'm glad you're here, Gideon," I said. "I couldn't do this without you."

"Neither could I, Mr. Kayle. We should go. Let's keep walking."

Gideon lent a hand to lift me from the rock. He cupped a hand on my shoulder and then turned and navigated his way over the rocks. The birds broke their formation and flew towards the turn in the valley, perhaps towards something freshly dead beneath the murderous sun. We followed their lead.

As we walked, the shadows of the valley shifted, the day bled away. Once the sun went down, the temperature would drop drastically and we'd suffer the night.

Finally, the valley tapered and we had to climb over a pile of enormous boulders. We rounded a bend and the valley came to an abrupt end. Past the exit to the gorge there was a flat expanse of brown desert sand. Gideon and I stood atop a boulder and stared out.

"There," Gideon said, pointing. "Do you see that?"

I could see it perfectly. At the edge of the horizon, a colossal black structure wavered through a mirage of heat. It was a man-made craft, the largest astromining ship ever built, the size of a small town. We were staring at Chang'e 11.

"We need a single day to get to it," Gideon said. "There's no point going now. Come the night, we'd be stuck in the middle of the desert. For now, we should find a place in the mountain to camp. We need shelter and water. More than that, we need to prepare ourselves, Mr. Kayle—our bodies and our minds. The desert does not forgive fools."

Time

I opened my eyes and I could hear and feel the rush of water beneath me. It took me a moment to figure out where I was. Finally, it came to me, with absolutely no sense of relief: I was on the ocean. I was on the raft.

I must be dreaming. Another cruel dream.

"Kayle," I heard. I rolled my head to my left. It was Daniel, the young man who'd first brought us to the whale. He was holding the side of the raft. "You did it. You made it. It's over." He was standing in the water beside me, smiling awkwardly.

"*Gideon . . .*" My throat seared with pain. "*Andy . . . Chang'e 11.*"

"Take it easy now. Everything will be all right," he tried to comfort me. "It was a long stretch, but it's all over."

I tried to sit up but was still shackled at the neck, wrists and ankles. Daniel put his hands on my chest to calm me.

"What's going on?" I muttered. "Where's Gideon?"

"They've pulled him out already," Daniel said. "Everyone's out of the water; you're the last one."

I shook my head, my neck tight under the leather neck-strap. My eyes rolled, taking in what they could, looking for a crack in the shell of a convincing delusion.

"It's been three days," Daniel said. "Three days. The longest sentence yet."

There was no crack. The world shaped itself into a terrifying reality. The indentations in Daniel's acne-scarred skin. The powdery tufts of cloud above and the birds that flew freely through them. The caress of the breeze on my face. Icy seawater lashed my back, the sun lashed me from above.

Cold water. Hot sun. Cold water. Hot sun.

In a dream, can we tell the difference between the burn of cold and the burn of heat? I wasn't sure. A lucid dream can trick us, but never with the complexity of wakeful thought. Could it really be that it had all been a drug-induced fallacy, that I hadn't gone anywhere?

No! You were there! my mind insisted. *You were on your way to Chang'e 11, to confront Quon and rescue your son. Wake up, Kayle . . .*

But I didn't wake. I was still there. I probed my new reality, as tender as the reddened skin on the edge of an inflamed swelling. I felt sick. I wanted to throw up, but I didn't. I stared at the broad blue sky and breathed in a deep ocean breath. I let the air out, and with it, myself.

I thought about that quest—so full of coincidences—and the more I thought, the more ludicrous it began to seem. How could I have believed I had been set upon a quest of such importance? The simplest explanation was, in the end, the most likely; all of it was nothing more than an elaborate fabrication of the ego, the invention of a man desperate for purpose, for meaning and resolution. I'd even made myself the hero of the story.

I felt like a broken idiot.

I would never see my son.

I would never leave that beach.

The raft had done its job; it had crippled my will, demonstrated the uselessness of mutiny, emphasised our individual insignificance. Not long after waking (*dreaming, Kayle, you're only dreaming!*), I felt the raft being pulled through the water. The water rushed over my forearms, soothing my blistered skin. My exile was over, my sentence had been served and I was being pulled to shore.

I was not permitted to see Gideon, Theunis or Angerona. I was taken straight to the white house on the hill and put back in the chair. The plugs were attached to my head and the grey machine read my thoughts, as it apparently always had.

The Body sat behind their long table and asked me about my time out on the raft. They asked if I had seen the error of my ways and if I regretted having helped Jai-Li escape the beach.

I could barely respond to their questions. The light of the overhead lamp seared my eyes. Even then, sweating in that big chair, I thought I would wake up to discover it had all been a ruse, a chilling new trick of the mind. I didn't want to tell them anything, but they waited, silent, until I was left with no choice but to speak. They were curious about my experience. No two raft experiences were the same, they said, but there was always *some* kind of experience.

In the end, I submitted and told them what I remembered so clearly: the island of fruit, Anubis, the family of machines and Gideon. I told them many things, but I did not say a word about Shen and Quon; they were my last two cards: my king and my joker.

Once I had told them the story, they said they were impressed by my fabrication, that I had always been gifted with imagination. And then, almost as an afterthought, they mentioned that they'd found Jai-Li; she hadn't made it very far from the cove before her boat had tipped, sending both her and her child to their watery deaths. My first reaction was shock, and deep sorrow, but then I remembered the story they'd concocted to cover up Moneta's fatal escape. They were seasoned liars, and I decided not to believe them. They asked how I felt about that news and I said nothing—they could *read* my answer if they wanted it.

Next they said I would no longer have contact with the other offenders. They added they were pleased with my co-operation and hoped I'd make the most of my reintegration into the commune. They expected great things of me, they said, which meant great things of doing nothing at all.

I was taken back to my tent where all my things were waiting for me. I climbed into bed. *Maybe when you awake, you'll be back there, Kayle, back in the desert.* But when I awoke the next day, I was still in the tent.

I was put to various tasks. I helped the fishermen with the lave nets and the young men and women with the cleaning. I'd stare at the ocean frequently, wondering if I'd ever be able to get back. It pained me to think how close I had been to finding my son. Or, at least, how close it had felt. Memories of my journey flew about my mind like the orange-tipped embers that blew from the nightly bonfires. I ran through the details over and over again, but the more I tried to remember them, the dimmer the flames of my certainty grew, the greyer the ash of my doubt.

I saw Gideon a few times, wandering through the commune. I tried to call him, but he wouldn't look my way. Was he deliberately ignoring me or simply obeying the orders of The Body? I couldn't tell. I'd go back to my chore, wondering if he resented me asking him to help with Jai-Li's escape. Whatever the reason, I had lost my one friend. That was difficult to accept. I thought I had been lonely before my time on the raft, but this was true loneliness: it isn't simply the difficulty of being by yourself; it's being near the people you care about most, and having them deny you.

I did end up on the raft once more, a few months after my first sentence. This time, I hadn't saved anyone's life or helped anyone off the beach. I was convicted because I had tried to run, to escape through the woods against the mountain, only to find my plan thwarted by an immense wall that I knew nothing about. There was no way over it and no way around it; we were truly imprisoned on the beach. Somehow the story of my attempt to leave got out and I was put back on a raft. I remember thinking that perhaps that would be the clincher; I'd lie back on the raft and pick up where I had left off with Gideon, in the desert, but over the course of my second sentence, I experienced nothing but a watery day and cold wet night before being pulled back to shore.

The time following my second return from the raft was long and painfully mundane, one long day recycled for all eternity. The nights were even longer than the days, sleepless and formless, offering nothing but a black wall against which I tried to paste the faded scraps of my memories. Over time, there was hardly anything to think about. Slowly, irrevocably, I was losing every last drop of my hope. And then, one day, I forgot to hope at all. That was the day I put to rest the whole idea of returning to the world and hope became a faint and faded glimmer, seldom seen, seldom felt.

Months turned into years, and the years rolled on.

Every now and again I sat and thought about that first time on the raft. I would never completely let it go, even though I felt that it somehow wanted to let go of me. I was on the beach for good, that was obvious now, and I told myself to accept it. Nothing hinted otherwise. The Renascence proved to be some kind of farce (the omega point of The Renascence had either not occurred, or was vastly less ceremonious than we had imagined), and everything simply, and gradually, wasted away. We had been on the beach for so long the water level of the ocean had risen and eventually there was barely a beach at all. We were forced to move our tents to the woods.

The dictatorship too had simply come to an end. Trawlers stopped bringing new communers, and nobody was called up to the white house on the hill (which was no longer a white house at all but a flaking, cream-yellow shack). One day, on a whim, I went up to inspect it. There was no longer any fear of being punished—The Body had already done their worst—and I knew there would be nobody inside. I was right. Bushes and trees had grown up to the entrance and the house was filled with little but dust and ruined furniture. The grey machine that once read our minds sat in its corner like a creature turned to stone by an angry god. There were no floating heads behind the table, no more *bearing witness*, no more questions and plugs and sentences for trivial misdemeanours.

Our commune had been forgotten by the world. We had no communication with outsiders, so had no idea whether The Renascence was being continued elsewhere. Nobody bothered dancing around bonfires (there was too little of the shore left to even make a fire), and we simply huddled through the seasons, keeping ourselves alive on fish and fruit.

Angerona was now a grown woman, but still hadn't uttered a word in her life. I had become an old and weary man. My knees were bad. I had arthritis in both wrists. I was the crumbling mess none of us ever dream of one day becoming.

I was often revisited by that old memory of a journey I thought I'd taken, but the memory had been hollowed of its worth by the chisel of time. It might as well have been someone else's memory, and someone else's quest—I had preserved every detail in my mind, but felt nothing for it. My son was either an old man himself, or dead; perhaps that, after everything, would be the one true way in which we'd finally be reunited. If I had thought such a thing was possible, I might have at some earlier time taken my life, just to see. But now I was too old to bother with suicide—a young man's escape. Time would do it for me, ungraciously and grudgingly, and I was prepared to wait.

We thought the rising ocean would be the means of our eventual end (we'd all be pushed up against the wall in the woods waiting for the ocean to claim us), but one ordinary day a communer began to cough in his tent. He came out, his mouth running with blood. Not long after that, someone else began coughing and appeared with the same scarlet patch of blood on her face. We did not know what the illness was, but over the course of a few months, it spread from communer to communer, claiming life upon life. Some people said it was the water we were drinking. Others said we had contracted a virus from mosquitoes. It didn't matter what caused it, though. There was nothing we could do about it, and people were dying. We dug holes in the dirt and buried the bodies to prevent the disease from spreading, but we may as well have dug pits for ourselves and gone to bed in them.

By the time winter arrived, I knew that most of us would not survive it. There would be less than a handful of us by the time the leaves returned to the trees. This turned out to be true. People died in quick succession. The woods were riddled with graves, and day by day our numbers shrank. One night, Angerona began coughing and spitting blood, and less than a day after the symptoms had first appeared, I was digging a hole for her too.

Within two months of that final winter only Gideon and I remained. We moved up to the house on the hill and made a fire with the furniture. Outside, the wind and the rain thrashed and thumped the earth. Gideon made the occasional practical suggestion, but apart from that said almost nothing to me. I didn't mind. All I wanted was to keep warm—warm and fed. That was what hope was reduced to. It was difficult to fish and find food. Some days we didn't eat at all and would go to sleep early, hoping the new day would bring with it some small, trifling fortune.

Then Gideon started coughing.

The first dry cough came in the middle of the night, Death's knuckles rapping on our door. I knew as soon as I heard it. Soon I would be alone. I loathed the thought.

I covered him with more blankets and started a fire in the centre of the room. He was sweating profusely, shivering beneath his blankets. I told him to hold on, *just hold on.* But I had seen enough of the disease to know what was coming.

I kneeled beside him on my old knees and wiped his hot forehead with a damp cloth. The first spurt of blood came from his mouth and I stumbled back. I edged closer, trying to pretend I hadn't seen it, continuing to pat his head and wipe his mouth.

He grabbed my thin wrist with his big hands and turned to his side.

"I'm so sorry," he said. "I'm sorry, Mr. Kayle."

He hadn't called me Mr. Kayle in years.

I told him to save his energy and pulled the blankets up to his shoulders.

"We had an adventure once," I said. "You and I. Not in this world, but somewhere. It was an incredible adventure, and I couldn't have done it without you. I remember that."

I could hear the blood gurgling in his throat. I sat at his side through the night, until the gurgling came to an end and he closed his eyes and died.

I pulled the blanket over his face and walked to the window. Outside, the rain was falling on the place we had once called a commune. Lightning cracked over the ocean. *This is it*, I thought. *This is the culmination of my long and pointless life.*

I walked to my blankets and lay down. The last stick of furniture in the house was burning. Soon everything would go cold and dark. I rolled myself in my blankets and tried to sleep. But it wasn't easy, not with my own dry and determined cough.

By morning the storm had ended and the weather cleared. I wrapped Gideon's body in the rest of the blankets and slid him to the door of the white house. My cough had worsened and I was sweating uncontrollably, but if there was one thing I'd get done before collapsing somewhere, it would be to give Gideon a proper burial. My last duty in this life. I rested his body on two long logs, clutched the ends and dragged him up through the soggy soil of the woods. I struggled, my frail body weakening with every step. The sun glimmered on the leaves of the trees. Water trickled from the canopies above. All around were the broken remnants of the commune—tattered tarps and tent frames. The area was deathly still but for the ceaseless slapping and gurgle of the waves through the vegetation.

My knees trembled and my arms began to shake and I lowered the logs to catch my breath. I put my hand to my mouth, coughed, and when I pulled my hand away, saw what I had been anticipating: blood.

"Kayle, is it?"

I looked up. The blurry figure of a person stood at the top of a muddy ridge. I blinked and the blur took shape—a man in a coat and a hat. He stood still, sneering down on me. He gripped a tree trunk and swung himself down to my level, his boots splashing in the wet dirt. He grabbed the rim of his hat and tipped it, then circled me slowly. I tried to turn with him, but could hardly stand. He hunkered down and pulled the blanket off Gideon's face.

"That's not very pleasant," he said, and whipped the blanket back before rising to his feet.

"Do I know you?" I asked.

"No," he said, slowly slipping a pair of leather gloves off his hands. He tucked the gloves into the top pocket of his coat and patted it. "You don't. But you'd like to, I take it. Or *would* have liked to, I should say. You don't have much desire or will left, do you?" He circled back to a stump of wood and sat down, crossing his legs. "It's a funny thing, human will. So cherished, and yet so fragile. So easy to break. Look at you, for example. You had will. You had hope. But where is it now? Gone. And what did it take to erode? Nothing but time. Lots and lots of time. That's it. All your dreams and desires crumbled by the weight of time."

"Who are you?" I croaked.

"It'll come to you. It's been a while since you last thought about me—well, a while to *you*, anyway."

He was waiting for me to say something, but I couldn't tell what. I was struggling to breathe and keep upright.

"No? Nothing?" he said, clicking his tongue against the roof of his mouth, like a strange woodland creature. "That's okay. I understand. Time is the great divider. Relentless. Incorruptible. It weeds out the meaningless and leaves the meaningful . . . Although, mind you, the funny thing is, over *enough* time even the most meaningful of things becomes meaningless. Things like hope. A pathetic, ineffectual charm you people hang around your necks to ward off the evil spirits.

"That's all I had to do to break your will, Kayle—dismantle your hopes. I simply had to flood you with a deluge of time, like an ocean washing over one little shell. And given time your will and your hope to find me became . . . *meaningless.*"

"Quon?" I hadn't thought of him in years but his name came back in a clear flash.

He sniggered. "Correct. Now I don't know why Shen bothered to send you to find me, Kayle. That I haven't figured out. He was obviously up to his tricks. I'm terribly sorry I had to do this to you—make you play out an entire lifetime in a moment—but that's really all I could think of doing to prevent you from arriving at my doorstep to do whatever foolish thing you've got planned. It was the only way for me to break you, hold you back from completing your mission. All I had to do was give you time and you discouraged *yourself.* Easy enough."

I clenched my teeth, fighting back tears. "I knew it," I said. "All this time, I knew . . ."

"You knew. So what? What did you do with what you knew? Nothing. Nothing at all, old chap."

"Where am I, really?"

"In a cave. In the desert, sleeping beside Gideon."

I wanted to scream. I wanted to dive forward and grab him, tear him apart with my hands, but my hands, my bony, spotted hands, could tear at nothing.

Quon's voice changed its tone. Still musing, but with a harder edge to it, the bantering note falling away. "I know you're looking for your son—that's obvious—but that can't be the only reason you were sent to find me. No, there's something else. Something I'm missing. The problem, however, the reason I can't snatch it out of your mind, is because you don't really know the big plan either, do you? Shen didn't tell you. He was just using you. He did that." He tapped a finger on his chin, pondering. "But using you for *what?*"

He stood again, dusting off the back of his coat. "All right, you know what? I've changed my mind. I was going to leave you here, make you believe in all of this *nonsense,* probably until you lost your sanity, but I have to admit, my curiosity is quite overwhelming. So see if you can pull yourself together. A tall order, no doubt, after a lifetime of dashed hopes and broken dreams—but if you can, and if there's anything left of you, stop by Chang'e 11. I'd be more than happy to meet you."

He paused then and added with a slight smile, "Just don't expect things to end in your favour. I'm inclined to be a little . . . playful with people's memories. I can easily make you think you're living a whole other life, like that!" He snapped his fingers. "One even longer than this, and far more boring."

I coughed and dropped to my knees. I grabbed my throat and bent over. Blood ran through my beard and onto the forest floor. I wasn't just spitting; I was retching at the knowledge that had come so late—so impossibly late. Quon stood over me and patted me on the back.

"There, there, old chap," he said. "It's a lot to process. I'm not going anywhere. Take all the time in the world."

I opened my eyes. Air rushed into my lungs. I knew instantaneously that I was my younger self. My body didn't ache; my flesh was firmer and tauter on my bones. I was in a cave on the edge of the desert, lying beside Gideon. I felt a gush of emotion—panic, joy and bewilderment. I could barely comprehend where I had been, and for how long. I put my hands to my face and sobbed. I had hoped I would return to the cave, but had lost all faith the moment would come. Now I was back, but not all of me. Something had been taken away, just as Quon had willed. Something in me had been broken by a mountain of wasted years, by the memories of an entire life that had never happened at all.

The world will be ash

When Gideon woke up, I was sitting at the entrance to our shallow mountainside cave, watching the sun creep up from behind the long, dull hem of the horizon. I'd been up for hours, studying every detail I could of the world, alert to flaws, on the lookout for clues. I rubbed the sand on the floor of the cave between finger and thumb, and it felt reassuringly gritty. I strained my ears to listen to every sound of the night, the clicking scurry of a scorpion, the manic whooping call of some wild animal. I wanted proof positive that what I was seeing was real. Either that, or it didn't exist at all.

Gideon sat on a cold rock beside me and wrapped his arms around his knees. Whether he was real or not, it was good to see him so young, and alive and well. As far as my memory allowed, I had seen his grey-faced corpse only the day before.

"I'm not sure I can do this," I said, shaking my head. The sun was beginning to ascend, hitting the wall of yellow light that lined the edge of the world. "I *can't* do this."

Gideon said nothing for a moment, and then asked, "What happened?"

"Quon knows we're coming."

"You saw him in your dream?"

I didn't respond. How could I explain what had happened, that I had lived an entire lifetime in a night? In my mind, I was still that old man and I had felt every minute of every day for countless years. My back had straightened and my blood had warmed. My bones had toughened upon waking, but my will had not.

"It's more than that," I said. "What he did to me . . . I . . . I just don't know. I can't tell if any of this is real. I've been sitting here, listening to the night, waiting for the sun . . . hoping that when it finally came up I'd know. But it's here now and I still can't be sure."

"What did you see in your dream?"

"It wasn't a dream. It was a lifetime. I lived an entire life in a night, as real to me as all of this."

I looked out over the desert, and my voice grew quieter as I continued. "I was on the beach. I grew old. I watched you die and I carried your body to your grave. After that, I woke up. I can't entirely explain it—it feels like I lived a lifetime; it feels like I was only asleep a night. But now, I can't believe in anything. You. Me. This place. My son. I *want* to believe it, but there's nothing I can't doubt. *Nothing.* And the worst thing is, I've seen the end, and it's absolutely meaningless. All of it. Nothing comes to anything. Nothing means anything, no matter what we do. No matter what we hope for."

"Whatever Quon showed you was to make you think this way, Mr. Kayle," Gideon said. "He *wants* you to lose hope."

"That's just it," I interrupted him. "I can't tell if *you're* really saying this, or if it's him, or me. No matter what you say, I'll never be sure of it! Whatever he did, it worked. I'm sorry, my friend. I'm not sure there's enough left of me to go on."

Gideon sighed. The sun was almost halfway up and the air was warming, taming the icy end of night. I went back all those many (imaginary?) years to Moneta, who had once made her choice. She had lost faith in the world, in memory, and ended her life. Her words slid into my jumbled thoughts: *One day, even the sun will burn out and everything will go dark. This earth will be a rock. We'll be ash. There'll be no meaning behind us ever having existed.*

"You're right," Gideon said. "There's nothing we can't doubt. But that has always been the case. And maybe this *is* all a dream. Maybe it's *always* been a dream. But at least we still have a choice, Mr. Kayle—the only real choice—because if this is nothing but a dream, we still have a choice. Either we end it all . . . or we try to make it the best dream we can."

Gideon stood up and rubbed his big hands on the sides of his shirt. His dark forearms were encrusted in sweat and dust. He swept his dreadlocks behind his ears. Bands of yellow sun and dark blue sky gleamed in his eyes. The dips and mounds in the plateau of desert sand threw exaggerated shadows towards us. In the far centre sat the black silhouette of Chang'e 11, looking like a crude replica of the beached whale we'd once found.

"Look, I don't know what you went through. I would be a fool to pretend to understand. But whatever Quon showed you, Mr. Kayle, he did so because he is trying to stop you continuing. Think about it. Why would he want to do that? He's scared of you. This Quon fancies himself a god, yes? Well, I don't know much, but I have never known a true god to ever be scared of a man."

We made our way across the desert under the full sun. The further we walked out into the open plain, the further we were from the refuge of the mountain. There was no place to hide, to stop and recover from the heat. The ground beneath us was hard and cracked. My feet were blistering in my shoes; my tongue was swollen and dry. Chang'e 11 broadened across the horizon with every step we took, rising ever upwards and outwards, but my thoughts dragged behind me like a heavy rock I had been cursed with carrying.

(*So see if you can pull yourself together, Kayle—it might be a tall order after a lifetime of dashed hopes and broken hearts—but if you can, and there's anything left of you, stop by Chang'e 11*)

I fought my way through the lies of the past, retraced my steps to the beginning of my journey out. As I looked back on the sad slippage of life on the beach, the disease, the death, that night's lifetime began to reveal itself as a forgery. The memories of my return to the beach were weakening and vanishing, time was contracting and regaining normal proportions. It was easier to pick up where I had left off before the life Quon had grafted onto mine. Gideon had been right. It was a lie.

(*Someone will put you to the test in order to find your son. He may try to deceive you, as he does to all people of the indomitable Now, and you should be prepared for that meeting, when it comes. So I'll tell you*)

Quon had done it because he didn't want us coming—but why? I searched for a reason. It was there, I knew, a thread woven loosely through my experiences, one that I only needed to grab and pull taut, if I could just find it. Moneta's connection to Anubis, Anubis to the family of robots, and the family to Jai-Li. What had been the point of it all? If Shen had planned all this, as Father implied, what outcome did he hope for? Why had he gone to the effort of guiding us through these many back doorways, simply to help a man he didn't know find his son? There had to be something more to it, something bigger. There was something Shen was expecting of us that we were not expecting of ourselves.

(*Time is the great divider. Relentless. Incorruptible. It weeds out the meaningful from the meaningless, and over enough time, the funny thing is, even the most meaningful of things become meaningless*)

Gideon and I kept walking, edging across the hot and sterile land, coming ever closer to the mountainous vessel. Gideon gave me a bottle of water and I sipped from it. The water did nothing. We were burning up. The earth seemed to harden with every step, straining my knees. My mind tumbled with memories.

(*You see, my father was the CEO of a corporation called Huang Enterprises*)

Though it was still far ahead, we could now make out the details of the vessel's structure—thick and immense black plates of wrought iron welded crudely to form what appeared to be a giant mechanical armadillo. There was nothing remotely refined about its design. This monstrous machine, created to haul millions of kilograms of raw ore across the universe, was now a castle from an ancient era, a religious site awaiting its pilgrims.

(And my father, as head of this monster, was the Ozymandias of the empire. King of kings, a wrecked colossus. A fair enough comparison, I think, considering the anticlimactic outcome of it all)

Rough stone walls had been built around the perimeter to form a type of citadel—to protect the vessel from the world or, perhaps, the world from the vessel. Two sealed iron gates hung in the centre of the jagged wall, supported by two massive obelisks on either side.

I felt my knees go weak beneath me, and stopped to bend over and breathe. Gideon put his hand on my back, though I could tell he was faring no better.

"We can't stop," he said. "Not here. We'll die if we stop."

"Andy," I said, panting. "I need to find Andy. That's it. Then we go home."

Home. What home? All I knew was that wherever we were, and wherever Andy was, it was not and would not ever be home. Home was peace, wherever peace resided.

Gideon turned and helped me up to stand, adding, "Then we go home."

(I ran into her, just as I'd imagined, and then I cried. She asked me what had happened. She asked me where I'd been, but I said nothing. She kissed me on the top of my head, rubbed my back in circles, and said to me the words I'd hoped to hear, but at that moment they sounded like the most impotent little words I'd ever heard: It's okay, sweet pea, everything's going to be all right)

Quon

The thick iron gates parted and opened slowly, squealing on their large hinges. We walked cautiously through the opening and entered what looked to be another commune. A number of tents and shacks squatted around the colossal vessel, each pegged into the solid earth with iron rods. Steam rose in the distance. There was the clang of metal on metal from an undetermined location, and then the clanging stopped.

At first, there appeared to be no one.

Gradually, men, women and children began to emerge from their shaded nooks. More and more of them, hundreds of people, slipping from the shadows. They walked into the dusty road that lay before us—the road leading to the entrance of Chang'e 11. They stayed close to each other and stared at Gideon and me with empty eyes and blank, impassive faces. Their clothes were torn, dusty and rumpled. Their hair was tangled and dishevelled, their skin leathery and dark. These desert people were shadows of their former selves, I could tell. For whatever reason they had chosen to dwell beside Chang'e 11, their time in that place had eaten away at them, their souls and their minds bled from their bodies by an ever-thirsty vampire.

They said nothing to welcome or rebuff us. It was hard to tell whether they knew we were really there at all.

"We're here to see Quon," I said, my voice whipped away by a hot breeze. For a moment they did not react to my words, and then, with perfect synchronicity, they broke into a terrible laughter. They cackled and howled and threw their wrinkled faces to the sky. The commune filled with their inflated roar.

As suddenly as it had begun, the laughter stopped. The joke was over. The vacant faces returned. The hollow eyes.

And then a collective breath, drawn in deeply before they roared as one: "I. AM. QUON."

I looked to Gideon but he did not look back. He wouldn't take his eyes off them.

The many synched voices rumbled: "PLEASE. COME IN. MAKE YOURSELF AT HOME."

"There was a man once," I said loudly. "Just one man. Quon. I want to see him."

"WHAT DOES IT MATTER?" they all said. "ONE MAN OR MANY?"

"You're a coward, Quon! Hiding—"

"HIDING?" they bellowed mechanically—men, women, children. And I could now hear something else under their collective words: the mutterings of individual voices, soft and distant. The droning white noise of the people they had once been, the inner stirrings of terror and confusion. A voice here, a voice there: *Don't go in, where am I, why me, no, no, no, I can't do this, oh god, oh god, help me, has anyone seen my child, I don't belong here, take me with you, I'm looking for my father, please, I don't know where I am, why, why, why, is anyone there . . .*

It didn't last long. A silence quickly befell them all, as if an anxious puppeteer had pulled their strings taut, and then the unified voice went on: "I AM NOT HIDING. I'M HERE. THIS IS IT. THE RENASCENCE. THIS IS WHAT IT MEANS TO BE ONE. THIS IS WHAT YOU ALWAYS WANTED, ALWAYS DREAMED OF—UNITY."

"You don't impress me," I said. "Show your face."

The communers paused. They edged back to the sides of the road, opening the path to Chang'e 11 . . . They raised their right hands and in perfect unison waved in the direction of the entrance. On each face I saw the same smirk, and then a quiet snicker hummed through the crowd. A cruel prank awaited us and they could not contain their mutual glee. As Gideon and I walked along the desert road, lined with those puppeteered people, their heads swivelled as we passed.

Had these automatons been lured into the desert or had they chosen to submit themselves? Perhaps they too had come on a pilgrimage. A journey not unlike our own, to meet their "maker"—to question him, or destroy him or even to hail him. Whatever the reason, their maker had not allowed them to leave. I promised myself then, no matter what happened, no matter what Quon said or did, I would fight with all my strength and will against such a fate.

Gideon said nothing as we walked through the commune. As we reached the end of the road the large section of the massive structure creaked into life and lowered to the ground, like the drawbridge of an ancient castle. I looked back at the hundreds of faces turned in our direction and then Gideon and I walked into the dark confines of Chang'e 11.

A long and dark passage stretched into the belly of the ship. A memory hit me: Jai-Li's walk along the well-lit corridor towards the underground house in the tower. I felt what she must have felt. She had wanted to escape her life of imprisonment. She had wanted answers.

It took a while for our eyes to adjust to the dark interior of the vessel. All heat was gone, replaced by the industrial cold of non-operational machinery. The walls of the passage were made of welded sheets of metal, studded with heavy levers and hung with faded warning signs. Each step on the iron grating of the walkway caused a clanking echo that rippled into the congealing darkness. I worried for a moment that the door would close behind us, sealing us in a gigantic mechanical tomb, but that was a chance we had to take. We would not walk back out until we had what we had come for: answers.

The interior was dank. Oily liquid gathered in the corners of the ceiling and dripped through the grate beneath us. Eventually we came to a corner and turned, deeper into Chang'e 11, away from the light of day. I could hear my breath, and Gideon's. We approached an iron door that stood partially open and stepped through into a large room sloppily furnished with defunct equipment and dusty panels of instruments. A dim blue light shone from the corner of the room, but we couldn't see any power source.

"There," Gideon said, and pointed his blue-lit arm to another door at the far end. We walked through another door and along another passage and then another.

The ship groaned, contracting and expanding under its own weight. The further we walked, turning and turning in endless, maddening circles, the more it seemed that the byzantine corridors would never end. We were dooming ourselves to an impossible maze. The air began to thin as we pushed forward into the iron gut of Chang'e 11. I could no longer see Gideon beside me, but I could hear him. I could feel the faint warmth from his body.

Then the warmth was gone.

The breathing had stopped.

I spun in my spot, fanning out my hands to get a sense of where I was. There were no walls alongside me. Gideon was gone and there was nothing around me but the darkness. Panic settled swiftly; my breath came out in ragged gasps. I swung my head from side to side, my hands flailing before me.

"Gideon," I called. There was no reply. "Gideon."

(*If the light won't have me, let the dark. The light, I've learned, is happier to whore itself*)

I stopped. Breathed deeply to calm myself. I closed my eyes then, embracing the darkness instead of fighting it. My breathing slowly returned to normal. My hands came down slowly at my sides. As the sound of my own fear began to subside, a faint sense of orientation took its place.

Listen, Kayle. Listen. You don't have to *see* where you are. You know where you are. You're here. You're not lost. You are here and you are *now*. You are here and now and it is all and it is everything. Do not fear it. Move forward, move slowly, and do not fear anything. You'll find your way.

Just listen.

"Mr. Kayle," I heard. "Here."

I opened my eyes and the hulking shadow of Gideon stood before me. There was a dull groan of metal on metal and then there was light. Gideon had his hand on the handle of a large door. He swung the door out carefully and the rest of his features materialised in the widening gap between door and frame. I smiled and made my way towards him, entering another division of the vessel.

Gideon stepped in after me, into what appeared to be a vast iron hall. (*The room was the hall of Valhalla itself: an incomprehensibly unwarranted amount of space with almost nothing inside it*) The far walls were lined with broken screens and dashboards and all was weakly lit by a large, circular skylight. Sunlight, struggling to reach the depths of the vessel, probably refracted into the hall from large mirrors lodged within the hull above. But such a skylight would be useless in space, I thought, unless it had been used to provide the astronauts with a heaven of sorts—to keep a long-travelling crew orientated beneath the cosmos.

Nine years in space was a long time to be away from home. What were the unspoken necessities for such a long voyage? Could we handle being away from something as matter-of-fact as an overhead sky? What would happen to us if we were denied the staples of our earthbound environment? Our bodies might survive these missing things, but could our minds? Could we truly last without a sky, an open plain, a horizon, or fresh air? Could Jai-Li?

Gideon and I walked towards the centre of the hall. The weak light met the floor, illuminating a man. He was seated on a big black chair—the throne of a commander, a captain, or a king—raised off the floor and attached to a metal pole that pivoted from the ceiling. He was wearing an astronaut's suit without the helmet, his arms loose on each of the rests. His head drooped listlessly to the side. He was frail and studiedly languorous, uninterested in our arrival in the court of his castle.

"Quon," I said. "*Quon!*"

The astronaut's head lifted slowly and he turned to look at me. He smiled drunkenly, twisting his neck from side to side, clicking it into place.

He sat up in his chair and cleared his throat.

"You," he said, leering. "Old chap."

Gideon and I stopped on the outskirts of the beam of light. Quon ran his tongue around his lips and gums, taking his time. He slumped back in his chair and wove his fingers into each other, cracking his knuckles.

"You've come a long way," he said.

"I want you to tell me where to find my son."

Quon snorted, amused. "Right, right. Your son. Andy. Is that right?" He leaned to his side and grabbed a can of Diet Coke. He sucked it down, his long, pallid neck convulsing as he swallowed. He crushed the can in his hand and threw it across the floor.

"That's right."

"Right," he said again. "*Young* Andy. But that's not all. Surely. Hm? And this man beside you. *Gideon*, is it?"

Gideon said nothing. Quon offered him a smile. The same smile as when he'd come down from the woods to watch me pull Gideon's dead body on the logs. I was acutely aware that at any moment he could cast us both into such a place, a place without time, with no escape. A place where we would live long enough to forget who we were, lose ourselves to lunacy. He could condemn us to such a place with just a thought.

I wondered how many people had attempted to stop him, if, indeed, there had been any. Perhaps every person in the commune outside had tried and each was now trapped somewhere in an incomprehensible version of reality. How could anyone have come close enough to pull a trigger, or take out a knife? He'd have simply looked them in the eye, and cast them into an eternity of his making. No paradise, either, I imagined.

"I want Andy," I said. "Do you know where he is or not?"

"What do *you* think?"

"I think you know."

"*I* think you might be right, Kayle."

"Then tell me."

"Why on earth should I? Can you give me one good reason?"

I said nothing. He was probably reading my mind, knowing I had no next play. I tried to think of nothing, to quell the fear that swirled in my thoughts like poisonous dust.

He looked up to the skylight. "The sun," he said, "is so weak. We fear it and admire it, but against the other suns in the universe, it's nothing exceptional. Trust me. Our sun is a dying ember. There are real fires raging out there, but to us they're just pinpricks in the night. Pretty little stars. Nothing like our precious and mighty *sun*. No!" he laughed. "You humans know nothing about who you are, or even where you are. So you scramble for scraps and paint them gold. You call what you do 'living', but you're just like the sun that bore you—nothing but self-important, dying embers."

"I'm not interested in your stories. I've heard enough."

"I see."

"I just want my son."

"Of course you do. And he's here."

"Where?"

"Hm, well . . ." Quon tapped his finger against the side of his head. "Somewhere in the mess."

"You don't have him. Only his memories. His past. Those aren't *him*."

"Ah," he said, gaining curiosity. "So there's more to you than just your memories, hm? Are you sure about that? Hasn't really been my experience, but I appreciate your conviction. You really believe it." He paused, stared me down, and then broke the gaze, rolling his eyes across the walls of the large room. "I must apologise for how things look around here; it's a bit of a mess. Not particularly homely at the moment, but . . . well, we are in the process of relocating. You know how these things go. We're expanding, you see, planning for the future." He held his bony white hands up to his face and seemed to study them, front and back. "My mental endeavours have taken a toll on my body, but then not much can be said for the human body. It's a flimsy vessel. Doesn't quite live up to the ambitions of the mind, does it? No, the mind, oh, it yearns to explore, to expand, to crash through barriers—to live a thousand years! But the body—the flesh is an anchor. A dead weight, as they say. And in my case, it seems the body has been less willing than usual to support the architecture of my . . . *vast* consciousness. Which is why I'll be leaving this terrible sack and moving on. I hear there's a temple up in the mountains that's quite lovely this time of year. A place where the fruit and vegetables are the largest and sweetest, the water is the purest, and the flesh . . . well, the flesh is less reluctant to rot on your bones. Yes, you know this place too, don't you? We have a mutual friend with a newborn child making her way there as we speak. Making her way to a man named Sun Zhang—still wandering around up there with his three daughters—a man whose slow-ageing body should accommodate my transferred consciousness most suitably, for a time."

Quon grinned. I shuddered to think he'd be waiting for Jai-Li in the one place she was hoping to find solace from this broken world, but I also knew he'd told me with the intention of throwing me off, of exposing my insecurities. I couldn't deny that it worked: Jai-Li had shared her tale of the secret sanctuary in confidence, yet Quon had fished it out of my mind and turned it against us with no effort at all.

"Tell me," he continued. "How were those long years on the beach? Did you learn anything?"

"If you can read my mind, then you'll know."

"That's true. And I am, as we speak. But actual conversation is so scarce these days. I really struggle to have a decent chat. Everyone's so preoccupied with everything they don't know. It's dull. So let's say, just for the sake of it, I won't read a thing, and you just go ahead. Keep talking, and I'll pretend I'm just a regular man, trying his best to listen."

I was not convinced, not for a moment, that he would hold his end of the bargain, but was left with little choice. "Fine."

"It's not easy being a god, you know," he added.

(*This Quon fancies himself a god, yes? Well, I don't know much, but I have never known a true god to ever be scared of a man*)

"Is that what you think you are?" I asked. "A god?"

"An archaic principle, steeped in rubbish. But by definition I suppose I would be, wouldn't I?"

(*After all, life is the will to connect. It is all life has over chaos. If you offer nothing to life you will be trimmed like the fat from a piece of meat. Similarly, if you choose to sit on a throne—to monopolise—you are doomed to stagnation, to collapse back into chaos*)

"Okay, so we're just talking," I said. "No mind reading? Man to man."

"I like that! Man to man."

"Then I do have something else to say. Something I know about you. And *you* can figure out whether I'm telling the truth or not. Like a game."

"Condescending, but okay. Why not? A game."

I smiled back at him, holding him in my grasp. No tricks. Simple fearlessness. The longer I waited, the greater his curiosity. I could see it in his eyes. What did a man like Quon need with such a thing as curiosity anyway? If he had the ability to know everything, what possible value could curiosity have?

My mind was a deluge of the details of every story and memory of the journey:

The first time Moneta had called me to the greenhouse, sitting at Jai-Li's side as she told me about her father's empire, Anubis's story about the activists, the prophecy of human evolution, the family of machines . . .

I saw the thread that ran through them all, the one Shen had woven through each connected experience, and the purpose of being sent out to find this twisted king.

I knew how to end it all. I knew what had to be done.

"I can offer you something you don't have," I said.

"You have my attention."

"On one condition."

"Andy."

"That's right. If I have something you don't have, something you want, you'll tell me where to find my son."

"And if you don't?"

"Then I'll give myself over willingly. I'll join your drones outside."

"I could make you join them if I wanted. Easily."

"I'm sure. But how often have you had someone *choose* to join you, knowing what you are? Surely that's worth something? That's real power, Quon. Having people *want* to join you instead of *tricking* them into joining you."

"Interesting," he said, and tapped his chin. "All right. Tell me something I don't know."

"Not yet," I said quietly. "First you tell me where he is. It's the only deal I'll make. It's not like you'd let me get away without giving you what I've offered."

Quon chortled. "I like you," he said. "I can see why Shen sent you, pointless as it will turn out to be. It's a deal."

Quon narrowed his eyes, a slitted smirk curling and tightening on his mouth. I held my resolve and offered no expression at all. He could read my mind but I'd never give more than I needed. I needed to be calm. Patient. Confident.

"He's here," Quon said, nonchalantly. "In the commune. I knew you'd be coming for him so I had him brought here. Always make sure you've got your bargaining chip close at hand—it simplifies transactions, yes? I had a feeling about your little visit. And, as it turns out, I was right. As usual."

Andy. Right outside. There was a swell of exhilaration, and my heart walloped, but I remained calm, controlling my actions since I knew I could not own my thoughts.

"Now," Quon said. He rotated his lower jaw and winked an eye. "It's your turn."

I waited again. He was fidgeting in his seat now, hands clutching the rests, his long neck extended like a turtle's from its shell, his head lolling.

Gideon and I didn't move. I held my poise, took a breath and said, "Before I tell you, I want to give you something."

I grabbed the shoulder strap of the bag on my back and lowered it to the ground.

"Oh, this is most interesting, Mr. Kayle!" Quon said.

I glanced up at him, got down on my haunches and opened the bag. I pulled out an object wrapped in paper: the apple Klaus had given me.

(It's from the jungle. Of course, I don't have to tell you not to eat it. You know that. But trust me when I say I think you should keep it. It won't go bad. It won't rot. It'll last for as long as you need it. And something tells me you will need it)

I held the shiny green apple out to Quon.

"An apple," he said. Was that a surprised look on his face? I couldn't tell.

"That's right," I said, rising.

He sat back in his seat. "I'm very tempted to read your mind, I must say."

He stared at me intently.

"You can if you like." I held his gaze. "It wouldn't change a thing. But if you want to keep playing . . ."

"I'll play," he said.

"This is what I know about you, Quon. You're bored."

Quon paused and twitched his head to the side. "That's it?"

"That's it."

He sat back in his seat, turning his head and biting his knuckle in contemplation. "That's all?"

"All and everything."

He burst out laughing. "My terrible secret! That I'm bored!"

"And you're becoming more bored by the day," I cut him off. "It's growing in you. And I know why. You may have people's memories, but that's all you've got. You can only know what everyone else already knows. Nothing more. That's not omniscience, Quon. Not even close. It's nothing but a trick. A cheap one. And *that's* why you haven't figured this out— because nobody has been able to tell you."

He waggled a long-nailed finger at the apple. "And you want me to eat that, do you?"

"It'll show you everything you are, everything you have and don't have. Truth. That's all I'm offering. If you don't believe me, go on, do your trick, read my mind."

"I already have."

"Then you already know."

"You're putting a lot of faith in that apple, Mr. Kayle, hoping it will end me, yes?"

"Yes."

"Then why should I eat it?"

"Because you *need* to eat it. You need to know the truth, whatever that truth is. It's the only thing you've got left. If you don't eat it, you're just another old man, scared of nothing more than himself."

"The truth could be that I am destined to be God."

"It could. There's only one way to know."

"But you don't think so."

"It doesn't matter what I think, that's why your mind-reading means nothing," I said steadily. My heartbeat had slowed to normal and I knew as surely as I had ever known anything that these were the right words to say. "You see, you thought killing Shen would complete you. Give you all the power. But there's something missing, isn't there? And it haunts you. And you're afraid it always will. Because life is the will to connect, and there's nothing to connect with, is there? You're at the top. Alone. Stagnant. And with nowhere else to go, you'll crumble, deteriorate, and slowly, slowly . . . waste away."

Quon paused for a moment, making sure I was done speaking, then threw his head back and chuckled. "Nicely done, old chap! Very convincing!" He clapped his hands twice. "This is all very familiar, isn't it? The forbidden fruit. The promise of knowledge. Very, very good, old chap. I know precisely what you're hoping for and, I must say, I appreciate the offer, but will have to decline."

"No, you won't," I continued without hesitation.

"Excuse me?"

"You'll eat it," I said. "They say you have our memories. But for what? A single man doesn't even have enough years on this earth to explore the expanse of his own consciousness, and yet here you are, laying claim to billions of them. You must only be skimming the surface of who we are. You'd have to live ten billion lifetimes to understand all the intricacies, the details of each one of us—every one of our dreams and hopes and fears. But you don't have that kind of time, do you? After all, you said it yourself, all hopes and desires are crushed by the weight of time. So what am I offering you? A catalyst. A chance to go from the highest peaks of our collective hopes to the lowest pits of our fear. To see what ten billion people truly desire, what they truly fear, and who we all really are. But I can't fool you. You've seen what this apple can do . . . to an ordinary man. An ordinary man's incapable of facing the paradox of his own existence. He might have to take his own life just to come to terms with his own realisations. But if you're a god, well, then there's nothing to worry about. You'd survive it. You'd thrive on it. If you're a god, then what I'm offering you is precisely what you want. The full spectrum of your supreme consciousness in a single moment, without the waiting, the dull figuring out, the time to sift through this, through that, to see which memories should be tossed back to us like small fish. A chance to confront the paradox of existence, the stuff that gods are made of, and come out the other side, Quon, more powerful than you are now. Right here. In my hand. All in a bite."

Quon nodded. "Everything you say is true. I can't fault you on your logic. And yet . . . you don't believe that, do you?"

"I don't think you're a god at all. I think you're just a man. But the question isn't whether I believe this; it's whether you do."

The chair lowered itself to the ground and Quon stood up slowly. Ponderous and awkward in the heavy suit, he made his way towards me. His white boots thumped on the ground. I could now make out the features of his face. A man, like any other man. Greying around his ears. Dark, tapered eyes. Cracked lips and rubber skin. I didn't move, just stood there, keeping the apple up, urging him to take it.

"Such a simple thing," he said. "Ridiculous, really."

Quon paused and studied the apple, the large shiny apple. He was thinking about what I had said, and knew it was true. He'd never go on without knowing; his obsession was with knowledge itself—a delusion of acquiring omniscience—and he'd take whatever knowledge he could get, even though, paradoxically, it was the very knowledge he secretly knew would destroy him.

But there was something else in his eyes. He was being compelled by something more primal than a need for knowledge. The irrational compulsion of ordinary men and women. And in Quon's case, billions of ordinary people, in that one place and one moment, desiring one more thing—just *one* more—as always. It was the scent of the apple. That sweet, *sickly* sweet scent. His lips began to work and his eyes began to bulge. His tongue flicked from his slit of a mouth. His nostrils flared and his torso heaved as his breath grew restless in his chest.

"Don't do it," he said, although I could not tell whether he was talking to me or to himself. There seemed to be a panel of voices, each fighting for its turn. "I must do it. No, that's what he wants and you know why. He doesn't know these things . . . he doesn't know things the way we know things, he's only hoping. This is a mistake. It's not a mistake. This is what we need . . . no more secrets . . . no more waiting . . . it'll destroy you. It won't! Oh yes it will! Look at it! You know he's right. No, you'll survive the truth. And then you'll see . . . you'll see that I was right all along. And you will be satisfied. Complete. And there'll be no more questions, no more doubt . . ."

I remembered the power of the fruit from my time in the jungle, but wasn't as overwhelmed by it as I had been that first time. Gideon wasn't reacting to the apple at all, but Quon . . .

Quon *was* reacting.

His desire to consume it, coupled with the need for its secrets, began to bubble up, rising in him like magma from beneath a cracked mantle.

Then, like the man in the woods who'd snatched Moneta's sandwich, Quon grabbed the apple from me and tore through it with his teeth. He took enormous bites, chewing and chomping and slurping it down. The juices ran over his chin and along his hands and arms. I took a step back.

"That other earth," I said, moving slowly away, "it knew. It had everything. But it sent you back here for a reason, Quon.

A reason you never figured out. As powerful as that earth was, as complete in itself, it was alone. It needed to connect with something else. So it sent you here to advance *this* earth. To help it connect with something new, with us . . . and now you're in a similar position, aren't you? Powerful and stuck."

Quon was still grinding and shredding off huge chunks of the apple, trying to swallow it all, but chunks were spilling from the sides of his mouth. After finishing the apple in his hand, he got on his knees and ate the remains from the floor like a dog.

"Yes," he said faintly, and then louder. The fruit was streaming through him, flooding him with awareness. It took almost no time at all. "Yes! I was right! I am! Oh yes, I *am* a . . . god."

Quon got to his feet. He was grinning from ear to ear, his eyes wide with horrific delight. He held up his glistening hands and threw out his chest. A laugh bellowed from deep within him.

"I am . . . a . . . god," he said, his voice a loud croak. "I am a god! There is nothing and no one above me! Nothing and no one!"

Gideon and I moved away as he strained towards the sky in praise of himself. I thought I had made a terrible mistake, but then I told myself to wait, just wait, because there were two sides—always two sides—and the other would come down like the ill-fated head of a flipped coin.

"Nothing and no one more powerful than me! Nothing and no one . . ." His laughter resounded through the hall and the iron plates creaked and groaned again. "Nothing and no one! Nothing and no one! Nothing . . . and no one!"

(*Stupid, stupid animals . . . stupid, stupid animals*)

The veins in Quon's neck bulged as the muscles tautened within the hard circular rim of his collar. His jaw cranked open, baring his big teeth. Saliva flew from his mouth as he bellowed, triumphantly, manically.

His words rolled on and on, becoming louder and louder: "Nothing and NO ONE! NOTHING AND NO ONE!"

Finally, he paused and breathed weightily, clenching his teeth, his bulging eyes flitting to the dark walls of broken machinery folded in the shadows.

"Nothing . . . and no one," he said under his breath. Something was slipping away from him. His own words were no longer a praise song, but a blunt reminder of what he had left in his life, whom he had left to conquer: "Nothing and no one . . ."

(My father shook my mother and told her to come around, come around baby, but her gaze turned on my father and all he could see in her eyes was fear. Fear like he'd never seen in anyone before, and it sent him reeling backwards in shock. A deep, deep panic grew and grew in her until she was screaming and she held up her hands and her hands were like gnarled claws)

Quon's grin began to shrink and wilt, but his eyes continued to race around the room. He was beginning to panic, fear sprouting within him, growing like a rampant weed from the seed of his own insecurities. He twisted his limbs, panting, frenziedly looking for an escape from the prison that had shot up around him. "Nothing . . ." he said with mounting fear. "No one. Nothing . . . and *no one* . . ."

He grabbed the rim of his steel collar and pulled on it, extending his neck, ricking his head up to the skylight (*of the weak old sun, right Quon?*) and shutting his eyes. He screamed—a scream of absolute terror, and loneliness, and acceptance of the truth. The damning truth: the dead end of absolute power . . .

(The rest of it, the levels of crazy, that's all you, man. Your deepest fears and insecurities brought to the surface, where you get to see how ugly and awful they are . . . horrible things in the basement of our s-suh-suh-souls, Raft Man)

"Nothing and no one . . ." he bawled.

Gideon slung the bag off his back, unzipped it and pulled out the knife we'd taken from the abandoned town. Quon didn't notice him. Quon was entombed in the hell of his own making, ripping out his hair and scratching his face with his long fingernails, just as Burt had done amid that swarm of angry hornets . . .

Gideon walked forward slowly, got down on one knee and placed the knife on the floor before Quon. The knife glittered in the light from above. Gideon got up and walked back towards me. "Come. There's nothing more to see. He'll end it when he's ready."

We walked towards the exit of the hall and I looked back to see Quon, contorting, trying to rip off his suit with his hands. The bulky gear seemed to be tightening around him, straining the air from his lungs.

"Nothing and no one . . . and no one . . . no one . . ."

Gideon and I exited the hall, turned, and sealed the heavy iron door behind us. Quon's screams rippled, echoing through the metal bones of the ship. And his screams were the voice of Chang'e 11 itself, the countless wails of stolen memories.

"He was a silly man," Gideon said dryly.

We walked back through the dim corridors of Chang'e 11. The way out was far easier than the way in, and finally we were at the exit, where the light of day was waiting like the warm and benevolent hands of something greater than ourselves.

Some true god.

The members of the commune were frenzied. Quon's anguish was being channelled through them, and they spun and twisted, ripping off their clothes and shrieking and digging their fingers into their own flesh. They clawed at their skin as if they could reach down to their true selves, layered beneath their fat and muscle. Some of them were curled on the ground in foetal positions, trembling and twitching and yowling.

Gideon and I walked down the lowered iron door and passed through the communers. There was nothing that could be done for them—nothing until Quon finally picked up that knife and put it to his throat, or across his wrists, or directly into his heart.

I searched for my son. I looked from tormented face to tormented face. My son would be older than the last time I'd seen him, but how old?

I grabbed people by the cuffs of their shirts and turned them over, hoping to recognise my son. They did not resist me; they were too caught up to realise I was there. I saw a boy lying on the hard ground, scraping away the chalky dust of the desert with his feet, his right hand shoved almost all the way down his throat. His eyes rolled up in his head as he spewed over his arm. I pulled out his arm and looked at him closely. No, it wasn't him. He was too young.

I spun around. Gideon was there in the distance, standing among the chaos like the last sane man alive, a rock amid the crashing waves of spinning, retching, scrambling people. He looked back at me through the crowd. I knew he couldn't help. There was no way to describe Andy. I could barely recall the boy myself. If he was under Quon's control, then he was on the ground somewhere, tearing himself apart like everyone else.

I looked to my side.

At the far end of the commune a number of huge trees reached up into the sky. They looked entirely out of place, thick towering trunks sitting flush against the side of Chang'e 11. The foliage was sparse but the branches stretched out on the sides like crooked arms. Perhaps they grew along the edge of a water source, an oasis that provided for the commune. My eyes ran up their trunks and then I noticed that one of them ended precisely at an elevated entrance in the side of Chang'e 11. An old docking station perhaps, or a runway for an escape pod. The cavity was about fifteen or twenty feet from the ground.

Gideon's eyes followed mine, and we hurried through the communers towards the base of the trees. I pushed and pulled people from my way, ran between the tents and found myself on the edge of a shallow body of water. I craned my neck and looked up at that one tree. (*I'm walking in a beautiful forest. That's how it starts. How it always starts. There are many tall trees. But I see one tree in particular in the centre of the forest, enormous in width and height. It's wider and taller than the rest*)

Gideon stayed by my side as I walked toward the base of the tree, my eyes fixed on the open mouth of the iron cavern.

"He's up there," I said. "I know it."

As I approached the base of the tree I spotted a red object lying between the surface roots and tussocks of grass.

(At my feet, a red shoe is lying in the dirt. It's a child's shoe. I recognise it as my son's, then look up and consider the possibility he dropped it while climbing that very tree)

I was staring at a shoe—a red shoe at the bottom of the tree—the one I had seen in my recurring dream.

"How do know you he's up there?" Gideon asked.

"I've always known," I said, turning my gaze to the top of the tree once more. "Right since the start. Shen's very first clue."

And then I put my hands up to the tree and, grabbing the first broken branch, pulled myself up and began to climb.

Xerox print test

I looked down from the great height of the tree and saw the clumsy sprawl of tents, shacks and people. Ahead, there was the flat and endless horizon. My hand clutched another branch and I heaved myself up. Sweat ran from my face. I gripped harder so that I wouldn't slip; I pulled myself up with a strength I should not have had. I hoped from a place in my heart I no longer knew existed.

I lifted my foot and rested it on another knobby protrusion, and pushed up to the next branch, and the next. I looked down over my shoulder. Gideon was climbing up behind me, one careful branch at a time.

We were far from the ground, and for an instant my fear of heights took hold of me, challenging my determination. I paused and closed my eyes. I took a deep breath and expelled it gently. I counted backwards from ten, filtering away my doubt, and then I opened my eyes and continued up, promising myself I would not look down. It was all behind me, and I would not fall back. Not this time.

Finally, I was at the top.

I stopped and watched as Gideon made his way to where I was crouching: near the mouth of the entrance into the high side of the vessel. I inched along the large branch that bridged the gap to the entrance and slid onto its iron grate. The wind lashed across us, one cold wave after the other. Gideon followed closely behind me.

We walked along the clanging iron grate until we reached a black wall. In the centre of the wall was a door standing slightly ajar, a faint glimmer of light shining through the gap. I reached for the handle and pulled it slowly open.

A room. A familiar room.

There was a grey box, rumbling a familiar sound, innumerable white wires extending to a chair in the centre of the room. The chair was turned away from us, but I could make out the shape of someone sitting in it, white wires attached to a shadowy head. Beyond the chair was a long empty table, hidden in the shadows.

I walked forward slowly, careful not to alarm the motionless figure in the chair.

"Andy," I said softly. I took another step forward. No response. I turned to inspect the grey box that groaned on the side of the room. It was similar to the one we'd had on the beach—the mind reader that had drained us of our thoughts. I ran my hand over the box and saw a number of buttons: *Start. Cancel. A4. A3. A2. Multiple copies.*

I lifted the thin plastic lid that covered the top of the box. Sheets of paper sat in a tray to the side. I grabbed a sheet and read: FX443—XEROX PRINT TEST (0076). FX443—XEROX PRINT TEST (0077). FX443—XEROX PRINT TEST (0078).

I dropped the pages and edged towards the chair, then circled until I was facing the person. Light brown hair. Darkly tanned skin. One missing red shoe.

It was him. Andy. My son. My boy. My *boy.*

I slid hurriedly down on my knees in front of him and laid my hand on his thin, cold hands. He looked through me, gazing into nothingness.

I took him by the shoulders and shook him gently.
Nothing.

I stroked his face, tapped him on the cheeks. "Andy? Wake up, big guy. *Jesus,* what did they do to you?"

Sluggishly and without blinking, Andy turned his head to face me.

"That's right," I said. "That's right, kiddo. It's me. Your father. Blink. Blink your eyes."

Andy did as I told him. He blinked once, mechanically, and paused before blinking once more.

"It's me," I said reassuringly. "It's *me*. I'm here. I've come to get you."

Gideon approached the chair and Andy turned his gaze on him, studied him. His eyes widened. He would not turn back to me, no matter how much I coaxed him, no matter how tightly I held his hand.

"Dad?" Andy murmured.

Gideon said nothing. He did not move.

Andy began to breathe deeply, emotion finally welling up within.

I didn't understand.

Andy grabbed the wires attached to his head and plucked them from their plugs. His eyes did not stray from the tall man with the long dreadlocks—the friend who had come all the way with me. The friend I had encountered in the abandoned town— *an exceedingly improbable coincidence*—I squashed the thought.

I released Andy's hand as the young man grabbed the side of the chair and got to his feet.

"You came," Andy said to Gideon. "You came for me." He threw himself into Gideon, wrapping his arms around him, clutching him firmly.

I rose from my knees.

And as Gideon's arms tentatively lifted from their sides and wrapped around Andy, I knew . . . I knew an excruciating truth. My heart clenched and I struggled to breathe.

It can't be. No, it cannot be . . .

I waited for something to confirm that Andy was muddled, projecting on Gideon in some way, but the confirmation didn't come.

And Gideon—his expression was changing too. The look of bafflement was lessening, replaced by something else. Painful awareness. Relief. Joy.

I edged back, away from the chair—away from Gideon and Andy, embracing each other as I had hoped to be embraced. I tried to accept what I was witnessing. The longer they held each other the more obvious it all became.

The room began to spin. Everything blurred. My face was hot, my arms and legs were numb, and then there was a heaviness—an aching heaviness I had felt only once before, a long time ago, in another place, as another person.

A wave of memories washed over me like the water in the room in my dream.

Jack Turning

Jack Turning did not appreciate his little meetings with the representatives from Huang Enterprises. They always sent some weedy, humourless man in a creaseless suit who never knew more than the information he had been sent to give. Jack had met one earlier that day, in an empty hotel conference room. The man was like all the others, dressed as if he was about to climb in his coffin, with a disposition just as cold and bloodless.

Jack had joined The Borrowed Gun with a belief in the cause—a powerful statement to the world that third-world countries would no longer tolerate the rape of their land and their dignity—but somewhere along the way, things had become complicated. Suddenly it was a non-profit movement backed by the most profit-hungry corporation on the planet. But they needed the corporation. Its intelligence. The weaponry. The money. They were consorting with the devil to buy a ticket into heaven, he knew. But the pressure from his Borrowed Gun comrades was growing too. It needed to be done, he was told. The Borrowed Gun was now larger than ever, with factions arising in cities across the world. The price they had to pay to save the rest of the world would have to be their few souls.

The meeting was short, thankfully. The representative from Huang Enterprises expressed his appreciation of The Borrowed Gun's compliance. He'd heard about the raid on the Gausen Tower, and said it was an unfortunate business, but there was a saying about omelettes and broken eggs.

Jack didn't feel the same way. A protest outside the telecommunication tower had been planned, but things had gone wrong, badly wrong, and now people were dead. Too many bloody people. It was a tragic mess, and they were all accountable.

The man in the suit nodded.

A tragic, *tragic* mess, indeed.

The plan had been to cut the power to the tower and raid the offices, not to murder people, but tensions had risen, violence had erupted, and more than sixty people had met the grisly end of their lives. Jack Turning hadn't been there himself, but he'd heard about it from his friend Charles, and he'd seen it on the news. No. It had been a disaster, and now the nation would overturn every table and crash through every door to find anyone in the region associated with The Borrowed Gun.

The man in the suit said not to worry.

There was a place they could go to, to stay low.

"There's an island," the man in the suit said, sitting in that conference room in front of Jack. "A floating island, perfect for your needs. And for ours."

Jack Turning sat in his parked car and explained the outcome of the meeting to Charles. Charles was a comrade, someone whom Jack could trust. Charles had been there when it happened. He'd tried his best to calm the crowd, temper the increasing agitation, but in the end he had been powerless to stop the horde. He'd even been injured in the process. A long red laceration ran from his forehead to his ear. His eye was blue and swollen. His clothes, ripped.

Jack grabbed a box of cigarettes from his top pocket. The lighter shook in his hand as he lit up. "The island's a few weeks away by ship. It's ours if we want it. He promised. You, me, your family, friends. We can take it. Make a new home for ourselves."

Charles sighed and closed his eyes. It had been a long day. A long and terrible day.

"Why? Why would Huang give us an island?"

Jack dragged on his cigarette. "It's owned by a former Huang employee. The guy's a geneticist gone rogue. Had the island built. Stole equipment for himself and is now sailing the ocean at Huang's expense. He's dangerous, they said, needs to be stopped. So that's the deal. We take him out, and we take the island."

"I don't know," Charles said. "I don't know."

"Look. Today was bad, and it's not going to end. They're going to hunt us down for what happened. We're not safe here anymore. But we can be—you, Jane, Anubis. I guarantee that, Charles."

Charles stared out the window into the night. "How we gonna get there?" he asked.

"A ship. There'll be a ship in two weeks. That's a lot of time to hang around here. We'll have to lay low."

"Jesus. This wasn't what we wanted, Jack."

"I know."

"It wasn't supposed to be like this. We were supposed to *help* this world."

"And we will, we will. Once we've helped ourselves. We'll make it what it's meant to be, do what we have to do, but for now . . ." He didn't finish his sentence. He'd said enough. Charles was hurting and exhausted. They were parked outside Charles's house, a pretty little single-storey on a quiet street that offered no hint of the madness and mayhem that had occurred only a few hours earlier, less than twenty kilometres away.

"I'm going in. I need to see Jane, and Anubis," Charles said, and unlocked the door.

"Okay, my friend," Jack said, his hand hovering over the blue console beside his wheel.

"Come in," Charles said. "Come say hi to Jane."

"No, I—"

"Come on, Jack. Have a coffee. You need to come down from this. You've got a long drive back."

"Okay, just a quick cup, then I need to get going." The two men walked up to the house. Jane opened the door and Charles hobbled in. Concerned and confused, she led him to the bathroom to clean his cuts and find out what had happened.

Jack stood in the living room by himself. He looked at the framed pictures on the walls. Charles, Jane and their young son Anubis.

"What happened to my duh-duh-*dad*?"

Jack turned and saw a boy standing in the doorway, wearing a yellow nightshirt and blue shorts. The boy was no older than eleven, perhaps twelve. Anubis. Jack once asked Charles why they'd named their son after a jackal-headed god and Charles said his wife simply liked the sound of it. She thought it was strong. Jack wasn't so sure; he thought it was weird. A weird name and a weird kid, but then what did Jack know about kids?

"Your dad was a hero today."

"Bed, Anubis. Now!" Jack smiled awkwardly as Jane rushed into the living room to usher her son out of the room. He sat on the sofa, grabbed a magazine from the coffee table, flipped through it, and then stood back up. He could still hear Charles and his wife in the bathroom. She was crying and he was saying, over and over again, "It's okay, I'm okay."

Jack walked to the bathroom. The door was open and he could see Charles sitting on the edge of the bathtub. Jane was dabbing his cuts with cotton wool.

"Charles," Jack said. "I'm going. You get some rest."

"Okay, Jack."

"And remember what we talked about. Think about it. It's the smart thing to do."

"Okay."

"Goodnight, Jane," Jack said. "Everything will be all right." She bit her lip and nodded.

Jack closed the front door behind him and walked quickly down the path. The moment he was in his car he lit another cigarette. He inhaled deeply, filling the car with smoke. Then he flicked the butt out the window and started the engine. The car hummed to life and Jack pulled out of the quiet street. Before long he was on the highway that would take him back to Beaufort West where he'd been staying for a few weeks, in a tacky dive called the Blue Caribou.

As he drove through the dark night the rain began to fall, lightly at first, and then harder, heavy sheets pouring down. Jack thought about his meeting with the Huang representative, the man's thin white skin, his unflinching eyes. The way his hands sat on the table, as if he had imprisoned some small powerless creature under his cupped palms. The man was unnerving. Zombie-like. Jack smiled wryly. Fanciful, maybe, but the bottom line was he didn't want to have anything further to do with them, much as they wanted him to maintain contact. The Gausen incident had gone too far. Too bloody far.

He hoped the representative had meant what he'd said about the island. He didn't trust the man, but in Jack's experience they didn't ever lie. Not outwardly at any rate. Outward lying was for amateurs. No, there was an island, and they could probably have it, as discussed, but Jack would be a fool if he didn't think Huang Enterprises had reserved the best part of the deal for themselves, whatever that best part might be. He didn't want to think about it. He wanted to go back to the motel and pour a tall glass of rum and coke, forget about it all—get a good night's sleep. If he wasn't awoken by a squad of police vans outside the motel in the morning, he'd figure the rest later.

The rain kept coming.

Jack passed wind-battered farm stalls and rolling open lands, all blurred shadows in the stormy night. He instructed the car to increase the temperature and demist the windows. At least another hour to go before he reached the motel that sat on the edge of the desert. It was nothing special—his room had only a bed and a bathroom—but at least nobody asked too many questions. The place was run by an elderly man who dozed behind the counter and his elderly wife who made sure there were always fresh flowers in the hallways. The only other tenants were businessmen and their mistresses and a few loud-mouthed families who reserved their holiday budget for booze and petrol. He rarely saw the same face twice. They came and went, and he sat by the piss-filled pool and observed them from behind his sunglasses over a warm beer. He'd been in Beaufort West a while already and people-watching was about as much entertainment as he could wring from the rags of that town.

After a few minutes, the rain stopped. The road curved and walls of trees flashed past on either side of him. He was driving along a mountainside now, weaving around corners, dipping and rolling. In the distance, further below, he could see the bright lights of a recharge station.

His receptanode rang.

"Private call," Jack said.

"It's me." It was Charles.

"How are you, my friend?"

"Fine, fine. I'll be okay. The family's shaken up, but we're all fine."

"What can I do for you?" Jack asked.

They both knew it was best not to use names and specifics. There was no such thing as secure communication, not in this world.

"I want more information on the proposal," Charles said. "The vacation we were chatting about earlier."

"Okay. I can arrange that. You've spoken to your wife?"

"Yes."

"And she's sure?"

"Nobody's sure," Charles said, and no wonder. There wasn't a sure thing left. "But for all intents and purposes, we're in."

"Good. I'll send details to your palm-plate. We'll need to make moves. I'll book with the travel agent."

Book with the travel agent: dance with the devil.

He'd picked up speed as they were talking and the AV was swinging around the mountain, screeching on the corners. The night ran on ahead, barely illuminated by the glowing headlights of his car.

"And Charles," Jack said, then stopped. He'd used his friend's name when he hadn't intended to. "I mean—"

The recharge station was just ahead of him now, bright and empty beside two big rigs and one lone autovehicle.

"Thanks again for everything. Goodnight. Sleep well. We'll chat later," Charles said.

"Right. Absolutely—"

Thump. A small sound.

Jack shuddered as his car struck something in the road. His heart jumped, but then he realised he was still on the road. Whatever it had been had taken the worst of the collision. He looked in the rear-view mirror but saw nothing behind him. Nothing but darkness.

"Everything okay?" Charles said.

"I—" Jack looked in the mirror again. "I hit something."

"Are you okay?"

"Ja, ja, I'm fine. It's just . . ." He turned his head back over his seat. The recharge station was disappearing behind him, the lights dwindling in the distance. "It must have been an animal or something."

"Did you stop?"

"No."

"Are you going to?"

"No," Jack said, "I probably should, but it's pretty far back already."

"Maybe it was a dog," Charles said.

"Ja, a dog. Maybe. Dammit."

"Well, take it easy on the road. Get home in one piece."

"I will. Thanks." He looked back again. It was too late to see anything now. Charles was right. Probably a dog. A baboon, maybe. Or the branch of a tree. *I should stop. Turn around, go back.* But the car sped on and Jack could think of nothing better than getting back to the Blue Caribou and pouring himself a nice tall, stiff rum and coke.

What a bloody day.

The next morning he woke up in his drab room and looked out the window. No squad cars. No sirens. Nothing but dust and desert. He took a shower and ordered bacon and eggs from the elderly lady in the empty dining hall. As he sat and sipped his coffee, the morning news flashed up on the television against the far wall.

"Volume," Jack said. "Louder."

They were interviewing a tall dark man with dreadlocks. He was standing beside a blonde-haired woman. His wife probably. A young boy was leaning into his mother.

"We just pulled over," the mother was saying, sobbing. A reporter held his mike closer and her voice grew in volume. "On our way to a lodge. She climbed . . . she just climbed out. We didn't realise . . . It all happened . . . It was too fast."

Her burly husband put his arm around her and pulled her in close. The boy looked at the cameras, unblinking.

Jack Turning sipped his coffee and watched them, trying to grasp the story. Their names appeared on the screen: Kayle Jenner. Sarah Jenner.

Jack put the cup back on his saucer. The old woman arrived with his breakfast and placed his plate neatly before him. The toast was on its way, she assured him.

"And this car just came out, it came out of nowhere. Speeding around the corner," Sarah Jenner said, fighting through the tears. "Speeding! If he hadn't been . . . he would have seen her, had time to swerve, stop . . . And then . . ." She turned and buried her face in her husband's broad chest. The reporter moved the mike up to Kayle Jenner.

"I didn't see the car," he said. "I ran as fast as I could. But I couldn't see it. And then I saw Maggie . . ." His face creased and he turned away from the cameras, holding out his hand, palm up to ward them off.

The old woman returned with his toast, but Jack Turning didn't notice her. He began to sweat a little, his blood suddenly boiling with a horrifying notion.

The reporter took over and spoke to the camera: "At approximately eight thirty-five last night, Kayle Jenner, professor of Theology and Folklore at the University of Tulbagh, and his wife, physiotherapist and business owner Sarah Jenner, were parked at this recharge centre on the R44 pass when a car struck and killed their five-year-old daughter, Maggie Jenner. The car sped from the scene, and police have no clues as to the whereabouts of either the vehicle or the driver. The police have urged anyone with any information to—"

The basket of toast fell to the ground.

Jack pushed his chair back and ran to the parking lot.

He stood in the blistering sun and studied the side of his car. There it was. Definitely. A dent in the side, just above the right front wheel. He'd hit something hard. And with sickening certainty he knew exactly what it was. He looked around. Was anyone watching him? Jack stood there a moment longer, scanning the dry land. Then he turned and sprinted back into the motel.

He returned to his room and paced the floor. What should he do? Should he come forward? Was he even sure it had been him? What if it hadn't been? He'd be forced to disclose his connection to The Borrowed Gun. Anyway, it might not even have been her. *Who's to say when that dent happened, anyway? I've been so distracted over the last few days* . . . It was just a dent. Nothing more.

He drew the curtains and fell back on his bed. That sound—that dull *thump*. Where precisely had he felt it? Had it even been near the station? He didn't know. No, no. He didn't think so.

An hour later he was on the phone with the man from Huang. They were in, he told the man. All of them. They'd board the ship and find that island. They'd overthrow the geneticist and take it for themselves—go drifting around the world, far from their many sins.

Their Huang connection sent back the details and Jack forwarded the details to Charles. Then he switched off his ear node and went to the motel bar. He sat at the bar and ordered one drink, and then another and another. The alcohol went down easily. After Jack Turning had added an appreciable amount to his running tab, he went back to the room and passed out on his thin and uncomfortable mattress.

Jack Turning didn't leave the Blue Caribou. He knew he was hiding out, but the longer he stayed, the easier it was to convince himself he was existing within the impenetrable fortress of his own isolation. If he put just one foot out of that place, he felt, the world would swallow him up. Charles called several times but Jack did not answer. He made no more contact with Huang Enterprises. Instead, he swam in the pool, drank at the bar, and sat on a white deckchair outside, staring for hours at nothing at all.

Two weeks passed and Jack knew the rest of them would be making their way onto the ship, bound for the island. He told the elderly couple that if anyone came looking for him, he'd prefer if they didn't mention he was there. Not unless it was the boys in blue, of course. He couldn't expect them to lie to the police—but anyone else . . .

Jack thought about his friends making their way onto that ship and starting their lives anew. He couldn't say why he no longer wanted to join; perhaps it was because a part of him knew that running would solve nothing. Perhaps he was hoping someone would come knocking on the door and end his misery—call him out on every terrible thing he'd done and mete out the appropriate punishment.

Until then, he'd stay put, right where he was, in the Blue Caribou.

Months passed and nobody had come looking for him. He hadn't received any more calls either, and assumed Charles,

Jane and Anubis were now enjoying their time on their floating island, sailing around the world. He no longer thought about that little girl, that small *thump* . . . Besides, he was pretty sure it hadn't been him in the first place. If it had been, someone would have come, he thought. By now, *surely*.

One morning, however many weeks later, he woke up and had his breakfast as usual. The old man had since died and the old woman was taking care of the place. The motel was no busier than it had ever been and she seemed to manage everything just fine. Jack did his best to demand as little from her as possible, and even assisted with the odd job around the motel.

Jack finished his breakfast but didn't watch the news. He had never again watched the morning news after Kayle and Sarah's story.

The old woman mentioned she'd be stepping out to get a few things from the store, and asked Jack to keep an eye for walk-ins. She left and Jack changed into his shorts to go for a swim.

The pool had recently been cleaned and he stood on the edge of it, soaking up the harsh morning heat. He plunged underwater and the cold water shot through his flesh, waking him instantly. He sat at the bottom of the pool and stared up through the silvery surface, into the blue sky. He closed his eyes and held the breath in his lungs for as long as he could. Maybe, he thought, he'd black out.

And then, suddenly, a screech. A deep, penetrating screech that slashed through his mind and forced the air from his lungs. He paddled to the surface and threw himself out of the pool. Holding on to the hot bricks at the edge of the pool, he clenched his teeth against the screech. There was heaviness—a throbbing heaviness that brewed and thickened and consumed his mind. The light of the sun was brighter and harsher, piercing through the closed lids of his eyes.

And then, everything in Jack Turning's world went black.

Jack Turning was gone.

Now there was only a man in a motel, by himself, with no idea of who he was and how he had got there. He wandered the corridors, took what he wanted, slept wherever he wanted and gradually emptied the bar and the walk-in freezer. Every so often, a memory came back to him. Each new one arrived without warning—the memory of a son, or a wife. A dead daughter. Sometimes the man would be woken by the recollection of some new thing. Memories struck him like bolts of lightning, jolting him from his mindless inertia. Sarah. Andy. Maggie. Two horses. A wooden house. A hill. He remembered things people had said to him once, things he'd once said back.

More memories arrived and soon he had enough to paste together—a collage of who he had once been and where he had once lived.

One day he woke up, and there was a man standing over his bed. A man he had never seen. Tall and old, wearing round-framed spectacles and a long brown coat. The man told him to shower and he did as he was told. After that, the man asked him to get dressed and meet him at the pool. The visitor claimed to be from a group called the New Past—his group had the answers, he said.

The man asked how long he had been staying at the Blue Caribou and the man said he didn't know. The stranger then asked his name and the man once named Jack, aided by his new memories, replied: "Kayle Jenner."

The beginning

I opened my eyes. Spears of sunlight and blue skies. Ocean. Wind.

I was on the raft.

And my son . . .

My son.

I didn't have a son.

I didn't *have* a son.

The water washed over my burned arms and legs—icy ocean water—but the true chill came from inside. The chill of the truth. My raft bobbed over the unsettled waters and I could do nothing but move with it, fixed at the limbs and exposed to the universe. I closed my lids against the glare of the mighty sun, the overhanging face of a god I could never look at directly, never negotiate my passage with.

I had been in Chang'e 11 alongside Gideon and Andy. I had watched as a father I'd never known reunited with a son I'd never had, and then there were the memories—new memories of old experiences like crumpled letters finally surfacing from beneath the dust and clutter of a dark attic. These memories had entered my mind as swiftly as they had once been taken, though they were now paired alongside the memories of who I *thought* I had been.

But Andy.

My Andy.

He was gone again. Gone forever.

The cold chill of truth could not change that I loved him, though he had never been mine to love. My hope that we'd be reunited had also been my hope of having some worth in this world, but it was a reunion that hadn't been mine to expect. As much as I still remembered him as my own, I had never been his father and he had never been my son.

The water ran over my face, splashing over my nose and down my throat. I didn't have the energy to tug on any of my straps. I moved with the water, as far as the rope would allow, but then there was a sudden bump; somebody was pulling my raft in, guiding me back to shore. It could all be another dream, I told myself. It didn't matter how real it seemed. I had been burned by the sun and cooled by the sea before.

I strained my neck to the side to identify the person pulling on my raft but I could only see a thin, pale arm.

I played through all the memories of my time in the Blue Caribou. A little girl standing in the road at night. A speeding car. A gutless plan to steal an island from an old man.

I was not a good man. I thought that Day Zero had erased the memories of a man with a life worth living, but that had not been the case. No. I was murderer. A coward. A waste.

I looked to my side again. The man beside the raft came into view. It was Daniel.

"Daniel," I murmured. "What's happening?"

"It's over," Daniel said. "All over."

"What's over? How long have I been out here?"

"Dunno. Maybe three days?" He was walking alongside my raft. "No one really knows."

I groaned and winced in the light. If I had received those new memories, I went on to think, it must have meant that Quon had finally picked up the knife Gideon had left on the floor, incapable of tolerating the truth of his own. The memories must have returned after he died, but if that had all happened, as I still believed it had, how was it possible for me to now be on the raft?

"Where's Gideon?" I asked, forgetting for a moment it was not his true name.

"He's being pulled out as we speak." Daniel turned to look at me. "You've been through quite an ordeal. Take it easy, Kayle. Everything will be explained in a bit."

"It's Jack."

"What?"

"The name," I said. "It's Jack."

I was unstrapped from the raft and slowly got to my feet. My arms and legs were numb. Stinging red rings of broken skin circled my wrists and ankles. I barely had the energy to stand, but I pulled myself up and twisted my neck to the side, clicking it into place. There were people on the beach, most of whom I recognised, but there was something different about them. There was a commotion. People whom I had never heard utter a word were now talking freely to each other.

I stood and stared at them, amazed. I had never seen them behave in such a way. I rubbed my wrists and wiped my burning eyes with the back of my arm, but my salt-encrusted arm made them sting even more. I stepped clumsily on the sand and felt the grains slide between my toes. I closed my hands into swollen fists, pumping the blood up my arms. I scanned the beach for Gideon (who was really Kayle), but couldn't see him anywhere. Daniel was crouched beside me, rolling up the leash the raft had been attached to.

"Daniel."

"Mm," he said, preoccupied.

"What's going on?"

I looked from face to face. The communers conversed animatedly with each other. Some were laughing, some were crying, but most stood clumped in small huddles, talking. Simply talking, nothing more.

"Like I said," Daniel said. "It's over."

"What's over?"

"Everyone remembers," Daniel said. "Everyone remembers. One moment we were going about our business and the next . . . it all came flooding back."

I studied Daniel's expression to determine whether or not he was joking, in on some elegant hoax, but he seemed to believe what he was saying.

"Where's Angerona?" I asked anxiously. "And Theunis?"

"Angerona's around here somewhere, but Theunis . . ." Daniel paused, and then added mournfully, "His raft broke loose in a storm, we think. We lost him at sea. We don't know when it happened but it was some time in the night, we imagine. There was nothing we could do, man."

I ambled away from Daniel and up the sandy shore. I trudged through the soft sand and made my way to the top of the beach, through the lively crowds, and onto the path that led to the white house on the hill. I caught a familiar smell, the faintest whiff of beachside greenery. The trees that lined the edge of the sand wavered in the wind. Clumps of white cloud floated across the sky like man-made islands on a perfectly still ocean.

I looked through the muddy windows of the white house. There was nobody inside. The back door stood open, unattended. I thought about all the times I'd been made to bear witness in there, to recite the lines of the script, plugged to a useless machine.

I walked back down to the beach, passed through the crowds of known faces and went to the water's edge to study the outlying horizon. The silvery ocean moved as it always had, rolling eternally, without memory.

The foamy water swirled around my feet. I stared as countless bubbles grew and burst on my skin. I looked again for my tall friend, the one who'd covered the world with me. I couldn't see him anywhere in the crowd. I wasn't even sure I could still call him my friend. His daughter had lost her life at my hands.

I wasn't a friend. I had ruined his life.

And then, from the depths came a painful reminder. Andy. My misplaced son. I had loved Andy, and still did, but there was nothing I could do about it. The universe had deliberately torn him from my clutches. Someone had raced around a dark corner in a speeding car and struck him in front of my eyes.

The sense of surprise at my return to the beach was subsiding.

Now there was only pain.

Deep, irreparable pain.

As I stood looking out at nothing, I suddenly knew: we do not own our memories; our memories own us. It didn't matter what I remembered or how I felt. Memories are their own strange creatures, flitting between the tall trees of our experiences, inviting us to enter the dark and uncharted woods of our lives, promising nothing.

I sat on the beach by myself and watched the sun set over the edge of the world, layering the sky in yellows, purples and reds. I thought about the strange journey. If our memories had returned, then so had the memories of everyone else. Jai-Li had left the beach with her child to find the Silver Whisper, but now her purpose must have changed. I imagined her walking back into her parents' farmhouse beside the muddy pig troughs— the parents she had forgotten and denied—not as Jai-Li, but as their daughter Jun. The dream of another girl had given her the courage to set forth, but the truth of who she was had brought her home, where she now belonged. Home. Where we all hoped to belong.

Three days, Daniel had said. I'd been on the raft for three days. If that had been so, who had spent days, months, travelling across the world? Who had washed up on that island of fruit, sailed through the sea of rooftops and flown across the landscapes in the Silver Whisper?

There was a moment on Klaus's island when I'd looked at myself in a mirror for the first time in years. I had hardly recognised myself. Had that been my face at all, or had my identity and my memories somehow leapfrogged from stranger to stranger until the very end? Theunis had broken free in the storm and was lost at sea. Had I actually seen and done everything through him, the man who'd believed in helping Jai-Li off the beach? Where was he now? In Chang'e 11? Dead? Still adrift on the ocean?

(*The only thing left to be in this world is a martyr. One day we'll look back and be forced to ask ourselves what good we've ever been to anyone*)

The man I once knew as Gideon finally walked up to me on the beach. I glanced up at him as he sat down in the sand, pulling up his knees and locking his hands around them. He stared across the ocean at the red setting sun.

"Do you know about the alp?" he asked, as he had once asked what felt like a hundred years earlier.

"It sits on your chest and steals the breath in your sleep," I replied, as he had once explained. "The woman with her hand nailed to the floor."

"The cat with its *tail* nailed to floor."

"Ah, right," I said, running the sand through my fingers. I looked at the lowering sun and for a while we said nothing to each other, sitting in quiet companionship the way we had in those first dateless days, weeks, months and years.

Finally, the big man named Kayle spoke:

"After my son was taken from my house in the night, I think it all slipped away from me." His voice was deep and measured, but his eyes did not veer from the cooling sun. "My memories—of my family, and of who I was . . ."

He shook his head and started again. "I don't think it even had anything to do with Quon. After my daughter was killed, my wife ran away, and my son was taken . . . there was a great emptiness. I never did remember my own name. 'Gideon' was a name left in a note. Of course, that's what I remember *now*, now that we've got it all back . . ." He paused a long while and then added, "It doesn't feel the way we hoped it would, does it? Having our true memories."

"No. It doesn't."

"Perhaps we expected more. Perhaps there were things we forgot long before Day Zero," he said. "But at least I now know what I have to do."

"And what's that?"

"Get off this beach. Get my son. Find my wife."

"Do you know where they are?"

Kayle nodded, pulled out a folded piece of paper, and gave it to me. It was a drawing of a house on a hill beside four crosses. Or were they tombstones?

Angerona had drawn the same image for me in the sand with a wooden stick, an incomprehensibly long time ago.

"I've seen this before," I said.

"Angerona. She had my wife's memories. Sarah's memories. So, in a way, Sarah was right here, on the beach with me all along. Angerona also knows where Sarah is," he said, holding up the page. "She's known all along, and she's decided to come with me. She wants to join my family; I don't think she has family of her own."

"I see." My heart ached to hear him speak about his family. I recalled nothing of Sarah, his wife, but, of course, those memories had been reserved for him alone. A story of a beautiful woman who'd lived in a house of students, who had once kissed him on the cheek, commencing their future love.

But Andy—I missed Andy.

Kayle took the paper back from me and slipped it away. "I don't know what happened after we found Andy in that room in Chang'e," he said.

I was startled that he recalled it too.

"I was holding him . . ." Kayle continued, "There were memories, endless memories, and then I was here. I can't explain it. Can you?"

I shook my head. "No."

"Strange days."

"Well, maybe it's happened already," I said.

"What?"

"The Renascence. Maybe this is the start of collective consciousness, as was always intended. Maybe we're sharing a dream right now. Maybe that was a dream. Or maybe we got more help than we realised."

I thought back to the scripts we'd been made to learn and recount to The Body in the white house. Perhaps there were some seeds of truth in those words after all.

(*Evolution demands more. In the end, we will not need to be the fittest, for competition itself will cease to exist for us. Subsequently, we will neither disown nor denounce the remaining organisms with which we share the planet. We will simply exist in a state of being of which they will have no concept and to which they will have no access, on an alternate stream of time—within the one true reality*)

"Indeed," Kayle said.

He watched as the sun sank over the brink of the ocean. Then he stood and dusted the sand off his pants.

"I couldn't have found him without you, you know," he said, tucking his dreadlocks behind his ears. "I was lost, and didn't even know it. You helped me."

"Kayle," I said. I needed to tell him who I was and what I had done. I couldn't bear to hear him praising me, not after all the pain I had caused him and his family. "I—"

Kayle held up his hand, a sign for me to stop, not say any more.

"I *know*, Jack," he said. "I know what happened. And I forgive you. I forgive you and I thank you."

Without another word, Kayle scuffed out the print his body had left in the sand, and it was as if he had never sat beside me. He strolled away and I watched as he headed along the beach towards the communers. Bonfires were burning bright, a celebration of recently acquired selfdom. I caught the final sliver of sunlight, the last breath in a dying thing.

I forgive you and I thank you.

His words lingered on the cool and misty scent of the ocean. I released a long breath, a breath I'd been holding for a lifetime. As it left my body, a sensation I hadn't felt in longer than I could remember, even with a lifetime of memories at my disposal, flushed through me. Whether I deserved it or not, I could not say, but I felt it.

(*Remember, Kayle. Victory isn't getting what we want. It's getting what's owed to us. And what's owed is balance. Balance between right and wrong, the guilty and the innocent, the saved and the damned. We might not ever have the Utopia we've dreamed about—I'm not even sure it's what we really want—but balance: it's the first step towards retrieving Man's stolen destiny. Towards peace)*

The sky dimmed overhead and the stars began to make an appearance. I stood on that beach and thought: perhaps *that* was what we'd always needed to evolve. We would never move on, together, as one, unless we settled our debts with each other. Kayle had lost a child and his pain was now mine. He had forgotten to reclaim his family and I had remembered enough to lead him to his son. Perhaps, after everything, that other earth had finally succeeded in helping us. Perhaps, after Quon's death, that one unifying thought entrusted to nine astronauts had finally been shared with the world—and one day, if we made sure to remember, we would all find a way to connect.

In the months that followed, communers slowly made their way off the beach to find their ways in the world. Trawlers arrived every few weeks to take them home. The beach grew quieter. The tents and shacks stood empty. Work stations were dismantled. Gideon said nothing more to me after that last time we spoke, and he and Angerona climbed aboard the last trawler and sailed into their future—one I would never know anything about.

I watched from the beach as they stood on the deck and left the shore. I had decided I wouldn't be going anywhere. Not until a man came down from the woods to tell me I was living a lifetime in a night, that I was in Chang'e 11, that I'd fallen from that tall tree to my death, was bobbing on the raft, or this wasn't the same world (or universe) at all. No matter how long I lived on that beach, I would always leave room for any one of those possibilities. I might be trapped, but I would never be fooled. Not ever again.

Gideon and Angerona looked back at me from the deck as the trawler chugged away. He raised his arm and waved and I waved back.

Then they were gone, forever.

After they'd left, I walked across the desolate stretch up to the white house on the hill. I threw out what I wouldn't need, moved in my bed and the few trinkets from my tent: a blunt knife, a broken umbrella and a box of clipped pictures. I walked to Moneta's dome of plants and herbs. I swept it out, tore out the weeds and watered the dry, neglected soil.

I made a fire on the beach and sat beside it, remembering the nights the communers had once danced around it in hope of summoning the gods of reason and meaning. I watched the tide swell and wondered if one day the water would rise to claim me, as once, in a strange and faded dream, I had believed would happen. The sun set before me, stroking the sky with dark and beautiful shades of red.

I put the past to rest like a tired child, bared myself to the universe, and prayed for the grace of another day.

Just one more day to call my own.

Day One.

About the Author

Fred Strydom studied film and media at the University of Cape Town. He has taught English in South Korea and published a number of short stories. He currently works as a television writer and producer in Johannesburg, where he lives with his wife and son, two dogs, cat, and two horses. His next novel, *The Inside-Out Man*, will be published by Talos Press in late 2017.